HIS LIPS CLOSE[...]
AND HER WORLD CHANGED.

He had saved her, he made her laugh. She'd not thought to feel so secure with a man. Finola stared up at him and saw his mouth descend on hers . . . knowing what he would do, knowing she should stop him, but unable to stop herself from wanting more.

No aftershock jarred her, no fading screams or shouts penetrated the inner circle that enclosed her with the Viking. It couldn't happen this way. Fear had manacled her. Now she felt a bursting need that eradicated her fear and brought with it a pulsing energy unlike anything she'd ever known. A Viking! Devil take her, it wouldn't be. Then her thoughts dissolved upward.

All became soft, pink, and cream, like the blended hues of an eastern sunset when the solstice was turning summer. She felt an explosion like a torrid dawn rising in her soul. Finola knew at that moment that her life had changed for all time . . .

The VEIL

Helen Mittermeyer

WARNER BOOKS

A Time Warner Company

WARNER BOOKS EDITION

Cover design by Diane Luger and Elaine Groh
Cover art by Michael Racz

Warner Books, Inc.
1271 Avenue of the Americas
New York, NY 10020

W A Time Warner Company

Printed in the United States of America

First Printing: January, 1996

10 9 8 7 6 5 4 3 2 1

To Jeanne Tiedge, who made it happen

To all women who've fought for a place in the artistic world, or any world, where they had the brains and ability to succeed. To them, down through the years, and today, I dedicate this book.

OLD CELTIC ROMANCES

SHE LED THE CHILDREN TO THE EDGE OF THE
LAKE, AND TOLD THEM TO GO TO BATHE; AND AS
SOON AS THEY HAD GOT INTO THE CLEAR
WATER, SHE STRUCK THEM ONE BY ONE WITH A
DRUIDICAL FAIRY WAND, AND TURNED THEM
INTO FOUR BEAUTIFUL SNOW-WHITE SWANS.
AND SHE ADDRESSED THEM IN THESE WORDS—

Out to your home, ye swans, on Darvra's wave;
With clamorous birds begin your life of gloom:
Your friends shall weep your fate, but none can save;
For I've pronounced the dreadful words of doom

Finola, once my pride and joy; . . .
Struck down on Darvra's reedy shore
By wicked Eva's magic power. . . .

Dear Reader,

It's been a banner year, doing this follow-up book to PRINCESS OF THE VEIL. I, who'd not intended writing historicals, have found myself hypnotized by the wonderful Vikings, who for almost a thousand years had a strong hand in the world of trade, east and west. I don't think the crust of their lives has even been cracked. So . . . there's more to do. I want to penetrate the hidden tales of those intrepid folks and write about them. Many of you must feel the same because I've received a mountain of positive and enthusiastic response to PRINCESS OF THE VEIL. THE VEIL was born as another avenue into those years, and I think it's even more of a mirror of those exoticand dangerous times. Nothing in modern times has equaled the wonderful "chutzpah"of the Nordics. They laughed at barriers set up by men or the gods, and went where only fools would venture, pointing the way for the Wall Street gamblers of the future.

When Warner showed an interest in publishing THE VEIL, I wasn't even sure how far the characters were going to take me. Like Topsy they just grew and expanded, taking me along for one of the best rides of my life. Now I invite you on the same journey and wish you as wild a trip as I've had.

As always I wish the very best to you.

Helen Mittermeyer

Prologue

Reykjanes, Icelandia

The world was ferociously quiet. As though it teetered on one foot, caught in a balancing act of time and space.

Fog blanketed sound and sight, sending most shivering into the comfort of their stone-framed domiciles. They sought the welcome heat of the dried peat fires that were husbanded so carefully in the long cold days of winter.

Not so the solitary figure staring out toward the fjord that was hidden from his view by the puffs of undulating moistness. He stood tall, straight, as though he welcomed the frigid dampness, as though he'd don it like a cape. He inhaled and exhaled through his nose. Though he stood on his own land, where he was born, land that had belonged to his ancestors since before the time of the great Grettir, his senses sharpened to his environment, as though they would discover new sensations, new knowledge.

"I see you, child of my heart."

At first he thought it was his mother. His good sense knew that was foolish. She and his father had been gone for many years. "Birgit?"

"Yes."

The mists, like coiling wood smoke, swirled around his face and ankles. He inhaled again, loving the damp coldness of his native Icelandia. "Come out."

"I will." Cackling, she moved like a wraith, appearing in front of him. "Child of my heart, you ponder as you did as a child. You've been to the vast world, known and sometimes unknown, Einar Thorhallsson, arid, forested, freezing, boiling, lush and forsaken. You've roamed far and wide. You don't tire of the high seas or adventure. One day you, or your brother, will chart the unmapped and unnamed. You love it all. Yet always Reykjanes calls you home. You will be happy here . . . one day." She patted his cheek

"Good mother, you know I have no brother . . . and I'm happy now."

Birgit nodded. "Mayhap, but there is restlessness in you, though you've just returned from a great trade, Viking of Vikings."

" 'Tis true." There was no denying anything to his old nurse. "Not remarkable. I always itch for the sea."

"Yes. But you are bothered, child of my heart."

He shook his head and embraced her. "Who knows why there's a fog of the mind, old mother?"

"A fearsome voice calls you. Intrigued you seek answers in our mist."

"Only a fool dwells on the unanswerable." He shifted his shoulders as though he could shake the nemesis, as though he would expel a weight from them. "I care not for mysteries."

"There are grays of life we can't ignore, child of my heart. They can frost the soul."

He inhaled. "The fog can turn the mind to meal." He chuckled, but deep inside he accepted her truth.

"Your ships have returned with much booty. As always you've enriched our people with your generosity. None will go cold and hungry when Einar Thorhallsson shares so freely.

From Mercia, Rome, and Genoa you bring riches for all. Your wealth and power equal any in the consortia. Icelandia grows fat with it.''

"I'm grateful, old mother."

"So you are, but not content."

He was glad of the fog that hid his face. Not that anything could be hidden from Birgit. She was a seer.

"Among foreigners you're accursed as brigand and pirate."

"Not to my face." Einar smiled.

"Wotan and the Christian God will bless your ventures because you've provided for your people."

"Old mother, you hide your reason for seeking me in the perilous fog."

"Ho! Einar Thorhallsson, seek not thy weapon to chastise me," the old crone cackled. She grabbed his arm, her humor fading. "Use thy silver tongue, instead, as you go forth from here. You will need all your skills to win the day." She studied him. "You think on much that is hidden from you."

"I wonder how you find your way, old mother. You move like a girl, yet I can't calculate your years." She was highly respected by all and could have her freedom, but she'd refused it time after time. "Birgit, how did you find me?"

"I see thee at all times, young master, and I know you go to Sutherland." Her dry amusement increased when he leaned over her, frowning. "It's written in the runes." Her dry claw of a hand clutched his leather shirtfront. "I see much blood and war, and you are among the contenders, child of my heart." She shook her head. "I know not where you will battle, but 'tis not here in Icelandia."

Einar frowned, shaking his head. "I had no thought to do so, anywhere, Birgit. I have trading engagements. Nor will I go to Sutherland. I go across to the Volga to trade with the Rus and Bulgars. The Great Bartering commences." His last trip among the wild men of the Rus rivers had netted him great wealth in furs and precious Baltic amber.

He watched his old nurse. He smiled at the woman who should've been a slave, but who, in truth, ordered others about and generally had her own way on almost everything. Few gainsaid the soothsayer. Her hair hung in lank plaits, a dull silvered brindle, her bones could be broken with two fingers, yet not another in Reykjanes wielded such authority. She had wondrous powers. Despite the misty day her skin looked parchment thin and dry, as though it would crackle like the dry leaves of the giant oaks of Mercia, the trading area south of Sutherland.

Princess Iona lived there. He pondered his princess for a moment, smiling.

"You think of our dear, sweet Iona who lives among the savages," Birgit said, her mouth twisting downward. "How her mother would rage if she knew her to be there."

"She is most happy, old one. And had she not been, I would've had her back here."

" 'Tis true," Birgit muttered.

"What brings you to me, old mother?" he asked.

"Soon after you leave Sutherland you will go to Antioch, child of my heart," she said, as though she'd not heard what he'd said.

"Antioch? No! You do not hear me, old mother. I've told you I go to the land of the Rus."

"And I tell you not. You must honor your covenant and go to Antioch." She brooded. "Perhaps that is where the battle will be."

Einar sighed. "You talk in riddles, little mother. There will be no battle, and I go—"

"Oh, but there will, and you will go to Antioch." She sighed. "Must be a demon's place. Your blessed mother was taken from her pilgrimage there along with the blessed Cup of Antioch. Those brigands took them for a long time. Curse their heathen souls."

"My mother returned safely to her home. My father's warriors rescued her," Einar said, wondering if Birgit was entering the forgetfulness of old age.

"Aye, she came back, but not unscathed, child of my heart. Even I could not plumb the inmost secrets of her heart."

Einar frowned. It was not the droplets of fog that coursed Birgit's cheeks. Tears! He'd never seen Birgit cry, not even at his mother's funeral. He patted her shoulder, gently. "My mother was happy to be returned to Reykjanes and live here until she died."

Birgit's words troubled him. He'd seen the sadness on his mother's face. No matter how many times he queried her about it, she would shake her head and say all was well. What had fretted the much-loved wife of Thorhallsson?

"I did not come to speak of your blessed mother, but rather of your journey to Antioch."

"Antioch. That's a great distance across the inland sea and past the pirate strongholds of Tripoli and Barka. I seek no treasure that way. It could cost many lives."

"You will go, Einar Thorhallsson. I've seen it. 'Tis your destiny." She sighed. "I like it not. Once your mother was captive of such pirates who roamed beyond the Bosporus."

"The Tartars and Seljuks are there," Einar said. "I've heard the story. But she was ransomed unharmed, and the leader was killed." His skin prickled with an alien awareness. "She lived many happy years with my father and me, until he died. Though she grieved for him, she was strong until the spotted fever struck her down, old one."

"Praise be," the hag muttered. She gazed upward, as though her watery old eyes could pierce the mist and see the future. " 'Twill be a battle. I like it not."

A powerful urgency forced him to grasp Birgit by her shoulders. Though his touch was soft, he couldn't hide his tension. "Tell me again about my mother."

"She was most beauteous . . . and sad, Einar Thorhallsson."

He shook his head. "She was happy. Have I not said so?"

Birgit nodded. "There were hidden tears that not even I could see, child of my heart, though I begged to give her solace."

Einar shook his head. "No, she was happy. Mayhap she grieved for the cup that belonged to her family. Why worry of past times, old mother? My mother loved us." Angst limned her features. Were there secrets that not even Birgit in her wisdom could ken? A part of him wanted to seek out the truth. Another part of him said it was better left alone.

The crone coughed and spit. "You feel your mother calling to you," she said simply. "Your mother understood the spirits, and now that she's one of them, she will reach out to you from time to time. And when she wants you to know, she will steer you to the answers you seek."

Einar's eyes sharpened on the crone. Had she known his thoughts?

She touched his arm, cackling. "You will know, child of my heart. You will know."

"Tell me your thoughts," he said, his voice hoarse. He'd overheard the talk. He didn't know the complete tale.

She squinted into the mist. "Your father knew she'd been taken by the Bulgar called Atoli. He feared for her life, and was determined to have her back. It mattered only that she was returned to him alive. They had great love between them, and he would not lose her. It'd been part of a covenant to her mother that prompted the pilgrimage to Antioch to see and touch the Great Cup. Her mother and her mother's mother had done the same. It was a holy quest to them. 'Twas said that the Savior had drunk from the chalice. 'Twould be passing marvelous to touch it. Your father would've accompanied her, but he had pressing business, and as a trader who spoke for and dealt for his king and his people, he was bound to his duty. And you were left behind with him. Since Griselda had a strong vanguard of Vikings there was no worry on her departure, and she arrived safely, many moons hence. She should've been protected behind convent walls . . .

"While walking in the convent garden in Antioch, she was accosted by the brigand who'd climbed the high wall to get her. His men then ransacked the convent, killing quietly, moving fast. The Great Cup was taken, so was your mother. The brigands galloped into the mountains where the Bulgars and Seljuks roam. She was kept beyond two turns of the sun . . . almost three.

"Vikings, through their spies, finally found the hiding place. They rescued her and killed those who'd taken her, including the leader. She was returned to Antioch, then put on a Viking ship for Icelandia. By God's grace she was kept safe until your father's ships intercepted the lone Viking vessel, and she was escorted home. All Icelandia rejoiced. She couldn't stop holding you, child of my heart. She often cried from the pain of it all," Birgit paused to spit again. She looked thoughtful, as though she had forgotten his presence. "The good Griselda was happy with you and your father, but sometimes the memories of that terrible time would overtake her, and she would cry. She told me that she left script for you to read, if you ever went to Antioch to see the Cup yourself."

"The Cup has been in the convent, safe from harm, for a long time." His face hardened. "Though were it lost, I wouldn't think to search for it," Einar murmured. "Tell me about the script." Why had Birgit never mentioned it until now? His mother had been gone from them for five turns of the sun.

Again she seemed to read his thoughts. "Child of my heart, thy mother wished you to be a man grown before you read the script. It's time."

"Then tell me what it says," Einar said, trying to curb his impatience. He'd loved his beautiful mother and grieved when he'd lost her.

"Mayhap I should give you the papyrus now, my dearest child." She tapped her chin, pulled at a hank of her hair. "Methinks she would've wanted me to read the words, but I could not."

Few slaves were taught Latin writing or Icelandic, the prevailing languages taught in Icelandia. Gently, Einar took hold of her shoulders, bringing her closer to him. "You've never given me falsehood."

"Nor shall I."

"But I know you can read."

"True. But not this. 'Tis for your eyes."

"And you still have the papyrus?"

"Yes. It's kept in the brass cupboard belonging to Griselda which is now yours. I will show you how to press the back so that it will be shown to you." She gripped his arm with her clawlike hands. "But I've come to warn you, child of my heart. You go to danger when you seek the Swan East. Even your silver tongue and golden sword will not free you from dreadful challenges that await." She sighed. "I have seen the fire and the flood."

Einar didn't need to have those signs explained to him. To see the fire and the flood in the runes was to see great peril. "Danger? Swan East? Cup? Script? What speak you, little mother? You say I go to Antioch——"

"First to Sutherland——"

"I had not thought to do so."

"You will. The call comes as we speak. A messenger from Asdis Iona, our beloved princess. You will go, child of my heart, because the pull is there, and you can't fight it. But I tell you to beware. I've seen the blackness in the runes. I cannot put a name to your peril but I know it's great, and you must be watchful." She put up her hand when he would've spoken. "Question not, child of my heart, for I know not what the peril of the Swan East is, but it's there in my vision like a bronze star with those words writ upon it in flames in our own beloved Icelandic." She spit again. "And the golden Cup of Antioch is there." Birgit's face creased with sorrow. She patted his arm. "First you go to Sutherland."

Einar took hold of her again. "You are confused, good woman. I don't go to Sutherland, and you must mean Swan's Road, not Swan East. You know that's how some of our people refer to the sea. They call it Swan's Road."

Annoyed, Birgit struck his hands away from her. "My mind's not addled, Einar Thorhallsson. Think you your brain grew with thegnship and wealth, and those of us who have not your goods cannot ponder. I know full well the sea, and its name. But that's not my dream or my fear. I've seen Swan East, and found it fearful." She nodded, her teeth clenched. "And soon you will take ship to Sutherland."

Sutherland! "I haven't been there since the twin spawn of Princess Asdis Iona came into the world, four winters past." He'd not soon forget those who'd betrayed the princess and her consort, and tried to kill them.

"Even now, child of my heart, you remember the evil ones who tried to thwart our princess. What has become of them?"

Einar's mouth twisted. "The one called Cormac has been dead these past years, as you know, long before the royal birth. The others, Elizabeth of Asquith and Abbot Petrus, are no doubt dead as well, since Sinclair banished them." Banishment was the same as death, even more so for the woman. The abbot might be able to find shelter elsewhere, in another abbey where his infamy was unknown, but, if he was alive, and that was doubtful, he could no longer set foot on Scotland's shores, as Sutherland was called by its own people. For a banished woman, most doors of good families would be closed. Death by starvation was not uncommon. And that could be the plight of the abbot as well, if all monasteries had learned the truth. Einar hoped that neither had died a happy death.

Birgit nodded. " 'Tis better to destroy evil. 'Tis good that they will be dead. Banishment doesn't find good companions. Yet there's more for you to take heed of, child of my heart. Listen to my warnings. Remember. Beware Swan East. I've had grave forebodings. Perhaps if you find the sacred Cup of your mother, it will protect you." She touched his cheek, moved, and, like the mist, she melted away.

"Birgit! Come back." Only pulsating damp silence and the haunting call of a sea tern answered his demand.

1

Antioch, 1060

All our power lies in both mind and body; we employ the mind to rule, the body rather to serve; the one we have in common with the gods, the other with the brutes.
Sallust

Antioch! Wild amalgam of learning and ignorance, grandness and poverty, paganism, cultism, Islam and Christianity. It groaned with caravans, people, animals, and vendors, every stall piled high with goods: wearable, edible, warlike, housewares. Antioch wasn't fussy. It embraced them all.

Above the teeming, blaring marketplace, the sky was a sizzling copper bowl, tinged blue, not a cloud to cast a shadow or break the heavy, dry heat that no breeze off the Mediterranean, no wisp of air from the Orontes could temper.

Dust rose at every movement, coating all, human animal or inanimate with an ecru, reddish layer. It was midday. All would sleep in other cities so afflicted with such heat, but there was no rest in Antioch, the world's great trading center.

Nothing interfered with trading or bartering, not even nature. It was told that in the great earth shaking of Anno Domini 526, when 300,000 Antiochans perished, business still thrived in some quarters: camels sold, scimitars fashioned, leathers tanned.

Heathen, heretic, and holy one, harangued side by side for the best booth at the market or at the gate, their goods bulging upon the backs of donkey, camel, yak or spilling from a cart.

The twisting, tessellated roads were choked with hurrying patrons or sellers. A few sedan chairs, well guarded, moved among the populace. Beautiful round-domed structures, turreted and fashioned with stone, rose several stories into the sky. Some were larger than any Roman edifice. The great citadel that protected the populace stood guard upon the highest vantage point, like a monument to strength. Its lancets faced in all directions, ever vigilant, ready to warn the people of any foe. Antioch was considered by the world to be the third-greatest city, and by Antiochans to be the first and foremost.

It bustled. People dashed hither and yon in the pre-midday preparation of the buying frenzy that would soon fill the market. Hordes of people from all corners of the known world would mingle, shout, barter, whisper, and trade. Beasts of burden would vie with sedan chairs borne by human slaves, chained about the neck and ankles, bent almost double, eyeing nothing and no one but the ground.

The marketplace! Business center where most deals were made, overtly or covertly, loudly or softly. Gold passed from hand to hand as though it were pence. Cabochons of every gem were tossed into the air to catch the eye of potentates, caravaners, and those rich enough to present the baubles to their favorites. Leathers, so fine that not the skin of a houri could match it, were draped from shelter supports. Armoring, so intricate not a lace maker on the Iberian isles could mimic the beguiling patterns, glittered as brightly as the jewels.

Voices were a cacophony of levels: screams, shouts, hails, melded with whispers, pleadings, sometimes threats. Above and below the human clamor, the donkeys, camels, and dogs were a discordant accompaniment.

But, even in all the busyness, she was noticed. Most glances were admiring. Some were assessing. Others didn't look away, but followed her every motion. She was an object of lust, but also of business, as slave traders calculated her worth. Some hazarded the cost to life and limb if she were taken. Many were not so foolish.

Finola MacDonnell, from the island of Iona off the coast of Scotia, which some now called Scotland, was too intent on sketching the market to heed much of the clamor. It irritated her guardians that she would pause to do so, but she couldn't resist.

Her mantle fell back in her eagerness to sketch.

"Milady, please," Petros, the chief guardian, whispered, bending toward her.

Finola nodded, yanking her mantle back on her head. She was not to be seen bareheaded. Her guardians would've had her veiled, as well, but she drew the line at having her lower face covered. It was already hard enough to breathe in the heavy atmosphere. She was cloaked in the coarse, unbleached hooded wool garment insisted on by the convent whenever any of its students ventured outside. The Arabic garb, called the djellabah, draped her from shoulders to toes.

"I won't tarry, Petros. Just a few strokes that I can use when I paint."

"Yes, milady."

Finola smiled to herself at the guardian's sigh. Then she forgot him in the urgent need to get down as many details as possible. The pieces of charred olive branch that she used for sketching blurred some of her clusters of people on the crackling, precious papyrus. Tossing the blunted piece into her sack, she fumbled for another, coming up with a stalk of the whiting she'd brought from Iona, to be used on dark surfaces such as smooth black rock or granite. Finally, she extracted one freshly sharpened charred stick that she'd honed to a point with her dirk that morning.

With swift, long, and curving strokes she outlined what she wanted to capture. Then once more, in spasmodic glances, her hand flying over the paper, she worked. Catching a child in tunic and turban toting a jug, a man who seemed immobile, statuelike, only his eyes seeming alive. He stared at her, or at something behind her, so she had a fine view of his features. She sketched him as fast as she could. The boy and man would be important to the foreground of the painting. When she looked up once more, the man and the boy were gone. Others had filled their spaces as the throng and noise grew. Others were cast down on the parchment, though not as clearly as boy and man. Camel, yak, and dog weren't ignored, but they could be filled in at a more leisurely pace.

Hungry to gather it all, the charred stick flew over the papyrus. She was indeed lucky to have the precious Egyptian material to use. Not everyone had patrons as generous as hers. Her artistic necessities were rarely ignored, and Finola had ample raw materials for painting and sculpting.

Stabbing her special mark on the items was important. That would give her the exact color, hue, or blend she'd need when she transfered the sketch to the fine skin, tanned and stretched as smooth as papyrus. Her eyes flew as fast as her hands. She brought tents, booths, shelters, people, and animals into clarity. Striped, marked with holy faces, crosses, or pagan symbols, the tents and stalls delineated their owners. Hung with family crests and charms, they would give life to her work. The final effort would be a feast of hues, alive and shimmering with activity. That was the part she loved the best, giving her sketches souls as she molded them in stone, cast them in iron, or swept them to vivacity in tempera.

"We must tarry no longer, milady."

"Only a moment more, Petros." Her guardians were impatient to get to the armorer's, purchase the iron she needed for her fashioning, and be gone from there. They'd always been most cooperative in accompanying her or any of the other students and staff, but Finola knew they felt uneasy in the market. And why not? More than one female had disappeared forever because her guardians hadn't been vigilant enough.

* * *

"That's the one. She was described to me."

"For a *faranghi*, she's quite beautiful," the other answered, his voice muffled by the djellabah he wore. The wrappings round his face would not be taken as a disguise in the market-place in Antioch, where desert men, their goods and camels, moved in and out of the winding streets, all in similar garb. "That flame hair would bring much in the market of Malta. Would it not?"

"Fool! Such a one at the slave auction would have the vultures cawing from market to market. And our master would be first to hear of it. Would you risk disembowelment while alive, your innards cooked while you watched and the rest of you to join them later when your screams faded?"

The other shivered, shaking his head. "You speak too clearly, my friend. I do not chance it."

The taller of the two nodded. "We'll follow them back to the convent, enter when they do, kill the guards. Our men will dispatch the others." The small hand sign he made was responded to by a host of other robed men who mingled with the populace. The job would be done and they'd be gone ere any could wonder.

"They will rouse the watch."

"Not if we're quick, and quiet. And we will be. When they return, it will be in time for late matins, which takes up the turn of the glass ere they partake of the meal eaten well past midday." The smile was hard and sure. "I've watched these fools who pray to their God, for many turns of the sun."

His companion nodded. Then the leader gestured and they moved behind some shelters, so that the trio approaching the armorer's shop would not escape their scrutiny while there, and when they departed. Nothing would go wrong.

2

There is no calamity greater than lavish desires.
Lao Tzu

Einar Thorhallsson was not new to Antioch. He'd been there many times, trading, dealing, making fortunes, losing some monies, but more often making a profit. Birgit prophesied he'd come. He had. He wouldn't dwell on that now. He was here for barter. He was a Viking, a Nordic trader. He was from Icelandia, where trading was the proudest of professions. It would've angered and shamed him if he'd done less than well at it.

This trip he had another objective besides trading. He would visit the Convent of Saint Mary of the Cross, and seek out the cousin of Princess Iona, Lady Sinclair. He'd make sure that all was well with the beloved relative of the Icelandic royal. No duty, large or small, could ever be an effort when commissioned by the honored Iona, revered by Viking and Scot alike.

"Have you seen this cousin to our princess, Lord Einar?"

"I've not met the woman called Finola MacDonnell, Darg." At least he didn't recall if he had. Of course, he'd heard of her, and he might've seen her, if the one described to him fit the memory.

"'Twill be a short visit, milor?"

Einar nodded. "Yes. I have a rendezvous to keep with Corin of Antioch, to exchange goods and information, along with this visit to the convent." He ignored Darg's frown. Corin was a confidant, and in some business ventures they'd been partners. His eastern liaison was known to his men, as he was known to Corin's people. Few others knew of their connection. They wanted it that way. His men didn't always give their trust to outlanders, anyone not a Viking. He hadn't always. Corin and he had shared dangers. It'd bonded them.

"You find him useful because, like you, he belongs to no consortia."

"True." Plus other bonds they shared. Corin had saved his life, as Einar had done for him.

"You feel this association has paid well for us," stolid Darg pursued.

"I've gathered information for many profitable trades from Corin."

"As has he from you."

"Yes. Ships belonging to us, and to him, have avoided pirate entrapment."

"Vikings don't shrink from battle, milor."

"They don't. But our cargoes have been safeguarded by avoiding confrontation."

Darg frowned.

"Look at it this way, my friend. We've returned to Reykjanes with treasures we could've lost in pirates' ambuscade. The marauders on the Mediterranean are well armed and hungry for our goods."

Darg expelled a sigh, nodding once.

Einar grimaced. He probably hadn't changed Darg's mind. He looked down at the leather goods in front of him. "As always the Antioch market has first-class barterings."

"They do, milor," Darg said. "Their blades are finely honed."

"Indeed. We could use some for our stores." He shook his head. "The covenant to the princess comes first."

"We would not disavow our princess."

Einar smiled. "We wouldn't."

His contingent of Vikings found the works interesting, though their vigilance didn't change. No man of substance traveled alone in any of the great markets of the world. Disappearances were common, if one was unwary. Einar had brought five men and Darg, his chief lieutenant, who captained his other vessel.

"Why would any female of marriageable age sequester herself in a convent, milor?"

"I don't know, Darg."

"A Viking woman would choke at such strictures."

Einar chuckled. "She's Ionan." At Darg's shrug of acceptance, he laughed. "The princess said her cousin is a most accomplished artist. She came east to study. The convent has masters who instruct neophytes."

"Freedom is too important to a Viking. Mayhap she is ugly and without means."

Not if she was the flame-haired one he remembered. But she'd been a child. "I will see to her welfare, leave some monies, and be gone."

Darg grunted.

Einar smiled, letting his eyes rove the stalls.

Leather fashionings! Damascene steel! The east produced high quality in both goods. He touched the intricately fashioned vest plate. Light, strong. The leather shirt that would hide dirks, throwing knives, and protect against an enemy's thrust.

He'd begun bartering, getting the vendor down many drachmas from his original price, as was expected in any good trade. Einar enjoyed it. One moment he'd been intent on the kill, closing in for the final price.

Then he saw her.

She floated through the market, the djellabah belling out around her, not masking the warmth of her coloring, the grace of her movements. Her lissome frame was revealed when the full-length cape parted at any motion.

The beauty strolled the circuitous path twining round the stalls, shops, and sellers' wagons, unveiled, between two protectors. Was she aware she turned heads, invited lascivious gazes? The puffs of dust about her person were like a hazy bronze halo outlining her vivid loveliness. Einar wanted her hidden from all eyes but his. They'd turned down a narrow path of shelters and tents that would take her to Antioch's many armorers, skilled craftsmen, known throughout the world.

He was on the opposite side of the wide area that constituted the main market. It'd been fashioned after the Roman amphitheater, with two wide terraces above it for the lesser vendors.

Throngs of people were between them. Because of his height he had a clear view until she reached the top of the street. Then she could turn sharp left or right to myriad shops, or go straight to the many diverse artisans working in iron, copper, and leather. Weapons were made. Leather seats for horse and destrier were fashioned. Iron stoves used in baking the wonderful eastern bread were hammered out in the same places as the spears and swords.

She paused at first one shelter, then another. Einar noticed how her protectors eyed no goods, only their charge, the marketplace, and those around them. He approved.

There was something familiar about her. She seemed so unaware of the stir she was making. Was it a mirage or was her skin tinged like the rare creamy cloth of Cathay, with rose in each cheek? The graceful sway to her walk gave her a royal air. She wasn't short, but there was a tininess to her, a fragility. She could've belonged to a Caliph or emperor. Had she come from Baghdad? As far east as Cathay? Was she free or slave? A memory nagged at him. He had the feeling that he knew her, or had seen her at another time. No! He wouldn't have forgotten, and, from that moment, he would've sought her.

"You wish to barter for the leather, honored one?"

"What?" He stared at the vendor, who inclined his head, his smile fleeting and unsure. Angry at his lapse, Einar nodded.

An eerie prickling of the skin made him turn. She was gone! Where?

Would she go on the block that day? If so, he'd purchase

her. No, that couldn't be right. She would've been veiled had she been saleable. Every day in the far corner of the market, penned and enclosed, were the slave blocks, always busy in their exchange of life for gold. There a man could find a child, a beauteous woman, a powerful Nubian. All crossed the block. Most were sold, never to be seen again.

What if someone else owned her? No matter, he would find a way to change that. There was a price on anything and everything in Antioch. A fortune in amber and garnets might be the price. He'd lay it down, every jewel and precious piece in the holds of his two ships.

"Lord Einar?" Darg, his first in command, prodded him. "Do we barter for the leather and steel?"

"Yes. The leather is fine and supple, Darg. You handle the sale." He strode away without looking back, or worrying. His ships, his men were used to his ways. He waved away the two who were intent on staying at his heels. They'd also been trained, to the last man, to take over the ships, or be in charge of any dealings. He commanded the finest Icelandic Vikings. Their shares in any booty were great. And each could assume responsibility as easily as another would don a cloak.

Six frowning faces watched him depart.

"Will he pay on his return?" the vendor inquired.

Darg scowled. None should question his captain. "We will talk of pay later. Let us settle on price first, merchant."

3

He who commands the sea has command of everything.
Themistocles

Finola MacDonnell of Iona stood between her two guardians, stifling a sigh. "Sometimes, Petros, I long for the freedom I had on Iona or on Sinclair land." She smiled at the expressionless guardian. "I walked alone over the hills and crags, down to the sea, where I would sketch." At his horrified look, she lifted a hand. "Don't worry. I won't go off alone—"

"We would not let you, milady," Antonios muttered.

What if she disguised herself as a boy? Then she could move freely, even in the Antioch market. Too dangerous. Still, she was tempted to explore the city. Mayhap, one day . . .

She and the other students at the Convent of Saint Mary of the Cross were protected. Women alone were frowned on in Antioch. Not only could they be the victims of slave seekers, they could also be injured or killed by footpads. For the most part, Antioch was a rich city, serene in its power. Unfortunately, as in great metropolises, not all the wealth was evenly distributed. Those who wanted more were willing to divest the uncautious, sometimes with dire consequences.

"We will be done, soon. Then we return, milady," Petros told her.

"Of course." It was Finola's dream to sculpt and paint. She would not give in to society and the confines of marriage where a husband would dictate her comings and goings, denying her great desire to be an artist. She was grateful she had a little dowry, but not too much. An abundance of wealth would shackle her into nuptials, instead of studying the great masters.

"You can continue sketching the Great Cup," Antonio said.

"True." She didn't want to make them uncomfortable. Her guardians were only doing their duty. "It's been a joy to sketch the Cup of Antioch." She smiled at both men.

"It blesses the convent, milady. I recall well when it was returned to the convent, after being held by heathens."

Finola had heard the tale many times. Vikings had retrieved it and brought it back to the Convent of Saint Mary. "As wonderful as it is here in the east, I miss my cousin." And her only family. If it hadn't been for Iona, her husband, and a wealthy Roman patron, she might never have had the chance to learn her craft.

"At home, Petros, I whittled on wood and painted on rough metals and stone. In Antioch, I have teachers and have learned to use the wonderful fine hemping called canvassing, smooth granite." She stopped and looked at the belching fires coming from several booths. "As well as versatile iron from Antiochan armorers." She inhaled the acrid odor. She had much to learn, but she was no longer an untried Ionan, who'd done most of her work with crude berry dyes on slate and rubbed wood. Here she had wonderful textured paint, fashioned from melted minerals, brushes made from the finest hemps, furs and feathers, and chisels of Damascene steel that were sharp as scimitars.

"This way, milady." Petros had a relative he considered far superior to other armorers.

Finola nodded. When she stumbled, putting out a hand to balance herself, she thought it was clumsiness.

Her guardians were more aware.

She staggered, blinded by sudden rising dust and a cascade of stones underfoot.

"Hurry. We must leave here, milady. The earth is moving!"

Finola understood. She'd been told of the mysterious shaking of the dirt and stone that could topple markets, the crackings in the ground that could swallow camels, even whole caravans.

"We must run."

She nodded to one of her guardians, lifting her skirts as she increased her pace. "Where will we go?"

Her words were lost in a sudden loud burst of sound. Then the city exploded in panic. A melee of shouting, milling, flailing populace, streamed out of shops and shelters. Blinded with dust, deafened with howls, out of balance with the moving earth, Finola was soon disoriented, lost in a river of people and thunderous cacophony.

The ground heaved and she fell against a tent pole. One of the protectors reached for her, but he was pushed back by the crowd rushing past.

In moments she was caught in the throng, spun away from the shelter, and carried by the pell-mell panic away from her guardians, tossed like flotsam on the sea of persons. Finola struggled to get her balance, to break away from the river of people before she was lost, or worse, pushed down and trampled. Nothing she did seemed to stem the cascade of humans running from fear.

A strong arm curved around her waist, lifting her high when she would've been buried in a sudden glut of flailing limbs.

"Thank . . . thank—"

"Shhh, I have you, milady," her savior said in formal Icelandic.

"Thank you," she replied in the same tongue. Being lifted up so high allowed her to breathe air into her dust-filled lungs. She noted his surprised look. He was as taken aback as she. Icelandic! Viking? Of course. Then she saw nothing for a moment when he wrapped his cloak, woven in finest wool, around her and lifted her even higher in his arms.

She began to cough, as others were doing. A sulfur smell rose around them. It was lemony and sec, pulling all moisture from the atmosphere. Every time she tried to gulp air, she choked more. She writhed against its insidious capture, and the man's hold.

Choking, she felt the panic around her which caused her own to rise like a flood as people screamed around her. "Save . . . yourself."

"I'll save us both, milady," he whispered into her ear.

Finola closed her eyes. She'd never feared people or gatherings, but now she felt as though she was being smothered by them. "Let me down. I can run, too."

"I'm sure you can, but it's better if I keep you high," her savior said, his voice grim. "You could be caught by the throng and thrashed underfoot before I could catch you up again."

Finola nodded. She was sure he was right when she opened her eyes and peered round the edge of the cloth. The crowd had increased. Mouths were as wide open as eyes, no voice defined in the din. They rushed like the Nordic lemmings to the unknown, perhaps to death. "Where will we go?" Her mouth was almost on his ear.

"Where it will be safe." He turned his head so that she could read his lips.

"Where can that be?" She didn't expect an answer. She thought he'd head for the port as most were doing. Instead he went back toward the hills behind Antioch, climbing steadily, legs pumping, breathing evenly. Her savior was well conditioned. What would it be like to cast him in bronze? Head and arms up, not stretched, just lifted. She could picture it. Building it in her mind, she stored it for later use.

Past them, and all around them, crowds tumbled and raced, voices raised above the unbelievable cracking and splintering sound, the cascades of dirt, dust, and stone. Then they were beyond the people, high on a shelf of rock, tufted with coarse grass, small stones rivering off its surface.

The statuesque form braced himself against the rock, not releasing her, as the shaking threatened to throw them down the incline again. Little by little, the tremors stopped. The trees stopped whipping like wild things. The awesome whistling of grinding rock rippled away and was quiet.

Slowly, Finola's savior placed her on her feet, though he dared not release her from his arms. They didn't speak. Instead, they listened, every sense on alert for more tremors.

Finola lifted her hands to push back from him, but he wouldn't let her. She looked up. "It should be all right. Shouldn't it?"

"Yes, milady, I think so. Sometimes the earth will shake again after a period of quiet. Mayhap not this time." He touched her skin with a fingertip. "You are alien to this area, with your skin tinctured coral and cream. Such as this I've seen in the skeletal crusts off the coast of Afrique, in deep warm water." He grinned at her. "Even through the dust and grime of the shaking, it shines with its own luminescence, milady." His fingers danced over the surface. "Every pore has its own warm light."

The man was shameless! 'Twas not seemly to address her in such intimate terms. Yet, she didn't fear him. Lord's truth, she would hear more. "You are kind to save——" Her formality was shattered when another tremor shook them.

" 'Tis moving away from us, milady. Have no fear." Surrendering to impulse, he sank to the ground, holding her, so that she didn't bruise herself, but landed on his thighs. "I'll brace you against further shock."

More disturbed by him than the tremor, she leaned into him and found comfort. His reaction had the blood pounding through her. His loins'd hardened under her. She would've pushed back from him when another tremor catapulted her against his chest. Was the heart pounding his or hers? Her chest was too tight to keep air. She expelled it in a sigh. Her savior was a dangerous man.

Finola lifted her head. "I would thank you, sirrah. You saved my life. I am Finola MacDonnell." His beaming grin had her staring. "What is it, sirrah?"

"There was something about you, milady. I have a memory of you. Your hair. I am Einar Thorhallsson, Thegn of Icelandia——"

"Captain of my cousin's fleet!" Finola exclaimed. "You spoke Icelandic to me."

"And you answered me."

She nodded. "Iona taught me."

"And you learned well."

There was a shuddering, grinding sound as the earth quaked once more.

Encasing her in his cape more fully, Einar pressed his face into her hair and let the moment stretch out in front of him. "You have a more fiery effect than the tremblors, milady."

"What?" His hands were going over her, as though he searched for something, as though he savored the touch. Nonsense! She was giddy from the earth shaking. Finola lifted her head from his shoulder.

"Nothing, milady," he muttered. "You have a softness and a toughness that intrigues me. Your wondrous beauty . . ."

"I beg pardon, sirrah. I cannot hear you over the shouting."

" 'Tis just as well."

Her smile fluttered away. "You've been most comforting. I thank you for the cherishing." She tried to smile. "I'm not so afraid now. I thank thee for the care." Exhaling she stared at her rescuer, then stretched to look about her. "'Tis only past midday. Yet, the day has a darkness cast upon it, as though night intruded before its time." She lifted a corner of the djellabah, covering her mouth. "It's hard to breathe."

Einar nodded. " 'Tis the sulfur that comes from the earth. We can get such an atmosphere in Icelandia when our hot springs are disturbed." His smile was faint. "Some say it's the anger of trolls arising from Perdition."

"Do you believe that?"

"Now and again." He angled her against him.

He was scanning her face as though it were a map. Was she so dirty? She swiped at her mouth.

"Are you thirsty?"

"No . . . yes." He entranced her. She felt the tautness beneath her. She knew she should move, but she was frozen in place. Raised on a holding that catered to its farm animals, she was not unacquainted with their coupling. She'd seen the mares and stallions. She understood the hardness under her hips. Fearful to move, to even breathe, she tried to pray and couldn't. Focusing on her art was no help, for when she closed her eyes, she saw his face.

"You were not my focus whence I came," Einar muttered. "Now your form drives me mad with a desire to bed you. Your loveliness sends Thor's own lightning through me. You test my lust, milady."

Finola shook her head. "I cannot read the words upon your lips, good sir. What say you?"

"I daren't tell you, little one. My life, my mission has been the Viking way: trading, exploring, opening up new markets, finding goods to sell and barter, crossing uncrossable seas as my ancestors did with Eric the Red, warring when needed."

"Eric the Red?" She shook her head. "I dinna ken you, Viking." She reverted to Gaelic, distressed not to be able to hear him.

He smiled. "I care for women, my beauty. Some as friends, others as lovers. None has put me off my course. You could." He enjoyed telling her things propriety would never let him say if they hadn't the din of screaming voices to mask the sound. "You're but a waif of a woman with the smile of a goddess. Your eyes of the color of Tripolitan palm fronds after a rain, smoky rich green, their gemlike luster caressing me. Did you know your gaze has such fire? Could you be a coquette like the dancing girls of Alexandria?"

Finola shook her head. "No, I haven't been to Alexandria. Why do you ask? I would ask you about my cousin—" The earth shook and the thought wafted away. The din subsided so suddenly, she feared. "Are all safe?"

"I would think most are." He turned his head. "Many are beyond us now, over the crest, taking their noise with them."

She exhaled, reveling in the quiet world where they seemed alone.

Huddled into the gnarled bole of a cedar tree and the rocky ledge, they touched, clung, neither moving.

Einar tented his cloak over her, filtering some of the impurities they breathed.

A person or small group went past them, but there was an aloneness to Finola and Einar. The noise didn't build again. Did people bind themselves from fear, pull into that deep hiding place inside every soul? An essence that could be the only bulwark against the world and all its upheavals?

A wisp of breeze lifted, caught, and dissipated a heavy bundle of the yellowish atmosphere. In the clear hole of the world, Finola looked her fill at him, as he scrutinized a larger group who ran, walked, and stumbled past them. She breathed great gulps of lighter air.

He settled back, as though what he'd seen had allayed his suspicions.

"What is it that you fear, Einar Thorhallsson?"

He eyed her, his half-smile hot . . . but so comforting. "The kind that prey on the fear of others would find this to be a high-water moment, milady. Cur dogs abound in most worlds, east and west. They would take advantage of those weakened or frightened. Vigilance is the only guardian against misfortune."

"Oh. I understand the necessity of taking care. My guardians are ever watchful."

He frowned. "My men, if they live, will be searching for me."

"As will my guardians."

"Rest, milady. 'Tis not wise for us to move before the populace settles back into their nests. And that could take a little time." He tightened his grip.

She was glad. She didn't want him to release her. It was cozy, safe with the two of them half concealed under the cape.

He closed his eyes. He was smiling! She relaxed in his firm grip.

Finola stared. He was more than beautiful. With all the scars on his face, arms, and neck, he had extraordinary, flexive skin and flesh, mobile, pure and strong. She ached to capture that masculine beauty with brush or chisel. She didn't want their moment of closeness to end, nor the hour or day, despite her fear. Her body and spirit had turned, reversed, rejuvenated. There was a flood inside her, building and bubbling. Such foolishness. She would sculpt him, paint him, then forget him. 'Twas a knell of untruth, ringing round her head.

His eyes snapped open. "Do you fear me, milady?"

Finola shook her head. His smile had her heart racing, the air more constricting now than the yellow aura had been.

"Good. You'll be safe."

She felt the stabbing, hot truth of that in the sudden inability to breathe that had little to do with sulfur residue. Swallowing, she strove to get her heart back in rhythm and loosen the tightness in her throat and chest. "I can see that you've broken your arm ... more than once, above the wrist and elbow." When he inclined his head, his eyes questioning, she licked her lips. "I'm not a healer, but an artist. 'Tis my work to understand the bones and skin of man and creatures, as well as the texture and makeup of rock and tree."

Einar nodded.

She felt trapped, but happy. Set free, but chained. "You have scar tissue on the back of your hand, and just past the junction of elbow and arm. Knife or sword wounds here ... and here." When he shifted so that he was closer, she felt a pearling of nervous moisture cross her top lip. Her hands slipped back from him. "Have you ever been sculpted?"

Einar's smile drooped and twisted. "No, milady, I haven't. Have you? I would barter much to have such treasure for myself."

Flustered, fluttering, she spread her hands, shaking her head. "I mean ... you see, I do that sort of thing ... I would have you comprehend that I stare but to hold the image in my mind, so that I might call upon it at some other time."

"Fine. I do understand you." He laid a large hand along her face, cupping chin and forehead. "Pardon me if I must do the same. I do not sculpt, but I recognize beauty." He smiled. "You fill my mind, and I won't forget you. I'm glad you're alive and not carved in stone."

"So am I." Her voice quavered.

Again the earth heaved, seeming to rumble away beneath them.

Einar caught her close. "Give thanks to the Deity and

Wotan, we'rc safe, milady." He looked down at her. "Though demons might have sent the tremors, they've allowed me to transcend custom. Fear not, milady. I will see you safe."

"I believe you." And she did.

Under most circumstances in the polite world, civilities dictated he touch his lips to her fingertips only in the company of guardians. If she were alone, he should only eye her from a distance. But earth heavings were not normal. He'd succored her; they were companions trying to survive disaster. To hell with mores.

He kissed the top of her head. When she looked up, he grinned. "I needed to do that, milady. That's all the answer I can give."

"Then I'll not question you more." Breathless she sank closer to him. Surely it was only because he saved her, because he was her bulwark against the black forces that made the earth tremble. It could be nothing else.

Why Thorhallsson? Her focus had never been on men and marriage. Rather, she'd sought to escape its manacles. Be her own person. Happy with her work, she'd needed nothing else. Along came a Viking . . . and she was beginning to question her life's plan.

"You'll not be hurt," he whispered.

"How can you be sure?"

"Wotan wills it."

Again he'd spoken Icelandic, and he'd called upon their ancient god, as Icelandians were wont to do. The Church would call him blasphemous. Vikings would laugh at such admonishment. She knew enough about them to be sure of that. She opened her mouth to ask him about her cousin.

The earth rumbled.

People ran past, screaming about getting to the sea.

She tried to move out of his arms, forgetting what she would've said to him. "Perhaps we should try to get to the sea."

His shrug settled her more firmly in his arms. "I'm not sure even the sea is safe. We'll have to wait. Many things can happen now. It could end. But it isn't always the same.

Now and again the sea will erupt with monster waves after such an earth shaking." He frowned.

"You're thinking of your men and ships. Surely they will do the right thing."

"They will. Vikings need not be overseen."

But he feared for them. She could see that.

Finola glanced in the direction of the sea. She couldn't see the undulating blueness of the great water. The yellow clouds seemed to have flattened into a noxious cover, shrouding all, earth, sea and sky. "And have you seen such? The monster wave."

"Yes. It was not to my taste." His smile twisted. "Even unshakable Vikings pale at the power exuded by the great water."

When he closed his eyes again, breathing better under the cape, Finola studied him. Yes, she wanted to sculpt him. But she'd need to sketch him first.

How long would she have? For, like ships on the sea, they would pass each other, move on, and soon become part of the horizon. Sadness cramped her. She bit back a groan of protest. Soon it would be finished. She would search out her protectors, he would go to his ship. Where was it anchored? Would she recognize the guidon? She knew of Thorhallsson. He seemed to know of her.

She'd seen him one other time when a gathering of his people had come to Scotland when she was visiting her cousin. Other Vikings, south of the Orkneys, on the holdings of Iona's husband, Lord Sinclair, had been polite but aloof. He'd been among them. He hadn't seen her. He was hard to miss. Head and shoulders over all men but Magnus Sinclair, spouse to her relative. Her cousin was fond of Thorhallsson, treating him as a brother, not as captain of the Icelandic fleet.

Finola could comprehend the caring. He was such a beautiful specimen. Sculpting, or the thought of it, had never made her heart pound in such a way. She loved her work, but there was a different sensation akin to fashioning a bronze of her rescuer. Her hands ached to touch that scarred skin, that tough flesh. Despite its mars, it had a smooth richness that she coveted.

She liked his ears. They fitted the contours of his well-shaped head. No man should have such lashes, thick and curling, tinged with red, glinting gold, and bronze. What were his eyes like? It'd been so hazy she hadn't caught the hue. Her usual sangfroid at contemplating an article or body to sketch or sculpt deserted her when she thought of his frame. She felt a nervous, hot aching as though she'd come upon a rare mineral that she could fashion. It went beyond such excitement to a core of herself, unknown . . . untapped.

Hand out, pulled back. She itched to touch. He was a most beautiful specimen. Faugh! He would've put Achilles to shame. The great war god never had such burnished locks. Large . . . more than that. Lean and tall. Not burly. A sleekness to his sinews reminded her of the polished Damascene steel, so sought after by Antiochan armorers. Yet, there was a silky hardness no armorer could match.

She'd never felt unladylike assessing a model. Now she did. Loose. Unfettered. Naughty. Hungry. Mouthwatering. Such could not be countenanced in a lady. Close your mind. Her artist's sense was famished, her body and limbs quivering with a need that wouldn't be denied. All of the woman opened to the man. The artist took her place behind that.

"And what think thee?"

The question in formal Icelandic startled her. She could feel the blood rising in her face. "As a sculptor, I know you would cast well." She answered in the same formal Icelandic.

He studied her. "You speak our language well."

"I like it."

"And I like hearing it on your lips and tongue."

He had no decorum! She reeled with a strange wanting.

"Princess Asdis Iona was a good teacher."

She nodded, feeling a wonderful shivery heat. "Thank you."

His eyes narrowed, the smile slow and steady. "I knew there was something about you."

Finola looked puzzled.

"I saw you in the market." He moved, keeping her close. "I followed."

Finola shook her head, delight flooding her. "You've never met me . . . not truly."

"You were a child. In Scotland." He smiled, one finger tracing her cheek. "You incline your head like the beauteous birds on the coast of Afrique."

"One day I would like to see such." She looked away from him, smiling.

"You take my mind from my words. I spoke of seeing you."

"There was something familiar about you, as well," she said, wondering if she should tell him.

"I've visited Sinclair land many times. One of those times . . . I met you, after a fashion."

Realization was a burst of sunlight on that dark day. Her head whipped his way. "You know!"

"Yes." His grin widened when she laughed.

Not thinking, she grasped his arm with both hands and squeezed, feeling safe. "You must know it was an accident."

"Or you were trying to rid the world of another Viking." He laughed when her eyes widened.

"Mayhap I was." Mirth escaped her. She was in the middle of a maelstrom. Her survival was not a sure thing. Yet, she'd never felt so comfortable, so secure.

It was a social solecism for her to touch him. She pulled back her hand.

He put his other hand over hers, keeping her still. "You're no longer a child," he whispered. "I'm glad for that."

She frowned, not sure of her feelings or his meaning. "No. And happy I am. I would not be in Antioch if I was." She rushed her words, flustered, unsure, but not wanting to move.

His smile widened. "I can only be happy you're unarmed."

Relaxing, she smiled back. "Perhaps I'm better with weapons than I once was."

He threw back his head and laughed. "I hope you stay with sculpting." He shook his head. "What a surprise when your arrow struck the small branch above me, breaking it. I ducked when I heard the sound, but not quickly enough—"

Finola bit her lip. "I know. I ran after Glam when we heard the bellow . . . shout—"

"Bellow?"

She grinned. "You rattled the trees. I saw you then, for a moment." Her grin faded. "Iona told me I'd scored your face, drawing blood—"

"A scratch, milady. Would that I'd kept the scar." He drew her hand to his face. "See. Nothing."

"Yes." She was in turmoil. The earth had moved again. She felt upside down and spinning.

"When Darg told me that it was the cousin of Iona who tried to skewer me, I was careful when I went abroad in the glen. Children with weapons can be most lethal."

"You're trying to rile me, sirrah, by calling me a child." She enjoyed the sparring. She'd never had such an easy converse with a man, other than her grandfather and Lord Sinclair.

"And you were not?"

"Two years ago, I was not a child. Eighteen summers." She'd surprised him.

"You don't look old enough to have lived twenty rounds of the seasons, milady."

Stung, she lifted her chin. "I have."

"More waif than woman, though I'm glad you're not a child. You're quite beauteous, milady. I should've expected such. Mayhap, though, I didn't foresee Finola MacDonnell to be like the goddesses."

Finola gulped, unfledged in flirting. For the first time, she wished she'd paid more heed when her grandfather had held his courts. She'd been more interested in sketching the people than observing the customs and manners. She felt swamped by his words. She sought another tack.

"How is it that you come here?" Caught and tossed into Thorhallsson's earth-shaking grasp, she needed to regain balance.

He'd saved her, he made her laugh. She'd not thought to feel so secure with a man. Finola stared up at him and saw his mouth descend on hers ... knowing what he would do, knowing she should stop him but unable to stop herself from wanting more.

No aftershock jarred her, no fading screams or shouts penetrated the inner circle that enclosed her with the Viking. It couldn't happen this way. Fear had manacled her. Now she felt a bursting need that eradicated her fear and brought with it a pulsing energy unlike anything she'd ever known. A Viking! Devil take her, it wouldn't be. Then thought dissolved upward.

All became soft, pink and cream, like the blended hues of an eastern sunset when the solstice was turning summer. She felt an explosion like a torrid dawn rising in her soul. Finola knew at that moment that her life had changed for all time.

4

The scent of flowers does not go against the wind, not sandal,
rosebay, or jasmine, but the scent of the good goes against the wind.
A good man is wafted to all quarters.
Suttapitaka—Theravada Buddhists

Einar became aware of the world around them first. He used his back and cape to shield her. With the greatest danger past, the focus would be on other things. Prying eyes would mark their place, wagging tongues would repeat what they'd seen, and Finola's reputation would be in tatters, in less time than it took to barter an Arabian steed.

He cursed himself for being all kinds of a fool. He'd risked much to hold and kiss her. Discovery would bring it all down on her. In the eastern world, where some believed that women were intrinsically evil, just as some did in the west, she would be the victim of the nastiness, the suspicions, the antipathy. The man with her wouldn't be mentioned. The blame, the viciousness would descend on her alone. There was even the danger of being shunned at the convent, asked to leave without proper escort. That could presage being taken and sold into slavery.

"What is it? What has angered you?"

He saw the blood stain her cheeks. She felt shamed by him! Damn!

She tried to free herself. "I . . . I would not have you think me common, sirrah."

He cupped his hands around her face. "'Tis not you, milady. I ask your forgiveness if I've been forward. I would protect you from the yapping herds that abound in this or any other area. 'Tis never my wish, nor will it ever be, to bring shame upon you." He smiled at her, but he never ceased eyeing the world about them.

Her look softened, her mouth shaking. "The formal Icelandic you speak soothes me, Einar Thorhallsson. Not all the flowery phrases in Greek or Latin could bring more solace."

"I would never hurt you."

She touched his hand that touched her. "I feel better now." And they both understood.

Einar inhaled, lifted her hand to his lips, grimacing. "We must go, and—"

"Milady, milady, we've searched for you."

Einar eyed the two above him, their faces tinged with concern for her, their anger directed toward him. He rose to his feet, bringing Finola with him. He stared back at the two men.

"Petros, you've been hurt. Antonios, are you all right?"

"We're both fine, milady, but we feared for you." Narrow eyed and ready, Petros watched Einar, his glance dropping to the hand that clasped Finola's.

Einar's jaw tightened, though he understood their ire. He would talk to the two protectors when he returned to Antioch. Turning his back on the two men, he faced Finola. "I must go to my ships and see to my men. I have a commitment to trade meetings involving Icelandia and the Sinclair holdings in Constantinople, for the next two days. I'll be back here in three, and come to you at the Convent of Saint Mary of the Cross." He smiled at her sudden confusion. "Surely you knew I'd return to you," he whispered.

Her eyes widened. "I . . . I didn't know."

He squeezed her hands. "I would've returned at any rate to check on the cousin to Iona." When her smile faltered, he urged her closer. "And you must know, I now return for a deeper reason."

" 'Twould please me, Einar Thorhallsson." She bit her lip to keep it from trembling.

He wanted to embrace her. The urge was so strong that the sinews of his body strained to her and his teeth clenched as though he bit on steel as he'd done numerous times when his wounds had been stitched.

As though she could feel his wanting, she curled her fingers around his. "I thank you for saving me." She smiled and whispered, "I dare to tell you that you're giving me a glimpse of a life I've eschewed." She blushed, turning her back on her guardians. "Never have I been able to understand the power between men and women, that which draws them back to one another from great distances." She swallowed. "You saved me. Now you take a part of me as you go." Her smile faltered. "Bold of me, I know, to speak thus. I know words can have little meaning at times . . . that one can say one thing and mean another, Einar Thorhallsson—"

"I'll come to you because I could do no other." He lifted both her hands, kissing the knuckles, not the tips as custom dictated. "I will return for you."

She nodded, pulling her hands down, unable to speak for fear she would weep.

"I'll be back, Finola MacDonnell. Believe in that. Look for me." He lifted her one hand again, turning it, angling his body so that the gesture was hidden from the guardians.

When his tongue touched her palm, she almost jumped out of her skin. Then he dropped it and strode away without looking back.

"Milady? He was a Viking."

"I know. He is confidant to my dear cousin."

"I see. 'Twas unseemly for the Viking to approach."

"Don't look so fierce, Petros. He saved me."

"God be praised," whispered the Nestorian Christian, bowing and gesturing that she precede him. "Come. We've been gone too long."

"Yes, I know." Einar, Einar, Einar Thorhallsson. She couldn't call him Einar, except in her mind. It was not good custom to do so. Faugh! Hadn't she broken a great number of mores that very day? She smiled, remembering. Her smile faltered. Could it've been a dream? An aberration caused by the moving of the ground? Could beauty be so sudden . . . and real?

She walked between the custodians, down the winding streets. The return trip took longer because of the debris that lined their path. It sickened her to see the litters carting the bodies away for burial. Despite the pain she felt for those wounded, she couldn't stem the happiness inside her. Einar Thorhallsson!

Lost in thought of Thorhallsson, she was content to walk between her two guardians, letting them guide as they climbed the stony roadway to the convent.

As always, she placed herself to one side as the two guardians used their keys to unlock the heavy gates. As they swung open in rusty protest, there was a sudden flurry of activity. She turned as someone grabbed her, stunned by the muttered ferocity of the two men.

"Wait! What are you—?"

An arm closed over her mouth, gagging her. She struggled but couldn't free herself. Her eyes were wide open, but she couldn't comprehend what she was seeing. It couldn't be true. No one would violate a convent. Women and children were safe there. It was desecration.

The convent seemed to explode without a sound, persons and goods pouring from its orifices.

Nothing stopped the pillage or the carnage. No alarum or knell sounded, no succor appeared.

She choked behind the gag as she watched custodians and staff dragged from the convent. No screams issued from those muffled mouths. The intruders silenced most as they carted them forth and began killing them.

Whirling sea birds cawed overhead, too far from their feeding grounds Were they the only dissenters to these silent murders?

A horde of robed intruders had charged Antonios and Petros, their unbleached cloaks belling out as they'd dispatched her two custodians in bloody silence. The convent was at late matins. Some were still in chapel. The singsong Latin could be heard. No other sound disturbed the rising, deepening heat of early afternoon.

Finola bit down on her captor's arm. She had to warn the others. She opened her mouth to scream. Swearing in guttural Arabic, the man had her before she could utter more than a syllable. His arm encircled her face, muzzling and bruising her. She struggled to be free, but the chokehold tightened and she saw stars and darkness before she subsided.

In swift efficient moves her captor wrapped her in a cape of rough-hewn material, only her nose and eyes showing. Binding the sack in coarse hemp, like a camel pack, she was tossed to one side to witness the horror when she waked.

In the next hour she prayed for death as she watched the quiet extermination of the convent. Nuns and students were dragged from their prayers, slaughtered in a deadly near-quiet. She waited her turn.

Finola saw the Cup of Antioch. It was held aloft by one of the intruders, laughing as he tossed the precious artifact to a friend. She screamed behind the cloth that wrapped her mouth. When a nun, tattered and bloodied, tried to reclaim the relic, she was decapitated for her efforts. Tears of rage and fear coursed down Finola's cheeks. She knew they'd kill her, too. She only wished they'd hurry. Watching was its own agony. She prayed for a clean, quick thrust. Einar! Einar Thorhallsson, let him be safe.

The sun was declining as the marauders finished their tasks, loaded up pack animals with booty, and began to leave. Stunned at the blood loss, and at still being spared, Finola was thrown like a sack of grain over the back of a horse. Swaddled with heavy clothing that almost throttled her, she became just another bundle on a beast of burden led out of Antioch. Her ribs felt broken and bruised, her breathing was constricted and her thirst was a torture. She could see the bottom of the convent gates as they were closed. Overhead another bird was calling. Would any see the carrion and wonder?

The marauders left as undetected as they'd arrived.

5

Because of deep love, one is courageous.
Lao Tzu

Landing at the port of Antioch with two ships would seem as nothing. Einar Thorhallsson's guidon was seen in many trading ports. Busy Antioch, the greatest of the trade ports, recognized his tall, square-masted ships and the tall, fair-skinned man who captained them. Not only did he stand head and shoulders over most men, native or visiting, his gold hair and very short beard were arresting in a city of olive-skinned, dark-haired personages. Many times he'd come and been welcomed. He liked the east and rarely came away empty. The bargains were plentiful if one knew how to barter. But he was a cold-water man, and didn't come unless the trading rewards would be high.

Perhaps it surprised those, who kept track of such things, that he'd returned so soon. 'Twas but three days since his last visit.

Einar Thorhallsson gave no thought to what others pondered. His mind and spirit were only on Finola MacDonnell.

"We had not thought to visit here, again so soon, had we, Lord Einar?"

Einar smiled. His men knew his itinerary as well as he.

"No, Bren, Antioch had not been our prime port of call. My plan was a sweep of the western segment of the sea, perhaps as far as Sicilia or Malta and across to Tripoli. If time permitted, we might've sailed beyond Constantinople to the trading posts on the Sea of Marmara."

Bren nodded. "A dangerous hegira at any time, Darg says. One could become the prey of the Bulgars, the Rus, and the Tartars, if not wary." Bren excused himself when duty called.

Einar looked out over the sea. Constantinople was often the main objective. The center of the Byzantine power, sometimes still called Byzantium by the older prelates of the Church, it was a nucleus where all caravaners came at one time or another.

On this journey, he'd limited himself to Constantinople, the meeting place of the world's traders. Much had been accomplished, but he'd been too impatient to return to Antioch, to be overly impressed at the covenants of protection he'd gained and granted. Einar Thorhallsson was well aware of his power and stature in the world of consortia. Somehow it all paled next to the need to see the Ionan once more.

"You've sent runners out to your friend, Corin?"

Einar nodded. "I have. He was to oversee the safety of Finola MacDonnell, cousin to our princess."

"It would seem passing strange to have a heathen protect the Convent of Mary of the Cross."

Einar shrugged. "His beliefs are not the same as ours. His God could be the same."

"I've heard such," Bren admitted.

When a sail needed attention, Bren left him again. Calling instructions to the men, Einar tried to tamp down his hot eagerness. Soon he'd be with Finola again. Day and night she'd been in his thoughts. He'd gone over every word and gesture they'd shared. Not all admonitions to himself that she couldn't be as desirable, as sweet as he recalled, smothered his growing urgency to be with her.

She came of old warrior families on both sides. She donned not armor, rather she used a brush and chisel. An artist! He'd not thought to be so enamored of one. She didn't fit the mold of her family. A winsome lass with glorious coloring and rare beauty.

He watched as Darg came, hand over hand, from the other ship to his. "Well met, Darg."

"And to you, Lord Einar." The lieutenant glanced up into the sails and around the deck before he spoke further. "Lord Einar, in Constantinople they spoke of fierce Tartars on the move—"

"And you think Antioch is at risk."

"I'm no longer surprised that you can read my mind, Lord Einar. It's true. I must wonder if the relative of the princess could be safe in such a city."

"I, too, have thought on it." Einar gripped the polished railing. "Why would her patroness send her so far east? There are fine art centers in Mercia, Normandy and Rome."

Darg nodded. "Antioch is important for trade. It's also dangerous. A woman is at great risk."

Einar inhaled, his insides knotting. "I've thought this," he said through his teeth.

"Lord Einar, the city is a weakening bastion against the barbaric hordes that push at it from the wilderness. Tribe, clan, and consortia have all warred against Antioch in one way or another. The city is lacking in protection. It has no army as other cities, like Rome, Constantinople and Athens, have." Darg waved his arm. "The populace is not trained to protect. Their talent is trading, bartering, milor."

"I know," Einar said, a muscle jumping at the side of his jaw.

"I don't see a great future for the city, milor. If the barbarians break through, all will be lost. They'll lay waste to the city, kill its people and its main method of surviving, trade. Antioch would be lost. The barbarians aren't builders, but destroyers." Darg bowed to him. "I use your words when I speak, milor."

"Go on."

"Why do we not take her back with us to Reykjanes, milor? 'Twould be safer."

Einar swelled, breath pumping out of him. The smack on

the shoulder he gave his lieutenant would've dropped a horse. "Your plan is a good one, Darg Jansson." Einar nodded. "I'll convince her."

Darg nodded. "You will, milor."

Einar bellowed for more sail. His men responded before his voice died in the wind.

"I've heard stories of this one. Did she not shoot an arrow over you?"

Einar laughed. "She did."

"I would hear this, milor."

Einar could've brushed him off, but he was too full of the new plan, too excited at the thought of seeing her. He wanted to speak of her, to bother. "A simple tale. I was on Sinclair land—"

"A most noble leader."

Einar nodded. "She was practicing the bow and arrow with Glam, the princess's protector, instructing her." He smiled. "Her shot went wild, hitting a tree branch. It fell, striking me on the head and cheek."

"She's a better sculptor than a bowman, I'll be bound."

"I hope so." Einar chuckled, very happy. He'd see her soon.

"How did you know she'd done it, milor?"

"She raced down the hill to apologize. Glam wouldn't let her. He did. I saw her peeking from behind a tree." He'd noticed her coloring, her natural grace. "I'd thought her a child."

"Child or woman, 'tis best we get her out of Antioch."

"We will, good Darg." She'd intrigued him then, and more so now. He ached to see her, to touch her. Did she feel the same? This lack of confidence was alien to him. Women, always important, had presented little challenge. Now, not sure of his place in Finola's affections, he felt threatened, off guard.

They steered into the harbor. He'd never felt such an itching need to be gone from his ship.

"Shall I accompany you, Lord Einar?"

Einar nodded to his second in command. "The usual contingent." He noted Darg's acid tongue. His lieutenant hadn't been happy last time, when they'd become separated. Einar thanked the gods for that time.

"As you say."

Einar frowned. "There are too many vessels clustered at the quai. We'll stand off and use our landing craft." He eyed the vast assortment of trading vessels sporting every important guidon.

"Yonder must be a fire, Lord Einar."

He looked up the hill, his frown deepening. "I see it. It looks to be in the city proper." Antioch had a port on the Orontes River and the sea. But the city itself stood back from the water. He studied the plume of black smoke. Fires weren't an uncommon occurrence. Einar squinted against the sun. "Mayhap the residential area."

"No doubt the abode of an eastern potentate, Lord. Several have palaces in the inner city, and they insist on their lighted braziers in every room."

Einar smiled at the veiled scorn in his lieutenant's voice. "True. And they are known to topple. But it could've been ground movements again, my friend. More than one domicile has been destroyed by them." He didn't want it to be the Convent of Saint Mary of the Cross. He hurried his men with a slight gesture.

"Why do the people stay in such a place?"

"To leave would be foolhardy to those who love Antioch. We love Reykjanes, for all its storms and dangers, do we not?"

"Aye."

Einar didn't bother to leave instructions for the boatmen left to guard the two vessels. They knew their worth and concerns. The ships would be kept in good order.

As the small boat was about to bump upon the strand, Einar stood and jumped from it, turning to watch as it was beached. Vikings would stand guard over it. The rest, seven strong, well-armed men, would accompany him.

"We've not had trouble here, milor, but I feel better with our contingent."

"You're right, Darg. Brigands and footpads prey on the unwary." He'd not lived as long as he had in the toughest ports in the world without prudence. Besides, Darg and the men had been voluble about their worry last time. He didn't want to hear any more.

The port of Antioch was an ideal place to trade and barter, but to get to the city proper that housed the market, the rich tall houses of trade, and palatial private domiciles, they would need to ride or walk. It was built back from the sea on a rise, its stone citadel guarding it from aggressors.

He looked around with a smile when he heard hoofbeats. As was the custom, horses had been brought to the strand. Corin of Antioch, his liaison and partner in the east, a trader of great renown, would've arranged it. Last time he'd not used them. This time he wanted to get to Finola with all speed.

Einar's smile widened when he saw the man who led the mounts toward them.

"It would seem none can keep a secret from your friend, milor. He knows of our coming." Darg frowned. " 'Tis not the usual attendant." Darg drew his sword.

Einar stayed his hand. "Wait. He has numbers of spies, runners and spotters along the east coast of the great sea, Darg. One would tell him. He could send one of them with the mounts."

"Your friendship with him is strong."

"Our shared jeopardy and escape from the galleys forged a bond."

"I understand." Darg didn't sheathe his sword.

Einar was taken aback when the man whipped off the head covering. "Corin! Have your fortunes declined so much you've become a horse tender?" Not too many men could joust with the powerful and very sensitive trader chief of the east. When he used his powers of persuasion to barter, few could gainsay him. "I'm glad to see you. All goes well with you?"

"It does." Corin grinned, but he never stopped scanning the strand.

Einar's smile faded, his eyes narrowing and following the other's scan. "What's amiss, my friend?" Moving swiftly, he took the first horse off the string. The action brought him closer to Corin. "There's trouble?"

"There is. Yonder." Corin jerked his head toward the city and the curl of black smoke from its center. "A convent burns and—"

Einar grasped the front of his tunic. "Mary of the Cross?" His teeth bared. Acid burned through him. "Finola MacDonnell. What of she?"

" 'Twas the Convent of Saint Mary of the Cross." Corin's gaze sharpened. "On your first trip, you had told me that you would see one called Finola MacDonnell upon your return, that she was kin to your princess." He sighed. "That I should provide protection."

"True." His insides squeezed and twisted.

"I was too late, brother."

"What happened?"

"She wasn't killed, like the others," Corin said.

"But?" Blood dropped to his elkskin boots, his innards knotting.

"She's been taken by one called Albai—"

"I know the name. A raider of caravans, though he professes to be an honest trader." He'd disembowel the bastard. Finola! He had to get to her.

"The same. All others were killed, the convent looted. No one heard anything . . . not even screams." Corin shrugged. "None knew until the following day. My men and I were the first to approach. One of the wounded spoke the name of Albai before he died."

"How could it be that none would know of the battle?"

"Surrounded as it is by stone walls, no man could see over without climbing its slick sides. Few paid heed to the columns of smoke, or so 'tis said." Corin grimaced. "They lit small fires, so that much damage was done before anyone thought to look. Many were burned. One that lived outside the gate told of seeing the marauders wrap up the lady with the flame hair and take her from the city.''

''Which way? How is it that no one would know to follow?'' Einar ground his teeth together.

''Most are not of the Christian persuasion near the convent. The quiet, the burning, that could've been caused by cooking fires, the lack of moving about was not remarkable. Those within the walls had always kept to themselves—''

''And the Ionan?'' He couldn't say her name again. It was burned on his brain. Finola! He'd skin the hides from their bodies when he found the culprits.

''Alive. I've had word of her imprisonment, though I've not been able to free her. Albai's holding is well fortified.''

''Why was she kept alive?''

Corin shook his head. ''That I don't know.'' His shoulder lifted and dropped in the eastern way. ''Caprice. Value on the slave market. Who can tell? Perhaps she was taken three sunrises past when the earth shook—''

'' 'Twas then.'' He'd felt it. He hadn't wanted to leave her. Now she was in mortal danger. He should've carried her to his ship and taken her back to Icelandia.

''No one knows for sure.'' Corin shrugged. ''All others were killed. My runner heard they wrapped up the girl and took her. He told of her fiery hair.''

''How can no one hear the ruckus of battle?'' Einar ground his teeth.

''Well planned, carefully executed.''

''No Viking enclave under attack would go so unnoticed. Were the people blind? Stupid? Or partners to the infamy?''

''Those are questions for which we have no answers, my friend. I hope to know more soon.''

''Fool's game.'' Fury rivered through him.

''It was done thusly, friend Einar. They have taken the girl and the Cup of Antioch.'' Corin gnashed his teeth, his free hand flexing and unflexing.

Only years of training in self-control, in battle and negotiations, kept Einar impassive and silent. The Cup of Antioch! Rearing up again. It'd been back in the convent for some years now, but once before it had been the cause of great pain to his family. Was its wickedness repeating? When he'd been but a stripling, his own mother had been kidnapped by Bulgars, along with the Cup of Antioch, from the very same convent. His mother's family had been guardians of the Great Cup for generations. It'd been his mother's family that had given it to the Convent of Mary of the Cross for safekeeping. When his mother had been rescued by his father's Vikings, the Cup had been returned to the convent. Cursed vessel!

"What ails you, brother?"

"Nothing," Einar said through his teeth. He'd seen the replica more than once, but he felt no awe for the relic. He considered it'd been a source of pain for his beloved mother while she lived. More than once he'd seen her cry while she held a replica, made for her by a Viking artisan. For that reason, he'd never cared for it. Nay! He despised it.

Now, Finola, cousin to Princess Asdis Iona, had been taken by brigands along with the Cup. That damnable Cup of Antioch rose like a specter once more in the abduction of another committed to Viking care, one who'd become dear to him in a few short hours, one whom he'd dreamed of during the days they'd been apart. He'd consign it to Hades if he could. Not now. He had to find her. Finola MacDonnell would be safe. He made a vow. To hell with the Cup of Antioch.

If the Cup were discovered, mayhap he'd destroy the accursed relic, once and for all.

6

There is no calamity greater than lavish desires.
Lao Tzu

Moments before, silence had stretched its neck into an arcane heartbeat. What had woken her? She'd been dreaming of Einar Thorhallsson, how warm and safe it'd been under his cloak. More than once she'd fallen asleep while sketching him. Her captors hadn't removed the metal tube fashioned to keep her sketching materials intact. In fact, they'd shied away from them, as though by reproducing features, she'd conjured up demons. She hoped they thought that. It might keep them from stealing her precious stylus and pressed papyrus. She'd done a few sketchings the day of the earth shaking. A man. A boy. The market. Einar Thorhallsson. They'd disappeared. Thorhallsson. She'd done him from memory since coming to her captors' holding. She rolled up the precious remnants of her art, depositing all in the metal cylinder, the one possession she had from the fateful day. She'd never forget that time.

Then Finola heard the sounds. A struggle! The muffled screams told the story. They'd woken her. She knew what was happening. It'd not been the first time in her captivity that she'd heard the wrestling, as a woman fought against rape. The adversary usually won. More than once she'd covered her ears at their piteous cries and howls. More often than not, the victims were little more than children. Female children were as much at risk as the adults.

In the east females were prized in their youth, which came quickly, and they aged just as fast, and could be killed or abandoned when unwanted. Not much better happened to them in the west, unless they were protected by family. But, in the east, a woman was rarely more important than trade goods, which in essence was what she was. Sometimes in the east, as well as the west, a child could be loved, as Finola had been loved by her grandfather. At times, in the west, a woman was given the choice of life, as she'd been. It was unheard of in the east, unless the woman was a ruler. Even then the spectrum was narrow.

Another scream! Even more terrified. Finola clenched her fists, biting her lips. One of their captors, not a eunuch for they protected the harem, had broken into the outer holding area, adjacent to the harem.

Though the captives were not inviolate, not untouchable, like the members of the seraglio, they'd been promised protection until their hearing. Each day new promises were made to them; each day more covenants were broken.

Once more an agonized yowl! At that moment she recognized the voice. One of their captors was attacking Dalia, the young handmaiden who'd been captured about the same time as she. No! She couldn't let it happen. Like many young ones in the east, Dalia didn't know her exact age, but Finola knew she was just a girl. She could die from assault.

Grabbing the small knife, she'd kept hidden in her clothing, she took a deep breath. Why they hadn't discovered the small, slender dirk that she'd been able to secret in the diaphanous folds of the harem garment, Finola didn't know. The women who'd been in charge of disrobing her had seemed disinterested in all things. Their apathy had worked for her.

What could she do? She moved toward the anteroom, cold sweat pearling her body, praying that the clumsiness so often decried by Glam wouldn't manifest itself. She was an artist, not a warrior, but she'd learned the rudiments of self-protection. She needed to be strong and sure. Her heart thumped so hard, she was sure it could be heard.

Patting the small dirk, she moved toward the door ... Before she'd come east to Antioch, the seamstress for her cousin had sewn cunning pockets into her clothing where the dirk might be hidden. She'd thought it fustian at the time. She'd needed nothing but her stylus, whitings, soft brushes of combed feathers.

Not now. She had to remember all the things Glam had tried to teach her. She hadn't done well, but she'd tried, for Iona's sake. She'd never thought to need the dirk. Since her capture she'd kept it close at hand at all times. She'd fight before she'd be violated, die if need be. Somehow her attackers had never discovered the weapon, but even if they'd done so, she would've found a way to fight for her life and soul. Now, she hesitated, gripping the dirk. Would she die? Never again to see Einar Thorhallsson. Where was he now?

When another scream split the air, she bit her lip and charged from her small cell to the anteroom where young Dalia stayed.

She saw the great beast of a man atop the slight child-woman, and leaped upon his back, hoping the girl beneath wouldn't be crushed. Dalia didn't have the strength to defend herself. If the ogre penetrated her, surely he would tear her to pieces. He was built like the great fighting oxen brought from Nubia.

Before the beast could react she thrust her knife into the front of his neck, quite sure from the rudimentary healing she'd picked up from her cousin that she'd hit the jugular. Jerking in and back with all her might, she felt the first tension, the rush of life's blood. God! It was not her destiny to kill, but to create. His great roar of anger became a gurgling, choking gasp. He released Dalia, struggling to staunch the flow, grab the knife and Finola, all at the same time.

She scrambled off his back as he twisted and turned, fighting to keep the life force that gushed from him. Then he sank to the floor, trying to bellow but only able to hiss as he drowned in the rush of blood from his throat.

Finola fought nausea. If she could escape it, she'd tried not to even hunt. Her method of sketching animal life, rather than trapping it and killing it for eating, astounded those around her. The few times she'd been forced by her parents to take part, she'd killed a few creatures, big and small, and hated it.

It was a nightmare. She'd killed a man, broken God's law, and she didn't care. No! She was glad the hulk had been dispatched. She pressed her hand to her mouth to fight the retching. Never had she thought to take a human life. It was her dream to study all living things, commit them to canvas or cast them in metal or carve them from marble. Now, she'd killed, and though she thought it justified, she wished she'd had another option.

She shook her head. How her cousin would laugh at her queasiness. It'd been a righteous killing, if any could be such. Those months she'd lived at Sinclair Castle after the death of her grandfather, it'd been drilled into her how important self-protection was, how necessary quick action was. She shuddered. She'd done it. She could never be happy about it, only glad that Dalia had been saved. Now what? Her world was a whirling morass.

So many things had happened. Her mother and father dying of ague, one after the other, her dear grandfather MacDonnell, following them a scant two turns of the sun later. Then she'd gone to Sinclair Castle to live. It'd been at the urgings of Iona and Sinclair that she'd accepted the patronage of Contessa Eva Lisetta di Marchi, and embarked on the trip to Antioch to begin her studies. For a time she'd been sure she'd found peace, direction in her life with the work she loved.

Then she'd met Einar Thorhallsson, and her world had exploded in a different beauty. At that moment she'd begun to question if her work could really be her whole life ... because of one golden man from Icelandia.

All those wonderful happenings had led to this? Taking a life? She'd be consigned to perdition. What would Thorhallsson say?

She shivered. She couldn't think of the Viking. She'd killed a man. It made her sick.

She swiped a hand over her damp face, staring down at the pile of flesh that had once lived. Her soul was consigned to Hell for the greatest of sins. Yet, another part of her shook with relief that she'd been able to stop him.

"You've done well, milady."

"I've killed, Dalia."

The young girl shrugged. "I'm glad 'twas him and not me."

"As you say." Finola bit her lip. She wished she had the sangfroid of the handmaiden. Her stomach kept heaving! She took deep breaths.

Both women stared down at the ponderous slab, pooled in blood. Then they gazed at each other for long, breathless moments.

"Oh, Lady Finola, you'll surely be boiled alive for this," Dalia said, wiping her mouth with the back of her hands, then pressing them down the sides of her tunic, as though she'd cleanse her person from the dead man's touch. "As will I. May Allah make my death a swift one," she said. She grimaced at Finola. "But I still thank you for your deed."

"Did he violate you?" Finola reached out to the fragile young woman.

Dalia shuddered but didn't seem embarrassed by the query. Young as she seemed to be, she understood. She shook her head. "He tried . . . his hand . . . almost."

"Wash yourself to remove his stench, while I decide what we'll do with him." Finola could only bless the eastern ways of washing constantly, of having at hand a myriad of lavings that both cleansed and perfumed.

Mouth agape and wincing a bit, Dalia backed around her cot as she rushed to the bowl of scented water. She soaped and rinsed over and over again. Glancing over her shoulder, she shook her head.

"What can we do, milady? He'll be found and then we'll die, or worse, we'll be given to the caravaners going to Cathay.

They will use us like the mountain sheep they favor." She groaned. " 'Twould be better to be boiled, mayhap."

"Do not jest," Finola said, her voice hoarse with angst.

"I don't," Dalia responded, puzzled. "Why recall the child and the maddened bull. He tore her and trampled her," Dalia said, shrugging. "The watchers were entertained. There was none to save her."

Finola fought the tremors that threatened as she pictured the many aberrations they'd witnessed since becoming the prisoners of the Tartars. Women used as sport in the center of a ring of men, having them converge on her, abusing her until she was dead. Easily discarded, they would look to other diversions at once. Children, boys and girls, were often the targets. The world was cruel to women and children.

"I will not think on it. Better to discover our location and find a way out of here."

Finola wasn't quite sure where they were, but she thought they could be north of Antioch, whence she'd come, toward the land of the Bulgars. Tartars roamed there, along with their nemeses, the Bulgars. And, since it was custom to placate the enemy when at disadvantage, she knew they could be given over to the hated and ferocious Bulgars as a peace offering or a barter, and that might be the best that could be done to them.

She didn't like to tell Dalia that she was sure that whatever the future held, neither of them would like it, nor would they be likely to survive. Women, except for ransom or barter, had little value.

Even if Einar Thorhallsson knew by now she'd been abducted, he wouldn't know her location. Would he try to find her? There was no other who could rescue her.

She wanted to be realistic and calm, as Glam had instructed she should be in a crisis. Think! She shook with indecision, the tremors starting in her soul. All she'd wanted was the solace of her art. Then she'd met Einar Thorhallsson, and he'd become a most important part of her life's dream. All was naught. She'd become the prisoner of Albai, the Tartar, a man renowned for his cruelties.

Dalia's fatalistic acceptance of the ill treatment she might receive made Finola both admire and wish to berate the other girl. She couldn't just accept that she'd die.

She fought her fear, glaring at the girl. "We'll get rid of him."

"Milady, we cannot lift him," Dalia said, shivering and glowering at the dead.

"We'll get Gregor the eunuch to help us. He hates the Tartars, and will be glad to serve them a bad turn."

Dalia yelped, shaking her head. "He's most cruel."

"We have few choices," Finola said. "We know for certain we'll be boiled in the courtyard caldrons for killing one of them. We should try to put that off for another day, I'll be thinking."

"You jest, milady. Why do the faranghi be mirthful at such times? You are all mad," Dalia said, grimacing.

" 'Tis truth you speak. And I still say we must use Gregor." At times Finola longed to speak her Gaelic tongue, but since coming east, she'd had to rely on the Greek and Latin which were the universal languages. She'd learned a few Tartar phrases, but she found the harsh singsong of the tongue difficult.

"Gregor is for gold, only," Dalia said. "He would sell his mother, had he one, though I do not think it." She looked over her shoulder at the ornately scrolled door as though the person in question would come through it.

Finola waved her hand. "The Tartar has gold. Turn out his pockets."

"Aagh, milady, I cannot touch the beast. He's covered with gore." Dalia waved her hands in the air.

"I can." Trying not to gag at the feel of blood on her hands, and gasp at the heaviness and stench of the Tartar, Finola went through the capacious pockets in the coarse, loose-fitting smock. When she felt the telltale jingle of drachmas, the coinage much favored by the Tartars, she swallowed her misgivings and dug out every round, hole-centered coin.

"Here! Look. We'll call Gregor. He'll be glad of more gold."

"I trust him not," Dalia said, speaking the Greek common to the Byzantine empire.

"Then I must go."

"No!"

"Then hurry."

"We are doomed," Dalia said, moving to the door. Only once did she look back at Finola.

In moments Dalia returned with a man almost twice her height and surely more than that wide. He was garbed in flowing robes of finest cotton, light, and striped.

"What you want, *faranghi*?" The sharp question was followed by a quick scrutiny of the room, the almond-shaped eyes barely touching on the dead form before they returned to Finola's face. "You will be boiled in oil, *faranghi*." He smiled.

Finola eyed him when Dalia gasped. "What a bit of sunshine you are, Gregor. Are all you Rus the same?"

"Bulgar!" He spat the word at her. "Rus are like Tartar, stupid. We are people of the spirit and the mind."

"Yet you'd enjoy seeing us boiled." Finola didn't glance at Dalia when she groaned.

The eunuch shrugged. "You're not Bulgar, and a fete is a fete. Why not enjoy the distraction? Many sweetmeats."

"Didn't I say he was—"

Finola waved aside Dalia's angry wail before an insult could alienate the Bulgar. He was not much, but she had few choices. She needed him. "Gregor, I offer you the Tartar's gold. No, don't bother with his pockets. I have it."

Gregor straightened, his eyes narrowing to slits. "I could take it."

"And I could cut your throat as I did his, Bulgar. Are you so caring of the Tartar, you'd not strike a bargain?" Finola watched his greedy mind work, a dot of spittle at the corner, a muscle high on his bulbous cheek twitching in angst. "Well?"

"What say you?" Gregor glanced over his shoulder at the door. "Make it quick. The watch comes."

"Not in here," Finola said, sounding surer than she felt.

Striding across the capacious chamber, she lifted one of the ornately crafted rugs that were so favored by the Byzantine families. "Roll him in this."

"No, *faranghi*, it's too costly for that. I will get another ... less well woven." Gregor spun about, his soft slippers making the merest whispering sound on the marble flooring. Everything was of the richest, not just the buildings and tents they'd been in, but all the accoutrements. More than once Finola's artistic soul had wondered about the fine architecture, building materials, furnishings and art used in the east, but now her mind was filled with the idea of escape. All previous plans had seemed too risky. Now any plot seemed a viable choice.

With Gregor's aid, for she fully intended to exploit the strength of the eunuch to help her gain freedom, perhaps she and Dalia had a chance of getting away. Which way to go was a puzzle, but she would discuss it with the eunuch.

"He'll bring back the guard," Dalia said.

"He's too greedy. He'll want the money before he turns us in," Finola said, hoping it was true.

Dalia grimaced.

"Come, Dalia, get a mop and some scented water. We must get the stink of the Tartar from this chamber. No need to give those who'll come after us any help in finding us."

"We'll be chopped up alive, then boiled," Dalia muttered, hurrying to her task while keeping a distance from the dead Tartar. She was still at it when Gregor reentered their chamber.

"Here, we'll wrap him in his." He closed the door, proffering a moth-eaten camel blanket that gave off a distinctive stable odor.

Finola eyed the eunuch but said nothing. She had no doubt that he would somehow commandeer the rug at their feet.

The job took longer than expected. Not only was the Tartar heavy and unwieldy, he was tall, making it hard to conceal him.

After much tugging and tucking the unlikely trio managed to cover the body, then Gregor tied the foul rug with the woven hemp favored by camel drivers, binding the corpse in it.

"Where will you take it?"

"Never mind," Gregor said. "Go back to bed."

"No. We're leaving," Finola said, shaking her finger at him. "And you'll help us, Bulgar."

Gregor bared his teeth, shaking his head. "Not I. You'll boil alone, *faranghi*."

"I knew it," Dalia whispered.

Finola struggled to hide her mounting fear, not so much of the oversized eunuch, but of what could happen if he raised the alarm. There'd be no chance for them then. And the punishment would be merciless, and not swift.

"You err in this. You may try to kill us now . . . or Dalia and I will kill you, but we'll not stay to be violated once you confess that you know we did the deed. No, we leave. Now." She waved the knife. "And if you don't aid us, I'll swear on my mother's grave that you forced us to go free."

The Bulgar stepped back at the curse, muttering unintelligible words. "You will die anyway, *faranghi*. Mayhap 'tis better I get you out of here."

"We'll be free, not confined elsewhere." Finola glared back at him. She had no intention of waiting for someone else to chart her destiny. If she had to die, it would be on her terms.

"How?" Dalia breathed.

Gregor smiled, his two broken teeth looking silvery in the shadowy lamplight, his shadow quivering on the stone walls looking eerie and monstrous. "You'll not get away."

Finola nodded. "We will, Bulgar." Her mind stumbled and fumbled for the right words. "You'll lead us to the emir's quarters, and let us out that way."

Gregor's mouth dropped. "How know you of this?"

Finola didn't, but she'd been in the east long enough to know that the leaders provided escape hatches for themselves just as men from Iona were wont to do. And she'd been shown the tunnel that led down from the tower room in Castle Sinclair. She'd found it exciting, though her cousin hadn't liked it much.

"You either help us, or I'll die with your name on my lips as perpetrator." She balanced the knife on the palm of her hand as she'd been taught, alert for any sudden offensive movement on the part of the eunuch. She hoped she'd be accurate. She gestured for Dalia to get behind her. "Do we go?"

Gregor nodded. "But you won't get far. I'll sound the alarm."

Finola nodded. "I was sure you would. Hurry, Dalia, bring little, some of the food, another weapon, something warm for the nights. Quickly."

"We'll boil twice," the girl muttered.

In moments, they were out of the anteroom that'd been a prison for the two women for too many turns of the moon. Since that fateful day she'd been accosted, Finola hadn't been her own master. The convent, and all its rules, hadn't bound her as had Albai's holding. The fear of violence had been a constant companion since her abduction. Albai's palace was a tower of horrors. Many times in the night, the screams of those massacred at the Convent of Saint Mary of the Cross had reverberated in her head, awakening her and bathing her body with moisture while hot tears streamed down her cheeks.

She'd hated the long, frightening journey to Albai's, the ignominy of the slavelike treatment. Though she hadn't been beaten, there'd been other agonies. She'd been forced to watch others eat and quench their thirst while her tongue swelled from dryness, and her stomach growled. Even the moments when she needed to relieve herself were without privacy. She didn't understand their lingo, but she'd been humiliated by the men watching her and laughing. Then came the most horrible moment of all, when she'd faced the sharif of the Tartars, Albai. A most dirty, unkempt man, he'd laughed when she'd demanded to be released.

"Released, milady? Never. Not until your ransom is paid. I'm patient. I'll wait. Perhaps you'll even be returned unused if the price is high enough." He'd shrugged, then had begun to eat and drink with complete disregard, leaving her standing in front of him.

"I'm thirsty."

Albai had looked up at her, smirked, then offered her his goblet. When she would've taken it, he guffawed and tipped the liquid to the ground.

"You're a pig," she'd said in Greek.

A tattered-looking scarecrow of a man whispered to Albai. The Tartar had roared to his feet, backhanding Finola. He all but knocked her senseless before she could react. She'd been carried from his presence.

In short order, she'd learned not to show her feelings, speak her mind, or let her fear show.

Since that time she hadn't seen Albai, but she'd felt his presence. She sensed that whatever would happen to her she'd be at the mercy of a cruel, uncompassionate tyrant. Better to die fighting for freedom than wait for a questionable, but no doubt horrible, outcome.

Even now as she followed behind Gregor, she could recall how nauseated she'd been when she'd watched the Tartar consume too much before he'd even looked at her. Then he'd lost his dinner over the trencher board. None of the others seemed to think it was extraordinary, but Finola had been glad for the first time that her own innards had been empty or she might've imitated him.

Though that was only mere turnings of the moon, it'd seemed like eons that she'd been a prisoner.

"*Faranghi*, pay attention," Gregor growled.

"Yes," Finola said, angry with herself for daydreaming. "Let's go."

"You will follow me, closely. If we're seen, I will say I've caught you escaping."

"Noble Gregor," Finola murmured, urging Dalia to stay close to her.

When he turned away to check the outer chamber, she reached up to a shelf and picked up a heavy seal, much favored by easterners for making their mark on their goods. The heavy iron could be either heated or dampened with indigo root. All traders had a mark, and were eager to make sure that none could lay claim to their booty. It'd been left the first day by

Gregor and she'd kept it, never letting on when he'd searched for it that it lay among some dried weeds on the ledge above the laving dish. In plain sight, it was effectively masked by the weeds. Now Finola had a second weapon. She kept her hand down, concealing it in the voluminous folds of the harem pants both she and Dalia wore. The clothing would give them little protection or warmth if they did manage to get free, but there was no time to worry about that.

The outer corridors fascinated Finola. She'd only seen them on her arrival, and had had scant time to study them. There'd once been paintings on the stone, but the dampness of the walls had peeled and rotted them away. How wondrous to see if they could be reclaimed. What a story they might tell. Art was the true road to past times. She hadn't time now to dwell on that. Survival was her only focus.

She wrinkled her nose. The mustiness surprised her after the colorful opulence of their quarters. And she'd not thought of anywhere in the east as being moist. Always it'd seemed dry enough to choke one. But these walls reminded her of many Hibernian and Scots castles. Albai's holding was damp, not chill.

Down one corridor, up another. Down one set of stairs, up another. Their padded foot covering masked sound, but it was a hollow comfort in a place where the slightest whisper was magnified by the empty silence.

"Shh, now we must go slowly. There will be guards. We must wait until the changing. They will move down toward the master's main door, then."

Time was a moment of danger, a breath of peril. No sound could be made that would bring discovery. It would mean painful death. Finola feared to draw air into her constricted throat. Surely Dalia felt the same. Heartbeats were loud in the stillness. There was a gritty whisper of wind that plied through the lancets. No other sound.

"Now."

At the eunuch's words both women started, but didn't hesitate to follow.

Gregor led them through a narrow door, closing it behind them. He pointed downward. "There's your escape."

Finola was about to nod, when the weak flickering light from the wall sconce licked across Gregor's sallow features. He was smiling. He looked eager. What hell waited at the bottom of the stone steps?

"Thank you. Go now, Gregor. We won't need you."

When Dalia would've spoken Finola pinched her, and waited until the eunuch was turning to leave. It was then she hefted the heavy seal, bringing it up high, then down as hard as she could on the back of Gregor's head. What would Glam say about her clumsiness now?

"You can keep some of your gold, Gregor, and I hope you'll be found with it. We'll take some for your treachery. It wasn't enough for you to sound the alarm, later," she said, her mouth tight. "You had a terrible end planned for us at the bottom of those stairs. Heaven help me, I read your twisted mind." She turned to the agape Dalia. "We go up, not down. Hurry, Dalia, and don't question."

7

There is strength in the union even of very sorry men.

Homer

"Make sure she's brought to me."

"That was not the agreement. I was to have her in exchange for the Cup."

"Your memory serves you wrong. She must be brought in secret to the bargaining table. When all is completed, she will be yours." Dealing with Albai was never easy. The man was a dog, never given to compromise. Intrigue escaped him. He'd not wanted to deal with him. There'd been no other way. "I would see the prisoner, Albai."

"No. She's locked away."

His skin bristled with alarm. "You know she's to be untouched."

Albai leered. "I didn't swear to that."

Cold sweat pearling his spine, he strove for an even tone. "It must be that way. I should see her."

"No!" bellowed the chief of the Tartars. "She's safe."

"See that she stays that way until the bartering . . . or you'll get nothing."

"You threaten me in my holding?"

"I urge you to stay within the contract." It was a struggle to keep from spitting in his fat face. "If members of the consortia discover you've deflowered one under your guardianship of great power, your use in the business world will be over. You know that as well as I."

"I like it not."

"The rewards will be great for the patient ones."

Albai turned his back and strode from the room tearing down the silken curtains swathed in the opening.

"He's in a fury, lord."

"I know. I know. We have to go. Damn his soul if he ruins all because of his lust."

"It will destroy your plans if he touches her, lord. What will you do if he does?"

"Draw and quarter the swine, and be glad to do it."

The two departed on horse, riding in the center of ten protectors, djellabahs hiding their faces. The desert wind was strong, the sand stinging. Beyond were the hills, a two days' ride. Over them would be the sea, their destination.

8

Great deeds are wrought at great risk.
Herodotus

Finola expected to hear an alarm at any time. The rounded staircase widened and was hung with richly woven rugs. At the top was a door.

Swallowing hard and shaking off Dalia's admonishing grip, Finola studied the area. When she saw the stairs leading down on the other side of the landing, relief made her knees tremble. They had to take it. Praise God!

"We'll go this way," Finola said, leading the reluctant Dalia. "Hurry."

"It won't be a quick death," the handmaiden said.

"So you keep telling me." Resentment at the everlasting doomsday prophecies of the eastern girl did much to steady her. Dalia was steeped in the eastern fatalistic acceptance of a poor life and a worse death. Finola was not. Fighting was not for her, but she'd dare anything rather than face recapture and the lingering horror that would accompany it.

The winding flat-stoned stairway seemed to go down forever. Were they going beneath the earth where they might encounter worse than Gregor? Were they going to Hell? Then they rounded a turn and were in front of an elaborate grillwork.

The sharif's quick exit! They'd found it. Beyond was a stable. Before trying the door, Finola studied the area. She noted the two guards and several young slaves who must've cared for the cattle. They bustled about, bedding down the creatures for the night, pampering the equines as though they were royalty.

"We should leave now."

"Shh, Dalia. We'll go when it's safe."

"We should take the road south, to Antioch," Dalia whispered in her ear. "'Tis safer, smoother."

Finola shook her head. "We'll go north and west, across the mountains. They will expect us to go to Antioch, and search for us there."

"No, milady, not north and west, 'tis a fool's journey," the servant said through her teeth. "None but Bulgars, wolves, Rus, and Tartars travel that way."

Finola shook her head. "I'm quite sure we're not more than three days from Antioch. I recall my terrible journey here, counting the moments until I could breathe again. We must not allow ourselves to take the obvious way back to freedom. We could be overtaken and recaptured. We'll take our chances the other way, the caravaners' way."

She hoped she could recall all the caravaners' routes she'd been shown. The cloth scrolls had been exhibited as part of the study program at the convent. A noted cartographer had been brought from the artisan's school in Antioch. It'd been part of learning the method of using Egyptian styli to study the maps. The first time she'd held the stylus in her hand, working it over easel and metal, she'd felt triumphant. Another step forward. At the time she'd been mildly interested in the maps. Now she wished she'd paid closer attention. She had an artist's memory for detail. Praise Saint Columba it would stand her in good stead, be strong enough to lead them to freedom. Using her artist's mind as a helpmate in an escape hadn't occurred to her. Now she plumbed every scrap of tutelage.

Einar Thorhallsson! Despite all her fear and desperation, he was there, in her mind. Had he returned to the convent?

Was he looking for her? Did he know she was missing? Would he care?

"Milady, we must go."

"I know. We go north and west. I will go alone, if I must."

"I'm sure of that," the handmaiden muttered.

There was little protection for her in Antioch, even if they managed to reach it. She couldn't forget the carnage, the destruction. Why had they done it? Was the Cup of Antioch so important? She could recall their exultant cries when they held it aloft. Why hadn't she been among the slain? She might never know. But she was determined to live if she could.

Escape and concealment were paramount. As a stranger in the east, she would be looked upon with suspicion. No matter where she went she would have to exercise care, keep covered and disguised as best she could. Perhaps along the way she'd find succor. No! Best to rely on herself. Even those that would be so inclined would be too fearful of Albai to render aid.

Go west! Then to the sea. With good fortune they'd find a ship going to Iona or Scotland. A ghost of a hope, but it was all she had. She wouldn't despair. "I go north and west, with or without you, Dalia."

Dalia nodded, grimacing.

As Finola stared at the antics around the stable, her hand hovering over the grille door, she noted the two extra guards in the small building just to one side of the stable. "What's that?" She whispered, pointing.

"'Tis the holding area for the booty," Dalia answered. "Many of the marauders have such. Their wealth stays there until they can assay it for keeping or put it up for sale. It's the way of things." Dalia peered at the building, nodding. "Some keep their booty vaulted in the ground or in caves."

"Then the Cup that was taken from the convent could be there."

"What cup?" Dalia eyed the guards who wandered the perimeter.

"The Cup of Antioch! It belonged to the convent where I was studying. As you said, if Albai has it, 'twould be there." Hope rose in her, her heart thudding. Could she escape and claim the great artifact too? Risky. Dangerous. It would be some small vindication for the loss of her friends. "It must be returned. It's kept at the convent, safeguarded by the Church."

"Milady, 'tis not important. We must flee," Dalia pleaded. "Let your church reclaim it." Dalia shook her head. "We must leave at once."

Finola nodded, biting her lip. "We can't let it be lost again, Dalia."

Dalia frowned. "It's not lost. 'Twill be with the other booty. There." She eyed Finola. "'Tis nothing to us, milady. Let us go, quickly."

"Albai cannot keep such a precious goblet. 'Tis said Saint Peter himself drank from it."

Dalia stared at her, dawning horror on her features. "What is that to us? We must be gone."

"Fear not," Finola said. "We'll be most quiet."

"Milady," Dalia all but squeaked. "We cannot."

"We can. And we'll carry it north and west with us. Would you leave it for the heathens?" When Dalia nodded, Finola frowned at her.

"There's other wealth, milady. I'll show you," Dalia said, her voice cracking.

Finola frowned at her. "'Tis not riches I seek, foolish girl, but the restoration of a relic." And it might make some of the nightmarish memories fade. If she saved it, it would be her memorial to her martyred friends at the Convent of Saint Mary.

Dalia gasped. "But, milady, can't you see how foolhardy 'twould be?"

"No!"

Dalia looked dumbfounded, then despairing. "We're lost. What does it matter if we die here when all's said and done? Even if we escaped from Albai, and could cross to the mountains and wilderness, the Bulgars are there, and more Tartars and the Rus." She rolled her eyes.

Finola didn't answer. Precious moments had elapsed. They had to move, get away. She was eyeing the watch. They tended to talk at the end of their tour that took them back and forth in front of the well-constructed mud, wood and thatch enclosure for the animals. They did the same at the smaller structure that contained the treasures. How dearly the Tartars prized their steeds . . . and their booty.

The young boys, who'd been busily hopping about the horses and bedding them down, now seemed to have settled for the night, too. "I will get the horses first. You will wait on the other side of the smaller building."

"But, milady—"

"Shh." Heart in her mouth, Finola edged the grillwork open, blessing the smooth workings. She moved through the gloom as quietly as possible, hoping that the intermittent sounds of the equines snorting and stamping would keep the guards from hearing her. God and good Saint Columba protect her!

She made it to the shadows of the enclosure. Exhaling, she waited, propped against the structure.

When she heard a sound on her left, she froze, then turned. She was almost face-to-face with someone her own height and much the same weight. One of the stable boys, who had white-blond hair that gleamed silver in the flickering light of the one lit torch, stared at her. She heard the hissed rattle of Tartar and shook her head.

"Then you're Greek?" the youth whispered.

"No. I'm a Gael from the Isle of Iona off Scotland's coast. Who are you?" Tense, she looked around her. Was the youth keeping her at bay until help arrived? She noticed the guards at the far end of the compound.

"Reric is my name. I was taken by marauders, as a child, from Norway, then sold. I don't remember it all. I've been here since I was six summers. Next year I'll be made a eunuch," he said, his face quivering once. "Why are you here?"

The impulse was to lie. How far could she go if he gave the alarum? She eyed the lad. "I'm leaving with my handmaiden." Finola shaved the truth.

The youth's mouth dropped. "Nay, you'll be boiled—"

"Yes, yes, I know all about that," Finola whispered. "I'm

going to get two horses. Now, please get out of my way." She fingered the seal in her left hand. The knife was in her right.

The youth shook his head. "You can't. They'd scream. They're like Albai's children. Any sound of mischief will bring his personal guard." He grimaced, then inhaled. "But I can do it, and release the others who will roam far afield by morning."

"You would do this?" Suspicion rivered through her.

"If you take me with you."

Lord! Finola reeled with the impossibility, the enormity of it all. She'd soon have a caravan. "We could be caught and killed."

The youth shrugged. "I was going to make a break anyway. They've done all else to me. Now, they would castrate me." His smile twisted. "I've lost all but my manhood, lady. I don't fear death."

Finola nodded. "All right. You get the horses. I have to get something out of the holding area."

The boy grabbed her arm in a surprisingly strong hand. "You can't. It's bolted."

Finola nodded, her mouth tight. "So I would expect. But I must try."

The youth grimaced. "Mayhap we'll die, lady, but I will aid you. I have greased those bolts many times, myself," Reric said.

Too shook with joy to speak, she only nodded. When he turned away she followed him to the back of the stables, imitating his steps and quiet movements.

Too quick for her to follow, he took three horses from their tethers, shushing another waking boy and speaking to him softly. It stunned Finola when the smaller lad rose to help, barely glancing at her. She hurried to the youth's side.

"We can't—"

"I must. He's brother to me, so I'm told. They killed our mother and took us for their uses. They'll tear out his tongue when they find me gone. After that, he will be given to the men who've—"

"Yes, yes, I've heard the screams," Finola said.

"Then we'll take him?"

She glanced toward the area where two other boys were lying, deeply asleep.

"I don't care what happens to them," Reric said. "They raped my brother and tried the same with me."

Understanding, Finola nodded once.

In moments four small desert horses were led to the back of the stables. The youth called Reric spoke Tartar to his brother, who went to the animals and soothed them.

Finola saw Dalia cowering beyond the stable, between it and the holding building. She moved toward her, gesturing for silence. Dalia stared wide-eyed at the two males. She shook her head but said nothing.

"Stay concealed. The boy will help me."

Dalia closed her eyes, shaking her head. "We'll die."

"Everyone dies," Finola muttered and crossed to Reric's side, keeping to the shadows, crouching as he did. It was slow going. Moisture pearled her body in expectation of discovery. Then, they were there. A few sticky moments when he moved the torches near the door, farther along the wall. Her teeth were welded together to keep from screaming. Surely the guards could hear them breathing.

"From a distance it can look as though they're in place," Reric whispered, jerking his head toward the guards. "This way they'll not see a shadow."

Finola nodded, praying it was true.

It took many sweaty moments to open the holding. Reric worked at the bolts. When they popped, with a cracking sound, the group froze.

They opened the door, inch by inch. Finola's hopes were shaken by the lack of light. In the dimness, only silhouettes, outlines of treasure showed. There were coin bags, gold, artifacts, carpets, and many unrecognizable shapes. It would take too long to hunt, too noisy.

"Tell me what you need, lady. I know where things are kept."

Hope flared. "A chalice—actually the reliquary that holds

it, and the chalice—" Finola clamped her lips shut. No time for detail. "A chalice."

To her surprise, Reric was quick and sure in the semidark, scouting out the relic in a shorter time than she'd dared hope. She stared at the Cup and its reliquary, believing for the first time they could escape . . . that she might see Einar Thorhallsson again. Finola quickly replaced them in the chamois bag, squeezing the arm of the youth and preceding him out of the holding. He locked it and followed her.

Finola tried to calculate the passage of time since leaving Gregor. Was he dead? Coming to consciousness? Had it been minutes or hours? It felt like ponderous turns of the glass. Reason told her minutes, but more than a few.

A few beats of the blood and the four of them were with the horses.

At Reric's direction they walked the animals through a large pen where other horses were kept. Along the way, Reric and his brother kept up a soothing Tartar conversation with the beasts. Though they milled and moved about, there were no loud or threatening noises from the steeds. Beyond the stable, in the faint starlight, Finola could make out the shapes of other horses grazing as they walked farther and farther from the holding pen.

Then they were out in the open. The starlight brightened. The hills and trees were pitch black silhouetted against the deep-blue night. They walked with their heads down, more hopeful each passing moment there wasn't an alarm.

More than once Dalia slipped and would've fallen. Finola kept a tight hold on her and bit back the pain of lacerations that came from wearing indoor slippers over rough, stony ground. Reric led them on a circuitous, rough path, up and down hillocks, into deep dales. Brambles and thorns tore at their clothes.

Dalia leaned on her more and more. But despite her own fatigue Finola was determined to keep going. So far there'd been no alarum, meaning that none had discovered the horses wandering away, the missing stablehands and prisoners, or the wounded or dead Gregor. What were blistered, bleeding feet to being boiled in oil in the courtyard?

"Now we can ride. Whither we go, lady?" Reric asked.

"North by west," Finola said, ignoring Dalia's groan.

Reric nodded, not seeming put off by this direction. He spoke to his brother, then swung bareback onto the first horse.

Dalia and the young boy also mounted with ease, seeming unperturbed by lack of the leather seat that could cushion their bodies.

Finola eyed the bare back of her steed and swallowed. Not since babyhood had she been on an unsaddled horse, and then it'd been a pony. She was adept at riding to the side, but, unlike her cousin Iona, she'd never ridden astride. Hell's fire! She'd learn. She could've cursed her stern father who wouldn't allow her the freedom enjoyed by her cousin. It was so foolish to closet women, to control them by denying them the freedom enjoyed by men and boys. More and more she saw the strictures as male control. She wanted none of it.

At that moment she wished with all her heart that she'd been raised as was her royal cousin, Iona, free and unfettered, daring anything a man could do. Viking women from Icelandia had far more options than she'd had. She'd had the heart and wish to try, but her unbending parents hadn't honored the worth of women as had good Queen Margaret and King Sigurd, parents to her cousin.

She clenched her fist in the horse's mane. By all the saints, nothing was going to stop her, not when she'd come so far.

Gritting her teeth, she avoided looking at her companions of the night and threw herself on as best she could. The others were already disappearing as she righted herself and urged her horse onward, her hands twisted into the mane. She glanced once over her shoulder. She wouldn't go back. Death in the wilderness was better.

She'd no doubt they'd be followed. And wasn't it said that a Tartar could track like a mastiff, sniffing the air and the ground, finding trails hidden to most. And always by their sides were the trained hounds from the mountain area, their long fur much like the Yaks that they were used to protect.

A sudden burst of movement under her had her almost toppling over the side. Already her companions were out of sight. She gripped the mane and kicked her horse's flanks. She had to catch up. Being alone in the Tartar wilderness would be even more dangerous.

All through the night they traveled, by the stars. Finola noted that Reric gazed at them as often as she did. Thank God and good Saint Columba for the clear sky. Iona and Glam had taught her to find her way by the stars, and she knew the vast collections and their different paths that changed with the solstice. If only she'd had a compasso. She'd been shown how to use the wondrous circle from Cathay, and had been intrigued by its power. But, until now, she'd never thought she would need one.

Onward they moved, up and down stone-strewn ground, riddled with holes that endangered their mounts, along paths that hugged the cliffs. Below were deep gorges with streams running like silver ribbons, the sides coated with scrub and brambles. It was never-ending torture to Finola, and she sensed that Dalia was suffering, too, though they never communicated with more than a few glances.

Reeling on the slippery back of her mount, Finola looked up when the others paused, noting that though Reric said little his arm and hand gestures were quite clear to her. Since this was a method of communicating that Viking and Scots used, she could comprehend most of it. How had the boy learned such signals? Did the brigands use them too?

They dismounted and drank from a trickle of water coming from a rock.

Reric walked back to her. "We cannot rest long. They'll be looking for us," he said as he handed her a chunk of grayish bread.

She nodded, chewing the heavy, grainy piece. "I want to keep moving."

Before they mounted again, Finola looked about her, then studied the sky. They were traveling west by northwest. It'd gotten colder, and she'd welcomed the coarse woven mats that'd been tossed across the necks of the horses by the young man and boy who accompanied them. They wore them over their shoulders to keep warm.

As the sun rose, they were moving a bit faster, but the pace seemed snail-like when she pondered what could be coming up behind them. Finola was braced to hear the unholy battle cry of the Tartar.

When Dalia swayed, she reached out to steady her. "We will be free, Dalia. Have faith."

"I trust that Allah will let me die quickly," the girl replied. "But I'm not sorry to be away from Albai."

"Neither am I," Finola murmured, falling behind her.

Reric had heard them. He paused, the others stopping behind him. "I, too, welcome the release whether it comes in freedom or death."

"Trust in God and Saint Columba," Finola muttered, ignoring Dalia's disbelief, Reric's obvious skepticism. The younger boy just stared. Finola hoped desperately that the Deity and the patron saint would indeed take their plight into account.

9

The bee is enclosed, and shines preserved in amber, so that it seems enshrined in its own nectar.
Marcus Valerius Martialus

Waves tore like snapping hounds' teeth over the bow of the Viking vessel, the full wind belling out the sails and propelling them at top speed through the rough seas. Sudden storms on the eastern end of the great sea were not uncommon, and were usually short-lived. But like most, this one was fierce and buffeted the Viking vessel, sending it hither and yon as the helmsman fought to stay on course. Not even their passage through the Pillars of Hercules had been rougher.

"Why so solemn, Einar Thorhallsson? Can thou speak on it?" Darg, his lieutenant, inquired in formal Icelandic. Though he usually captained the other ship, Lord Einar had wanted to confer with him.

Einar glanced at the man, more broad chested than himself, and almost as tall, his face scarred and weathered. "I wish to make all speed back to Antioch. There was no trace of Lady MacDonnell, cousin to our princess. Not even at the trade markets was there mention of her capture. I'm uneasy."

He was more than that. He'd never been more afraid in his life. Had Finola MacDonnell dropped through a hole in the earth? Why was there no gossip about her capture? If she were to be put upon the market, there would've been some rumors about it. To hear nothing was worse. Had she been taken to a harem? He glanced at the sky. Clouds were gathering. An omen?

"You have great enemies, as well as friends, Lord Einar. If an enemy knows you're looking for the Ionan, he might strive to smother any word on it."

"True," Einar spoke through his teeth.

Darg looked puzzled. "I, and my men, heard many other tales, some hinting at trouble in our wake, and ahead."

"And they didn't explain?"

"No. Nor did I comprehend." Darg frowned. "I suspected wrath from the consortia. Yet, I couldn't figure how that would fall on our heads. We've done nothing to gainsay them."

"Sometimes it doesn't take much." He couldn't worry about nebulous threats from unnamed sources. Finola Mac-Donnell was his focus. He had to find her.

"How is it that they speak in such veiled ways, milord? Are they in touch with the sea trolls?" He was half serious. No true Viking seaman discounted the water demons.

Einar eyed his lieutenant. "We've traveled long enough in the east to know that the most deeply hidden factors can surface and be known to the most unlikely. I questioned many of the members of the different consortia still present at the temple. I thought one would know of Finola MacDonnell." His jaw tightened as he stared at the water creaming by the hull. "None did."

"Would they dissemble?"

"Yes, but why?" Einar squinted at the horizon, wishing he could fly like the sea birds back to Antioch. Corin was his only hope. "Such posturings are not normal among those powerful men, unless they feel they could be threatened by greater powers." He feared for Finola MacDonnell. His two ships had coursed up and down the sea, taking to land whenever there was an inkling they might receive information. Nothing.

Darg stiffened. "And are we threatened, Lord Einar?"

Einar hesitated. "I'm not sure. Mayhap our ships are safe . . . but there's peril, and I would know what it is." He would've sworn on his father's grave that it had to do with the Ionan. There was no good reason to think that way. He couldn't shake the certainty, but he said nothing to Darg about it.

"We stand with you, as always."

"I know that."

"Your friend may have new information, milor."

"With good fortune he'll still be there, and not gone searching inland. I would question him. If anyone knows of a great conspiracy, it will be Corin."

"But why would that involve Lady MacDonnell?"

"I don't know that it does. But I will look for a connection."

"You trust this Tartar, I know, lord, but—"

"I learned to trust him under most adverse conditions." He bit back his exasperation. Darg was the most loyal of seamen, the best lieutenant a man could have at his side. Still, Einar had to admit that sometimes this rooted distrust of easterners annoyed him.

Darg nodded. "Then we make all speed back to Antioch."

"We do."

"I and all the men are with you, Lord Einar. We will find her."

"Yes." And he counted the minutes. Was she well? Had she lost hope that he would find her? She had felt the power between them, as he had. She must be strong until he could be with her. His lungs emptied in a powerful gust.

"You fear for her, Lord Einar?"

"Yes." Longing and trepidation. She had to be safe. Perhaps at the moment, Corin had her in Antioch. The ship couldn't travel fast enough. He'd tasted her mouth and found it a treasure beyond compare. His hands had floated close to those luscious curves, and he'd been fired hotter than the furnaces of Damascus where armorers fashioned the Damascene steel.

Never in his life had a woman lived in his mind in such a specific way, making a new space that no other could fit. She'd made a hole inside of him, and he needed her to fill it. Not all the women, east and west, who'd warmed his skins, had given him such a want . . . a need. With others he would anticipate the lovemaking, the completion. Then he could put thoughts of it aside until next his body demanded coupling. And he had the distinct impression that his lemans felt the same way. He'd always amply compensated them, and there'd been mutual satisfaction under the skins.

"Lord Einar, Corin spoke of the Cup of Antioch. 'Tis the same relic our people rescued for your mother?"

"Yes."

" 'Twould seem their destinies are tied."

Einar gripped the rail, his blood running cold, the vision of his sad-eyed mother swimming with Finola's.

"Land ho!"

10

He is a fool who leaves things close at hand to follow what is out of reach.

Plutarch

"Fools!" Albai laid about him with a whip. "She must be found. Today."

A servant ran into the room, dropping to his knees, banging his head on parquet. "Lord, thy horses are gone!"

"Allah's greatest curse be on those who took them, and those who allowed it." His bellow shook the silken curtains on the doorways.

Many cowered as more were brought before the master.

Albai sweated when he flailed at his servants. Not exertion but fear had him in a fury. That very day an emissary would come—

"Lord Albai!" Another slave entered, bowing but not kneeling. "One is in the outer chamber who would speak of the prisoner. What would I tell him?"

Now! Too soon! He swiped at the sweat upon his brow, handing his whip to his lieutenant. "I will come."

All the words he'd tossed about his brain seemed suddenly clogged in his throat as he faced the man.

"Where is the woman?" The emissary was unknown to

Albai, but he wore the right colors, the scroll had the right stamp.

"Not here."

The emissary inhaled, flaring his nostrils. "Whither?"

"Gone."

"Where?"

"I know not. I will find her and—"

The emissary left him standing, racing from the enclave, shouting for his steed.

Albai sweated and cursed. Many would die for this.

11

Give me where to stand, and I will move the earth.
Archimedes

And what of Corin? Had he found her? Einar paced up and down the beach waiting for his friend.

If there was a threat to Finola MacDonnell, he'd take it to heart and wage war on those who'd hurt her, until Wotan called him.

When he saw Corin on the strand, he hailed him and began to run.

Einar gripped his forearms. "Friend, I'm glad to see you. What news?" His blood congealed at his friend's solemnity. "Tell me."

"The prisoners seemed to have vanished into the wilderness." Corin barely flinched when Einar's hold turned crushing.

"Alive?" His throat was so tight, the word caught.

Corin nodded. "We've had no word to the contrary." He coughed. "She'd be too valuable to kill. She's saleable in the market."

Einar ground his teeth. "Someone must know where?"

Corin shook his head. "I'll keep searching." He sighed. "But there's little here for them to reclaim. If they hadn't sacked the convent so completely, they might've returned for some of the treasures. All is gone, as I told you, including the Cup of Antioch."

He could scarcely breathe. "This Albai . . . give me some direction." When Corin shook his head, he scowled. "Why?"

"She's no longer there. Somehow she's escaped."

"What?"

" 'Tis true. I know because runners have brought her description to the marketplaces. A high price is on her head." Corin's mouth twisted. "'Twould seem the Cup of Antioch is with her. None know if Albai is worried about the Cup or the female. I would say both. Albai hates to be crossed, and he is searching for her."

"As I will."

Corin nodded. " 'Tis your way. And knowing this, I have put out my own runners. It seems, if truth be told, as though she heads north by west."

"What? It cannot be." She'd be in Bulgar country.

"My runners will watch for your guidon. There'll be horses for you and your men when you go inland."

"Thank you, my friend."

Back on his ship, Einar gave sharp orders. The stoical Vikings jumped to do his bidding, his urgency infusing them with speed.

Soon they were out to sea, wake creaming out behind them.

Until dark shadows began falling they sailed, finding shelter in a cove before dark. It was useless to seek her without light.

Einar paced the deck filled with dismay.

"Lord Einar, would you have me stay on your ship?"

Not looking at his lieutenant, Einar nodded.

"You're sore troubled, milor."

"I am."

"Corin has brought bad news."

Einar shook his head. "There's hope." He struck the rail with his fist. "That damnable Cup, Darg! The cursed Cup of Antioch. It brings its evil upon me once more. I swear on my honor as an Icelandic Viking that I will destroy it."

"Was it not sacred to your family, milor?"

"Not to me. Because of it, my mother was sacrificed. Even when she was returned from Hell, she mourned. Not all the love of my father and myself could give her lasting joy. Now it would rob me of Finola MacDonnell. Why have the Fates dealt with me and mine this way?"

"All is not lost, milor. We'll make all speed. Wotan will let us find her. There's safe harbor a league from here."

They'd anchor there. Einar couldn't rest. He took the watches, his eyes straining into the darkness.

They broke out full sail at dawn.

By midday they'd traveled a good distance.

"Can they have gone this far, milor?"

"They had a good start on us. I look to be beyond their place when we take to the land and search."

" 'Twill be easier."

"And we'll do it."

" 'Twill be great fortune if we find them," Darg pointed out, immune to Einar's glare. "I heard Corin tell you she could be deep in a harem—"

"That's one of the places she could be," Einar said through his teeth.

"Or dead. Though 'twould sadden our princess."

"I'll not think of that." Einar turned his back on his lieutenant. Dead! No! If he had to turn over every rock, search every seraglio, sift though a sandstorm, he would do it. He'd not lose her. The enormity of his need, his covenant to find her pushed him as he stared out over the rough sea.

"Would you have me take the other ship and try the other way, Lord Einar?"

Einar pondered splitting his forces. "He said north and west. We go that way."

Darg nodded. "I would that I could trust the man as you do, milor."

Einar smiled. His stolid captain was slow to trust any but Viking, and even then, he didn't commit to anyone or anything without testing the waters, checking every facet of the person or thing. Darg was as solid as the glaciers of Icelandia; he was never impulsive. Einar might take chances; Darg would not.

Einar turned to give new directions to his men. They'd been approaching the shoreline. Rampant danger in the eastern waters kept them cautious, one ship staying farther out than the other. All were alert now.

For two days they sailed, curving in and out of bays, scanning headlands and cliffs.

Einar relied on his skill as a sailor, his factoring as cartographer, to tell him when to drop anchor. There would be scanners on land, sending messages as to his progress and direction.

"We land here?" Darg eyed the cliffs of brush and rock, the wide strand.

"We do."

Deeper water near the strand allowed for a closer mooring.

Einar leapt off the prow into the waters, welcoming the short swim that cooled and refreshed him. He waded ashore, looking around while studying the rock-strewn hillside that rose sharply a hundred feet from the water's edge. After several minutes, he gave the signal to lower the boat to bring the others in. There was no need to give further orders. The Vikings knew their jobs and didn't need any directive about shipping oars, furling sails, making all ready against a surprise attack from Corsairs or other renegades. The two crafts would be as secure as possible against marauders, with armed men aboard and on the strand.

Einar scanned the cliffs that rose behind the beach. Though not as forbidding or high as those in Sutherland, they were ample for hiding the enemy.

When a barefoot man came running over the rocks to the beach, Darg drew his sword.

Einar stayed his hand. "Nay, 'tis the courier Corin promised would meet us at every landing."

Einar strode ahead of his men, collaring the man as the other Vikings took up the semicircular position they always assumed for defense, one section facing the land, the other the sea.

In minutes the courier had turned back the way he'd come and was soon out of sight.

Darg moved to Einar's side. "Which way?"

Einar's smile was acid. "Still north by west. She's on horseback and not alone, but she is still free of the Tartar called Albai." Einar shook his head.

Darg frowned. "Hard to believe, milor. She must be blessed by the gods. Though she is free, she cannot know her peril, Lord Einar. She heads into Bulgar country. Albai will have trackers on her. Front and rear she'll be besieged. There's little to protect her."

"I'm aware." Einar ground his teeth. Even now she could be recaptured. Where in the damnable wilderness of the east could she be? Was he ahead of her or behind her?

Darg studied his lord. "Mayhap she has bought her protection."

"She has no means. She's but a student, under a patron's care." Einar's fist came down on his other hand. "She's but an untutored babe . . . a painter, a fashioner of iron and granite. Only the gods have preserved her this long."

"Then they will continue, lord."

"We follow."

Darg opened his mouth and closed it again.

"And don't speak to me of the danger. I know. I'll take only volunteers. Put the booty on your ship, and make all haste to Icelandia—"

"We follow you, Lord Einar." Darg ignored his lord's glower. " 'Tis our way. And you cannot gainsay the wishes of the men. 'Tis the rules of Viking trade."

Einar nodded, knowing it was foolish to argue. He was well aware his men would trail him, even if he insisted they leave. "They travel the high country. They've horses, but little else."

"We'll be in the country of Tartars, Bulgars and some of the wild Rus. Not to mention the Seljuks." Darg licked his lips. "We will have to see to our weapons."

Einar's mouth twisted. "A veritable crusade."

"Yes."

"Rig all sails. We must be in time. We must land at the right strand."

"We will."

"I would have your Icelandic pragmatism, my friend."

"You have it, lord. You are only distracted."

Einar didn't question how Darg could know of his desire for more speed, a need greater than any quest he'd undertaken. His lieutenant and the men knew this was no ordinary chase and hunt. His men were intuitive. They'd been chosen because of their ability to factor, to conclude, to think ahead of their adversary. Besides, though he'd not spoken of his feelings for Finola MacDonnell, they weren't hidden. His perceptive Vikings understood. He looked to the horizon, tamping down his fear. He would find her, and soon.

12

Fortune helps the brave.

Terence

Pausing to rest in the craggy hills, tufted with coarse grass, smooth stones, rough rocks, the quartet tried to forget that their lives could be forfeit at any moment, and that if they were caught by Albai's men, they'd pray for a quick demise.

Finola reeled with fatigue, well aware that her companions were in the same sorry state.

Sea birds dove above them, and it seemed as though their cawing and crying had some elusive message of doom. It was past daybreak, but no sun touched them. Thick, doom-gray clouds hovered like a tattered blanket above them. Rain threatened, but no drops fell from that low-banked heaven. The area gave them little shelter from the cold wind that sliced off the sea; the rocks echoed back the cold starkness. It was not the usual weather in the land of everlasting sun, surely a welcome respite from the penetrating heat, yet a touch of the sun would've been most welcome. Somehow the cold seemed more frigid because it was alien to the environment. None could shake the rawness from their bones.

Early-morning mist coated their clothing and persons, making their tresses and garb damp prisons. They shivered with apprehension, chill, hunger and thirst. They'd been three miserable days on the run, without a fire to warm them, little to shelter them, and even less to sustain them.

More than once they'd heard horsemen, but not knowing whether they were friend or foe, they'd kept hidden with their hands over the muzzles of their steeds. A few times they'd seen shepherds and their fires, but they'd given them a wide berth, not wishing to give themselves away by disturbing the flock, thus causing the guard dog to signal their presence.

"We might be given shelter, milady," Reric said, hesitating, when they'd spotted the third herder.

"Yes, let's try," Dalia begged, shivering.

Finola shook her head. "No. They might feed us and shelter us, and wish us well, but a word to one of Albai's men who came on them would be the end for us. And they would tell, for they would risk much if they were caught in a falsehood. Even a chance word could seal our fate."

"We will die anyway. I'd prefer my belly filled first," Dalia said.

"No."

So they went hungry, relying for moisture on the grasses dampened by dewdrops to slake an everlasting thirst. Finola knew that trusting no one was the only way to gain freedom. Though Reric and his brother complained not, Finola saw how they swayed from fatigue. And Dalia had to be aided, time after time, or fall from the steed.

They couldn't give in, they wouldn't. Death was one thing, but if they were caught, the long tortures that would be prescribed for them were too barbaric to ponder.

Each incident, each near accident, made Finola feel guilty over the condition of her friends. Dwelling on what could happen to them if captured, what had been done to other hapless captives when they'd attempted escape from Albai, hardened her resolve.

Choking on huge quantities of dust and dirt at the tail end of the ragtag cavalcade was better than Albai's holding. Her mouth was so dry that she couldn't salivate; her eyes so encrusted with soil she could barely open them. So she kept her head down as she crossed the flatlands. Hunger made her queasy and light-headed. Her clothes and hair crackled with dirt. Her companions fared no better.

Reric moved back to her side. "Milady, I should get some game. My brother is weakening from our spare stores. The green figs we had yestermorn have griped him. He has emptied his innards," he said, licking his cracked lips. "Yon rocks could have a spring."

Finola sighed, shaking her head. "Too perilous, my young friend. We have to avoid the usual watering holes. Albai and his spies are everywhere."

Reric's lips tightened. "My brother falters."

"I know. Give him more of the bread and goat's milk." She raised her hand when he would've protested. "'Tis wise to push on. Let him have my share. When his stomach is not so empty he will travel better."

Reric nodded. "I will give him half mine and half yours."

Finola watched as Reric gave sustenance to his brother, though he didn't take any himself. When he looked at her and frowned, Finola moved closer. "What is it?"

"I thought we had more." He showed her the two chamois skins with the milk and bread.

Finola grimaced, her innards tightening with fear and hunger when she saw how littler there was. "We must push on, and hope we can steal something along the way from a passing shepherd."

Reric shook his head. "It's not easy to get close to them without their guardians giving the alarm."

"I know. Soon we'll have to try."

Reric nodded, his face grim.

Dalia lifted her head from the folds of her moth-eaten blanket. "I would like a fire to toast my toes, and I'm parched, milady."

Finola shook her head, eyeing Reric, who gestured to his brother to rise, even as he tied the chamois bags to the side of his horse. "Not to be. Come, we must push on."

Though Dalia groaned she didn't hesitate to knee her mount

and get in line behind Gar. As Reric led the way, Finola took her place at the rear.

Miserable, cold, hungry, they trudged forward. Distancing themselves from the enemy was their only hope.

Soon they'd turn toward the sea. Mayhap they could find a ship that would take them to Rome. In Rome they would be safe, as would the Cup she carried. She touched the chamois bag that hung from her waist. She couldn't return it to Antioch, now an alien, threatening place. Albai had penetrated a holy, inviolate convent. Barbarians had done it before, but they'd been castigated by the pope and the patriarch. Did no one know of the latest atrocities? Surely that was impossible. Was the great patriarch at risk from Albai? Better to take the artifact to the center of Church power. The papacy would protect it.

Finola still had the drachmas she'd removed from Gregor and the ogre who would've raped Dalia. With good fortune, they might be able to buy their passage to Rome. There would be a number of traders on the inland sea . . . and an equal number of Corsairs to prey on them. With God's help, and Wotan's, they would choose rightly.

Where was Einar Thorhallsson now? Had he ever returned to Antioch? Or had he forgotten her? He'd kept her so safe, so warm. Did he remember? Did he know her to be taken? Would he not care?

Some leagues beyond, Reric paused. Again, his weary face turned to Finola. "The path leads downward."

She nodded, her heart fluttering in fatalistic acceptance. The strand! Both safety and peril awaited. Which? They'd be in the open, vulnerable to attack very soon.

The horses picked their way delicately down the rock-strewn path that was little more than a goat track. When the wind died a trifle as they traversed into the lea of the hillside, they could hear the sea pounding up on the sandy swath below them.

"Your gods and saints have forsaken us, milady," Dalia said.

"Not so. We're alive, aren't we? Come, we must go on. Soon we'll find berries and greens to eat." 'Struth, she wasn't sure what was perilous to try and what was not. She knew some of the herbs for healing, but she'd not paid much attention to the edibles. Now she wished she had. Still, she'd gathered medicaments along the way. One could always use them if stomach gripes occurred or the ague overtook one. But whatever came, she'd survive. She had to, not just because she wanted to live so badly and not just because she wanted to sculpt and paint so many things, but because she needed to see Einar Thorhallsson. She ached to see him. She knew it was a fool's game, but she couldn't help it. Would she ever see him again? She would see him, she would!

Mayhap if she reached Rome, she would see him there. And there would be time to talk again. There was so much she wanted to say to him. They would be safe in Rome, as would the Cup and its reliquary. 'Twas known far and wide that the precious Cup belonged to Antioch. Mayhap 'twould never be returned there because of the danger of brigands and earth movements. The Church would decide.

Her patrons were in Rome, as well as the central monastery of the friars who'd taught her about the treasures of Antioch when she'd lived on Iona. It was they who'd submitted her work to the patrons in Rome, without whose support artists had little chance of producing any volume of work. She owed them the effort it would take to rescue the Cup. In her heart she needed to do the deed as a memorial to her fallen comrades at the Convent of Saint Mary. It'd become her mission. After seeing to the safety of the Cup, there would be time to talk to the Viking . . . if he was in Rome. All traders went there from time to time. Surely he would, too. Not all her artistic dreams had fostered the urgent need that one golden-haired man had wrought in her. No other person could command her visions and hopes for a tomorrow as he had done.

Life was so strange. She'd thought that nothing could ever be more important to her than her craft. Now, there was Einar Thorhallsson, and he'd claimed a piece of her life; a portion of the importance and the memory of him lingered inside her, heating her, making her sure, yet very uncertain. She could barely understand the myriad emotions that'd assailed her since meeting him. Even swamped with fear at Albai's holding, a part of her had cloven to Einar, to be soothed by him, to be protected by the great emotions he'd engendered in her.

The horse sloughed sideways. Finola gripped its mane, berating herself for daydreaming. Yet, 'twas sinking into reverie that had kept her from going mad.

She turned her mind to her craft. There'd been a friar from Genoa at the convent who'd taught the students to recognize the great original works, separating them from clever fabrications. Many of them were considered masterpieces by some.

Segregated in most of the teaching, male students rarely mixed with females. All were protected or indulged by wealthy families. Her cachet had been the Roman patron who'd acquiesced to the pleadings of the Ionan friars and agreed to underwrite her expenses. It'd been a great honor. And now another reason she felt obligated to see to the safety of the relic.

Rome? Would they reach it? Would she ever see Einar Thorhallsson again?

Her horse stopped, almost jolting her from its back. Reric was looking back at her. He had his finger to his lips. Nodding, she moved around the other two horses to his side.

"What is it?" Her whisper seemed to echo into the wind. She could smell the salty spray.

"Milady, I don't feel good about this. We'll be in the open on the strand. Perhaps even now Albai's men await us."

Finola stared at Reric. "I share your anxiety, Reric. We have little choice. Finding a ship is our only hope."

"And if we're seen?"

"We'll not be taken," Finola announced.

Reric nodded, his face grim and purposeful.

"I will lead," Finola said.

Reric swallowed, his throat constricted. "I will, milady."

"Allah protect us. We're undone! Run for your lives."

At Reric's alarm, the neighing of frightened horses, and men shouting, Finola leaned over her mount's neck, kicking at its sides. Direction didn't matter. Get away! Hell! She'd rather plunge to her death down a rock-strewn slope than submit to Albai. She wasn't giving in without a fight.

"Flee, Dalia, flee."

All at once her steed leaped and landed hard on flat, solid ground. They'd made it! Kicking harder at her mount, she laid over it and prayed she could outrun the marauders. She had no idea in what direction she was riding, or if she was anywhere near her companions.

Thundering hooves behind her kept her spurring her small horse. Then a much bigger equine pulled alongside. Panic had her kicking her horse again and again.

When rough hands pulled her from her steed, she screamed and turned to fight. There was no chance. Strong arms imprisoned her, rendering her immobile.

Swathed in dust and tattered veils, she could only fume and curse, shake with fear when she was put on the ground. "Touch me at your peril, beasts," she said, her voice shaking. She struggled to get her dirk free, aiming the puny weapon at her attacker. "And release my friends. They are free and belong to no one."

"Pray do not smite me, Finola MacDonnell."

The laughing voice above her head froze her. "Who are you?" It couldn't be! She'd conjured him up.

"Einar Thorhallsson of Icelandia at your service, milady." He leaned close. "We meet again . . . and once more in extraordinary circumstances." He touched her arm. "Are you all right, milady?"

His voice and touch had her reeling. Giddy with relief, she reached out. When he grasped her hands, she almost cried.

"I'm here, Finola."

His caressing tone shook her. "I can't believe it. How did you find me?"

"I searched."

His words were simple. His tone said she was a holy grail. Shivering with reaction, she reached out.

"You're cold. Dammit!" He flung off his heavy cloak that had been tanned to silky softness not quite imitating the cloth of Cathay. The skins were warming, though not heavy. He scooped her close when he draped her in it. "Are you well? Did they harm you?"

She saw the fear, fury, an amalgam of hot emotions crackling in his eyes. "No . . . No, I'm safe . . . untouched."

"Unharmed is what I wish to hear."

"That, too." When he leaned down through the gloom and dust, touching his mouth to her cheek, she gasped.

"I will keep you safe, Finola MacDonnell."

She gripped his tunic, fighting back the tears that threatened to storm her. For the first time in so many days, she had hope.

"I . . . I thank thee," she said in halting Icelandic. She put her hands to his chest to balance herself. His heart pounded as hers did! Did he feel the same?

"My language sounds sweet on your tongue, Milady MacDonnell."

"Does it?" He was really there! With her! Not a dream, but a truth. If she died at that moment, her joy would be boundless because he was there.

"I feared for you."

At his scowl, she would've moved back, but he wouldn't let her. "What ails you, Einar Thorhallsson?"

"I had visions of your body broken, Finola MacDonnell, your blood spilled across this accursed land." He pulled her closer. "A man could go mad."

His whispered words ran over her skin like a caress. She shivered.

"You're not cold now," Einar told her. "You quake from reaction, milady." His hand stroked her. "Now that you're here in front of me, I can release the demons from my spirit."

She looked up at him, joy bubbling out of her . . . and more. "I, too, was bedeviled, Einar Thorhallsson." She couldn't stop looking at him. That hot, unfathomable wanting that she'd experienced when they'd been together in the earth shaking surfaced like a flood. She tried to laugh. "Glory be! Are you truly here, Viking? How can it be? You have horses. Ships." The Gaelic words slipped from her tongue. She couldn't stem her words. Relief made her giddy. Her knees had turned to water. "Thegn of Icelandia, you're most welcome."

Why had she said that? Beyond his arm, she could make out the dusty outline of his vessels, shadowy forms of his men. "You saved us. My thanks to you."

"As thegn of Icelandia I'm honored to serve, milady. No thanks necessary."

She heard the pride in his voice. His placement in the world was well defined. A sweet sadness overtook her. He could be king in his country. She knew about him. When they'd been together, they'd talked of other things, not his powerful situation. She couldn't deny his importance. He would have to marry to his station. Her happiness plummeted to the sand.

She pulled her hand back, but he caught it again. He seemed larger, broader. His laugh curled around her like his warm cloak. He was here. She could touch him. She had touched him. No! Mustn't dwell on that. Think of the moment. Freedom.

"Truly we're here, Finola of Iona, Vikings of Icelandia to save you."

"How is it you have horses?"

"They were brought to us in Antioch by Corin, my ally in this part of the world. How right he was to think we'd need them. Each time we landed we brought them from the ship to help us search. Soon emissaries of my friends will know we've found you. They'll retrieve the equines. I couldn't have snared you afoot." He grinned and squeezed her closer to him. "It seems a miracle we landed on this strand on this day, at this time. We've sailed, back and forth, along the shores, hoping to find you. More than once we ventured inland." He smiled down at her. "And you appeared from the hills, thundering to the strand with traveling companions. Our days of searching have seemed eons."

"I would thank your friend."

"I, too, give him my gratitude."

"I'm glad that you're here, Viking." When she saw the rush of blood up his face, she felt heat rise in her.

"I would we could talk in private as we did the day the earth shook."

Shaken, she could only stare. Unseemly of him to talk of such intimacy. She wanted to hear more.

"I've never prayed for an earth shaking, Finola MacDonnell, but if Wotan sent one so that we could have speech beneath my cloak, I wouldn't decry him."

She swallowed. It must be the lack of sustenance that made her tremble.

He touched her face again. "I can't believe you made it here."

She scanned his harsh features. "Does that anger you?"

"Fear is the fury in me, Finola MacDonnell. My head envisioned many perils. How did you escape unmarked?" He scrutinized her features. "Are you truly well?"

She nodded, never wanting to move from the comfort of his hold, though it be unseemly, too forward. She fought against collapsing against him, pleading that he never let her go. At that moment she wanted her tools more than she ever had. Though her limbs shook so much she might not be able to stand alone, nor hold a chisel steady, to mold him in precious bronze would be joy.

13

The gods love the obscure and hate the obvious.
Upanishad

"I've sent the scroll to Rome."

"Why?"

"They should know."

"What good would it do to tell them?"

"Because the one called Finola MacDonnell might go there, with the Cup."

"Why would she do that?"

He bit back his ire. Albai was a fool, but a powerful one. One day he wouldn't be needed. For now he was. One day the coveted Cup of Antioch would be his, and his enemies along with Albai would be eradicated.

"She's devoted to the relic. Probably she wants to return it to her church for safekeeping," he explained.

"It belongs in the east."

Albai's bellow annoyed him. "Had you kept her safe, these steps would've been unnecessary."

"And how would I know she was cursed with demon skills, that she could walk through stone? She's in league with the dark world. How else could she have escaped me?"

He took deep breaths trying to contain his fury. If it weren't for Albai's clumsiness, all would've been completed. He would be rich, his revenge taken. He would be rejoicing with friends and cohorts. Damn the Tartar!

"What do we do now? I want my horses, and I must kill those who escaped my holding."

"Another time. For now do nothing."

"What if she doesn't go to Rome?"

"We adopt another plan. I must go."

"How will I know where you are?"

"I'll keep in touch with you." There was not enough gold in the east to make his plans known to Albai. He was a fool, and a vengeful one. He had no desire to wake with one of his henchmen slicing his throat.

14

Lead me from the unreal to the real!
Brihadaranyaka Upanishad

Darg approached. "With your leave, we supply sustenance to the others, Lord Einar." He jerked his head to the group behind him. He bowed low to Finola. "We give thanks for your safety, milady." He slapped his closed fist across his chest. "I am Darg, milady." He handed her a skin. "'Tis watered ale, milady, to quench your thirst."

"Thank you, Darg." Finola lifted the skin. When she would've gulped, Einar took it from her.

"Sip only, milady."

She nodded, retaking the skin, slaking her thirst.

Einar felt a peculiar ire catch in his throat. He wished his loyal lieutenant to perdition. He coughed. Darg glanced at him. "Prepare something for Lady Finola to eat," Einar said.

Darg gave the Viking salute of respect, including Finola, when he tipped his head and slammed his closed fist across his chest.

"He honors you," she said, handing back the skin. "Are all Vikings so large?"

Einar nodded, not taking his eyes from her.

"You stare."

He nodded. His hand moved to the coarse cloth that covered her, pushing it back. Her skin, though coated with grime, still had a winter rose hue. Hair that would be more fiery than his own had it not been caked with dirt and dust swept across her cheeks. Her eyes, gleaming like smoky green gems, proclaimed a spirit he'd seen on first meeting. A hot gladness that his memory had not forsaken him, that she was as wondrous as he recalled, that being captive hadn't broken that wonderful spirit, made his hand curl around her jaw. The other one, that still gripped her hand, edged her even closer.

"You must rest."

"I would see to my friends—"

"They are being cared for, milady." Like a goddess of old, she faced him, body swaying, burned with fatigue and the elements, in filthy tatters, but more beautiful than Homer's Helen. She'd not come to his shoulder, yet there was a power about her that awed him.

He glanced at the toes showing through the ripped slippers. She was dirty as a swamper, indomitable as a warrior. He'd thought her vulnerable as a child at first meeting. No longer. Some men at arms wouldn't have survived her trek. A veritable Titan of courage. Athena, the beautiful Greek goddess of wisdom, couldn't have been as noble. "Milady, methinks you could be Viking. Your exploits will be sung far and wide."

Finola smiled up at him though she was tired. "In truth, I surprised myself. Fear is an amazing impetus."

He laughed, pulling her closer, his eyes scanning the area.

First light was softening into day. The traveler's dust had all but settled. The world was turning into rosy morning. He wasn't lulled into thinking it could be safe. "We will feed you and slake your thirst, milady, then we must make all speed from here." A burgeoning urge to protect Finola Mac-Donnell from all peril lent an edge to his voice.

"You think Albai follows us?"

He heard the fear in her voice. "I cannot lie to you. His reputation for hanging on to what he thinks is his is well known. A friend has told me this," Einar said as he remembered not just what Corin had told him but what he hadn't said.

"I'm not his."

"You're not, milady." And one day, not just Alp Arsian, the brigand who'd imprisoned Corin and Einar, sentencing them to death on the galleys, would feel his wrath. He would also draw and quarter this Tartar who'd dared to capture Finola MacDonnell. His innards felt shredded with Damascene steel when he pondered what could've happened to her, how empty life would be without her.

"First you glower, then smile, then frown, Einar Thorhallsson. What mystery do you contemplate?"

"I worried."

She exhaled, a smile trembling on her lips. "Thank you."

He leaned closer, his breath mingling with hers. "Though I like to hear you speak, you need not thank me further, milady. You've warmed me with your gratitude."

Forcing his thoughts to other things, he eyed the Arabian steeds they'd used. "These would be Albai's best, by my judgment. How is it that you walked with such fast, agile mounts?" He pointed to her ripped sandals.

"We were on dangerous trails, not the more open ones."

"You should've taken a lower trail."

Finola shook her head. "We sought to hide from Albai and his men, so we often took to high ground. From the first moment we left, we took great care to hide. If we hadn't, Albai and his hordes would've been right at our heels."

"True." An incredible risk. He could hardly credit that she dared to escape. She wasn't adept at weapons. She was an artist. She'd mentioned sculpting him. He'd never had a notion of such. Now he wanted her to do it. He'd seen some great examples of the arts in his travels. None was more breathtaking than the woman in front of him.

Finola MacDonnell hadn't had the advantage of being a Viking woman, not the freedom of movement, the skill with weapons, or the travel expertise. Yet, she'd chanced all for freedom. He wanted to embrace her, never let her go. He hadn't realized that he'd brought her even closer, lifted her, until she made a sound. "What?"

"I'm all right, Lord Einar. I can stand."

He bit his lip, stunned at the smile poking through the tired, soiled visage. "You're weak."

"We escaped from Albai."

There was pride in her voice. He bowed. "I'm relieved, and I honor your brave effort."

Her barely suppressed shudder told him much. He had to fight the rage rising in him. He'd seen, too many times, the horrors visited on women in the east. He'd see to it no such atrocities would befall her. Better they should embark and leave the area. Einar was loath to move.

She enthralled him even more than she'd done in Antioch. Not once, since he'd found her, had she broken. No tears, no demand for cosseting. She had spunk.

"Had you no boots for the trek?"

"My raiment was taken from me. I had only these light garments, ye ken," she said, switching to Gaelic in her agitation. She looked over her shoulder when food and drink were brought. She barely touched the food, though he knew her to be hungry. She drank as though she'd not stop. He made her take her time.

"You need food—"

"I need water more . . . and privacy."

He bowed, and gestured. A man came running. Einar whispered.

Finola handed him back his cloak. He shook his head, whisking it about her again. "Wear this, and follow Sven. You'll be safe."

"I know."

He smiled.

"Thank you." She stared after him when he strode away.

"This way, milady." The Viking spoke in halting Greek.

15

Everything comes about by way of strife and necessity.
Heraclitus

When she returned to the beach, from her rock shelter where she'd laved and relieved herself, Finola moved toward her erstwhile traveling companions. Her feet were sore, but the bandaging and elkskin boots given to her by the Viking made the discomfort bearable.

"Milady."

She wheeled to face Thorhallsson. He was tall, broad, and his well-muscled torso was scarcely covered by the leather shirt and apron, war gear of the Vikings. "Are we to leave now, sirrah?"

She'd go anywhere with him. If someone'd told her that she'd gladly relinquish her talent to follow a Viking, she'd have laughed. Not now. A part of her railed at the suddenness of the commitment to a person she barely knew. A great part of her rejoiced that she'd found a man she'd give her life to save, to nurture, to want with her through all life's trials. Perhaps it was wrong. A voice deep inside said it could be. She wouldn't change her feelings, if she could. Blinking, she realized she'd been staring at him while in her reverie. He must think her mad.

"We are." He'd not let her out of his sight. He slung a lighter, full-length elkskin cloak about her, all but swathing her from neck to ankle. "This is for you. My men are passing good at tanning. You'll find this clean, and odorless."

"I thank you." Overwhelmed all at once by her near nakedness, Finola snuggled down into the warmth, unable to meet his gaze.

"Milady, my men and I honor you as the brave woman you are. Vikings will never scorn you."

Suffused with heat and a radiating joy, she lifted her chin.

He swung her up into his arms, ignoring her faint yelp of protest. "It's necessary that you be carried when your feet are so sore and covered with welts. One of my men shall salve them when we board . . . or I shall."

Finola gripped his shoulders. "Einar Thorhallsson, could we go to Rome?"

"Rome?" Surprised, he glanced down at her, almost tripping. "Nay. We head for Scotland or maybe Reykjunes."

"I must get to Rome."

" 'Tis safer to get to Viking waters."

"Rome," Finola said, her voice weak.

"Why?"

She hung her head. "I have something that must be returned there."

He crossed the strand to the longboat, stepped in, and sat down, still keeping her close to him. He nodded at the coxswain, and they skimmed over the water to his vessel. "Tell me."

Finola sighed. "I must, I suppose."

"Yes."

"At Albai's holding I was able to find the Cup of Antioch among his treasures."

"What?" Disgust shivered over his skin. That damnable Cup. "You didn't risk your life for that stupid—"

"What're you saying? It's a true relic."

"Not to me or mine."

"What do you mean?"

Einar ground his teeth. "Never mind. 'Twas foolish of me to cause you concern. Put it from your mind."

"I cannot."

"We must be gone from here."

"What do you mean, Einar Thorhallsson? We take ship at once. You have said it."

"Not soon enough."

All at once he was a stranger. The person who'd shared the perils of the earth shaking, who'd held her, keeping her warm and safe, was gone. In his place was a bleak-eyed man who seemed to stare beyond her, over the cliffs and into Bulgar land. "What is it?"

"The Cup is cursed." His mother'd had no happiness after her captivity and release. Deep in his soul he knew the Cup had caused it. His mother had been lost to him and his father much of the time even after she'd returned to Reykjanes. He blamed the Cup.

Finola stared. "How can that be? It belonged to the Savior, some have said."

"And it could as well have belonged to Beelzebub. You cannot know the pain this relic has caused, the evil it engendered, the agony of a child."

She was stunned, hurt by his brusque tone. He'd cushioned the world for her, rescued her, endangering his ship and men to do so. How could she castigate him? Whatever reason had him hating the Cup, she had no right to question. She looked away from him, struggling with ambivalent emotions. If only he'd explain, perhaps she could understand.

On deck, he led her to the small enclosure at the stern. "You'll be warm and safe here."

Finola was so upset when he walked away, stiff backed, that she reeled.

In moments a sailor came to her with a pile of clothing, which he deftly separated, handing some to Finola, some to Dalia, and the rest to Reric and Gar.

"Whither bound, milady?"

Startled, Finola stared at Dalia for long moments. "Rome." She sighed. "I hope we can go there."

"You have family there, milady."

"No, my patron is there."

"Who?" Dalia looked puzzled.

"Someone who has sponsored my schooling in the art I love."

"You're eager to seek such once more."

"I've never met Contessa di Marchi, only her emissaries."

"Then why would you go there?" Dalia dropped down the flap that consisted of elkskins, giving them a measure of privacy.

"We need a lamp," Dalia complained.

She'd hardly finished speaking when a hand came through the flap with a small oil lamp, lit, its flickering flame adding a semblance of warmth, as well as light.

The two women stripped, laved themselves again with seawater, and donned the heavier clothing.

Glad to be rid of the tattered reminders of Albai, Finola piled hers near the entrance, on top of Dalia's. She knew they would be disposed of momentarily.

Einar watched the closed area from his position on the bow. He was so relieved to have her back. Yet, he was hotly annoyed that she'd endangered her life to rescue the Cup that'd been the bane of his family's life, that'd been the cause of much sorrow to his mother and hence to him, as a boy. He couldn't forget his parent's tears, the sad looks, even when she tried to smile at him.

He wouldn't let Finola go, now that he had her. She'd come to find out that his protection, his name were what she needed if she wished to live in the dangerous areas of the world. She needed his protection. The woman was too sensuous, too beautiful and bright not to excite foul temperament in those with whom she'd be in contact, women and men. Jealousy was rampant among aristocrats. His name would be her bulwark.

The urge to explain, to apologize for his sharpness, overcame him. He hesitated, reluctant to speak of his family, yet wanting her to understand his antipathy toward the relic she revered. More than that, he needed to be near her!

As he approached the enclosure, he heard her talking to the handmaiden.

"When I travel to Rome, I shall contact my patrons."

"What good will it do, milady?"

"It will protect us."

"All of us?"

"Yes."

Einar called to her. "Come out, milady, I would speak with you."

Finola hesitated. "I'm coming." She left the area, huddling into her elkskins. The wind wasn't cold, but she was chilled from the night ride in her thin garb.

She gazed at the sea as the craft sped over the waves. "You wish to speak with me?"

She was still hurt. He heard it in her voice. "I didn't mean to cause you pain."

She swallowed. "I've known you a matter of hours, Einar Thorhallsson. I had no right to demand you take me anywhere."

"I feel it's been a thousand years."

Her head whipped his way, words faltering on her lips "I . . . I don't understand you, Einar Thorhallsson. You say kind things after you've had frost in your eyes. The Cup of Antioch did this. I don't know why."

"One day I'll tell you."

She nodded once. "I was wrong to insist we go to Rome."

Einar shook his head. "You may tell me anything." His smile widened. "Even the direction I must take." He touched her cheek when she reddened. "I would give you no discomfort."

Einar stared down at her. She was lovely, perhaps not as beautiful as she'd been when he'd seen her ride down to the strand, coated in dirt and dust. That'd been the most beautiful sight of his life. He touched her cheek. She was more than passable when she was clean. He didn't know why he'd burst out at her about the Cup. He'd never wanted to talk of it, not even with his trusted confidante, Princess Iona. Why had he railed at her after so many years of silence about the relic?

There was something about her attitude toward it that'd made him rant. Was she, as Darg suggested, tied to it by destiny, as his mother had been? A cold hand gripped his heart at the thought.

"You wanted to speak with me?"

He nodded. Then he gazed out to sea. "'Though I sometimes don't think I know the whole of it, I will tell you about the Cup of Antioch . . . and my family." He hadn't expected to say that, to make such an admission. Yet, he wanted her to know.

When he stared down at her, he forgot the Cup and his family. He couldn't tamp down the sudden ardor, the hardening of his body. In his life he'd known many women. The depth of his desire for Finola MacDonnell was new to him.

This was no light lady with whom he could dally and dance. She was Iona's cousin. Even if she'd had knowledge of men, and women of the world who traveled generally did, he'd given his covenant she'd be safe. She would be, now more than ever. She was most special to him. He fought his aroused being that recalled the moments in Antioch when the earth moved.

"I must tell you that taking the Cup of Antioch to Rome could be foolish. If it is one of Albai's treasures and he learns that we have it, he'll come after it."

Finola gasped. "But it isn't his. He took it from the convent, and killed many innocents. The Cup belongs to the Church."

"Albia will not see it thus."

"He must."

"He won't." Einar shrugged. "What makes you think the relic would be safe in Rome? There are thieves there, I can assure you."

"But surely they wouldn't steal from the Church, as heathens are wont to do."

"They might be more inclined," Einar said, irony in his voice.

She bit her lip. "I must make it safe." Her voice turned husky. "You can't know how many suffered and died because of Albai."

"I've seen the convent."

"Are they all dead?"

He nodded. "Dwell not on the past. It can't be undone."

"I know."

She was fighting tears. He touched her hand, wanting to comfort her. He could feel her struggle to stay calm. His hold tightened. "Tell me what you wish."

"I would go to Rome, if it pleases you. I would not endanger you."

Einar's smile twisted. "Milady, we're in the most dangerous waters in the world, at our peril, even as we travel." He frowned. "If you remain in Rome, it's within the power of the Church to name another as your guardian." Einar's blood ran cold at the thought of some of the wealthy lechers that fluttered about Rome.

She shrugged. "Only if I had vast properties and holdings. I don't."

"And if you're left alone without guardian, what will you do?"

"I'll survive. And I have no fortune that a man might covet. I have my art to sustain me and give me happiness. I will remain unwed." The thought of that had never hurt . . . until now. Images of Einar Thorhallsson and his wife and children wafted through her head like a smoky viper, stinging everywhere.

Einar was irked. Didn't she know how lovely she was? Many men would covet her, with or without dowry. And there were those who'd take her for a mistress whether she gave permission or no.

He'd allow none to touch her! He'd never let a woman inside his soul. He was too private for that. He liked women, but only his mother, and Birgit, his old nurse, and Iona had ever been close to him. With lovers he was generous, but when it was done, it was done. And he'd left none of his seed behind him. It was not his way, nor did he wish to give bastardy to any child of his. With Finola all was changed . . . and would never be changed back. More of him had been given over to her, without volition, than had been given to any living soul.

The Ionan would stay in his thoughts no matter how far from her he sailed. "To venture to Rome when you have marauders at your heels could put you in jeopardy."

Finola bit her lip, nodding. "I see that. And I would not be ungrateful, Einar Thorhallsson, nor ungracious."

"I didn't ask for your gratitude," he snapped. Had she forgotten their closeness during the quaking, how he'd held her? Fury was an acid in his blood.

She stepped back, cheeks flaming, her mouth opening and closing.

He whirled away from her.

Biting her lip, she retreated to the relative quiet of the enclosure.

"Why is the Viking angry, milady?"

Finola ground her teeth. "Vikings are always angry."

Dalia's eyebrows rose. "Truly? And they are such massive men. That could make them most interesting, could it not, milady?"

"I couldn't say."

Reric glowered at Dalia. " 'Tis not for us to conjecture about the men who saved us."

"Why not?"

Dalia and Reric glared at each other.

Fatigued, Finola moved away from them. Gar was staring at her. She angled herself closer to him when Reric began whispering to Dalia. "Are you all right?"

Gar shrugged, spreading his hands.

"You don't speak Greek?" At his uncomprehending shrug, she switched to Latin, then to Gaelic. Then she muttered something in Icelandic, and he nodded. Surprised, she turned to Reric. "Your brother speaks Icelandic?"

Reric nodded. " 'Tis a Nordic tongue and I've spoken it to him right along. That's how we communicate without the others knowing," Reric told her in faltering Icelandic.

Finola nodded. " 'Tis much like the tongues of other Nordic peoples, then?"

"I don't know, milady, but I suppose. 'Tis the language our family spoke."

Finola nodded, then turned to Gar.

Reric went back to his low-voiced conversation with Dalia.

"Gar, do you not speak?"

He shook his head and smiled.

Reric turned to her once again. "Not since they raped him, milady."

"Those evil ones," Finola muttered.

"It's the way of things." Reric shrugged. Dalia nodded.

"It's wrong. A child should be protected."

When Gar produced some ivories from his tunic, Finola laughed. From a very young age, boys learned about dicing and they did it well. "I have naught to dice with," Finola said, spreading her hands.

Gar grinned and pulled pebbles from his pockets, evening them up between them.

"Good." Finola took the proffered dice and rolled them across the skin spread on the deck. She frowned at her low number.

Einar heard the laughter as he was giving hand signals to Darg about changing course. He moved back toward the enclosure, checking the sails, looking over the side at the waves, the sky, the chasing clouds. All had messages for the wary sailor. Einar paid attention to all the signals of nature. In front of the enclosure, he scanned his ship once more, nodding his satisfaction.

When he lifted the loose end of the skin to see into the sheltered area, his mouth dropped. Finola MacDonnell was running a piece of burnt wood over a section of well-tanned skin. Even in the gloom of the one flickering oil lamp he could make out the features of the handmaiden. Finola's hands moved like the wind, and she seemed to be wholly absorbed in the task.

The other three were dicing with pebbles.

"You are most talented, milady."

Finola looked up. "All is well with the ship?"

He had a moment's twinge of conscience. He'd been too sharp with her. Had she stayed in the stuffy enclosure to keep out of his way? "Fine. Might I speak with you, again?" He ran his eyes over her friends. "Are you comfortable?" At their nods he smiled. "I will send a cask of fruited ale." The liquid was often used for those who suffered sea gripes. It also served as a soothing drink that didn't dull the senses.

When Finola rose from her position on the throws, he noted how she put away the skin on which she sketched and carefully wrapped the burnt wood.

He lifted the flap and waited until she was standing next to him. "Have you nothing else on which to sketch or fashion but the skin?"

Finola shook her head. "I lost most of my work in the fire, even the papyrus I'd been using the day I was captured."

"I saw you sketching in the market that day." His heart thundered against his breastbone when she colored up and nodded. She'd not forgotten! He leaned over. "I thought of you many times, milady. But I'd thought you safe with your guardians, or I'd not have left you." At that time or any other.

Finola stared up at him, swallowing. "I hoped and prayed that you'd look for me, that you'd find me."

Einar steeled himself to keep from clutching her to him. He would not humiliate her so. "I would've scoured the world for you," he said, his face riven with anger and determination. "Had I an inkling when I spent those three turns of the moon in Constantinople that you were captured by Albai, I would've gone after him at once." He shrugged. "His holding is well hidden. We had many men searching. If I'd found him, I would've torn his caravans to pieces and burned him out."

Overwhelmed by his intensity, she could only stare up at him.

"I frighten you. I ask your pardon."

"I'm humbled by your caring, good Einar, and most grateful that you've taken my fears away." She touched his arm when he would've spoken. "I know you don't want my gratitude."

"I spoke too roughly, milady."

Finola smiled up at him. "You have a way of making me feel safe, Einar Thorhallsson . . . much like the day when the earth quaked." She took a deep breath. "I was foolish to tell you to go to Rome. I would ask your pardon for being overbearing and—"

"You weren't, milady. And I called you out of the enclosure to apologize for my harshness and to assure you that I will take you to Rome." He grinned when she stared at him wide eyed. He couldn't resist touching her slack lips with one finger, just a graze, nothing more, but the power went through him. The charge he'd felt since the first time she'd eyed him was magnified. Blood thundered through him. Words fought up his throat. He needed to tell her so much. "But I must caution you, milady, that we'll take our time getting there. 'Twould not be in our best interests to be followed, to be marked." He stared down at her until she nodded. "I will protect you."

"I know that."

When her lips fluttered, her cheeks blushed and fire hardened his loins. He wanted her like none other. He had not fathomed that he could have such sensations for anything, or anyone. "Finola," he whispered.

She looked up at him, trembling. "I . . . I would be most grateful." She bit her lip.

"That word again," he said, his voice so low that it couldn't be heard over the combing sea off the gunwales. He looked about him, but good-mannered Vikings were looking anywhere but at their leader. "Walk with me a bit."

She didn't pull back when he slung another fine tanned elkskin about her shoulders. The garment was light, yet it kept out any bite of breeze. Though they were in warm waters, the wind was cool coming out of the north.

Einar shielded her by leaning over her, so that not even the sailor who'd climbed into the rigging could see her. "I must warn you that we could be followed." He forestalled her speaking by placing a finger on her lips. "We won't be going directly to Rome. We'll take precautionary measures to protect ourselves and send any predators off the scent."

"And how will we do that?"

When she turned to look up at him, he became more caught in her hold. She'd snared him with a look. He couldn't take his eyes from her splendor. "Finola!" he whispered as he brought her hand to his lips.

16

Thy rays are in the midst of the great green sea.
Ikhnaton

With the sea all around her, nothing but the birds above, scurrying sailors, and the few passengers on board, Finola had found a peculiar solidarity, a serenity, a completeness. She sketched everything: birds, sailors, the striped sails, the dragon masthead, Einar Thorhallsson . . . over and over again. As much as she loved her work, and that was a great deal, her life's need for it had watered down since meeting Thorhallsson. He'd become the sun in her life, making her work a moon to be treasured, though it no longer obsessed her as it once had.

Einar Thorhallsson! His face and figure appeared constantly under her stylus. More than once she was startled to look down and see him looking at her. Some images of the sea, sky and his men she wiped off her skins, so that she could fashion other sights. His visage she kept, the skins rolled away and protected. The meager amount of papyrus she still had was hoarded in its tin cylinder. One day, perhaps, her fingers would fashion again that precious day when she'd met him. All those drawings had been destroyed by Albai's men. Mayhap the beauty of that day would return to her, that wondrous time in Antioch when the earth moved, when Einar Thorhallsson appeared, when she went to Hell accompanied by Albai's men. There was an urgent need to record that time, though she was sure nothing could blot it from her mind. One day her fingers would answer the call. Then those moments would find themselves on her canvas.

The men on the Viking vessel began to pause in their chores, angling to see what she did. Murmuring among themselves, they smiled and nodded. Little by little burnt pieces of wood, honed fine and sharp, skins tanned to satin finish, mixed tempera from the ship's stores, appeared where she'd stationed herself at the stern.

The tanner, who worked long and hard to keep the sails in shape, took on the extra chore of adding to her store of skins. He stretched them on iron hooks so they'd be flat, usable and accessible to her. Many of the skins were more malleable than papyrus.

Einar moved behind her one day, careful not to block her light. "You smile at my men and they rush to bring you any joy. We'll be happy not to crash on the rocky shore."

Startled, she could only be glad that she was sketching a tern that dove over the ship, not another image of him. She smiled. "Your men are expert. And I don't need to be to recognize their skill. I cannot see you dealing with men of less stature, Einar Thorhallsson."

Hunkering down next to her, he studied the outline of the bird. "You're very good." He smiled. "Rose colors your cheeks when I pay you homage. 'Tis only truth I tell."

"It pleases me to hear you praise my work."

"I'm proud of my work as a Viking. You should be equally so, Finola MacDonnell. You have entered a world dominated by men, and elbowed yourself into the rich place you deserve."

She swallowed. "I need to learn more." She smiled up at him. "You . . . you honor me, Einar Thorhallsson."

He leaned closer and caught the soft skin she worked upon when it would've slid from her lap to the deck. "One day you might gift me with a work. I would pay you, of course."

He smiled into her eyes, handing back the picture of the bird, careful not to smear the charcoal rendering.

Glowing, Finola pressed it back to him. "Keep this, Einar Thorhallsson."

Einar was going to protest that she didn't have enough skins to give any away. When he saw Lars Bjornson approaching, he laughed. "It would seem our tanner feels you must have raw material for your work."

Finola's mouth dropped. "My dear friend, how kind you are." She grasped the hard, callused hand of the ship's tanner and main sail mender. "You are most good, and I tell you true, I've not seen such fine work in all my days."

Einar didn't smile as the burly Lars sputtered, reddened, then executed a stiff bow. He waited until the tanner was out of sight, then leaned closer. "Bjornson is one of the most stalwart of all Vikings. He's seen many battles, never flinching from confrontation nor backing down against great odds. He could lead and win with the best of the best." Einar shook his head. "Never before have I seen him out of balance."

Finola turned to Einar, her arms laden with skins. "What a fine gentle man he is, to be sure."

"I don't think Lars has ever been so described." Einar chuckled.

She didn't respond. Spreading a skin in front of her, she stretched it and smiled. She picked up her utensil. Her hands flew over the skin, bringing it to life. It startled him that in just a few moments she was able to bring Lars Bjornson into view.

"Bjornson looks more like an adjudicator than a warrior. What magic do you have that you bring dignity to such a ribald rough Viking? 'Tis touched by the gods, you are, milady."

"I thank you."

Silence stretched between them as she completed her picture, letting it fall in her lap. She leaned back against the housing that kept the weapons and furs.

Einar dropped to his backside, leaning back on his hands, scanning the sky and his ships.

"Whither bound, Einar Thorhallsson?" She glanced at the sun.

"So you can read the directions?"

"Yes. It helps in our work to know where the sun is pointing at a certain time. But long before I studied art, my grandfather would take me out on the sea and show me how to manage his small craft. I enjoyed the water, and the many lessons on the moon, the sun and the stars." She smiled. "On the few calm days we had off our coast, I was allowed to sail alone. I was never caught in a storm, but I was shown how to manage if there was trouble." She laughed softly. "I'm not sure I would've been too able if one of our great winds arose."

"You've shown your warrior's ability by the way you led your friends to freedom, milady."

"You humble me." Embarrassed and excited by his praise, she looked at the sky.

"Can you tell we take a circuitous route to Rome?" He grinned when she smiled.

She shook her head. He warmed the air when he smiled. Her lips trembled. "You've gone against your better judgment in doing this. I thank you."

"You're welcome." He moved closer. "You must have been fearful when Albai had you."

She nodded. "He's an evil man."

"I've heard that."

"He did unspeakable things to innocents." Swiping at her eyes to wipe away the remembered horrors, she tried to smile. "You spoke of an island?"

"Yes. We could be in great peril if our destination was known to some, so we won't take a direct route. Albai has long arms." Einar frowned. "I was fortunate that my friend Corin knew of him." His smile was acidic. "I'm not an unfledged boy. I have hiding places."

"You trust this Corin."

"I do. We were imprisoned together on the galleys. We became like brothers in our desire to escape. We did, together."

Finola nodded. She enjoyed listening to him, pleased that

he would spend time with her. If proprieties were served, she should be in the stuffy enclosure. It was her great happiness to be on the deck. Einar Thorhallsson had made her safe.

"What are you thinking?"

For a moment she was tempted to lie. The truth was out before she could call it back. "I was thinking of the earth quaking." How foolish he must think her! Her voice had shaken as much as the earth that first day.

"Not a time was it out of my mind, after we'd parted." He gazed into her sparkling eyes. "If I'd foreseen the danger for you—"

"You could not. None could."

"I should've wrapped you in my cloak and taken you to my ship. I thought of that every day I was away from you." When her head lifted and spun his way and her lips parted, Einar couldn't be sorry he'd made such an admission. "It wasn't easy to remain at the conference. I wanted to come back to you. If I had thought Albai was near—"

"You must've been just on your ship, or barely under way when it occurred." Her eyes darkened. Her hand gripped the burnt wood tightly, soiling her fingers. "They were so quiet. They killed my guards without saying a word."

Horror washed over her. He could see her waves of fear, the pain of losing friends and allies. He took her hand, wiping at the charcoal marks, trying to infuse her with strength.

She swallowed. "Day after day, I saw and heard what they did to the women and children. You can't know—"

"I do," he said simply.

"How can you not kill such beasts." Her gaze moved to the enclosure. "Did you know that Gar was raped by other slave boys? His brother couldn't protect him. Reric could barely protect himself."

Her tear-drenched eyes rended something inside him. He thought himself inured to the agonies of the world. He'd seen much, had his share of pain. But looking at the torment in her eyes magnified the horror.

"They're safe now. And they wouldn't be if you'd refused to bring them." He took her hands.

She looked down at their clasped hands, knowing she should protest at such intimacy, that his crew could see and her friends, had they looked out of the enclosure, could spy them. What did it matter? She needed his touch.

"They wouldn't intrude," Einar said, his voice soft, reading her thoughts.

She smiled, her lips shaking. " 'Tis unseemly to say so, but I'm glad that you are here, and I'm with you." She looked away from him. "I've become shameless. I cannot blame my incarceration for that."

Chuckling, he squeezed her hands. "How foolish you are. My men revere you, for they set great store by courage. Your young friends are in awe of your bravery. You are a noble lady. All who know you would honor you. I do."

Finola felt giddy. Her arms couldn't be connected to her hands. Her fingers floated. The rest of her tingled. "You have indeed honored me—"

"Call me Einar, milady. I would call you Finola."

"But custom says that we—" She extricated her hands.

"We'll resort to custom on land. The sea makes us free."

Finola smiled. "It does."

It would be different then. Einar Thorhallsson had a very full life. Sadness squeezed her heart. Such an urge to live for the moment almost swamped her. She caught her breath. Having a precious moment, was worth more than an empty lifetime. She'd discovered that the day the earth shook in Antioch. Impulse had her stretching out her hand.

Einar caught it and kissed her fingers, cursing the prying eyes of his crew and her friends . . . down deep, not caring if the world sat in judgment.

No matter how she tried, Finola couldn't stop drawing Einar that day. Sometimes parts of him, sometimes the whole. Finding herself enamored of his nose, she sketched it over and over. His eyes pulled her. Nothing could make her stop painting them. She ached to use her chisel on the fine stone used by the Hindi. What a sculpture Einar Thorhallsson would make.

Increasing in power each passing hour came the shaky awareness that awed her, stunned her, causing her to become shy and feel uncomfortable with the Viking captain.

Day segued into night, then into dawn, from thence to twilight. The moments ran together too fast, and she prayed for the hours not to pass. Yet, she wanted to reach Rome so she could see to the safety of the Cup of Antioch. It was her covenant. The urgency of her duplicitous feelings turned her upside down.

Each minute that he could, Einar was with her. When he first arrived, she wouldn't meet his eyes. Her responses were desultory, sporadic. He would turn the conversation in several directions. "Soon the waters will change color and become like your eyes."

After a time, Finola would lose her shyness, begin to respond. "I look forward to seeing the island. Why won't you tell me more about it?"

"I would surprise you."

They had so much to talk of, so many things to discover about one another. Though they rarely touched, she experienced an intimacy with him that made her tremble. And she could tell from his warm gaze that he was not unaffected.

Each day she sketched more and more, passing out the skins to the various Vikings whose images she'd fashioned. She kept the ones of Einar. She was sure he knew that she'd sketched him, but he never asked to see any of himself. He was not penurious with his praise. Over and over he extolled her talent, showing what she gave him to his men. Finola bloomed.

At night, bedded down, far from him, she had the sensation he was touching her, that it was not Dalia at her side but the Thegn of Icelandia. Such dizzying results had her feeling she'd almost lived the moments she dreamed. Shame should've suffused her. Instead she felt increasing heat and awareness. When Einar was near, the hairs on her neck would stand straight out.

Gar and Reric slept with the men on deck, and many times

they worked with them. But each day they would spend a few minutes with her. She came to respect and like them.

Finola was both content and restless, with urgings that were alien to her. Wrapped in his skins, she was warmed by Einar. It was as though he could hold her and keep her warm. She closed her eyes, clinging to the roll of skins that had his visage in charcoal.

One fine day when she was sketching, the wind was mellow and the sun shone like a copper plate on the azure sea. She was startled at the lookout's call.

"Land ho!"

Where were they? Too far for Constantinople. Athinai? Certainly not Rome. That was days more, she was sure. How good of Einar to take her there, despite his reservations. And she knew he had many. It would be all right. He'd see that once the Cup of Antioch was given to the right people, he'd share her feeling of well being.

She'd see her mentor, or at least the emissaries. They could protect it. The papacy was there with its powerful army.

Putting her sketching aside, she moved to the rail, leaning over to see the faint outline of land. She climbed the narrow steps to the level where Einar stood. "Where are we? Are we near the isle?"

Einar took hold of her arm, pointing. "Through the mist. A small mass of land. Not inhabited for many years, though it once was. It's off the traditional sea-lanes. Many moons ago, it belonged to a wealthy personage."

"How do you know?" She smiled up at him.

He leaned on the rail, the action bringing him closer to her. "My ships have used this as a resting place many times. We've explored the island and seen the remnants of a fine estate . . . including several hot baths, much favored among the Romans."

"And the Icelandics, if I remember correctly my cousin's stories about the hot springs around Reykjanes."

Einar smiled. "Yes. We are most addicted to that manner of cleanliness."

She could imagine him in such waters, the steam rising around his . . . Flustered she turned from him.

"What were you thinking?"

"About the hot baths."

"I, too, can imagine you in such, Finola."

A hail from the ship following them caught his attention.

Finola was grateful. Her knees had turned weak. A hotness ran over her from ankle to eyebrow as she gripped the rail for support.

Einar looked back at her, noted her confusion. "Have I been clumsy with you, milady? I would not have you think me too familiar."

She looked up at him. "I don't. I admit to alien sensations. They don't threaten me. Neither do you."

There was relief in his smile. "We've headed west. The cartographer tells me we're on safe course, that we can moor here. When we're sure we're not followed, we'll sail off the coast of Crete, then turn north. We'll find more cover there."

"Crete? Isn't that a thieves' nest?"

Einar shrugged. "Some say it is. 'Tis a better choice than Antioch, or being caught upon the delta of the Danubis."

Finola nodded but she didn't fully understand. Her geography was not as good as his, nor did she know all the small islands that could hide them. It didn't matter. She trusted her rescuer. Her spirit was intertwined with his. Had she become fatalistic in the east? Perhaps. Mayhap it'd occurred one day when the earth moved, scattering many in fear, but she'd found warmth and safety with the Viking. Feeling flustered, she excused herself. She could feel his eyes on her as she made her way along the rolling deck to the enclosure.

When Dalia would've questioned her, she waved her away, pleading fatigue. In truth, she was tired. As though all the harrowing moments of her captivity had caught up with her, she sank to the cushions, covering herself with a soft mat. Sleep drew her down like a fall into a deep well.

17

In truth, we know nothing, for truth lies in the depths
Democritus

"Safe depth, milord!"

The sound of the watch brought Finola awake. The short nap had refreshed her. They were landing! Following her travelmates out to the deck, she strove to shake the wrinkles from her garment. She saw Thorhallsson at once.

Einar scanned the area. It could scarcely be called any type of landmass. It was clustered with windblown gnarls that had once been trees, and black, porous rock strewed the narrow strand. The nearest landfall beyond was a scant lump on the horizon.

He and his men studied the area long and hard, the ships cruising in slow zigzag pattern about the island. He signaled to Darg, who came aboard his ship.

"You don't worry, Lord Einar."

Einar smiled at the stolid Icelandic's certainty. "I'm always concerned, my friend."

Darg lifted his shoulders. "This is not on most charts, lord. As you know, we Vikings sail where none other dare. None would find us here but our own."

"We'll make sure."

"Our great Sigurd founded it," Darg said, pride in his voice. He smiled. "And none but us know its surprises."

Einar laughed. "I look forward to some of them."

Darg nodded, his stoical expression creasing in amusement.

Einar had seen Finola go to the rail with her friends, their chatter fading as they noted the grim readiness of the Vikings. He could've told her that all was well. It behooved him to let her see the readiness of his men, their ability to protect her. He tried to ignore his feeling of disappointment when she returned to the enclosure without approaching him. Was she more than fatigued? Fears of what could've happened to her at Albai's surfaced anew.

Finola swayed and moved in the depths of the ocean. If she cried out, she would drown in the water. She opened her eyes, blinking, realizing she'd fallen asleep again. How could that be? She'd been most interested in the island. Then she'd dreamt she was in water. She stared at Einar. He was carrying her! That'd been the sensation she'd thought was water.

"I can walk." Her voice was thin, sleep ridden. It was so silly to be tired all the time.

"You're fatigued. 'Tis no trouble." He hefted her over the side of the ship, smiling at her when she gasped. "Have no fear."

"I don't." It was the sheer strength of the man, lifting her, lowering her and himself into the smaller boat. "What is the name of this place?"

"It has no name, just a number on our charts. This is known only to Vikings, milady."

She clung to his shoulders when he seated himself with her on his lap. 'Twas unseemly. She didn't want to move. "Are we in hiding here? From Albai?"

"From all who might seek to follow us. I would know who watches us, or who would seek to waylay us."

She nodded, settling herself more comfortably. She eyed him when he groaned. "Do you ail?"

"No!" He glared at his expressionless oarsmen.

"Oh. I thought I heard you ... never mind." She looked around her. "It has a strange beauty. I would sketch it."

"You have your skins?"

"Oh, yes. You know Bjornson supplied me with much. I feel rich, indeed."

"Good. You are unspoiled, milady. 'Struth it takes little to please you."

Surprised she stared at him. "You've done nothing but please me."

He stared down at her, feeling the run of blood up his face. He wanted her! 'Twas his duty to protect her. He looked away from her, over the water.

She was silent for a moment. "I cannot see why Albai would be so persistent about the Cup. It wasn't his."

Einar didn't think it was just about the Cup, but there was no sense alarming her. "Some men don't give up prizes easily."

She nodded. "I ken your meaning." Not realizing she'd switched to Gaelic, she shivered. "To be a fair distance from Albai is a good thing."

"Think not of him."

His ferocious tone brought her head up. "In your own way, Einar Thorhallsson, you could be as unswerving an enemy as Albai." She paused. "Though you couldn't sicken me as the Tartar did. You, I respect."

Shaken, he held her close.

They landed on the strand with a soft bump.

Einar lifted her through the shallow water, setting her on the stone-littered sand. He kept her behind him, as his men scattered left, right and to the center.

"You needn't guard me, Einar Thorhallsson. Go with your men."

He smiled. "They know their work, and will be back in short order—"

"Or there would be an alarm."

He nodded.

Finola took a step closer.

He felt her heat. She drove him wild, and yet he was content when she was with him. Madness.

She felt safety and warmth with Thorhallsson. His aura was her shield against a cruel world. She smiled and moved even closer.

Einar looked over his shoulder. "You've not said much about Albai and his hordes."

She shook her head. "I saw too much of cruelty . . . children." She bit her lips. "He does not respect women."

"In his world, there's no need."

"In my world, there is."

"That I know."

Fascinated, she watched the quirk of that strong mouth. "You think I jest. I see a light in your eyes." Could the fjords be that blue?

"You make me smile because I wanted you by my side those days I searched. Now you're here."

"Your Icelandic directness does take my breath," she muttered.

He smiled, his gaze going up and down the beach.

"Do we tarry long here?"

Einar pondered the shore. "I'm not sure. One of the ships will cruise this area, and farther asea. The information they glean will determine our course, and when we embark."

She nodded. "I'm happy to be ashore, though I would sail the River Styx to be done with Albai."

"You don't mention Rome."

"You've told me we sail there."

"If all is well, we do."

Content with his leadership, she smiled. "It's good to be unafraid."

"I share your well-being because you're safe." He grinned. "I couldn't face your cousin otherwise." He touched her arm.

Finola bit her lip. It was foolish to want his hand upon her. There were things in her heart she wished him to know. " 'Twould be wondrous to return the Cup to Rome, but not at the risk of your men and ships."

" 'Twould be foolish, I agree."

"And you are not that, Einar Thorhallsson." He turned toward her, so close, their garb touched. Relief, and a certain fatalism, made her weak. Without thinking, she pressed her face into his chest. "I think I may learn to like this island."

When she looked up, smiling, she sustained a shock. Einar was pasty hued, biting his lip. Then, as though he'd spoken of his dilemma, she felt the hardness of him against her belly. She'd not grown up on a holding that lived off the land without understanding coupling. And she'd seen graphic examples of what could happen between a man and woman at Albai's enclosure. Had she caused it? No! She couldn't. She went statue still, but that only made her more aware. She stared at his leather chest plate.

Taking a step back, she looked up at him with a reddened face. "I cannot thank you for all you've done for me and my friends—"

"You've thanked me many, many times."

She looked away. "Yes, well, I am most grateful."

Einar watched her long moments. "You're most welcome, milady."

"Yes . . . Well, I must see to Reric and Dalia and Gar."

"They've landed." He pointed behind her.

"Ah, yes . . . well . . . I shall see thee anon." Why had she switched to the formal Icelandic speech?

"Anon," Einar whispered.

His eyes were burning into her back. When she reached the others, she could barely speak. The urge to turn and look at the Thegn of Icelandia was too great.

The ship's tanner gestured to her. "There will be shelters for you and your retinue, milady."

Taken aback, Finola looked around her. "Where? Will you stretch tents upon the beach?"

He pointed beyond the thick stand of trees that stood well back from the strand. "In there."

Finola would've questioned further, but he was called away by a shipmate. She and her companions had little to do when the one ship was unloaded of stores and the other made ready to set sail again.

* * *

When the sun was curving down, Einar approached her again.

"This way." He let her walk ahead of him along a path through the greenery.

Finola was entranced at the bird life and the sounds of small animals. " 'Tis not completely deserted."

He smiled. "There's more."

She expected thicker wooded areas, or brambles that one could use like a cave. Instead the path took them to a clearing. "Are we in the middle of the island?"

"Not quite." He pointed to some structures almost hidden by greenery.

Agape, she stared. "Oh. 'Twould be wondrous to sketch such. Roman, are they not?"

"We think so. And very sturdy. They would be better if the underbrush was cleared away. But then they might be discernible to others."

"And you want to keep the hideaway to yourself."

"Yes." Einar urged her forward, directing Dalia one way, Reric and his brother another. "Come, you will shelter yonder."

She looked around the marble-floored area. "These are Roman baths," she whispered. "What beautiful marble. Oh, to have such for sculpting."

There was hunger in her voice. "I will get you some."

She shook her head. "I must sound foolish to you. Thinking of sculpting when we've just been through such an arduous time."

"I think you devoted to your work."

"I am." She hesitated. "Not as I once was. There are other things that now take my thoughts at times."

"I would give much to have you sculpted . . . or painted. In Florence and Venice I've seen the beautiful temperas that artists have begun using. Not just your face, but your hands should be fashioned as well." He lifted one to his mouth.

She pulled free and walked ahead of him. She kept one hand pressed to her chest while she rattled on about the architecture, thinking of him.

"You make me see this place with new eyes." He touched a graceful column and looked up at the coved ceilings.

"I can't believe the many apartments. Those marble pilasters and floors are works of art." She looked over her shoulder. "Have Dalia, Reric and Gar seen these?"

"I'm sure they've seen ones very like these."

"Where are they?"

"Don't worry. I think they've already bedded down. They were exhausted."

She nodded.

"You're too restless to sleep, milady?"

"Yes. It feels so strange here, as though we wandered into another world."

"Yes." Einar followed behind her as she wandered across a round space, overrun with weeds that had once been an atrium.

Then they were in a separate building away from the others. They could hear the sea, but no voices. It was quiet, more serene.

"I often think my mother would've liked this place," Einar blurted, then looked away, scowling.

"You don't like to speak of her?"

He shook his head.

"Did you not like her?"

"I loved and respected her. She was beautiful and kind," he said, his voice hoarse.

"Then what is it?"

"Sometimes I think it's a nightmare." He swallowed. "I thought she was happy. But sometimes there was such pain in her eyes, when she thought no one noticed."

"Can't you tell me?"

He'd told no one of his mother . . . or of that misty day on the cliffs. He still didn't fully comprehend any of it.

"Einar?"

''Perhaps my mother would wish you to know.'' There was a rawness to his words.

She sat on a marble bench. ''Then I will listen.''

''It was before the time of the Great Bartering.'' He took a deep breath. ''I was readying to take ship . . .''

18

Evening star, you bring all things which the bright dawn has scattered.

Sappho

Finola waited, hardly daring to breathe. She'd seen into his soul and had found love behind that harsh Viking facade. He'd loved his mother and wanted to share her pain. Finola felt his, and wanted to give him her love. Had it happened that first day? Mayhap. It'd grown with every sea mile they'd covered since he'd found her. He made her feel safe, wanted . . . a woman. Yet the power he wielded over her was gentle, and she would've given him more. He was a beautiful man, who'd suffered. She could've cried for his pain. Instead she queried him.

"And what did the papyrus say?"

He blinked as though she'd struck at him, instead of touched his arm with gentle fingers. "I . . . I don't know. I've not taken it out to read it. I will one day. I keep it with me," he blurted.

"I wound you when I speak of the papyrus—"

"No." He shook his head, his smile twisting down. "Telling you the tale unlocked some truths." He touched her face. "You're the Swan East Birgit spoke of, milady." When her eyes widened, so did his smile. "I know it's true." He looked away. "I don't know why I haven't read my mother's words. One day I will." He patted the chamois bag inside his leather breastplate.

"You'd rather not." His slow twisted smile made her heart ache. "I don't mean to probe your feelings."

"Mayhap I'd choose not to read her words, milady. Are you a witch who reads my thoughts?" He touched her tender cheeks. "I told you what I've said to no other. I'm not sorry I did."

"Thank you." She bit her lip. "I didn't mean to salt your wound, Viking."

"You didn't."

" 'Tis precious to you, a legacy from your mother."

"Yes."

"I thank you for her story. I think I would've liked her."

"And she would've liked you. She, too, was brave."

Her pulse quickened at his praise, her heart pounded against her chest.

In tacit agreement, they moved deeper into the catacombed marble structure.

Einar indicated a chamber. "You will sleep here. I will be outside. There's ample privacy and torches for the ensuing darkness."

"It's a wondrous place." She turned, holding out her hand.

He took it in both of his. "I will bring you adequate clothing." He jerked his head toward the back of the structure. "Come let me show you your own bath. Then you may rest." He pulled her one hand to the top of his arm when he turned.

She felt such an urgency when she walked beside him. She could hardly notice the wonderful swirl of water. Touching him had fired her. Keeping him near became paramount.

Einar smiled. "See. A natural spring that stays warm all the while. We have them in Icelandia, and they are most salubrious." He scanned the area. "I've been on many of these small islands. They're mountainous, many are rocky to the sea, without a strand, covered in moss. Some explode in their innards, and some like this have wondrous hot springs.

Most sailors do not land upon them. They fear the Circe, even as Odysseus did."

"You do not."

He smiled. "A Viking is more than passing curious. He forgets to be fearful."

"I think you underrate yourself, Einar Thorhallsson. You are the bravest of warriors. I have seen that."

He swallowed. "You have my blood thundering, milady."

As always, his bluntness shook her.

"My veins are too paltry to keep the life liquid in check."

She glanced at the water, then back at him. He scanned the bath area and its surroundings. He had great beauty. Casting him in bronze was becoming an obsession. His coloring brought to life on the stretched hemp brought from the east would make a most memorable work. And she would do it. Plus, she would keep all the paintings she'd made of him on board ship. She would make a collection of Einar Thorhallsson. Her artist's soul, her woman's spirit cried out for it. Her heart pounded just looking at him.

When he looked back at her and their gazes held each other, she couldn't breathe.

He licked his lips, swallowing. "I'll give you time to rest. Later, I'll bring food. My men will prepare it."

"What if—"

"None will attend you here but me. The handmaiden will've been told this."

"Thank you." She would've thought that Dalia would come to her. She didn't question why it wouldn't be so. The privacy was not unpalatable.

He turned to her, lifting her hand to his mouth, caressing not the back as was custom, but the palm. "I thank you, Finola MacDonnell."

"What do you mean?" He was gone. The words wafted on air.

She felt bereft ... drained without him. He'd given her strength. Tired to the marrow, she could scarce move. Stripping off the dirty, water-streaked garments, she decided she would use the lightly woven covering on the marble platform bed as sleeping garb. Twisting it about her form, she sank down on the layers of woolen batten someone had placed there.

She'd been staring up at the coved inlaid ceiling, closing her eyes numerous times. Sleep wouldn't come. It was locked away in the throes and cascades of her mind that appeared in visions of Einar Thorhallsson. He blotted out all the remembrances of her time with Albai, her escape, her fears. He covered her with the heat of his eyes. Surely such want and need were unseemly, mayhap sinful, but she couldn't chase them away, nor did she desire them to vanish. The passion she'd had for her work seemed paltry compared to the river of feeling that Einar Thorhallsson engendered in her. Though she couldn't contemplate a life without sketching and drawing, he'd become the largest canvas in her thoughts and sensations.

Finally, she rose, wrapped in the bed covering. She wandered about the apartment with its ceiling of slate, cracked and open in some areas.

She went out to the front section, eyed the hot bath with its slow bubble of water. Then she stripped off the makeshift robe and moved down the wide semicircular marble steps. The heated water swirled around her. She sank into the depths and closed her eyes. Dirt, fatigue, care, guilt all swirled away in the bubbles that dotted the surface.

Einar had gulped down his own plain meal, ignoring the flat stares, knowing glances, and smothered smirks of his men.

Done, he left them, almost running. Finola! He was a fool!

"We could take the food to her, milord," Dalia called out as he passed her, Reric and the young mute.

"I'll do it." He strode by them. He had to see her again! And he didn't give a damn about Dalia's sly looks and Reric's agape ones.

It was as though a dam, like the wooden barriers he'd seen on the Volga, had burst inside him. She'd been with him on his ship, under the expressionless gazes of his men. Even out of sight, she was never far from his thoughts. Fastened to his mind and spirit, it was as though he'd taken on part of her.

She'd been on his mind since that day when the earth quaked. They'd weathered the bad moments. He'd kept her close and dreamed of her when they'd been parted. Now, after seeing her again, talking to her, he hated being separated from her. Without her, there was an emptiness as hollow as though his life lacked flesh and blood.

All the feelings that'd begun when they'd met had boiled up in him. They were now coming through his skin, churning his lower body to hardness, and twisting his innards with a want he couldn't put a name to. He couldn't battle this with his war ax, and he couldn't wish it away if he had wanted to try.

This desire was intangible with him, not a necessary searing of the spirit that grew, not dissipating as other sexual needs had done. Oh, Wotan! For her. He laughed at his own folly as an alien excitement raged through him. He longed to see her. And he was damned if he'd fight that. They were together, on an island, at peace for a time. He would care for her, if only for a little while, until she need return to her life, whether it be in Rome, Antioch, or Iona.

He approached the structure, his stride lengthening.

When he crossed the threshold, he realized it was very silent. Caution, sudden fear of Finola in peril, gave him pause, Einar scrutinized the area, ferreting through the dimness of every nook and cranny. He saw the movement to his right and flung around, not making a sound while drawing his dirk, his teeth bared. The hot pool! He saw her hair first. It floated out behind her like a fiery wave. She was there, under the water ... He dropped the dirk and froze for a blink of the eye. Nothing could happen to her!

19

Deathless Aphrodite on your rich-wrought throne.
Sappho

Panic had him running. He flung himself through the outer room to the bath area, thrusting his body forward in a dive. He hit the water hard, his hands grasping her before the hotness closed over him. He had her! Was she dead? No! He wouldn't let that happen. He lifted her up, bringing his mouth to hers, opening, breathing.

Finola pushed at him. "Wha ... ? Einar?" She coughed, taking deep, shuddering breaths.

He lifted his mouth, stunned, his heart slamming into his ribs. "You're alive," he choked.

"Yes ... yes." She clung to him, confused, dizzy, coughing hot water. "Has ... has something ... happened?"

"No ... No. I thought ... you were ... Never mind." He clutched her to him, fully aware of her nakedness and not giving a damn for the proprieties. She could scream the place down about the amenities. He'd see for himself that she was fine.

He set her on the side of the hot pool, his hands going over her, lingering on the satin wet skin, but clinically assessing every bone. More than once he'd doctored his own men with good Icelandic treatments. He used all his skills of touch to ascertain her good health.

When he cupped her jaw, her eyes fluttered shut, then flew open. "This cannot be . . . Einar Thorhallsson." Yet it was not shame she felt, but a heat more torrid than the baths. "I cannot be alone with you . . . unclothed."

"But you are."

"Cannot be." Her voice was thin, shaking.

He leaned over her, pressing his mouth to her. "'Tis not unseemly." He didn't give a damn if it was. He had a need to make her well, to keep her so.

"I think 'tis." She swallowed. "Passing strange. I feel spun in a wheel of light. 'Tis early evening, though it seems that stars whisk around me. Does the hot water give such a hunger, Einar Thorhallsson?" She touched him. "In many ways you've taken my life as you rescued me. Has my life been given over to you?"

"Are you sure you're unhurt?" He spoke as though fevered. He couldn't tell because she was so warm, soft . . . glowing like a sun.

"Yes."

"Your voice is faint and you shiver." He swept her up into his arms and stepped down into the pool. "I will warm you, milady, and keep you safe."

"Haven't you from the moment of our meeting?" Dazed she stared up into his eyes. "Your garb will be sodden."

"I care not."

"You bring great heat with you. My blood boils from it, my skin prickles." She bit her lip. "I shouldn't speak so."

"I want you to be free with me." Her form floated in the steaming water. He couldn't look away from the sheen of skin, rosy nipples peeking from the surface. They drove heat to his loins and made them throb.

"I have been. We know that. I can't get out now."

"No!" He modified his tone. "Do you want to?"

"No. I like the heat. A very new sensation."

"Yes." He was burning alive. He wanted her, more than he'd ever wanted anyone. His hands feathered over the taut, smooth skin, and he almost choked on the desire that rose in him like a flood. Einar pulled back. He could frighten her. Longing flooded him. He reeled with it. Not since his unfledged years had he known such unbalance, such emotional impact, such sensual necessity that blotted out purpose. At that moment, not his vocation to serve his people as Thegn of Icelandia, not his men, his ships, nor his wealth, were important to him. Finola was his everything. She was life, none other, nothing else. He sought her joy, ached for it.

Years of control, eons of leadership, millennia of good blood that kept a man in power of his world, faded. He was left shaking, never so weak, never so strong. "I'm . . . I'm your guardian. I can't. The covenant."

"What do you mean? I don't feel threatened." She touched his cheek. "So strange."

"What?" He would fly apart like the mountains of Sicilia when they were packed with heat.

"In my life I've sought order, artistic truth, perhaps perfection."

The shrug of one perfect shoulder had him quivering. "And have you found it?"

"Mayhap today. I feel such a newfound passion. I can't explain . . ."

Einar shook. "I understand."

She beamed. "I knew you would." She squeezed his jaw. "Don't pull back, Einar Thorhallsson."

" 'Tis prudent that I do, milady," he said through his teeth.

She stared up at him. "You feel it too?"

"Aye." He couldn't look away. He pushed back the wet strands of hair that clung to her brow and strung out on the water.

They were suspended in bubbling time. The only conversation, an almost noiseless rumble of surf as it filtered from the strand through countless trees and brush, had a cocooning effect.

"Milady," Einar said, his voice raw. He struggled to pull back even more.

With a gasp, Finola leaned to him, pressing her fingers into that strong jaw. "Soft and hard," she mused. "I don't want you to go." She bit her lip. "Propriety says I should run from you." She pressed her hand to her breast. "Something won't let me. Nay! I want to be closer."

They stared into each other's eyes.

"Milady, I—"

"Einar Thorhallsson, your eyes are azure ... so Nordic. When I paint you again, I will mix the hue. Make it like the hottest part of fire. The blue flame. Yet, they don't scorch me. You've saved me, cleansed and healed me." She couldn't resist. She moved up and kissed his eyes, delighting when they closed. "You're soft, Einar Thorhallsson. How can that be when you're so hard, so strong? 'Tis a fool's game that we play, is it not?"

"Wotanhelpme." The words ran together in a strident whisper, ground together like grain under a stone miller's wheel. His resistance was becoming barley meal. His blood was hotter than the outdoor iron ovens in Reykjanes.

His hands wouldn't stay away; they ached to touch her white velvety skin that floated half in, half out of the water. His hand smoothed over her back in slow strokes. She should tell him to leave. He shouldn't need the admonition. How could he go? He caught her about the waist, feeling Finola's smallness, her delicious bones, soft curves, her silky skin, the provocative gentle fullness of her hips. If he ever kissed her hipbone he'd be lost forever. That muddled, errant thought was his last one of clarity. Then he succumbed to the flaming need, and devoured her in kisses, only lifting his head when she gasped.

Glassy eyed, breathing hard, he stared at her, fighting the greatest battle of his life to free his hands, to move away.

"Why are you so still?" Her fingers curved over his twisted smile, feathering over his hard mouth, strong cheeks, and hawk-like nose. Einar's full lips quivered once ... twice ...

He turned his mouth into her hand, grazing her palm with his teeth, sucking the softness between her thumb and finger joint. When she caught her breath, he lifted his head and dropped his mouth to hers. He kissed her hard, bringing her around, letting her float up to him in the heated water. Was it true what some said in this part of the world? That the hot water came from Hell. It was in truth but a tributary of the River Styx. Those foolish enough to test its demonic warmth would be cast among the devils for all time. "The Romans didn't believe it." Einar kissed her lips, stunned and delighted when she didn't pull back.

Finola tilted her head. "Didn't believe what?"

"That Hades is at the bottom of a hot pool."

"Oh. I don't fear. You're with me."

When her mouth drooped in the first flutterings at passion's entry, he stiffened. "No."

"No, what?"

"I should not." Or he could, in truth, take her to Hades. In his world, men could covet, rape, take women at will. But a woman could be castigated forever because she was a victim of such. Even in Icelandia, where such practices against women were frowned upon, women were sometimes put aside when they became the victims of rape. Those that put women aside were not admired nor respected, though the law said that it could be done. As Thegn, he'd let it be known he could not countenance such, nor would he command men that did. Now he was ready to cast a most beautiful virgin among the unclean, the unwanted, the unprotected, knowing what could be her fate. "I cannot."

Again the admonishment was more for himself than for her.

"Is it sinful to feel this warm wanting, Einar Thorhallsson?"

He frowned. Now she was uncertain. Her heart didn't lessen its fast rhythm.

"I . . . I should go," she said as she began to back away from him.

"No!" He enveloped her in his embrace, sloshing the water around them, swirling the steam in tighter folds. "What's between us is beautiful, Finola MacDonnell. I would not have you think otherwise. I want this for you, and for me. But I fear to take you on this course, little one. I could hurt you with my passion. I would not have others call down names to you."

"And that is what pulls you from me? I do not repel you?"

"You could never do that." The huskiness of his voice, as he swept back her thick wet hair, had a tremor to it. "You are all of loveliness, Finola MacDonnell. In all my life there has been no other who had your wonder. 'Tis truth I tell thee," he whispered in formal Icelandic. "Did you ken my words, little one?" He switched to Gaelic.

"I did."

She groaned when his arms tightened, his mouth slanting and taking hers with a gentle ferocity.

He lifted his head a fraction. It shocked him when the childlike look that was so much a part of her was belied by the seduction of her soft lips, the sprawl of her lissome body in the water, the hot look to her limpid glance. She was made for a man. No! She was made for him.

"Finola . . . you are a woman . . . untouched." He knew that as he'd known, from the moment he'd seen her that first day, that she was like no other. His heart slammed into his rib cage, the hardness of his root challenging the rebuke in his voice. "How can I touch thee when the vows have not been spoken between us?" Again the words were but a savage query to himself.

"I want you to love me, Einar Thorhallsson. I didn't expect this wanting, nor did I believe it lived in the world." She shook her head. "'Tis not like the greedy taking I saw at Albai's holding. This is . . . is—"

"I know, little one," he said softly. He should castigate both of them, himself and Finola, reject his throbbing need. He should go back to being the practical captain of a trader fleet who always thought actions through and calculated the dangers.

Now he was the one seeking, wanting what should've been an untouchable treasure. He couldn't back away. He could master the passion, the steam of desire, the illusory world of water. He could lose himself in her, even as he knew it was wrong to want . . . Finola . . . Finola.

"I . . . I have never been with a man . . . never thought to be." Her whisper shook as though her voice and body had been given over to another power. "I do not pretend to understand this feeling . . . but I don't wish it to leave—"

He shook his head. "I can't fight this, Finola."

"You sound so surprised, Einar."

"I am. Yet I succumb, gladly. This is our world, the only world . . ." His voice was so ragged, he had to pause. "Others will think us wrong, Finola. I will fear for you—"

"Don't. I want this sensation that fills one to overflowing. I know my cousin knows of it."

"She does," Einar said, smiling. "Sinclair does not try to hide his hunger, nor does she." His smile faded to a frown. "They have had their vows blessed. I would have it with us."

Finola opened her mouth, shut it, her eyes filling, tears slipping down her cheeks. "You wish for our vows?"

"I do." When she caught back a sob, he held her. "I wouldn't have you grieve, dear one."

"I grieve not. I'm overjoyed." She pressed herself toward him.

The undulating water allowed a pinkish view of her uptilted breasts, the supple middle of her body and her lower mound cluster of reddish curls. He'd not ever wanted a woman so much. It'd come like the bursting of the mountain when molten innards poured down the sides, often making another island.

Finola of Iona had made a new isle of him where fresh feelings filled him. A deep need to protect her had entered his bone and sinew. She would be part of him. He would be part of her. As none knew when the mighty mountains would pour forth their hot earthly gifts, he had not known that he could be so struck by a woman. Neither had he known when the great passion would take them, but it'd come, and could not be denied. He would have Finola. She would have him.

He lifted her clear, watching her for long moments before kissing one breast, taking the nipple into his mouth and rolling it between his lips.

Reason asserted itself. He would've pulled back. She wouldn't let him. Could the spirit of this hot desire come from Lucifer himself? No! 'Twas God-given. Only a holy love could be right for Finola MacDonnell. Society could try to put her in Hell, but he'd damn them all before he'd let it happen.

It was his last coherent thought. She lifted her leg and rubbed it alongside his.

He released her to tear the sodden clothes from his body. Then he embraced her again. "Finola, I give you my pledge to protect you with all I possess, to have our vows heard by a priest, to give you everlasting love and respect. That is my vow as Thegn of Icelandia," he said against her lips. "Can you give me yours?" He'd made the most solemn Icelandic covenant.

"I, too, vow." Her voice trembled. "I give you all freely, Einar Thorhallsson. My body, the care of my soul, my love, from now this day and into our next life." She pronounced the words of Gaelic spousing.

The huskiness of her words had him trembling. He brought her close, embracing her as his hands traveled freely over her body. He felt her begin the quake of need, even as his own body trembled with desire.

"I want you, Einar Thorhallsson."

"I am yours."

"And I am yours."

His fingers feathered over her wet skin. The sheen and slickness of it drove him wild.

She opened her eyes. "I might be clumsy at this."

"I think not."

She welcomed the invasion of his tongue, gasping as need intensified.

His hands never stopped their hot stroking, stirring her to writhing motions. Blood cascading at her giving, he moved his mouth over her bare shoulder, then eased her up to take a wet, pink nipple into his mouth. He pulled back.

"What are you doing?"

"Looking at you, beautiful one." He pressed his mouth to her breast once more, his hand in gentle search, stroking her hotter. The water would ease his entry. Even as his being exploded in want, he was careful, not wanting her to fear the first time.

When she moved beneath his touch, her body twisting in the water, making rivulets that splashed over the side, he eased her over him, keeping them submerged. "Look at me, Finola."

When her eyes lifted and gazed at him in adoration, he pulled her over him, easing her downward. He kissed her, gently working himself to her virgin's barrier. He moved slowly, though his body screamed to plunge into her essence.

Finola wriggled against him, deepening his thrust. "I want you, Einar Thorhallsson," she said against his lips.

With a groan he sank into her and felt her start of surprise. He passed through the barrier, pausing. "Beloved?"

"I . . . I like this. How surprising."

He laughed, though there was a tremor to it. Her body was pliant again. She moved against him. Again and again he delved and withdrew, until she was quaking, her nails digging into his shoulders. Over and over he moved within her, to give her joy, fulfillment.

"I . . . I can't . . . I . . . want . . ."

"Let go, Finola. I have you."

It went on and on, building. Then it exploded around them. She cried out. He called her name.

The words were a covenant to their joining.

Cries of joy, of desire were lost in the steam as they joined and pledged their love.

20

May the gods grant you all things which your heart desires, and may they give you a husband and a home and gracious concord, for there is nothing greater and better than this—when a husband and wife keep a household in oneness of mind, a great woe to their enemies and joy to their friends, and win high renown.

Homer

Time was running away. Long days seemed like moments.

" 'Tis well past time to leave, beloved," Einar told her as they lay together next to the hot tub, their bodies replete from lovemaking.

Finola moved the arm she'd had over her eyes, looking up at him as he leaned over her. She shook her head.

"What is it?"

"I know 'tis time to leave. Once we get to Rome, we can give the Cup—"

"To hell with it," Einar said, curving her to him. "First we say our vows. Then we worry about the damnable Cup."

Finola smiled, rubbing his beard with her fingers, becoming used to his bursts of temper when the Cup was mentioned. "I'd prefer that too, Einar."

He smiled. "There was something else on your mind. Tell me."

She laughed. He'd begun to read her well. "I was thinking how natural it seemed to lie here, unclothed, with you." She reddened under his hot gaze.

"You may dress if you choose, milady. Truly, I'll just remove your garments if you do. You entice me, dressed or no."

"I do not think you consider it a chore, this undressing."

"I don't. Since I like doing it so well, it's no problem for me, either way." He leaned down and kissed the valley between her breasts. "You're so beautiful, my own." Though she smiled, he glimpsed the pathos. "Now, what troubles you?"

She sighed. "I'm not. Truly." She glanced at him, biting her lip. "I have not conversed with Dalia or Reric or Gar. I've been closeted with you." Her face reddened. "They know, don't they?"

Einar preferred hedging. He nodded and ground his teeth. "Please don't be hurt by this."

"I'm not."

That was a falsehood. She couldn't hide the pain in her eyes.

"Forgive me for giving you grief, my love."

Repentant, she flung her arms around him. "No, no, don't think that. I wouldn't take back our moments together. I'm being a fool."

"No, I'm that."

"Einar, truly, I wanted you to love me."

"You have your wish."

She gasped a laugh. Did he love her?

In moments the banter was gone. They were locked in one another's arms; their hunger lifted them to a fiery plane where none could touch them.

Once more Finola was stunned by the cascade of emotion. Feelings that she hadn't imagined swamped her, overpowered her, and left her clinging and loving the man from Icelandia.

Again and again they'd loved. In bed, on the floor, by the pool, in the pool. Finola had had more than a moment of guilt at the way she'd ignored her traveling companions, though Einar often assured her they were fine and given care.

The mountain of sexual heat that built between them burst in a flood of molten love that welded them as no blacksmith's heat could do to iron.

They were almost asleep when they heard it.

"Milord Einar."

Einar reached for his elkskin cape and placed it over her. Then he sprung to his feet, wrapping his skin about his waist. He smiled down at her, blowing her a kiss. "I'll return."

Finola couldn't get over how warm, how romantic he was, how she never tired of being with him. She sighed, closed her eyes and turned on her side. Weren't Vikings called rampagers, monsters, destroyers? Not Einar Thorhallsson.

"Darg?" Einar studied his lieutenant. "Problems?"

"Mayhap not, milord. Our men who've gone foraging and scouting in the waters some miles from here report seeing several of the square sails with our heading."

Einar stared into the distance. "And you think it's Albai."

Darg hesitated, then nodded once, his mouth a grim slash. "My innards tell me so, Lord Einar."

Einar clapped him on the back. "Mine, too. We've tarried long enough. Make ready. We sail on the morning tide."

Darg nodded, a whisper of a smile. "We're ready when you give the order, milord. We'll send out one more scout to make sure our passage from here will be safe and secret."

Einar slapped him on the back hard enough to down a horse. Darg didn't budge. "We sail up the Mare Tirenno."

Darg frowned. "The Barbaries rest at Isole Eolie, milord."

Einar grinned his eyes on the horizon. "Let them attack. We'll put them on the bottom."

Darg nodded, slapping his arm across his middle, his smile hard and eager.

Einar returned to Finola, stripping off his clothes and lying beside her. He liked to watch her sleep and had done so often.

She opened her eyes and looked up at him. "Trouble?"

"No, but we embark at dawn." Her features mirrored the disappointment in his heart. He leaned over her, groaning. "We'll be together."

She clutched him to her. "No privacy."

He gritted his teeth. "I've thought of that." He clutched her. "Once our vows are said, none shall interrupt us."

She laughed in his ear.

He shook her in his arms. "Your mirth is unseemly, milady." He gazed down at her, his mouth moving over hers, his eyes open. "I love you, Finola MacDonnell."

Tears welled in her eyes, coursing down her cheeks to her ears, then to the pallet.

"Beloved, my words shouldn't upset you."

She pulled him down to her, her mouth opening over his. At his gasp, his tightening hold, there was once more the torrid rush of power that came whenever he touched her. "And I love you," she murmured when his mouth moved down her neck.

Their lovemaking was fiery. Indeed there was a hint of desperation to it, as though they needed to store up their emotions, their joy for the long days to come.

21

From their eyelids as they glanced dripped love.
Hesiod

Sailing through the rough islands that dotted the northwest coast of Sicilia was an experience. The waters were warm and wild. The islands with their black rocks had a mystery all their own.

Though Einar was with her much of the time, Finola couldn't shake the feeling that they'd parted, that there'd been an ending to them and their love. She was plagued by a feeling of trepidation.

"What is it, beloved? Soon we'll be along the coast of Italia. You needn't fear the dreaded pirates again." He touched her cheek. "You're silent. Do you fret? When we are alone together, don't worry. Our thoughts are open to each other. Don't fear. All will be well."

"You must see the love in my eyes, Einar."

"I do, little one."

His concern reassured her. Her gentle Viking was such a warrior. His men showed him the greatest homage. His valiant reputation was worldwide. The tanner had told her many stories of the great man, Einar Thorhallsson, who struck fear into the hearts of all his enemies.

"I'm well and happy," Finola told him.

Einar would've said more, but duty pulled him away.

She didn't mind. She watched him, sketched him, talked to the sailors who brought her food and drink.

Finola chuckled one day when Lars Bjorson was waxing strong on his tale. Reric and Gar were entranced. Dalia was skeptical.

"He cannot have done such, milady. Not the Ajax of Greek fame could do so."

Finola turned her head, puzzled. "How is it you know of the great classics, Dalia?" When the girl bit her lip and turned away, she stayed her. "Wait. Don't fear me. We've been through too much to hide from one another."

Dalia shrugged, sinking down beside her, facing away from the others. "I was not always a serving girl, milady. My father was a great desert chief. He loved my mother and me, and allowed me to be taught along with my brothers. When he died, and my mother followed him in death, my brother's wife contrived to sell me though I was but a girl. I was in a caravan when Albai captured it."

Finola knew there was much unsaid. She had no doubt the child had been raped as was the custom in many parts of the east. She touched the back of Dalia's hand. "I swear to you that you will be free when we reach Rome." She was unprepared for the flash of hatred in the girl's eyes. "Why do you look so?"

"Free to do what? Sell my body in the streets? No, I'll stay a slave . . . to live."

Finola bent her head, then gazed at the girl once more. "You've been hurt by life, Dalia. I promise you I will try to change that. You may stay with me, as my friend, until we are able to arrange a good life for you, one that you want." She smiled at the other's palpable astonishment. "I mean it."

"I think you do," Dalia said, shaking her head. "I do not think I will ever understand the *faranghi*, especially you."

Finola laughed, and patted her hand. "Listen to the stories."

"Wild, they are, but they entertain. That might've been my job, had I been lucky."

The troubled tone of Dalia's voice had Finola frowning again. How cruel a moment in time could be. Dalia had been in a loving family, then brutal fate changed that.

It'd happened to her when Albai had taken her. Perhaps up to that time she hadn't realized how life could be but a turn of the dice for females. There had to be a better way. Her cousin had found it.

Each night the stars and moon cast their light on the sea. The ships would sail through the silver and blue beauty of the entrancing night, with the moon her beacon. And Einar would be at her side, their arms touching.

"Great loveliness, is it not?"

"How can you sail at night? I've heard tell that Vikings do not."

Einar leaned against the rail. "I inhale your special fragrance, Finola, enhanced by the laves I've unearthed from the stores."

"I use them to cleanse."

"They drive me mad."

Her heart thudded against her breastbone. "Look at the wondrous night."

"I would prefer to lie with you, rather than discuss the stars."

"Einar! You'll be heard." Her whisper carried on the wind.

He looked down at her, smiling. "And you feel the same."

"I do."

" 'Twill be well for us to be wed."

"I think so." She was breathless, desiring him so much that she could've dropped him to the deck. Shameful! True. "How long to Rome?"

"We'll be there on the morrow, beloved. And I shall find a priest at once."

She inhaled, nodding, her mouth shaking. "I wish it."

"So do I."

"Do not look at me so, Einar."

"I can't help it."

"Speak of the stars."

Einar sighed, looking upward. "The stars. Yes. You asked how we could sail at night. Our good princess, your cousin, came by a wondrous instrument of Cathay, called by some the compasso—"

"I know of it. I've seen Iona's."

He smiled. "'Tis not readily used by most because it's deemed to be a demon's wand." Einar shrugged. "Iona's mother was given it by a Genoese sailor she'd cured of some ailment, for such was her great healing power. She gave it to her husband, Sigurd, who entrusted it to his daughter for the people of Icelandia. We know not why it always points to the north. But it does. And so, even when the stars and moon are misted, we can find our way."

"And that's how you've drawn such good maps."

Einar nodded.

"I'm proud of you, Einar Thorhallsson."

"Do not say such, beloved." His voice was hoarse. "Else I'll take you to the enclosure."

She smiled at his heat, not fearing he would do that. He was too jealous of their moments alone to risk anyone's knowing or seeing. Though if he did, she knew she couldn't fight him. She wanted him as a husband . . . for all time.

It was late when she retired. Dalia, Reric and Gar were asleep.

At dawn she heard the cry and rushed from the enclosure. "Sail ho!"

Einar sprang to the rail, his own eyes straining. "What guidon, Jarl?"

"One of our own people, lord."

A cheer went up.

Finola's rush of relief was so great, it almost brought her to her knees. She was in awe of the expert sailing done by the three ships to bring them together.

When the other ship was close enough, a line was thrown with a grappling hook. Then, from the other vessel, a man came to them, hand over hand.

"Ho, Tor of Orkney. Good cess to you."

The barrel-chested man slapped his arm across his upper

body, grinning. "And to you, Lord Einar. Many days have we sought you. Word came that you would have need of us."

Einar nodded, unsmiling. "And I would have. Wotan and God smiled on us, and we found our quarry." His warm gaze skipped over Finola and back to his guest. "Join me in warm ale and tell me the news. We sail to Rome."

The man blinked, then nodded. "We will follow, Lord Einar."

" 'Tis meet."

Finola knew enough of the standoffish Icelandics to know that Einar was glad of his friend's support, but neither he nor the friend would mention it. To Vikings it was assumed that one would help the other. To think other was not of their culture.

When Einar put out his hand to her, she was startled. Then she moved to his side. She made the customary bow when meeting a stranger, fighting to hide her mirth at the other's astonishment. She was to be included in the conversation. That was unheard of in some quarters.

"Like the princess," Tor of Orkney muttered.

" 'Tis true," Einar said, with a glimmer of laughter.

" 'Twould be the bloodline." Tor nodded when Einar explained Finola was cousin to the princess. He bowed. " 'Twould be an honor for me to sup with you, milady."

"I am honored by your presence, Tor of Orkney," she said in most formal Icelandic.

When the other man beamed and walked to the rough table set up amidships, Einar chuckled in her ear. "I would have you welcome him, milady, not captivate him."

Finola laughed, looking up at him. Her mirth died at the heat she saw there. "Thee must not."

"I cannot help it." He lifted her hand and kissed it. " 'Tis most happy you make me when you speak Icelandic."

"I like your language, Einar."

"Good. You will be happy at Reykjanes when you're not sailing with me."

Stunned, she gazed up at him. "And will I be doing that?"

He nodded. "With your tempera and parchment, if you choose."

Finola felt giddy with joy . . . and a wonderful power. To love such a man and be loved by him. Would he always love her? She pushed away the foolish thought and sat herself upon the pile of skins indicated by Einar.

He smiled at her and turned to Tor. "You've been to Rome?"

Tor nodded. "We looked for you there as well as in the east." He frowned. "I do not understand all the goings-on, but there is much I do not like."

Einar stiffened. Tor was a stolid man, of good character, unafraid and truthful. "What bothers you, friend?"

"When we docked in Rome, there was much excitement." Tor shrugged. "There are always throngs of yellers and vendors . . . but this was more." His hooded gaze touched Finola before fixing on Einar. "There is much sport in Rome, as you know." He tipped the horn filled with ale into his mouth. "I do not take part in these sports, but one name caught my eye."

"Which was?"

Finola could feel Einar's tension as though a lightning bolt had passed through him to her. Without thinking she put her hand on his sleeve.

Tor saw it and coughed.

Finola pulled her hand back as though she'd been burned. Einar took it and put it back on his sleeve. "Go on with your tale, friend Tor."

He sighed. "Albai. That was the name I heard."

Einar covered her hand with his own. "And how is it that you heard it?"

Tor swigged more ale. " 'Twas he who was to provide the entertainment. All who could, would attend. There was to be great wagers on the outcome."

"And the event."

"Albai had thought he'd found a Viking in disguise—"

"What?"

Tor put up a placatory hand. " 'Twas not so. It seems Albai

had captured a Bulgar, not a Viking ... for some reason he thought him to be Viking." Tor shrugged as though such foolishness didn't seem possible. "How could anyone think we could resemble those river vermin, I cannot see."

"Nor I." Einar wasn't laughing. "And what would they do with this Bulgar?"

"Staked him out against the bulls from Afrique."

Finola gasped.

"That's not entertainment." Einar was scathing. "'Tis slaughter. None but the beasts of Hell would call it entertainment."

Tor cocked his head. "'Twas what I would've said." He rubbed his hairy chin, the faded red of it crackling under his hand. "Mayhap not. 'Twould seem the Bulgar had been known to free himself and kill a bull."

Einar leaned back. "He would be wondrous strong."

Tor nodded. "Mayhap 'twould be a match, but my runner tells me that Albai will make sure the Bulgar fights more than one."

"The beasts are ferocious. 'Twould be folly to pit two in the same arena. They could tear each other to pieces and ignore the staked prisoner."

Tor took another swallow of ale. "True." His shoulder lifted. "Still, there is much excitement over such."

"And what happened?"

Tor blinked. "Oh. 'Tis not happened, Lord Einar, nor will it, until after the full moon."

Einar sat back, his laughter harsh. " 'Twould seem we arrive betimes, good friend."

Finola could barely suppress a shudder.

Einar leaned forward. "I do not attend such sport, beloved."

Relief colored her smile. "'Tis passing cruel, to my thinking."

Einar nodded. "If the man is a fighter, it could be a battle beyond credence. If not, the bloodbath will not be to my liking." He smiled down at her. "Besides, we must see the priest."

Finola nodded.

Tor hadn't heard the last whisper, nor did he seem curious about what they said. When enjoined, he told them other gossip about Rome and his other ports of call.

They spoke of many things. Tor had many tales to tell.

Finola noted he talked more than Einar, that much of the conversation was on trade. He told of many dangers of the upriver bargaining among the Rus, the growth of the Viking trade, and the eagerness of the young men to go beyond the Poison Sea.

When Tor returned to his ship, Einar joined Finola at the rail. "He honored you by speaking so freely in front of you. Tor is one who's clung to the ways of his father, who never allowed a woman to speak in the presence of guests. Tor has told me he respects you."

Finola understood that. "I'm honored by his trust."

"You honor me, fairest lady."

"As you do me."

He leaned toward her.

Finola pulled back, jerking her head at his crew.

Einar sighed and nodded.

"Tell me about Rome."

Einar smiled. " 'Twould seem that Rome will be more of a circus now than in Roman times."

He'd spoken lightly. She could hear the undercurrent. "You are uneasy."

His smile twisted. "You've begun to know me." He nodded. "I don't like Albai bringing his games to the west. Who protects him from the wrath of the western consortia, who are most powerful and can be rigid about such things?"

"You've said he belongs to a consortium in the west."

"Yes. But I didn't think his power truly extended out of the east. Albai grows beyond what is safe for honest traders."

"You are a match for him," Finola said, confidence in her voice.

He laughed. "I bow to your opinion, milady."

"You must. I know the man."

"So you do."

22

The shifts of fortune test the reliability of friends.
Marcus Tullius Cicero

Rome!

It smelled, not of roses, but of unattended garbage. Some said the Tiber was so thick with waste the fish fought their way to the sea to die in the salt rather than in the urine-and-feces brine of the Roman river.

After days at sea, Finola felt shaky on the ground. Perhaps she wasn't as bad as she'd been when they'd landed on the island, but an inner trembling had her more off balance. Much of her shakiness was akin to her uncertainties. When they'd been together on the island, when she'd become his, it'd all been so right. She'd belonged to him. Now, after days on the ship when they'd been forced to keep a certain distance, her angst had become a flood. Despite the many reassurances of his look and touch, the closer to Rome they'd come, the more unsure she was of their future. Einar knew she felt the Cup should be returned to the Church. Would his great antipathy to the relic supersede their love, bury it in bitterness? And what of her work? Einar's love had relegated it to lesser importance. Could she, in all conscience, allow that to happen when such great faith had been put in her by her sponsors?

Did her loyalties lie with them first? Would Einar resent this? Would he back away from her?

She couldn't shuck the uneasiness that she could lose him as fast as they'd come together. It all seemed so unreal. A fantasy.

If only they could discuss the Cup. Why did it have to divide them? Yet she was loath to mention it. In her heart she knew it was an honorable quest, to return the chalice to the Church. Her determination to do it was not only a memorial to her lost friends at the convent, but she felt the relic belonged with the Church. Her heart squeezed within her at the thought it could destroy the most wonderful commitment of her life . . . to be with Einar. It tore her apart that he might want her to choose between the Cup and him. His antipathy toward it was so great, it could cause a rift between them that couldn't be mended. Maybe if she'd come from a strong loving family, as had her cousin, Iona, she would've felt more confident of Einar's feelings . . . she'd be more sure of her power to hold him. It tore her innards to think of losing him. She was sure that Iona had never had a moment's worry about her husband.

Would she be Einar's wife? Was that also a fantasy?

"What are you thinking?"

"About Rome." The lie came easily. She saw a momentary flicker in his eyes. Did he suspect the truth? Could he know that she feared for their future, that nothing seemed solid? Would he trust her if he knew of her uncertainties?

"We have a house." Einar took her arm, gazing around the busy shipping area called the arsenale by the Italos.

"Do you look for someone?"

"Yes. I've sent word to those who've procured lodging for me at other times. I expected them here."

"You must have many friends here."

He wasn't looking at her when he nodded, so he missed her crestfallen expression. He wouldn't need her when his cluster of amis, men and women, gathered.

She was still watching him when she saw his visage lighten with pleased surprise, almost shock. He would've rushed away, but then he looked down at her and pulled her close, remaining where he was.

She turned and saw a tall man striding toward them. There was a moment when she was sure she knew him. When he came closer, she realized that she didn't.

He was as tall as Einar, built in the same fluid muscular way. There was even a sameness to their hawkish noses. However, the differences were far more than the similarities.

The man had swarthy good looks that went with his thick ebony hair that fell straight and shiny to his shoulders. His stride was long and purposeful, his head up, his eyes straight ahead, smiling. "Well met, friend."

Einar nodded, his arms going out to clasp his friend's forearms. "Well met, indeed. How is it you come west, my friend? I had not thought you to leave the curve of the east."

His friend laughed. "I don't like to, but I have business. What else? You and I know the value of following the gold path. 'Tis what has made us independent."

"True." As though he'd forgotten for a moment, Einar turned to apologize to Finola. "Forgive me. Let me introduce you to my friend. Finola MacDonnell, may I present Corin of Antioch."

Finola's gaze widened. "Antioch? But I lived there in the Convent of Saint Mary of the Cross."

Corin nodded. "I know. I was the one who had to give the bad news that you'd been taken by Albai." He took her hand, bending over it. "Milady, I don't know how you escaped. But you have given us all courage, those who would oppose the barbarian Albai. He's a cruel tyrant." Corin's mouth tightened. "He has no care for any living thing but his horses."

Einar stiffened. "I didn't realize."

"What?" Corin frowned at his friend.

"Lady MacDonnell and her friends used some of his equines to escape."

Corin bit his lip. "The barbarian has a long memory and a thirst for vengeance."

Finola shivered. " 'Tis true what you say. I was told he treats his horses like babies."

"And everyone else like dung."

Her gaze sharpened on him. "You've been his victim?"

"I have. Both Einar and I were in the galleys. That's where we met. Alp Arsian, the great pirate of the east, put me at the oars. He'd bought me from Albai, though at the time I didn't know his name." His lopsided grin touched Einar. "But we escaped, did we not, brother?"

Einar laughed at Finola's shock. "We're not brothers. Corin has called me such since we escaped and became business partners. He's the east, I'm the west."

Corin bowed again. "And we keep you standing, mistress. Forgive me. You would go to your house?"

Finola shook her head. "I must contact my patrons here in Rome. I have the artifact for them." Her glance skated from Corin to Einar. She noted how Einar's mouth tightened. She wished she could unsay her words. They'd brought a constraint among the trio. "Mayhap, we can speak of this another time."

" 'Tis safe to tell him, Finola. He knows many of my secrets."

Corin grinned and nodded. "As you know mine."

"I have brought the Cup of Antioch to the Church of Rome. I reclaimed it from Albai."

Corin looked stunned. Eyes narrowing, he stared from her to Einar. " 'Tis true?"

"Yes. They brought it with them when they escaped."

Corin shook his head. Then he bowed low. "Milady, I will pay you any price to join my business. With such tenacity, and touched as you are by the gods, I can only prosper."

Finola laughed.

Corin's gaze sharpened on her, smiling to his own amusement, and more.

Einar put his hand on her arm, drawing her back a fraction. She looked up at him, puzzled. "What is it?"

"You're fatigued, Finola MacDonnell. Why don't we go to my house? You may freshen up. Then I shall escort you to your patrons."

She nodded. "That would be fine." She looked around her. "Where are Dalia and the others?"

"They're coming. Tor and Darg will bring them and the stores. We'll go on ahead. Will you accompany us, Corin?"

Corin grinned, his head cocked. "Would I be welcome?"

Finola was surprised when Einar reddened. She was going to say something, but he spoke first.

"I'm sure Finola would like to hear tales of your many exploits and encounters with danger."

Finola nodded. "I would." She liked Einar's reckless friend, who seemed to laugh at adversity. "Oh, there's Dalia." Finola waved and moved toward her.

Einar kept his eyes on her, satisfied when he saw a few Vikings move closer to her.

"You guard her well ... I think, more than an ordinary prisoner."

Einar's mouth twisted. "You talk too much."

Corin threw back his head, laughing. "I will not poach, then."

"I wouldn't let you." Einar flashed him a smile.

"When I searched for her, I was told she was an artist, brother, not a beauty."

"Aye, she's blessed both ways."

"And is she skilled with the stylus as purported?"

"Most talented." Einar grinned. "She enthralls my men by setting their images on skin."

"Enchanting."

"Yes." Einar eyed his friend. "So you come with us?"

Corin frowned. "I would like that, though not all the way. I've given my bond I would be in the market. Count Sigla comes and he is most influential in getting the furs down from the Volga. I must confer with him."

Einar looked surprised. "He's here?"

Corin nodded. " 'Twould be most prudent of you to see him."

"I agree. Tell me where he lodges. And I will send a messenger to meet with him."

Finola turned back to them. "And do you come to the house with us, Corin of Antioch?"

"I cannot, milady."

"I'm disappointed. I'm sure you would have many exciting tales to tell, friend to Einar Thorhallsson."

"Indeed, I would regale you." He grinned, fumbling in his cloak.

"Ah, you carry a scriber. They are most useful, are they not."

"They are, milady." Corin scratched the name and address of Count Sigla and handed the small scroll to Einar.

"I like your scriber, Corin of Antioch."

"Take it, milady, in good health."

"I can't do that." She smiled. "You're most gracious. But I have one, and I know how precious they are."

"I want you to have it." He grinned. "Einar tells me that you do magic with your stylus. Have you work to show me?"

"Some. I had skins aplenty on the ship." Finola shook her head, a sad far-off expression in her eyes. "My other parchments and sculptings were in the fire at the convent in Antioch . . . as were my friends."

Corin frowned. "A great loss. I'm sorry."

"Thank you."

"One day she might show you the drawings she did on the ship." Einar smiled down at her.

"I would like that."

A Viking approached with an open-sided carriage pulled by a broad-chested horse. Its woven hemp roof swayed and flapped with every motion.

Einar helped her into the narrow conveyance. He turned to Corin. "Walk with us, until the great alley."

"I will." Corin walked on the opposite side of the carriage from Einar so that Finola was included in their conversation. Along the busy quai it was also an added protection. They made many turns onto wide thoroughfares, and some very narrow. Corin paused. "Here is where I leave you. Perhaps you and the lady will dine with me on the morrow, good

Einar." When Einar nodded, he grinned and strode away down a crowded alley, weaving in and out until he disappeared.

Finola ogled the mass of the people, goods, and pack animals. "I've never seen such a place."

"Trading alleys. There are many more, as in most cities. They're the lifeblood of the communities. Food, goods ... even persons are sold or bartered here."

"I had not dreamed of such in the west, though I've seen Antioch's."

"I will show you many of them."

She smiled at him, her hand reaching over the shallow side of the carriage to touch his sleeve.

He grasped her hand, looking into her eyes.

For a moment they were caught in their own magic.

Then a hawker yelled.

Finola blinked and blushed. "Your friend is quite educated. He is a highborn trader, is he not?"

"Blood heat fills your cheeks, beloved. Soon we'll be wed, and we can be alone."

She smiled, not able to speak.

He touched his finger to her cheek. Aware of prying eyes, he moved back from the carriage. "You're right about Corin, Finola. I feel he has good blood in him, though he decries such. His father was killed when he was but a lad. He's three years older than I. When his father was alive, they lived well. After his death, things changed. He and his mother were cast from their home. He was forced to live by his wits. Luckily he'd been educated. He did well in business almost from the beginning. His mother died, just a short time ago. He'd taken care of her these many years."

"A good son, too, as you are."

Einar smiled. "I'm glad to have shared my mother's story with you. It's brought her closer to me. Soon I will read the scroll of her last words ... with you."

"I'm honored, Einar Thorhallsson."

He smiled. "What think you of Rome?"

Finola gazed around her. "The Eternal City," she breathed. "I'd hoped to see it one day."

Einar shrugged. "It has charm. But I prefer Genoa, Florence, or even Venice. They smell better."

Finola laughed. " 'Tis blasphemy you speak, surely."

"Mayhap I do. Who knows? My opinion of Rome is already changing." Einar moved closer to the carriage. "It will have its own beauty now."

They looked into each other's eyes, happy to be together.

Other eyes trailed them, careful to keep out of the way of the phalanx of Vikings that followed the carriage. They wouldn't always be so guarded.

When the chance came, the right moment to strike, there'd be no saving them. Soon . . . soon . . . and they'd be ready.

23

When the people of the world all know beauty as beauty, There arises the recognition of ugliness, When they all know the good as good, There arises the recognition of evil.
Lao Tzu

The house was a palazzo!

That's what the first servant called it. Finola agreed. She'd spent a delightful time in the large tub filled with essence of roses, thyme and rosemary. Clean and refreshed, she reveled in the sense of well-being.

Dalia helped her dress, pleased with her own room and the new garb she'd been given to wear. "And I have other pieces as well."

"And so you should." Finola rejoiced with Dalia.

Reric and Gar had rooms above the stable at the back. Einar had given them run of the house, but neither had entered as yet. She was sure their obvious reclusiveness had to do with their incarceration at Albai's. She shivered.

"You're cold, milady?" Dalia frowned at the blazing fire.

"No. For a moment I thought of Albai."

Dalia grimaced. "Do not. I've put it behind me."

Finola was sure she had. Dalia was the most pragmatic of creatures. "I wish I were more like you."

Dalia blinked. "Surely not."

Finola laughed. Dalia didn't pick up the slightest nuance, intonation, or second meaning. Yet, she had the uncanny survival instincts of a ferret.

Dalia shook her head, walking to the window and pushing out the casement. "The carriage is being brought round, milady. Milord Einar looks most handsome in his Roman threads."

Finola hurried across the room to look over Dalia's shoulder out of the opened casement. He did look handsome. No other man could come close to him in stature or beauty.

"We mustn't keep him waiting," she murmured to the serving girl.

Dalia smiled, very much aware.

Finola rushed from the chamber, Dalia at her heels.

The stone walls of the curving corridor would've been damp, dank, even morbid, if not for the rich hangings that belled and swayed with their progress.

Finola's hand went down the stonework wall of the stairs that hugged the round wall. It was dry, but there was a dank roughness to it that made her think of dungeons and oubliettes. She shook her head to chase the gloom from her thoughts.

As they reached the large high-ceilinged foyer, Einar entered from the courtyard. "Well met, milady."

"Milord." Finola felt shy.

He laughed, moving closer, his body turned so only she could hear him. "You look most fetching, beloved. That baster woman Corin bragged of was as good as purported. Not so?"

Finola laughed and nodded. "And that he could have something we could wear at once is a miracle. Dalia and I are grateful, aren't we?"

Dalia nodded, moving toward the back of the house.

"These garments fit well, Einar. And I like them, truly."

"They gather beauty from you, my star."

Finola gasped at such intimacy. Men married years didn't address their wives in such ways. She loved it, yet she couldn't control the quick scan of the turreted hall.

"None heard, my sweet."

"Sirrah, you're bold."

"And I'll be bolder once we're wed ... which will be soon. When I have you back from your patron's place, I will seek out a priest."

Joy colored her pink. She nodded. "I would like that."

"I would love that." Einar laughed.

He enjoyed her confusion! She didn't mind. She was as excited as he. Soon he'd be her spouse. Such waves of pleasure she'd not dreamt could occur. Since meeting Einar Thorhallsson, 'twas a daily happening. Before twilight he'd arrange their nuptials. In mere turns of the sun she'd be his.

"Shall we go?"

"Yes." Out of habit that fear had honed fine, she touched the seam of her robe. Her small knife was there. She carried a knitted bag for essentials, her scriber and parchment. "I have the address." She bit her lip. "I don't bring the Cup with us. I fear footpads."

He laughed. "I fear nothing today."

Finola was speechless at the clutter of richness in the entryway of the Contessa's palazzo. She was so bedazzled by the opulence, she barely paid heed to the attendant that greeted her and Einar.

"A messenger was sent to apprise Milady MacDonnell that the Contessa di Marchi has taken to her bed. You must have missed the courier."

"No doubt." Einar was formal with the attendant. "Just a minor upset, I trust," Einar said.

Finola's disappointment was evident.

The attendant's smile was small, stilted. "The contessa has had these head pains at other times. They come on her rapidly, but usually fade as fast. She will send a messenger on the morrow, I'm sure. She's most distraught not to see her artist."

"I, too, have wished for the meeting," Finola said. "Please give the Contessa my best wishes, and tell her that I will await her message."

"I am called Michaela, milady, and I will convey your words to her." The attendant waved her arm toward a larger room, its double doors wide open. "Perhaps I could offer you some refreshment."

Einar interjected before Finola could speak. "We thank you, but since the Contessa is indisposed, we would not intrude. We will return when she is well."

Once outside and in the carriage, they sat in silence for long moments.

"Don't fret, beloved. You'll see the Contessa tomorrow or the next day, and all will be well. Now I have more time to contact a priest and arrange our nuptials."

She smiled up at him, glad to have her hand engulfed in his. "It's foolish, I know, to be so worried about the Contessa, but I'd counted so on meeting her."

Einar smiled down at her. "You're very lovely when you're worried, my beauty. Have I told you that?"

Finola forgot the Contessa in the welling heat and joy of being with the man who would soon be her spouse. "Tell me about Reykjanes."

Einar grinned. "You'll like it. But we won't live there all the time. I have land abutting Sinclair's. You'll be able to visit with your cousin whenever you choose."

Finola sighed, cuddling closer to him, and wished that they had a closed conveyance so that Einar could kiss her.

It was midafternoon when Einar left the house again. Kol guarded him on one side, Loki on the other. Two stalwart Vikings. Rome was no better or worse than any metropolis of the time. There were always dangerous footpads. Men went accompanied by a companion, or companions. Women were always in a sedan chair, escorted by four or five burly attendants. If they walked, and it was rare, they were surrounded by protectors.

"Think you to find a priest to your liking in any of the near churches?" Loki wrinkled his nose at the garbage-laden streets.

Kol and Einar noticed his disdain and smiled.

"Loki, my friend, you must rid yourself of this contempt

for any but Vikings." Einar laughed when his friend looked affronted.

"I don't discount others. I have the greatest respect for Sinclair and his people."

" 'Tis true."

"He's the only one," Kol said, his laughter loud.

Einar grinned. "I go to the monastery where some of the prelates of Icelandia reside when they come to Rome. We'll find one there who will hear my vows."

Loki nodded. "Good."

As all travelers in the cities, they were vigilant. 'Twould have been better with horses, but the stables wouldn't be ready until the morrow. They looked up at the houses they passed, their second stories right over the alley in some cases.

They moved down a narrow way between high buildings, eyeing the three men who were walking toward them. Cautious, the two trios scanned each other.

As careful as they were, none of the Vikings looked behind them. The runners approached on soft boots. Even as the three in front rushed toward the Vikings and they took precautions, the three behind wielded their cudgels.

Einar heard the sound behind him, turning with his arm coming up. He saw the cudgel and tried to avoid it. It struck him a glancing blow. Before he could rally, another was struck. It cracked his head and sent him spinning insensate.

Before Loki and Kol could retaliate, they were set upon and dispatched with cudgels.

"What of the other two?"

"Leave them to rot. The carrion birds can have them."

"But—"

"Quiet, fool, and help with this one. He's passing large."

The nervous felons said no more. It wasn't for him to say he thought the other two to be alive, that the blows had not rendered them dead. His five companions would call him fool. He'd been paid. As soon as the big one was taken to the dungeon, he'd be gone to drink and dice with his friends.

Leaning down, he lifted, grunting at the heft of the Viking. The man was a giant. Though blood trickled down his reddish-blond locks, he couldn't be sure he was knocked out. Nor did he want to test the theory. He'd heard stories about the Vikings, how they fought and they overcame odds that fell lesser men. He shuddered. Barbarians. All Norsemen were such.

"Come, hurry, shove him in the cart. Throw the skins over him. We must be gone from here."

Soon the giant was loaded, bound and covered.

The cart clattered down the street.

The two Vikings lay in the clutter of the *strada*, their lifeblood dripping over the cobbles.

24

Alas, I am struck a deep mortal blow.
Aeschylus

"I do not care to eat." Finola almost lost her innards looking at the food. Fear had made her nauseated.

Tor and Darg glared at her. "Milady, Lord Einar would want us to care for you. Others search for him. We guard you. You are suffering with concern as we are. The Thegn could've met men of business. He will be angry if you don't eat."

"I would wait for him." Forever, if need be.

"You must eat. And you needn't fear. Einar Thorhallsson will return shortly, and laugh at your misgivings," Darg continued.

Nothing they could've said settled her more. "You're right. Of course. Please join me for the meal. I'm sure Einar Thorhallsson has been put onto some interesting goods, and he is bartering at the main market." Worry etched her brow as she watched the door. "You've sent others to search him out?"

"We have, milady."

"They'll find him." Finola tried to smile.

The two men nodded. Then they stared at each other, then at the two chairs indicated by the lady.

"Please. Dine with me. I won't eat unless you do."

"Einar Thorhallsson will be angry if you waste away," Tor said, his face screwed into an affronted mask.

"Then we'll eat." Finola felt better. The two rough men were showing her more than respect. They expressed a warm caring, a recognition of her fear, and a willingness to help it recede.

Dinner wasn't festive. The conversation was stilted. Finola was relieved to have them with her, but they couldn't quite distract her from her angst. Where was Einar?

After they'd dined, the two men stayed close to her.

Finola was sure that Einar told them she was to be guarded.

When the stars brightened, the moon moved and he didn't return, she rose. "I'll go to bed. Perhaps he will be back later, and I will see you in the morning."

"Yes, milady."

The two Vikings bowed, followed her to the stairs, saw another Viking at the top of the curving staircase and nodded.

Darg and Tor went back into the capacious sitting room, pulling chairs closer to the fire. Though it was getting on to warmer weather, the nights were cool and damp. They huddled near the fire, looking toward the hall, then at each other.

"What think you, Tor?"

"I like it not. His lordship would send a messenger if all were well."

Darg nodded, rose to his feet. Before he could make a sound, one of Tor's Vikings was at the aperture. "You heard our lord is missing?" At the terse nod, Darg almost smiled.

"You know what to do. Take ten men with you."

The Viking clamped his fist across his breast, nodding.

Darg and Tor began to pace.

Einar had a terrible thirst. His tongue had thickened into a sausage. His throat closed and dry, he couldn't salivate. What desert held him in its sandy depths? Being a seaman he had no love for the oceans of sand, though he'd ridden the bad-tempered camels across its stretches. No head should drum as his was doing. It was twice its normal size. Fighting the retching that tore at his innards, the confusion that robbed his thoughts, he struggled to right himself. He couldn't move!

He didn't want to open his eyes. That would decapitate him. He knew his head would fall off with the pain if he did. He'd been wounded. That he knew. Too many times had he sustained blows, not to recognize the weakness. Battle? His mind was too fuzzy to factor and implement the details. He had to husband his energies. He tried to move again. Nothing.

"Wake up, Viking . . . before they come. You won't like the way they do it."

The strange guttural accent was not unfamiliar. Italo was not the unseen person's mother tongue. What was? Einar squinted in the gloom, his head banging in pain. There was a movement adjacent to him. Across from him was another. They were chained to stone walls. It was a relief to know that manacles caused inhibited movement, not complete debilitation.

"Who are you?"

"I'm Tariq, the Bulgar. I'm your fellow prisoner." He jerked his head at the limp form chained on the other wall. "He's been dead for a few days. Starting to stink."

Einar moved, flinched at the pain. His left arm was numb. There was a suspicious wetness down his one side. "What did you mean I wouldn't like the way they woke us?"

The other grinned, the flash of teeth white in the darkness. "They come to do their beatings twice a day. There's no food or water—"

"You sound strong enough."

"I'm a Bulgar. We draw within ourselves, Viking. Our strength is legend."

"How is it you know I'm Viking?"

"They called you thus."

"And you don't think they'll kill you?"

"They will, but not until they tire of the fun."

"And that is the usual torture."

"And the battling of the bulls."

Einar stiffened. "You're the one who's been on display."

"I've been in the arena once."

"And they'll send you in again."

"Until I'm killed."

Einar understood. "There's no way out."

The Bulgar hesitated too long.

Einar chuckled, the sound weak. "So, you wait for the right moment. I can do the same."

"You're wounded. You bled heavily when they carried you in. You haven't the stamina."

"Tell me your plan. We'll see."

"Why would I endanger myself?"

"Because if you don't, I'll warn our guards, and tell them you've a weapon. By the time they're through with you, your plan won't be much." Einar was prepared for retaliation.

When one of the Bulgar's arms struck him on his, he winced, but grinned through his teeth. "So, you're free . . . but not quite."

"My knife broke, or I'd have dug out the other arm."

"Can you—"

"You may not survive the battle with the bulls." The admonition hissed from the Bulgar's mouth.

Clanging, the cell door banged open. Three men entered, armed with whips and swords.

"Take the Viking."

Einar didn't put up a struggle. In fact, he acted as though he'd swooned.

"The fool can't take his wounds. Douse him in the tubs."

Einar didn't know what it meant. When he heard the Bulgar curse, he braced himself but didn't speak.

They tossed him, clothes and all, into a tub of steaming brine. He screamed, not just because it was expected, but because it was agony. Burning salt! An Italo favorite. Boiling brine, not enough to cook a man, some said. This wasn't. It was getting hotter. The brine boiled his wounds. Einar gritted his teeth and recalled the boiling that'd been done to cleanse sores, cuts, grievous inflammations.

They shoved his head under, holding it there. Years of holding his breath under water when he swam in the great fjords of Icelandia kept him from going unconscious. Lungs burst, he shot to the surface coughing, gagging, to the hilarity of his captors. Time after time they did it.

After they dragged him from the pot, boiling hot and red as the northern salmon taken from the fjords, limp and water logged, they beat him. He lay on the floor, feigning near unconsciousness. For their delectation he yelled, loud and long.

A man came running down the stair going to a burly jailer and whispering. The jailer began to curse, his manner changing to urgency.

"Hurry! The master wants the Bulgar and the Viking for the arena."

Einar struggled. Four of them subdued him.

"Dress him in the skins. The master wants them to smell of the female. The fighting bulls will go mad."

The men laughed.

Einar strained to think. A weapon. Anything.

He watched as five of them dragged the Bulgar from his cell. A momentary glance satisfied him. The Bulgar would fight . . . and he'd kept his puny weapon.

Einar scrutinized his surroundings as the others tried to help subdue the Bulgar. On the floor, almost at his feet, was a rusted dirk, something torturers' attendants carried. Not good steel, but better than nothing.

Groaning, he sank to the floor. Before his captors could turn, he'd caught the weapon in his fingers, slashing it into the smelly skins that covered him.

"Do it again, Viking, and we'll toss you in the tubs again. So we will."

Einar didn't even look the speaker's way. He concentrated on what it would be like ahead. There wouldn't be much chance to best the beasts. The bulls of Afrique had prodigious strength, cunning and agility. They'd be maddened by the female smell on the skins. That was the only chance. The maddened bull or bulls, for Einar had no hope that they wouldn't be teased and tortured into frenzy, might be off guard and not as careful. Slim hope was all he had.

Bursting out into the sunshine was another shock. Rome

was bathed in it. He blinked to clear his sight. He looked quickly over the scattered, not large, but vociferous crowd that roared lasciviously as the prisoners were marched to the center of the arena and bound to posts. They had their backs to one another.

When the guards deserted them, the crowd roared, knowing what to expect.

Wooden enclosures under the stands began to vibrate with roars matching that of the crowd. The latticed wooden barrier lumbered up. The bulls didn't charge forth. They were led in opposite directions by a host of men who kept them at bay and apart.

"They will loose them in the center, Viking. Then the dogs, who contain them, will scramble into hiding. The bulls will attack anything that moves . . . until they get the scent of the skins." The Bulgar's words tumbled over one another. "Has thee a weapon?"

"Of sorts. A dirk belonging to one of the dogs who guarded us."

"Save it until you get atop one, then jam it into the throat. Can you get free?"

"I'm working on it." Einar felt his bonds go just as the two beasts charged from opposite directions.

He had no more time to ponder the Bulgar's fate. His own was almost upon him. With strength born of desperation, he broke his bonds, when the beast's breath was on him. Ducking, going under the chest of the bull, he heard the roar and the splinter of wood as the behemoth hit the post.

Einar scrambled to avoid the hooves of the wild bull, coming out beyond the tail on his back, then coming to his knees, as the beast whirled.

Running wouldn't do it.

Leaping to his feet as the beast lowered his head, pawing at the ground, Einar imitated the beast, giving it mere pause. With a roar it came right at Einar.

He waited until the last instance, realizing that the beast had incredible energy and agility. Just as the horn was grazing him, he leaped to one side, then grasped the horn and swung himself on the back of the bull.

He neither heard nor saw the crowds. The thunder of their yells didn't penetrate the concentration it took to master the bull. No wild sea storm ever rocked and plummeted him about as the creature was doing. Einar hung on until he was able to bring the knife into play.

One turn the bull made pulled the head around, the throat exposed. Einar struck into the softness, again and again. Blood geysered from the beast, its caterwauling death throes rocketing through the arena.

For a moment there was a semblance of silence.

"They killed them!"

Swaying from exertion and the effects of his wounds, Einar looked around. The other bull jerked and quivered in death.

"Well . . . done . . . Viking." The Bulgar panted as he sank to his knees. "Husband your strength. They aren't through with us, yet." He eyed the throng who threw things at them as they departed the arena. "We've destroyed two expensive animals."

"So we have." Einar eyed the retinue that approached them in full circle. "You won't escape this Hell without me, Bulgar."

A hiss of mirth was his only answer as the men converged on them. Their hands and feet were manacled before they were dragged from the arena, down into the Stygian darkness of the long, dank corridor that led to the dungeon that housed the prisoners.

Perhaps if Einar hadn't been so shocked to discover that he was mere blocks from his own dwelling, he might've tried an escape before entering the hall.

As it was, he had to think. Who owned property so close to the center of Rome? Prime. Expensive. For the most part exclusive. Who had the power politic to run such games? Rome could be a wild city. It could be prickly conservative about anything that smacked of paganism.

The long walk back wasn't enough to bring him answers. He began to be aware of the angry mutterings of his jailers.

There'd be hell to pay. He braced himself when they reentered the octagonal room.

He was almost prepared for the blow on the side of his head, and another dousing in the boiling brine.

Penetrating the fuzziness of pain was his surety that if his captors knew the brine was salubrious to his wounds, it wouldn't be used as a method of torture.

After a time they removed him. By then, he was no more than semiconscious.

Little by little, things became less hazy. After he'd dripped on the floor for a time, they dragged him back to his cell, though not before he'd had time to size up his surroundings.

The octagonal room had many openings, with stairs running upward from some. One surely led to the arena. The floor and walls were stone, with a variety of equipment for torture that hung from the ceiling and walls. Despite the large flaming pit in the center where the tub had been suspended, the area was dank and clammy. The men were dirty, toothless, and dressed in rags. His torturers were no better off than he, by the look of them.

Three of them dragged him back to his place on the wall, rechaining him.

Einar didn't open his eyes or lift his head until they left. Then he looked right at the Bulgar. "Can you reach my boot?" He stuck out his leg, his mouth twisting at the stunned look on the other's visage. "I, too, can find benefit in subterfuge, Bulgar."

The Bulgar strained, heaved, pulled. "More. You must stretch."

"I'm manacled, dammit, as you are." Closing his eyes, Einar yanked against the steel. As he extended his arm, which had been medicated rather than harmed by the brine, he felt it pull and tear. There was a ripping on his side. Ignoring it, he tried harder. "In ... the ... leather ... sewn along the seam of the boot. Knife."

Ordinarily boots were removed from prisoners. Winners at dice took them. They'd been left on when they'd fought in the arena. He didn't know why. He could only be glad. Stretching again, he felt a blackness.

He didn't know he passed out until he opened his eyes and noted the Bulgar digging at his manacles.

Was it hours, days or minutes that went by? Then there was a groan, a clank. Neither man moved for long moments. Had they been heard?

"I'm free."

Footsteps. Three men entered with whips and buckets of water in hand.

Einar saw the expectation on their features, the greedy lust for pain that was perhaps their only hope of power in their powerless world. He glanced toward the Bulgar, noting he was bunched like a wrapped falcon before it's unmasked and can fire into the sky. He was ready.

As two of the men threw their water toward Einar and the third toward the Bulgar, they lifted their whips at the same time. Einar struck out with his feet, the dank wall behind him giving him the impetus and power needed. Though he hit each one a good blow in the chest, he couldn't follow up because he was chained.

Braced, he watched as they shook themselves, cursing, feeling around for their swords. Looking up at him, they cursed louder.

"How'd he free his legs?"

"Fool. I know not. Watch him. I'll skewer the dog."

As they rose to their feet, their heads flew off their necks with one powerful blow from the Bulgar, who'd commandeered a sword. The man who'd approached him lay behind them. Blood spattered Einar. He spat, turning his face away.

"Queasy, are you?"

Einar stared at the Bulgar, the three men dead at his feet. "I don't care for tainted blood."

The Bulgar glanced at the door, then pushed it shut, not letting it latch. "This will take too long. I should leave."

"Bastard."

"I think my mother was married to my father." He grinned.

Einar said nothing. He couldn't say why he trusted the

Bulgar would free him. He fought off the dizziness that made him want to puke.

"You're not too well, Viking," the Bulgar grunted, digging at the mortar around the manacles.

Einar knew that it'd been minutes, not turns of the hourglass, yet his yearning to be free had his body and mind sweating with the effort.

The chains fell off.

Both men were motionless, listening.

Einar staggered from his slumped position to his feet, reeling from pain and loss of blood. Swiping his hand across his face, he searched for a weapon.

"When I go, Viking, I don't look back. Follow me, if you can. I go to a hiding place I know."

"I'll keep up." He swayed, staring at his jailmate. "Where the hell are we?"

"In a junk pile of a palazzo, in the center of Rome. I came slung over a donkey's back, but I felt the way." He moved his shoulders, grimacing. "We Bulgars don't get lost."

"You're wounded, too."

"A scratch." He looked to the door, then leaped to it.

Einar stared. A tall, well-made muscular fellow, he'd leaped like a boy in the Greek plays put on at the Circus Maximus.

The Bulgar opened the door. Though it was rusty, its hinges were well oiled.

There were four ragtag men in differing degrees of emaciation suspended from the ceiling. No attendants were around.

The men looked at them, hopelessness in their eyes.

The Bulgar cursed, swinging his weapon, cutting down one.

Einar worked on the others.

The Bulgar cursed. "I cannot wait for you. We must leave."

One of the men on the floor pushed up. "We're . . . we're weary and sickening, master, but we serve you now. Bela will know the only way out. He once served this house. Above lies an army." He jerked his head to a skeletal fellow, who glanced up one stairway, put a finger to his lips, then went to the firepot. He leaned over it, and pressed . . . something.

There was a grating sound. Part of the support of the firepot screeched and scratched away.

One of the men started to scream and shout to cover the sounds. The others joined him. They pointed up the stairs.

Einar nodded, glancing at the Bulgar, who watched the circular stairway appear.

They all went down the stairs, Bela last. He placed three torches in the firepot and handed them down, then he pressed the hidden switch and scurried after them.

Black as death, it wasn't a cave. Rather, a tube of underground that wound down on crude far-apart steps, slippery and icy from the constant drips of ceiling moisture.

Though the four men they rescued could walk upright, neither Einar nor the Bulgar could.

Hunched over, they bumped one another in the close downward cave.

"We have tossed our ivories on an unknown game, Viking."

"That we have."

"Do you fear to follow such?"

Einar shook his head, then spoke, realizing the Bulgar couldn't see the gesture. "I don't fear men as desperate as myself. What the future holds, I'll wait and see."

"You sound eastern, Viking. You have a Bulgar's soul. I was told my mother was fatalistic, though some said she was not Bulgar, but Circassian. I was taken from her arms when merely a babe, but my nurses never stopped speaking of her beauty and wisdom."

Einar wasn't distracted by the voice. He gazed around him at every turn. He could feel himself weakening. It irked him when the Bulgar had to shore him up a time or two. He knew it was loss of blood, the broken bones in his arm and the crack on the head. He was impatient with all of it. He had to get back to Finola. She needed him. They were to be married.

"There. Up ahead. There'll be a boat on the river. We'll go from there. I know where we can hide." Bela had assumed leadership.

"Move, then," the Bulgar said, his voice rough, his eyes scanning the area, then fixing on Einar, who fell forward.

The one called Bela helped Tariq to lift him. "The Viking might not make it."

"Irksome," Tariq said through his teeth as Einar came out of his swoon. He turned back to the man called Bela. "Where are the boats?"

"We can't see them from here, lord." Bela pointed below.

"Let's go. Tell the others to find them and get them ready." Bela spoke in whispered, rough Italo.

The other three nodded.

The two turned toward Einar, the last of them to come out of the cave.

Bela grabbed at his torch, mashing it out in the soil around the exit. "It wouldn't be prudent for a lit torch to be seen. Many persons move on the river."

"True." Einar inhaled the air, pushing past the brambles covering the exit. He stepped into the watery sunshine and fell forward on his face. He would've gone over the cliff had not the Bulgar and the man called Bela caught him about the middle.

25

Every thing is soothed by oil, and this is the reason why divers send out small quantities of it from their mouths, because it smooths every part which is rough.

Pliny the Elder

"You cannot mope, Finola MacDonnell."

"Milady Contessa, you've been most kind to me, but I would prefer to have remained in the house that Einar—"

"So you've told me, many times, my girl. Surely you can see the inefficacy of such behavior. A maiden alone would invite riffraff. You could be endangered. And as the Viking fellows remain in the house, you could not do so without female escort."

"I could get that . . ." Her voice trailed at the shake of the Countess's head. They'd had the same discussion many times.

"It's been three months since you were abandoned by the Viking. I think you should be realistic." The Contessa grimaced when the girl whitened. "An unfortunate choice of words . . . but you will admit that Father Antonio also feels you should abandon hope on such a front."

Finola bowed her head. Sadness had been with her since those black days when Einar hadn't returned to their house with a priest as he had promised. "But what of the Vikings? Have they not called or asked for me?"

The Contessa shook her head, her lips tightening. "I fear to allow barbarians in my home."

"They are my friends." Deep inside she felt she'd deserted her Viking friends, yet she hadn't the stamina or inclination to argue against the Contessa. Since losing Einar, she hadn't cared about making decisions about Gar, Reric or Dalia, let alone the Vikings. The Contessa had taken over her life. Finola had let her. Though it went against the grain to be apathetic about her friends, she couldn't seem to muster the energy to do anything about it. Einar! Einar! Why did he leave her? "I must see to Gar, Reric and Dalia," she muttered.

"No need. It's been handled."

Finola closed her eyes. "I see."

"Don't fret, my dear. You have many friends. And now that you go about with Lord Corin of Antioch, your days will be sunnier."

"I . . . I don't think I should be going to these parties. I haven't felt well. I would rather remain at home." She looked at the floor. "Do not think me ungrateful, but I've written to my cousin and her husband and have requested their indulgence. I would go to their home in Scotia. Living there, I'm much closer to my own land on Iona, and I can be contented there, caring for my cousin's children . . . sketching . . . painting." She blinked. "I can take Gar, Reric and Dalia with me."

"And would they be happy in such a cold area? I think not. Besides, you can sketch and sculpt here."

"Yes." Finola sighed. It was so much easier letting the Contessa make the decisions. She'd already done a great deal of sketching since coming to the Contessa's palazzo. And she'd been given every modern accoutrement to do it. Much of her work had been framed. There'd been interest in it. Her patron had hung a few pieces in her own gallery. She smothered the guilt of not seeing to her friends. She was sure they would be cared for properly. The Contessa would do it.

In one of the wide heavy wooden settees that were throughout the palazzo, the Contessa sank down across from her. The roseate hue of the cloth of Cathay covering provided a perfect background for her luxuriant ebony hair and the deeper pink of her silken garb. "My dear, when I insisted you come to us, four days after you were ... after Thorhallsson didn't return, I vowed that every care would be given to you." She removed a roll of parchment from her reticule. "My scribe wrote to your guardians. And we have exchanged three missives since then."

Startled, Finola looked up. "But why?"

"As I've said," her protector continued, her tone soothing. "We worried about you. I've consulted Father Antonio and Lord Corin, and they agreed that my misgivings were valid." She placed the roll on Finola's lap. "You may read them yourself, of course." She hesitated. "When they told me that Lord Corin had petitioned them to seek your hand—"

"What?" Finola rose to her feet, then sank back again. She'd felt increasingly weak the last month, out of sorts.

"Easy, my little Finola. Are you ailing?"

Finola frowned. "I think not. I just feel ... not myself."

"Of course. You've had a series of shocks. Your imprisonment, escape, in the clutches of the Vikings—"

"I've told you, Contessa, I was treated very well."

"Of course you did. You are a most fair young woman." She shrugged. "We are of the world here, and know how the Vikings carry on, personally and in business."

Finola shook her head. "Truthful, milady. I was treated ... very well." She thought of Einar. Was he well? Did he remember her? Another thought intruded. She looked down at the scroll in her hand. She opened it, hands shaking. Surely she misunderstood. There was a seal at the bottom. It looked to be— "What's this? He and my cousin give their consent to my marriage to ... to Corin of Antioch." She stared agape. "This can't be true. Nothing was said to me—"

"Surely I told you that Corin had sued for your hand."

Finola shook her head. "Not until this moment. How is it that I never knew these negotiations were going on—"

" 'Tis not custom to discuss such things with the female in question." The Contessa's regal features tightened a trifle. "Surely you know that such business is transacted between houses, not between the principals."

"Yes, I do know that, but—"

"There you are. I was sure you would not be remiss in your duty. You do not have another whom you'd prefer to Corin?"

"No, but I—"

"Good. Then I shall have my scribe write to your cousin and her husband and tell her that the prescribed three months of betrothal will move forward, and we shall have a wedding in three turns of the moon." She rose to her feet and strode to the door.

"So soon?"

"Of course. Corin grows most anxious. And you will admit he's been all that a suitor should be." At Finola's reluctant nod, she smiled. "You'll see in the days ahead. You'll have much diversion and enjoyment. There will be no end of celebration." She opened the door, then turned back again. "Mayhap we might ask Cardinal d'Ontini to preside at the nuptials. How would you like that?"

Finola became aware the Contessa was waiting for her response. "Fine."

When she was alone in the ornate sitting room that was now hers, she put her head down on the gold-inlaid desk. Finola felt weary, helpless . . . so alone. She hadn't been as disarmed when she'd been in Albai's holding.

Corin! He was Einar's friend, as baffled as she by the disappearance of the Viking and his friends. Every day he searched, and other men were doing the same.

"Milady!"

The whisper was like the echo of a bee in summertime.

Finola raised her head, not sure of what she'd heard. She looked around the spacious room. Then she rose to her feet, frowning. Had it come from the bedroom? Had she dreamed it?

As she passed through the archway, she saw him. "Gar!" To her foggy brain he looked thinner. His color was so pasty. She frowned. It was so hard for her to think. She must help her friends. 'Twas not the Contessa's job, but hers. "Tell me—"

The mute boy put his finger to his lips, jerking his head toward the ajar door that led to the hallway.

Finola moved there at once, shutting it. There were no locks on any of her doors. No doubt the hostess didn't feel that her well-staffed house was unsafe. She returned to the sitting room, closing its door. The staff would think her napping as she was wont to do in the afternoons since coming to the palazzo. Strange. Napping had never been one of her constants when she'd been at the convent. This lethargy was irritating. She seemed not able to overcome it.

She went back to the boy. He was standing near the wall at the end of her bed. She touched his shoulder. "Are you well, Gar?" His curt nod slanted toward the wall. To her surprise, she saw a narrow door there, open a crack. "Is that how you came from the stables?" At his nod she took hold of his shoulders, pulling him to her. She'd been so lonely. She hadn't realized how much until she'd seen him. "And how is Reric? Have you seen Dalia? I've missed you. The Contessa said you were busy with your new lives, but I wished to see you . . . many times." When he seemed to unbend under her hands, his wariness seeming to dissipate, and a smile start, she frowned. "Did you think I didn't want to see you? I have. So much. I've been so alone." She fought back tears, touched to her heart when he grasped both her hands and squeezed. "Where is Reric?"

He pointed to the narrow door.

"How did you find the passage? Did a servant show you?"

He shook his head, scowling.

Finola tried to read his gestures. She bit her lip and shook her head.

"He says that we found it by accident, when we were sleeping in the stables. There are men here who remind us too much of Albai's place, so we've been slipping away and staying at Master Einar's some of the time."

Finola spun around, gladness at seeing her friends lightening her heart. "Reric! So that's why I haven't seen you."

Her brow knitted. "How could you stay there? Have not the Vikings left the city? You'd be alone. No one to feed you."

Reric smiled. "We find food. And we bring some to Dalia."

Finola scowled. "Why would she be hungry? Soon she'll be with me, as my maid. The Contessa thinks it's a good idea."

Reric shook his head. "I don't think so. She plans to come with us this night." He hesitated. "She thinks we shouldn't return."

Finola was frightened. "Don't let her. You could be thought to be Viking, if you're stopped by the watch. If the Vikings are not about to protect you and explain that you are part of their contingent, she could be thought to be a runaway, as you and Gar would be. You could be flogged . . . or worse."

Reric bit his lip. " 'Tis hard for her in the kitchen. She's been mistreated."

She gasped. "Is this true?"

Reric nodded. "They think of her as a thing."

Finola nodded. She knew how intricate the network of workers could be in a household, how each level had its caste system. The more powerful were often cruel and selfish with those on a lower strata.

Reric shrugged. "I'll tell her. But she feels betrayed and lost, milady."

"I will do something about it now." She went toward him. "I have missed you. Now I don't feel so alone. Perhaps we can help each other." She cocked her head. "You said you were staying at Thorhallsson's. Have you seen the other Vikings?"

Reric nodded. "Now and again. Most of the time they're gone . . . in search of Lord Einar. But there's no trace. Though they trade and carry on with bartering, and are not often in the palazzo, they will not leave Rome until they know his whereabouts."

"Good."

"And they ask of you, milady."

Finola slumped. "Tell them I'm to be married."

Reric's mouth dropped. "How can that be? You were to wed Lord Einar."

"The Contessa and Corin feel he's dead, though his friends still search for him. I am to marry Lord Corin."

Reric frowned. " 'Tis passing strange.... He is a good man. Lord Einar thought this."

"Yes. I had not thought to wed him, even so. But my guardians have consented to the match. They've signed a betrothal bond."

Reric was going to say more, when they heard a rustling at the door. He and Gar scurried through the narrow opening, pulling it shut behind them.

An attendant knocked, then entered.

Finola smiled at dour Michaela, the Contessa's woman in waiting. "Ah, you've come, how nice. And have you brought Dalia? I told milady how unhappy I've been without her, and she said I might have her with me."

"I brought clothes, not the girl. Nothing was said to me."

"Oh. The message hasn't reached you? Perhaps you might send someone to fetch the girl. I would be more comfortable." Finola walked to the door, noting a footman. "Pepi, will you fetch Dalia, my maid. The Contessa has been so kind. She knows I can't be happy without my handmaiden."

Michaela moved to her side, staring hard at Pepi.

Finola pretended not to notice. "Of course, I can call the Contessa and ask that she do it personally. She was working in the study this afternoon. You might get her there, Pepi. I'll tell her that you and Michaela didn't want to get Dalia for me." She smiled at first one, then the other. She'd often dealt with recalcitrant help when she ran her father's household after her mother's death. She hadn't liked it. But she'd learned how to manage. Her father's castle had been poorly kept, with the barest necessities. She'd learned how to handle those who would defy her.

"Pepi will get the maid for you though I do not see why you need one," Michaela said, her voice almost a growl.

"Thank you, both. That makes me happy. Now show me the clothes, Michaela."

"You're to wear them this evening at Cardinal d'Ontini's reception."

"How nice," Finola said, smothering the resentment. A staff member would tell her about an evening she was supposed to enjoy. "I'm most grateful to the Contessa for supplying the clothes." And she was, but she would've felt better if she had more say on what she did and on what she'd wear.

Michaela looked less disgruntled.

They put the costly garments away.

Finola wasn't sure about some of the richer hues. They might fade her porcelain coloring.

The door opened behind them as the two women discussed the heavy cloths.

"Milady?"

Finola turned around and saw a much thinner, dirtier Dalia, whose eyes brimmed with resentment. Swallowing, she grimaced. "Come in, girl, and close the door. You'll need a bath." She turned to smile at Michaela. "Thank you. Tell the Contessa I'm well pleased. This creature needs more to do."

A small smile all but cracked Michaela's lips. Petticoats rustling with disdain, she flung herself around and stalked to the door with her nose in the air, her lips frozen in prim malice.

Finola put her finger to her lips when Dalia would've spoken. She listened at the ajar door for a moment, hearing the unmistakable sound of retreating footsteps on the stone and wood floor.

Exhaling, Finola shut the door, pushing a small chest in front of it. She turned to her friend. "I've missed you."

"You needed only to come to the kitchen. I scrubbed the stone floor, the pantries and buttery every day before dawn."

Finola grimaced. "I know the lot of a newcomer to a household can be hard." Her smile wavered. "I hope you know I've tried to get you here. It's such a large household, and the Contessa leaves most of the duties to her major-domo." Finola frowned, rubbing her forehead with two fingers. "I do not seem to have the energy I once had. As for the majordomo . . ." She shrugged. "He doesn't seem

that efficient to me. The Contessa thinks him so capable."
She led Dalia over to the bed. "Tell me how you've been."

"At death's door with the work."

Dalia didn't look clean, but she was far from emaciated.
"Have they hurt you?"

Dalia stretched her hands wide. "Look. Not the hands of
a camel driver's wife look worse."

"They're quite red. I have some emollients." She went to
the huge dresser with its wall-sized mirror, grimacing anew
at the size and breadth of everything in the di Marchi palazzo.
It was the overpowering opulence she found distasteful,
though she couldn't have faulted the generosity of her hostess.
Simplicity was not a di Marchi characteristic. The Contessa
loved her home and was a lavish decorator. "Here. This
will help." When Dalia winced at the first touch of the oily
substance, Finola frowned. "I asked if they hurt you, Dalia."

"I've not been whipped, milady. But I'm worked like a
yak."

"You think I consigned you there?"

Dalia shrugged.

"I didn't. I wanted you with me. It's taken all this time."

"Why?"

"I don't know. I told her that I wanted you with me." She
sighed. "I needed to be more forceful." She shook her head.

Dalia's eyes slid toward her. "Truly?"

"Yes."

Silence.

"Reric and Gar told me where you were. I had asked for
you. The Contessa said she'd informed her majordomo." She
frowned. "It seems he was too busy to take care of it."

"Mayhap all he wants are slaves."

Finola nodded. "I've been in houses like that, and not just
in the east, Dalia."

" 'Tis not much better than Albai's."

Finola patted her arm. "I'll call for hot water. You can
bathe."

"They won't bring it for me, milady."

"I'll tell them I wish to bathe." Finola grinned. "There's

a reception this evening. I shall wish to bathe. I'll have them bring extra water and two tubs, one for washing, one for rinsing ... so I won't smell bad." She laughed.

Dalia wrinkled her nose. "Some in the west do."

"In the west they don't recognize the efficacy of bathing often. My sojourn in the east taught me to like it very well." She'd always washed, much to her mother's dismay. It'd been a delight to visit the east, where daily ablutions were not thought to weaken the back and addle the brain.

" 'Tis passing strange that the Vikings have not the offensive odor," Dalia said.

"They delight in their hot springs ... and bathing in freezing fjords."

"In a way they are wicked ... but they are wondrous, too."

"Yes." Finola looked at the floor. " 'Tis hard for me to speak of them."

Dalia looked puzzled. "Why?"

Finola winced at Dalia's plain speaking. "I'd hoped that I would stay with the Vikings ... that they'd return me home." That wasn't exactly true. It was too painful to bare her soul further.

"You had hoped to speak vows with the Viking."

Finola blanched. "Was there much gossip in the kitchen, Dalia?" Not that she gave a fig.

"Yes. They chattered all the time, but not to me. They called me slut."

Finola's face reddened. "They dare not."

"They did."

"You will remain with me, and never return below stairs." Her face hardened. "I will never understand the caste system in some of these homes. There are those who think they are God."

Dalia nodded. "What gossip would I hear?"

Finola looked away from her. "Einar Thorhallsson is dead."

Dalia didn't move. "So. They talked of a certain misfortune, over and over, and laughed. 'Twas this?"

"Mayhap it was."

"Will we never leave here, milady?"

Finola went to the door, spoke to an attendant and returned. "I won't be staying long here." A sadness overtook her. How could her guardians, Princess Iona and Lord Sinclair, consent to her marriage and not consult with her first?

"How is that, milady?"

"I'm to be married."

"Why did you not say that you didn't wish for marriage?" Dalia shrugged. "We cannot do that. I understand that western women can."

Finola shook her head. "Most can't. Viking women can, some northern peoples in Scotia and Scandia . . ." Her voice trailed off.

"But not you."

"My guardians signed the betrothal book. It's binding."

"Whom will you wed, milady?"

"I'm to marry Lord Corin of Antioch."

The girl sank down on the bed, mouth agape. "They don't even know that in the kitchen."

"And they know all about the missives that come?" Finola smiled.

Dalia nodded.

Her curiosity piqued. "How is it that they know what comes, what it is, and from whom?"

Dalia grinned, a sly cast to her features. "The majordomo reads little. Much must be explained to him. But he peruses all scrolls. They are read to him before he takes them to the Contessa. He won't let anything pass. He's far too curious for that."

Finola would've laughed with her if she hadn't felt so downhearted.

26

If any man hopes to do a deed without God's knowledge, he errs.
Pindar

"And is the deed done?"

"Yes, noble one, 'tis done."

"None know of your connection to this?"

"None."

"Good. 'Twould seem the weight of years is with us. Who could've known 'twould be so sweet, so finely done?"

"I would give credit to you."

"And I to you. Had not the information come to you, we might never have been allies."

"Only in business."

"Yes. Always there."

"We cannot meet again like this."

" 'Tis better we don't."

"I cannot see your face."

"Nor I yours."

"This will take time."

"Yes."

"She's under control."

"Yes. A sweetened drink laced with a poppy drink has kept her amenable."

"None know this is done?"

"Only the trusted one who does this for me."

"Good. Soon 'twill be completed."

Their voices echoed in the vaulted dungeon. Neither liked to meet in the room that pearled with fetid damp. The scurrying of rats was heard so clearly when the only other sound was the drip of water from the ceiling and on the walls.

Hands touched. Smiles flashed for a moment.

"I had not thought it could be this sweet."

Laughter echoed in the dimness, the scratch and scurry of the unseen turning to momentary frenzy.

27

One word frees us of all the weight and pain of life: That word is love.

Sophocles

There was a "light" supper before leaving for the cardinal's reception, consisting of capons in wine sauce, goose dredged in berries then roasted to a crackling essence, and goat meat marinated in sour arak and served with dumplings redolent of rosemary. Bread was served, leavened and unleavened, a honey pot at each place. Quarters of venison were thrown upon wood platters, trenchers of spiced bread awaited meat au jus. Sharpened dirks were thrust into the animal flesh. Root vegetables were shimmery with melted curds. There were fiery potables, as well as the interminable wines of shades and hues to match the finery, from clear as water to umbered burgundy. There were greens, cooked and raw, swimming in an array of vinegars. Olives brined and fresh were served with all.

"Come, come, Finola, you must eat something. Your intended will think we starve you."

Finola tried to smile at her patron who'd chided her. "Thank you for your solicitude, milady Contessa. I have found your breads delicious." She'd broken a large piece into bits, putting it crumb by crumb into her mouth, then washing it down with watered wine. Since she didn't welcome the attention of the guests who stared from her to her plate, she tried to eat. It was a relief when the focus of conversation moved from her to business and trade. Finances, bartering was paramount. It was often thus at the di Marchi palazzo. She had come to respect the Contessa's business acumen. It hadn't taken Finola long to ascertain that the long hours spent in the large sitting room she used as an office were not wasted. She had been able to glean enough from observation and questions to realize the di Marchi holdings were extensive.

Only by accident had she found out that her patron was a member of a consortium. That'd been enough to impress her. Women were just not included in the male-driven and -oriented business clubs that abounded throughout the trading world.

After slicing a bit of honeyed orange, she put it into her mouth.

"What think you of our Contessa, milady?"

The priest who'd posed the query was no stranger to the palazzo. Finola'd seen him many times from her window, though she'd never met him until that evening. Padre Antonio. Extremely reserved . . . which made him seem cold. She was surprised at his question, the first words he'd addressed to her since she'd been seated at his left.

She shrugged, pointing to her mouth, needing the pretense of eating to couch an answer. Though her time in Rome had been short, she'd learned the value of discretion. The gossip vine in Roma was exceedingly efficient and fast. Speak a word wrong, it could come back to you that very day, ruining you or putting you beyond the pale and below the salt. A true embarrassment to one of means and stature.

In many ways she felt so removed from the assemblage. Still, she was aware that the fifty persons the Contessa had invited to sup before the cardinal's soiree were powerful and important. The cardinal's palazzo was in reach of the Vatican, not a great distance from the Contessa's.

Finola dabbed at her lips with a square of finely woven

linen. ''Contessa di Marchi is a most accomplished and admirable person.'' She smiled at the priest, wishing she were back in her room, or better, back in Iona. As much as she'd desired to be in Rome, she now wanted to leave it. There was such an emptiness in her life without Einar. Mayhap she could beg her guardians to reconsider her marriage. If only she could return to Scotia . . . or even Iona. Why not make the decision and go? Had she not done so at Albai's? Why had her determination evaporated?

Lord Corin was a good man. He was worthy of respect and admiration. In his company she felt content. She didn't want to wed him, or anyone else. If only the betrothal papyrus hadn't been signed. When she'd seen her cousin's name, she'd been very disheartened. If the Contessa hadn't pushed her she wouldn't have signed her name below it. The Contessa had reminded her of the laws governing betrothal. Guardians had the right, nay, the duty, to choose a husband. Finola knew that. She'd thanked her patron for her good offices and tried to be courteous. Her heart wasn't in the festivities. She missed Einar Thorhallsson with a terrible ache. He'd not faded from her mind. Nay, his visage had grown clearer behind her eyes.

Yet, the contingent of private soldiers working for the Contessa who'd been sent to search for Thorhallsson had found little. They'd brought back his clothes they'd found in a dingy *vicolo*, torn and encrusted with blood. No doubt the body had been dumped in the Tiber. That was the conclusion. Footpads! Even now the thought made her stomach rise.

''Milady MacDonnell?''

Startled from her reverie, Finola eyed the clergyman, turning her mind to what had been said. ''Ah, yes, I would say the Contessa sets one of the best tables in Rome. Many agree.''

Padre Antonio inclined his head. ''I, too, have heard it said. Soon you'll be running your own household, milady. Will you rely on the Contessa for tutelage?''

''One would be foolish not to ask her advice.''

Again she sensed rather than saw his withdrawal, as though what she'd said disappointed him. She sighed. No doubt Padre Antonio would have preferred her to be more open with him.

Mayhap he was used to more sophisticated conversing. She couldn't manage it. Nothing took her mind from Einar Thorhallsson for long. Reason told her she was a fool. She couldn't help it.

Better to be silent. Words cast out in careless fashion could be turned around, twisted. Rome was a sea of chicanery. The people were like vultures waiting to tear and shred any who were not discreet. It was most tiresome. It also behooved her to keep a civil tongue. Though Gar, Reric and Dalia were under the protection of the Contessa, and she hoped that they were well, she worried. She hadn't seen her young friends since the day Gar and Reric had come through the passageway. She feared to inquire lest she cause them more discomfort. Was she being a coward? She wished she could talk to them. And if only the Contessa weren't so set against the Vikings. She'd been allowed to send missives. There'd been no reply to any of them. Perhaps if she could talk to Reric . . . if he could talk to the Vikings . . .

"Finola? Did you not hear?"

Finola blinked, trying to smile at the titters that went around the table. "Forgive me. Padre Antonio and I were having such an interesting conversation, I didn't hear."

She felt the clergyman's glance, but he didn't gainsay her.

"Duc de Seigne, a most illustrious collector," Contessa di Marchi indicated the man at her left, "has seen some of your work. He considers it admirable."

"Thank you," Finola bowed her head to the white-haired man who had the place of honor at the table. "I'm honored, sir."

"I would like to take some of your work to Paris, milady. Of course, there would be recompense."

Finola barely heard the subdued mutters accompanying the announcement. She was thunderstruck. "I can't credit it, good sir. You have great stature as a collector." She swallowed. "That you would want to take my work to Paris . . ." She shook her head. "I don't have much. I have been working since coming to the di Marchi palazzo. Some is unfinished . . ." Her voice cracked. "Much of my other work was destroyed in a fire—"

"I knew of this," the Duc said, nodding. "Perhaps you would show me what you have." He smiled at the Contessa. "Of course, Lisetta has shown me some of your pieces." His bemused gaze moved back to Finola. "But I understand you have bits of sculpture which you show to no one."

The silence at the table boomed over Finola. She felt every gimlet stare. "Some that I have are very personal. I would not show them, unless I must."

The Duc de Seigne bowed in his chair. "I would not press you, mademoiselle."

"Thank you." Finola lowered her eyes, lifting her glass and sipping her wine.

"You have becoming modesty, milady."

"Thank you, Padre Antonio." No doubt he thought her a fool for holding back any of her work from de Seigne. His beneficence could mean fabulous success in the art world.

The Contessa smiled.

Duc de Seigne eyed the protégé. "I would urge you to display your work at the Circus Maximus, milady. 'Tis our greatest show."

The murmurs grew loud, filled with incredulity. A neophyte at the largest art show in the world!

At the other end of the table, a thoughtful glance stayed on Finola.

"Your bride is most enchanting, Lord Corin, and highly talented, else the great Duc de Seigne would not have suggested the Circus Maximus. I wish you happiness." When Lord Corin turned, the prelate smiled. "I'm Monseigneur Campbell from Scotia, though I live in Rome."

"Ah, then you know my fiancée."

The clergyman shook his head. "I've not been back to Scotia for many years. My assignment has been Rome. But I know the isle of Iona whence she sprung. A wild and cold place. Her mother's ancestors, the Skenes, had a place on the isle."

"Thank you for your good wishes, Monseigneur. I look forward to our nuptials." Corin watched Finola, his brow furrowed.

"Something troubles you?"

"Yes. My betrothed and I lost a good friend not long ago. It has clouded the joy of our coming nuptials." He shook his head. "In some ways I wish Contessa di Marchi would not hurry our vows, yet I think my betrothed needs my support as a husband."

"True." The priest shook his head. " 'Tis passing sad that you have lost a loved one." He frowned. "Wait. You mean Einar Thorhallsson, Thegn of Icelandia?"

"None other."

"I knew him and the princess he served so well. I met them at Malcolm's court." The priest shook his head. " 'Twas such a tragedy. Have they never found his body?"

"No. But there were some who saw him set upon and stabbed."

"A good Viking."

Corin smiled. "He was well known."

The priest eyed Finola. "I thought the bride-to-be somewhat subdued." The priest shook his head. "I, too, mourn such a man. He was a good trader and good to his people, so I'm told."

Corin bit his lip. "You will forgive me, Father. I am Lord Corin, but in the hubbub of meeting, I didn't give you my name, Monseigneur."

They touched hands.

When the guest on the other side of the priest spoke to him, he turned away, excusing himself.

Corin looked around and found himself the object of scrutiny by his other dinner partner. "Do I know you, good sir?"

"I'm Latius, the gem merchant. I would compliment you on the betrothal ring you have bestowed on Milady MacDonnell. I've not seen its equal."

Corin's lips lifted in a smile. "Nor I." He turned so that his eyes were more fully on Finola. " 'Twas a gift to me from a benefactor who raised me. 'Tis said it belonged to my father.

My father was deceased before I have good memory of him, so I treasure the bauble."

"Ah, I understand. I would tell you, though it goes against the grain, that this is no bauble. The stone, I would hazard, comes from Cathay and is of the purest." He coughed. " 'Tis said that divers find them in the warm waters that touch on that faraway land."

"True."

"And the jade that surrounds the wonderful pearl is hand wrought by a master."

"You peered closely, I'll be bound."

" 'Tis my business."

Corin arched his head. "No doubt you make some of the magnificent jewelry that graces our hostess."

Latius grinned. "No doubt."

"Then, as I know not other lapidaries in the area, I might call on you for a trinket for my betrothed."

Latius bowed. " 'Twould be an honor."

"Nothing inferior."

"Alas, no. 'Twould not do my repute any gain were I to deal in inferior goods. I don't. They cost."

"We understand each other."

"I was sure we would." Latius's wide grin displayed a golden tooth.

Corin would've said more, but the Contessa rose to her feet, signaling the end of the meal.

"Time to go," the man called Latius rose. "Well met, Corin of Antioch."

"Well met," Corin returned the salute.

He moved around to Finola's side, where she was conversing with two men. When there was a pause, he touched her arm. "Are you ready?"

At her nod they walked out to the wide foyer.

He managed to separate her cloak from the others with ease, sliding it around her shoulders and clasping it at her throat. "You look very regal in the maroon velvet, Milady Finola."

"Thank you." She thought it too rich, too opulent for her taste, but since it was a gift from the Contessa she wore it.

"You would prefer not to go this evening."

"I'm sure the cardinal's soirees are most entertaining." Finola bit her lip when he laughed. Her lips quivered.

"You've become a discreet Roman."

" 'Twas necessary, Corin."

"You might be bored this evening. Much will be about bartering and business."

At his flat statement she looked up at him. "I feel I spoil your enjoyment."

Corin shook his head. "I feel the loss of Einar Thorhallsson as well."

Finola laid her hand on his arm, feeling comforted. They went out the wide double doors, held by footmen. She sighed.

"I think of him," he said.

Finola nodded. "I know you shared dangerous moments with him."

Corin smiled. "Many."

"And that your friendship was fired through these hardships."

"True."

"Perhaps you would tell me about them as we ride."

He climbed in beside her, tapping the roof of the open-sided conveyance, shrouded with curtains. His long-handled cane was an affectation, copied from the Bulgar and Viking cudgels used for hand-to-hand combat. Some of the sticks hid swords as fashioned in the east. Most were just adjuncts of fashion, used by both men and women. "You had an interesting contretemps with the Duc de Seigne. I'm most proud of your work."

Eyes alight, she looked at him. "How awesome, is it not, that he should express an interest in my work."

"Not at all. You are a true artist and artisan, milady."

"Thank you." Her smile faded.

"I know you feel the loss of your work in Antioch."

"True. At this moment I think of my friends, too, who died there."

"A tragedy. Perhaps when you display your works at the Circus Maximus you will salve your pain."

Finola tried to smile. "If I'm chosen for the finals."

"You will be."

28

We live, not as we wish to, but as we can.
Menander

It'd been three months since he'd escaped the dungeon. He remembered little of it. He'd lost a good deal of blood and had sickened with fever shortly after the escape.

Einar knew he looked like a shadow of his former self, but he would wait no longer to seek out his Vikings and assure them of his returning health. He was more than sure that many of them waited for him. Even if the one ship had gone on to Icelandia, it would make the return trip as soon as booty and stores were unloaded, shares were given and stories were told.

"You're a fool to venture forth, Viking."

"And I tell you I must, Bulgar. They will be searching for me—"

"Let them. 'Tis better we're thought dead."

Einar shook his head. "I can't do that to my men. They'll take our goods to Reykjanes, then they'll return. They'll trade, then they'll return. 'Tis the way with us. They won't give up until they find me or my remains."

"I am Tariq the Bulgar, leader of a powerful family, catered to by my friends and slaves." He shook his head. "But none would be foolish enough to continue to search for me when

I'm gone. That's up to the Fates. At times a man must die, or save himself.''

Einar nodded. ''We believe such. And we have saved ourselves. No matter, we cannot gainsay loyalty. 'Tis our greatest asset.'' His mouth twisted. ''Some would say it's also our foremost liability. We are what we are.''

''True.'' There was no mirth in Tariq's laugh. ''If truth were told, I'd say I envy you such comrades . . . but I'm not unhappy with my lot.''

''Mayhap you're a Viking at heart.''

''Mayhap you've insulted me,'' Tariq said, honey-vinegar on his tongue.

''Nay. I've lifted your station.''

Sour mirth bubbled from the Bulgar. ''You test my patience, Viking.''

Einar laughed. ''I will go. You must not join me.'' At the other's frown, he chuckled. ''Your size, Bulgar. They might pass me by, but two of us, almost of equal girth and height, could cause comment. I'll take Bela. He's a good man.''

The Bulgar nodded.

Einar strapped on a sword of poor quality, as were all the weapons taken from the dungeon. 'Twas better than nothing. He nodded at Bela and made his way out of the catacombs. Their hiding place was not much more than a cave of thieves, with a hidden opening on the side of the Palatine that they used.

Einar blinked at the sunshine as he always did when emerging from their underground home. They lived in the catacombs, where the Christians lived hundreds of years past. Now they were haven for many types of abandoned souls. Einar and his fellow escapees had found sanctuary, where none questioned why they were there, or who they were. That the haven could be riddled with traitors and those seeking to make a drachma on the pain of others didn't escape them. They'd been too long in the arms of danger to be unwary. Someone in their small group was always on watch.

''This way, Viking.'' Bela grinned, his blackened teeth given a dull sheen by the sun.

Viking! It'd become his name. And he'd honed a profession of stealing into a fine art since living underground. With it, he'd survived while his body healed itself. It'd taken too long, but they hadn't dared using an apothecary. So, with the help of the Bulgar, he'd medicated himself. He'd described the herbs he needed, and gotten most of them. More than once he'd blessed the boiling brine that'd cleansed his wounds, though that'd been in spite of his jailers' intent.

They'd managed to steal a fair amount of good food. Bela was a chef of sorts, so they'd managed. Even when he was reeling with fatigue and the effects of his wounds, he'd done his share of food gathering. Einar understood the code that a man's friends look out for him but a man survives on his own.

He stretched his arms and inhaled. Here the air was fresh, not as fetid as some of the Roman streets or the catacombs. Where were his Vikings . . . Finola? His heart cried out for her. Bela and Tariq had told him he'd called out to her in his fever. If only it hadn't taken so long to regain his strength . . . He couldn't return to her unless he was at full potential. He had to be able to face his enemies and care for her. Then they'd say their vows.

He'd damn well discover who it was who'd arranged his disappearance. Instinct, the same instinct that'd kept him alive in many a battle, told him that one or more had contrived to have him killed. He'd find them. As a Viking he'd always had enemies. He could accept that. Living with them at his back was something else. He couldn't allow it. He needed to find them, face them, eradicate them. And he would. Then he would find Finola and they'd wed.

Had she waited for him?

"Hurry, Viking. 'Tis wise for us to be gone from here. This is our main entrance. 'Twouldn't do to draw curious eyes to this spot."

Einar nodded, following the bandy-legged creature who'd clung to Tariq and him since his release. There was a certain alien integrity about Bela. They trusted him.

Their entrance into the city was not like the rattling carriages and drays that trundled in and out in constant cavalcade. They circled, dodged, eased around vendors, darted into doorways of shops, to exit past the tolerant owners and out their back ways.

"They're paid well," Bela told him for the hundredth time when Einar studied the shop owners.

"It pays to watch the man who sells his integrity. Any can put a price on it."

Bela shrugged. "The life of such would be taken, ere he could spend his spoils. Too many use this area. The people are well paid. They'd be fools to betray us."

Einar's mouth twisted. "Wariness is part of me. Even then, I was betrayed." His lips hardened. "It won't happen again."

"I'll watch your back."

Einar grinned at him. "Let's go."

The journey by foot, into the hub of Rome, wasn't far, but the many detours, the many hiding places they used took time. Making sure all was clear was paramount to survival.

Block by block they went deeper into the city.

Bela led him down a corkscrew street. "Yonder is the palazzo di Marchi. The lord is gone, but the lady is forging ahead as a trader. 'Tis been whispered she has ships that steal others' bounty."

Einar grinned. He'd heard that same tale about most of the wealthy in Roma. . . . "What did you say the name was?" He stiffened, his eyes going over the high walls that stretched around a block, shielding the inhabitants from prying eyes.

"The palazzo di Marchi."

It washed over him like the giant waves that sometimes built in the North Sea. Finola's patron. Was she there? Would she still remember him? Foolish question. She would. Mayhap she had changed her feelings. . . .

"Hurry, let us go."

"I have a wish to see this palazzo."

Bela shook his head. "This is not for us to rob. Too big. Too many guards."

Einar shrugged. "We'll walk around it."

Bela frowned. "We go to find your men."

"Yes." Einar inhaled. "But first, I wish to see this place."

The two men eyed the wall like the experts they were. They'd scaled bigger.

Einar wasn't as strong as he should be, but he had no fears that he couldn't do it.

Bela sighed, eyeing the strong-willed Viking. "Great respect for you doesn't blind me, Viking. Your reach can outdistance your grasp this time. Such tenacity saved your life when you'd lost much blood. Now it blunts good sense. We should be on our way."

"So we should. Still, I would see this palazzo."

"We could be killed. I'd like it not."

"Nor would I."

The two men looked again on the wall.

"I've scaled bigger, Viking."

"As have I." Not as strong as he once was, Einar didn't doubt he could do it. He moved around the wall until he saw it. A tree grew inside the barricade with a strong branch that leafed over the wall. Gazing around him, listening at the wall itself, he finally stepped back, then flung himself toward it at good speed. He ran up the sides, his elkskin boots sliding and kicking out, his arms grasping high.

"You'll miss. Not strong enough," Bela muttered. "The Fates know you're stones lighter than before imprisonment. Tariq told me." His teeth cracked together when the Viking tried for the third time.

He had the branch! Exhaling, he smiled down at his partner.

Bela nodded and imitated the maneuver, his body springing upward, his toes digging into the cracks left by the mortar. He pushed up and to the top, using the protruding spikes as handholds, then straddling the width. "Whither?" he whispered, his lips barely moving.

Einar scanned the garden, waiting, his eyes never ceasing the search of the classic formal area with the stone paths, the Greek statuary, the many fountains with benches dotted hither and yon. It was a place of peace, serenity . . . riches.

He dropped down into the soft soil, freezing in place for several seconds. He looked up at Bela, his voice lighter than the breeze. "Stay up there. You know the whistle. If you hear it, leave on the run."

Bela nodded.

Einar moved in slow, careful reconnaissance.

He heard voices, and moved into the shadows.

"Milady, you should be glad that tonight you go to the bal masque. The maids chatter of it all the time. 'Tis most eventful."

"I know, Dalia, but I'd rather not go. I didn't enjoy the cardinal's reception, nor all the soirees that preceded it. The palazzos are hot or freezing, and the crush of guests makes me queasy."

"Enjoy yourself, milady. 'Tis not a sin, even to your god."

Finola's answering chuckle was weak. More and more, she was in Dalia's company. "I enjoy your wit, Dalia. Sharper than the Damascene steel of the east, it is. But I adjure you to use it only with me. Such talk as yours can be looked upon as blasphemy in some quarters. There are groups in Rome who would see you drawn and quartered for it."

"Your Christian god was such a man of peace, you say. How is it that his followers are not happy unless they are killing, maiming, or destroying . . . in the name of this peace-maker? A profound puzzlement."

"To me, as well," Finola muttered, fanning herself in the unaccustomed heat of early spring. It should have been cold. Instead there was a balminess that allowed the fetid smells of the city free rein.

Sweat beaded Einar's brow. His hand shook as he pressed it against a gnarled grapevine. Finola! She was there! In front of him. He was about to step out and identify himself, when he saw another following Finola and the serving girl. What the hell!

It didn't look like an Italo, though he was swarthy and built like the kegs used to store the wines. Einar studied the stalker, fingering the dirk at his belt. It wouldn't take much to skewer the fellow if he became threatening.

Then the women turned on the stone path, retracing their steps.

Einar braced himself, cursing.

"Aiello, whence you came? Is something amiss? Does the Contessa want me?"

The attendant bowed. "No, milady. She wishes me to follow you wherever you go . . . so that you come to no harm."

Finola nodded, her smile strained. "'Tis my lot to know no privacy, in the name of protection."

"Tell him to leave," Dalia said through her teeth. She glared. Aiello glowered back.

When the man faded away, Dalia lifted her shoulder, putting her finger to her mouth. "'Tis like a pleasant prison." Her whisper was but a drift on the breeze.

Finola chuckled, her shoulders slumping a bit. "Come along, we will stay closer to the palazzo. I wouldn't want our walks curtailed in the name of safety." She sighed. "I wonder if Gar or Reric will come to see us this day." She frowned. "I thought they would, so many times. I've not seen them since they came to me and told me about you—"

Einar looked down at his trembling hands. Why he'd been compelled to remain silent, he wasn't sure. He was certain of peril. His skin and teeth shook with it. What would endanger Finola that even her guardian felt she should have escort? Damn! He could smell the jeopardy that surrounded her. Protecting her was more important than confronting her. Perhaps if she didn't know of his existence, keeping her safe could be done more easily. He thought of his Vikings. Before another scoop of sand dropped through the glass, before the water clock could drip away, they would be on guard for her.

He swung his body upward, hooking onto a limb.

At the same moment, an alien yet familiar intonation intruded.

Dropping to the ground again, he skimmed along the shaded stony path. An unreasonable anger built like a Volga flood in his system, percolating behind the barrier of skin and flesh, aching to bust through. All the hated moments and memories curdled his mind.

He'd been set upon and thrown unjustly into a dungeon. He didn't know who'd done it, or why. What crime was his? Who was so eager for his death, disappearance?

He stopped, forcing his brain into focus, refusing to allow the weakening vagaries of anger, disappointment and need to cloud his judgment. He was in enemy territory in Rome. He'd been imprisoned and tortured once. He could be again.

There was the sound again that'd sent his thoughts on a bitter caravan.

Wariness slowed his steps.

It came once more. He'd take care, but he would see what was amiss. His skin crawled with what could be. The sound had a familiar knell.

29

Those who know how to win are much more numerous than those who know how to make proper use of their victories.
Polybius

Inching around the bole of a gnarled olive, hidden by the greenery, Einar viewed the gore and the titillation of the onlookers.

"My turn! Let me at the rebel." A begrimed creature in a stained apron approached the lasher, trying to wrest the instrument from his grasp.

"My job, 'tis. Marco has spoken."

Einar's eyes narrowed on the one held prisoner by two of the spectators. Reric! Fixing on the sagging boy strung with hemp to the post, he spotted the hair. Yellow! Many a Circassian had lost his life on the galleys because his looks angered the darker-visaged easterners. Any and all excuses to use the lash and torture.

Wracking his brain, he sought a solution. He had no fear he could kill the seven attendants who dallied with the boy's life, but he wouldn't be quick enough with all of them to prevent an alarum.

"What do you plan?"

Einar would've jumped through his skin had he not begun

to get used to Bela's method of moving without sound. "Were you not to stay on the wall?"

"I was. I'm here. You undid my manacles in the dungeon, Viking." He eyed the panoply of men arguing over the whip to be used on the boy. "We kill the children or the men?"

"Men. Most quietly."

Bela nodded. "How?"

"You'll take the two. Bring the lad unharmed—"

"Why should you get so many?"

Bela's sour question almost had him smiling. He was too churned up with what he'd seen and heard to respond. "The four will be right in front of me. They'll die quickly."

"All right," Bela sighed. "I feel cheated, more's the same."

Einar jerked his head, not hearing the other move away, but sure that he did. He angled up to the quartet who were not quite ringed in front of the lashing post. He drew his dirk, flexing his fingers.

For long seconds he waited until he caught the hint of movement behind the duo. They all but strangled the struggling Gar, who fought to get to his brother.

His one hand exited the foliage. Catching the end of the lash that trailed on the ground, he snaked it up and looped it into a sailor's knot. Leaning out, he snagged over the two closest heads, yanking hard and hearing their bones crack. Ere either of the remaining two could factor the action, he cut one throat, then the other.

Gurgles were cut off as he threw the whip over the limb above him and pulled, making sure they were dead. He looked over at Bela, who had the lad Gar under his arm.

Einar removed his shirt, placing it over Reric. "I'm taking you from here. Can you hear me? It's Thorhallsson."

The nod was a mere wisp of the head.

Einar cursed. Reric mightn't live even if they managed to escape.

Bela released Gar, who ran to his brother. Bela dragged his two victims toward the stable. Einar followed with two of his.

Bela moved around the stable to the pit where offal and

refuse were deposited. "Caustic. Many of the houses use it now. The good alchemists of Rome have found it in the earth. It eats the bones of man." He tossed in one man, watched him sink, then the other.

"I'll get the others." Einar had the stomach for killing, and he was glad to dispose of the enemy. Yet, he found the ready use of the caustic alien to him. It was becoming common in the battles against sludge and sewage that threatened to overcome more than one metropolis.

When the last of the lashers was disposed of and straw was swept over the blood and around the post, Einar picked up Reric, holding him close. He smiled encouragement at Gar. Perhaps if there'd been an Icelandic healer . . . He felt no real hope for the limp body he held.

"I know where to take him," Bela said, slinging Gar up on his shoulder. "Though we couldn't use him for you . . . 'twould've taken too many to cart you and brought inquiring eyes, for the boy, 'twill do."

Einar followed with his burden, getting him over the wall and along the narrow *strada* at the back of the palazzo with as much care as he could muster.

In and out of the bending, winding *strada*, through *vicolo* so narrow that two men couldn't walk side by side, they wended their way. The two moved fast, but cautiously. Overhead was the danger of refuse being tossed upon one. Their only measure of safety was that few of the rabble took note of them.

They traveled many winding lanes until they came to an area of lopsided buildings.

Bela hurried to a gate and rang a low bell. They were let into a long tunnel, leading into the bowels of the building. It smelled of leeks, and the ever-present garlic. The white floweret was worn around the necks of many of the Italo to ward off ill humors.

There was a network of shops inside the building. It was in reality a shell, a wall that kept out onlookers and allowed only one person at a time to enter the enclave.

Einar studied his surroundings. He'd never known of its existence.

"From the east." Bela pointed to the shops. "The Italo hate them, as the Roman aristo hate the Italo, who don't think of easterners as people with souls. There are masters here of art, sculpting, medicaments . . ." As he talked Bela pointed at each overhead shop.

"I think we need to hurry." Einar looked down at his burden. Maybe they were too late.

Bela moved into a shrouded area, pushing back the hangings that had intricate workmanship in jewel tones, rich in texture, each seeming to tell a story. "His wife and children make the carpets. Iben heals."

The man who moved toward them, cloaked in a swirling cape, topped with a conical hat, looked skeletal. A limp mustache and beard drooped over his face, his swarthy skin shiny and pockmarked. He eyed Bela, Einar, then pointed to a long bench.

Einar put Reric down on his front, fearing to cause him pain.

The man sighed, throwing back his cape and pushing up his sleeve. He spoke over his shoulder. Two women and a boy brought a long tub and began filling it with water from a tub over the fire, the steam rising in the already close atmosphere.

Einar frowned, remembering the agony of being put in a heated vat. "You'll kill him in that. NO."

Iben studied him. "His skin must be cleansed and soothed. These are eastern salts used for such. His body must be purified. And it must begin now before putrefaction." He shrugged bony shoulders. "Once it does . . ."

Einar nodded. "No irons to close?"

"That could kill him. He's not strong enough to withstand more pain."

When the tub was full, Iben poured white powder from a bag at his waist. It hissed and bubbled.

Einar would've moved. Bela restrained him, shushing Gar, who struggled to get to his brother. "Wait."

Reric roused from his stupor when he was immersed, his mouth open to cry out. All that emerged was a croak. His eyes opened wide, glazed with shock, the intermittent agony that possessed him going through the skin and flesh, past the bone to his very marrow.

"Saving him will be a challenge."

"Meet it," Einar said through his teeth.

Iben studied him. "He's not yours, but your forces are joined with his."

Einar didn't answer. Used to the mysticism of the east, the powers that they could call upon, he didn't bother to question how the healer had come by his knowledge. Some said it came through the air to the easterners. They were more often right than wrong. "He has my interest . . . and he is under my care and name."

He sounded the international covenant of adoption, making even the stoical Iben blink.

One of the women kept her hand in the water. When it would cool, more hot water was added. Reric was up to his neck in hissing, bubbling steam, the skin on his face white as parchment, his breathing shallow.

Another woman propped his head, keeping the water from his mouth.

"He will be here many days." Iben looked at them. "You must know that he will be given every care. Despite my expert ministrations, others have died. This one could, as well."

"I know that."

"The pay?"

Einar was caught off guard. He'd always carried his gold. He shook his head. "I will see my people when I leave here. They will give me florins and pieces of gold."

Iben fixed him with a fiery stare. "I trust few of your coloring, Viking. I have suffered for trusting your ilk."

Einar stared back. "And I've had my troubles with your people."

Iben nodded, his glance sliding to Bela, who nodded.

Einar understood the look. Many of the "underworld" of the time relied on each other for good faith, balance in bartering and bargaining. Too many times the consortia short-changed the hoi polloi, stole their goods and didn't pay. The threat of reprisal kept most quiet. Over time, the commoners banded together in their own bartering groups, those on their own levels who would be less likely to cheat them. It worked, and to the chagrin of the consortia, it'd paid off. Men that were once destitute, or just scraping by, began to have shops, places of business. Ships that plied the bartering areas and collected goods from their own kind had grown into fleets. It was most galling to the aristocratic consortia that more and more of the merchandise had superior quality. Some consortia had approached asking for bartering agreements. It hadn't happened. No outright refusals. Evasions, dissembling, the "underworld" used the same techniques that had been used on them. Perhaps they were even more subtle, not wishing to call down the wrath of the consortia, and the Church who backed them, upon their heads.

"Well?"

Iben put his arms and shoulders through an undulating motion that seemed to pull bone loose from flesh, yet made the elder man relax. Trancelike, he stared at Einar for long moments. Could that gaze cut through flesh and bone? His nod was reluctant ... slow ... not quite begrudging. "We have a pact, Viking."

Einar went down on his knees in front of Gar. "You'll stay with your brother. I'll be back as soon as I can." When Gar touched his face, Einar was still. It was as though he looked into a deep well of pain. The boy couldn't speak, but a wealth of words was in his eyes. "I give you my covenant, I'll return."

Gar inhaled, a tremor running up his cheek. He bent his head.

"Nothing will keep me away, except death, on my honor as Thegn of Icelandia," Einar murmured. When the boy's head came up, he smiled. Gar almost did the same.

Einar rose, staring at Iben for long moments. "These two are mine."

"I understand you, *faranghi*."

"And I you."

Einar left with Bela. In the octagonal-shaped enclave, he paused. "You trust the easterner?"

"I do. In his world ... and mine, he's a pandit. He and his family were enslaved by the Goths for many years. He bought his freedom by tending the leader's son. Iben's father was a great sadhu. Iben was a maharishi and renowned healer. Visions have told him he must serve our people in Rome. He does."

Einar nodded. "Do you know the way to the house?"

Bela smiled. "I was shown it when you were ailing. Tariq had figured which it was from what you'd muttered in your delirium." Bela shrugged. "More than once he pondered breaking into your home. It could've been profitable."

"My men would've sliced all of you thrice."

"He factored that, too." Bela's grin revealed his missing tooth, the blackened others.

Einar smiled when Bela laughed. The Greek was a thief, but he had more honor than many titled men he'd known. "Let's go."

"It's a good distance. And we needs be wary."

"You think they've noticed the loss of the attendants?" Disbelief colored Einar's voice. "Most of the houses know little about their workers."

"Many of the household wouldn't grieve for the loss, but most keep accurate count of their slaves ... for that's what they are." He jerked his head back toward Iben's.

Einar heard the bitterness and understood it. It was taken for granted that slavery was acceptable, though it was called by different names. They were to provide households with the care needed in the cheapest way. The person behind the job could've been faceless. He'd always hired freemen because he valued loyalty, which was more apt to show itself among the free workers. He hadn't mistreated those who were enslaved, nor had he shipped any to ports of barter. However, he'd taken little note of their agony before he'd been put on the galleys. The overt desolation of being in the control of another hadn't penetrated until he'd been in the same place with Corin.

After he'd been returned to Icelandia, and taken command of his own ships once more, he'd stayed as far from the slave block as possible. If he was given a slave in barter, he freed him or her and gave each a scroll and chair that pronounced it was so. A slave that carried his own chair would not be again enslaved.

He shook himself out of his reverie. "Whither?"

Bela pointed.

Einar had always loved the outdoors, exercise, running. At the moment, he didn't care for any of it, and didn't relish the hot trot across the city in steaming heat. His almost healed body was still enervated by the effects of wounds and incarceration. Not long into it, he was winded and pushing himself.

Bela eyed him more than once, then began to scan the street.

Einar cursed, the words rolling out with every harsh breath.

Bela took his arm. "Do what I do. 'Twill solve things."

When Bela jumped on the back of a cart, burrowing into the soft goods, Einar ran behind, catching up, and doing the same as his companion had. He waited for the angry outcry of the owner.

"He won't notice," Bela whispered. "These carts are unwieldy and out of balance. They shake and twist all the time."

Long, circuitous twists and turns took them through the heart of the city back toward the area where the palazzo di Marchi was located.

They saw the hubbub when they passed along a nearby block.

"They look for something," Bela said from the side of his mouth, letting some of the goods fall onto his lap.

"Right."

"We should help them."

Amusement curled Einar's mouth. "Another time." Bela had been right. The household had noticed the missing slaves.

"As you say."

They passed the area, men rushing hither and yon, frazzled, shouting, cursing.

They rounded another corner without pausing. The din faded.

"We go." Bela jumped off, taking them down another very twisting, dark *vicolo* that was rank with sewage and deep with debris.

At a corner, he paused, not stepping into the light. "There. Up that hill."

Einar froze, not believing his eyes. He'd never used the route they'd just taken. His place! He'd thought it must've aged or fallen down or crumbled. It'd been an eternity since he'd seen it. So much had happened. He'd died to an old life, taken on a new one, fought back from death itself.

Bela fumbled under his coarse cloak, bringing out the curved short sword, an abbreviated cuirass, from his belt. Not of good quality, it'd been taken from their jailers. "We go in . . . killing . . . or quiet?"

Einar laughed, knowing that Bela was aware he didn't impugn his bravery or code of honor. "They would fight to the last man. Let's approach them with an olive branch."

Neither man ventured into the wide, clean thoroughfare until there was a semblance of cover.

A vendor's unwieldy cart, smelling of breads, wheeled past, no doubt going to the rich houses on the hill. Someone would be having a soiree, perhaps more than one house. That would demand extra rations of the succulent breads touted in Rome. It'd become a tradition to serve these special breads when entertaining. Few households bothered to fashion the great amount needed for their hungry guests. Though public baking ovens had not been unknown in ancient Rome, the fornos that'd sprung up in the modern city dotted many blocks. In them were the bread makers, pastry fashioners, incredible sugared sculptures done by master bakers.

To excite the taste buds of even the fussiest dilettante was the aroma of yeasty delights, almost overcoming the pervasive stench of garbage and refuse that rotted in the streets.

Using the cart as cover, Einar and Bela made it around the corner to the narrow *vicolo* that ran along the back of many of the high-roofed houses. Each domicile had a high fence on either side of the stables to prevent entry of the lesser classes. Deliveries were made to an iron door in the high wall, the large bell rung to let insiders know of a new arrival. Einar didn't bother with the door or bell. His incarceration had made him cautious and suspicious.

Scaling the fence was easy. Though he'd been weakened by his wounds, more and more of his muscle tone was returning. Each day he was stronger, more determined to find his enemies . . . and Finola. Balancing on the top where sharpened bits of steel were mortared into the surface to prevent such an assault, Einar glanced about him. Where were his men? Had they been taken or killed?

"You'll come down easy, or I'll skewer you on the spot," a Viking voice said in rough Italo. "There's an arrow aimed at you and a sword to finish the job."

"Bren?"

Silence.

"Bren, 'tis your captain who speaks with you."

"Show yourself," the man called out, his voice rusty and unsure.

Einar dropped to the ground, Bela at his side.

Bren stared, his mouth open, blinking. "Milord Einar?"

Einar nodded.

A Viking bellow tore from Bren's throat.

"Sweet prophet of doom," Bela muttered. "I jumped outta me shirt. It fair makes my skin crawl to hear such a sound."

Einar laughed, gulping a huge breath, for the first time feeling free. "For me 'tis a cry of joy. My men," he muttered, his chest bursting with pride.

From every corner, well-armed Vikings spilled from the trees and shrubs, their eyes riveting on their leader.

Many, like Bren, dropped to their knees. So unaccustomed was this behavior, Einar could only stand there, his hands limp at his side. Words were lost in his throat.

Darg appeared, his sword down, his face white. "Milord. You're here," he whispered.

"I am."

Darg gestured. Armed men aimed their heavy swords at Bela.

Darg banged his closed fist across his chest. "Milord . . ." He coughed, a muscle jumping at the corner of his mouth. "Milord Einar, we've searched for you."

The simple declaration told Einar more than any litany of explanations how hard they'd tried to find him. "I know that, my friend—"

"Your cargo is safe in Reykjanes, milord. All is divided as you would want, and in stores. The Cup of Antioch is safe with us. We stayed here." He indicated the men. "There's a complement out searching now."

Einar made the veriest hand gesture. The kneeling men snapped to their feet. He thumbed at Bela. "This is my friend and companion. He helped free me from the dungeons—"

"Whose?"

The swords pointed at Bela dropped.

"I know not, Darg, else I would burn the swine at the stake," Einar said through his teeth.

A servant rushed into the enclosed courtyard, bearing a bronze tray and goblets.

Darg gestured to a wooden table surrounded by the backless seats much favored by the Italos. "All is well here." He hesitated. "There've been changes . . ."

"And I shall hear them."

Darg flinched. "Forgive me, Lord Einar. I keep you standing. And you've been sorely wounded."

Einar laughed, his tone filled with menace. "I'm stones heavier than I was."

Faces darkened. Fury limned the features of the Norsemen.

Darg ground his teeth. "They'll journey past the Poison Sea, their souls on fire. I will bear the torch. They'll rue the day their mothers bore them."

Bela backed away. "I've been wrong about your Beelzebub, Viking. He doesn't have black eyes, stringy hair, a hawk nose and pointed chin. Nay! Forsooth the devil be square, tall, yellow haired, eyes like the sky, or green as an angry sea."

"You're being fanciful, Bela," Einar whispered back.

Bela shook his head. "'Struth yon warriors are the demons of perdition. Now I know how thee commandeered so much of the world's booty. Strong ties to black angels." He retreated one more step.

Einar gestured him forward. "Come, you'll have a place in my house—"

"I can't . . . the others . . ." Bela shrugged.

"They can stay here. In fact, I insist on it."

Bela's eyes widened. "Not all. Just our own queue. Right?"

"Right." Einar frowned. "And the boys when they're well enough."

"Boys?"

"Darg, small Reric and Gar were misused at the di Marchi holding. I don't think Milady MacDonnell knew this." He paused. Was this the work of the accursed Cup? Its darkness had dogged him for too long. If 'twere possible he'd melt the relic and put it under a blacksmith's hammer. Could Finola be a conspirator? If she'd betrayed those boys, she'd be the worst sort of traitor. His stomach clenched. When they'd loved, had she thought of betraying him? She was at the di Marchi palazzo. No one, in Rome for more than a day, wouldn't discover how powerful, how far-reaching the connections of the family di Marchi. 'Twas said the present Contessa was the most powerful of all.

"Where are they now, milor?"

Einar shook his head, trying to recall what'd been said. "We freed the boys. They're at a healer's. They will be brought here when it's time to move them."

Bela grinned, jerking his head at the solemn Vikings. "Do they not smile?"

"Only if I say so."

Bela's brows lifted. "I'll take it as mirth, Viking. 'Tis too painful to ponder, if 'twere true."

"'Tis not mirth. Now, there's only fury. Vikings know how to answer that. Those boys had been shipmates of theirs."

"But those wielding the whips are dead."

"Who gave the order for such?" Darg's whisper held a death threat.

"'Twould seem they were allowed to be pawns of the other slaves. Those that taunted and beat them are dead."

Darg nodded once, as did the others.

Bela swallowed, following close behind Einar when he entered the house.

Two turns of the hourglass, and Einar woke, realizing at once that his nightmare was just that. He was no longer chained to a wall with Tariq. There was no giant Cup of Antioch, burning and suspended over him. He was in his house. He had enough money and booty to purchase a good share of Rome, if he chose. Instead, he would buy information. Bit by bit, he'd discover who'd handed him over to be tortured and put to death. As soon as he rid the world of his enemies, he'd approach Finola, bring her back to his home.

He'd bathed over and over, cleansing his skin of the flea and bug bites that had scourged it, causing pain and itch. Already his skin scarred from the floggings. His health was returning.

He ground his teeth in frustration as he pictured how proud Bren had been, bringing the Cup of Antioch to him, as proof of its safety. He'd bit back the vitriol that'd cascaded through him at the sight of the artifact. He'd simply told Bren to put it away.

Runners had been sent to fetch Tariq and bring him to the house. He was, at that moment, laving himself. Bela had balked at such depravity. It'd taken two Vikings to immerse and scour him.

Clasping his hands behind his neck, Einar stretched his aching muscles and pondered the future. That very evening, he would go out in society because the prime opportunity presented itself.

A bal masque was to be held at the Duc de Lyons's palazzo. The aristos would come in droves. Included in the upper world would be a great many members of the numerous consortia. He would move among them, hidden from their view. Darg would be there, out in the open as his representative. Though Einar'd cautioned him not to approach Finola, if she confronted him, he was to tell her nothing of Einar's return. Bela, Tariq, and other Vikings would be there as guests, attendants, in assorted poses, all under cover. One person or more would know that much had gone wrong, that he'd been captured and was now freed . . . or dead. Some would consider it a crime, others a coup. He'd begin that very evening to know his enemies.

One or more, in particular, would know he'd been captured, and why. When Einar discovered the identity, he'd also know the author of the perfidy. Perhaps by some move or word, he and his cohorts would find the enemy that very evening.

Finola! She could be there. As a member of a prestigious household, her name could be included on the guest list. Would she know him, despite his disguise? His loins expanded in heat and want . . . yet a part of him knew he must remain hidden from her. The suspicion sickened him. He couldn't cast it off. If she was a manipulator, his people, his ships, his household could be in danger. Treachery! That couldn't be. He closed his eyes against it, wishing for a nirvana.

30

He who has a thousand friends has not a friend to spare, and he who has one enemy will meet him everywhere.
Ali Ibn-Abu-Talib

Much in the fashion of the day, the Duc de Lyons had eastern cymbals and strings for the step music. It was thought to be rather risqué in Rome, but there would be dancing! Hand reaching out for hand, moving about the floor, connected by fingertips! The Countess of Rothsay on a visit to Lyons was said to have swooned at the utter, immoral audacity. Surely only barbarians partook of such sport. Some agreed. Others thought it diverting.

At first there were but a few. Most watched. Little by little it changed, until there were more participants than onlookers. Soft slippers sliding over the smoothness of the polished stone floors had a unique whisper that caught in the music pauses. More than one was seen to smile. Bless the masks that hid the identity of the deviates enjoying themselves.

With Tariq at his side, both of them robed like desert caravaners, Einar entered the high vaulted room. Thousands of candles and smokeless lamps sent shadows skating over the tapestried walls. The light material of their garb contrasted with the less comfortable, heavier, beaded, bejeweled raiment of most of the other guests.

"What seek thee in this place?" Tariq asked in formal Greek.

"Anything that will lead me to my enemies," Einar had answered in formal Icelandic, quite sure the easterner wouldn't comprehend.

"Then thee could look on any face, I vow."

Einar swung to stare at him. "Your Icelandic is quite good. You picked it up in bartering, I'll be bound."

Tariq nodded, his eyes traveling over the throng, fixing on Bela, who watched him. "That, and I had a tutor who spoke to me in Icelandic when I was small. The language stayed with me. When I went on my first bartering, I met Vikings." He grinned behind the djellabah that draped over his mouth. "I was able to strike more than one good bargain because of my facility." He eyed Einar. "You speak Aramaic and Bulgar, and other lingoes. Why would I not speak yours?"

"Why not, indeed." Einar's eyes scanned the crowd. Some he knew well, others he recognized. A number were strangers. Some names caught in the conversations were familiar. None inspired him to reveal himself. Not even the great Count Sigla, who, with a coterie of statesmen, was the center of attention.

"That is Sigla?"

"Aye, Tariq, 'tis the man." Einar smiled. "Even you Bulgars know of his stature."

"We do. The man controls the Rus, and he barters with them. We have to know about him."

Einar laughed at the sour note. "He's an honest trader. If he were not, 'twould be a worldwide war among the consortia for everlasting turns of the sun."

Tariq nodded. "He controls the peace in the land drained by the Volga. I know that, too." His eyes never stopped their sweep of the room and its occupants.

They were the object of many stares.

Drawing eyes because they were taller than most in the room, head and shoulders over a great portion of the men, and all of the women.

* * *

"Are they twins? I've not seen such giants, though I've heard of such north of Cathay, in the mountains that climb to the clouds."

Finola turned to see the object of Flavio's high-pitched assessment. Tall men dressed as caravaners. Albai came to mind, and she shuddered.

"Are you cold, Milady MacDonnell?"

"No, no." Cold? In a room steaming with persons who'd eschewed bathing in favor of lathering leaded powder over their bodies to lighten their skin à la mode. It was also used to dry the heavy odoriferous sweat. It couldn't smother all of it. Finola couldn't bear the heaviness of the lead powder on her body and face. Despite the importunings of Contessa di Marchi's dresser, she'd prevailed. She agreed with those who figured bathing was less injurious.

"Would you care to take a turn around the floor?"

She was about to acquiesce when she noted the predatory glint to Flavio Cordia's eyes. Her fear of being whisked behind one of the interminable tapestries that covered the windows that prevented the smallest breath of air and subjected to a rough fondling that the nouveau riche Italos preferred stopped her. "I will decline. I've been too long from the side of my patroness. 'Tis most uncivil of me."

Flavio had such disappointment on his face, she almost laughed.

" 'Tis said you have a most wondrous artifact, milady."

His curiosity was rampant. Wariness had her wondering what he knew of the Cup of Antioch. " 'Tis true there is a relic to be returned to the Church which is now held in safekeeping."

"By Vikings, I've heard." Flavio shuddered. "Murderers and assassins. Not to be trusted."

"Italos are thought of in the same way in some quarters." Irate, Finola tapped his sleeve with her fan and moved away, chin high, wishing him to perdition.

"You need not fear that such would approach you, Milady

MacDonnell." Like most Romans, her name tripped hard on Don Flavio Cordia's tongue. Many Italos and Romans found it difficult to pronounce. He was not going to leave her alone!

"I beg pardon." She wasn't that interested in his meaning. Courtesy demanded she pause.

"The tall men who just entered are no doubt caravaners from the east, and should not even be at this soiree. I will protect you from them."

Finola glanced at his knobby knees in court attire, his narrow chest pumped out by layers of bunting. Then her gaze moved to the fine-formed men who filled the doorway. They were stones heavier, cubits taller, more sleekly sinewed than the pompous Cordia, and again she had to bite back a chuckle. "Thank you, Don Flavio. Your concern touches me."

He waved his handkerchief in front of his face, smiling as he bent from the waist. "I know you to be a most genteel person from a good family. 'Tis my duty."

Finola tried not to yawn. She'd been battling the malady all evening. It was so hot! The conversation was always the same. Business. Bartering. Trading. Fashions. Fabrics. Consortia. Gossip.

No one seemed to do anything but attend soirees, though they socialized little. Those that danced had little business connections. They banded together with their own kind, spouted the same clichés, nattered about others, and looked down their noses. It was everlasting ennui. Only Romans could love such a social life. Finola found it smothering and stilted. Some of the interesting aspects of such an evening were closed to her. Few women were included in business talks. Most didn't care.

The Contessa was one who wasn't shut out of such. Finola found that her cachet as a member of Contessa di Marchi's household didn't extend to the consortia. The faces closed when outsiders approached. This evening their disdain would be masked. Ridiculous!

Being knowledgeable didn't help, either. Finola had seen astute men rebuffed by the closed ranks of a consortium. Even her Roman guardian, intelligent, well known, a member of one, wasn't welcome in all consortia,

"Are women welcome in most of the consortia, Don Flavio?"

"Never. Well ... the Contessa ..." He shrugged. "How sad she doesn't see a woman's duties as her fulfillment."

"Tragic." She angled away from him.

"Few men of trade would deal even with her at a public gathering."

"They would behind closed doors?"

Flavio nodded.

She closed her lips on a retort. Flavio Cordia would think she'd run mad if she disagreed with the popular thinking. Finola found the hypocrisy foolish. Members of consortia generally had networks of spies at their disposal. Most knew what others did. Despite this, the pretense of secrecy was maintained. Only at the very top of power was there silence.

Flavio Cordia bowed, almost striking his head on the floor. "I would get you refreshment, milady."

Finola shook her head, wishing, not for the first time, the evening would end.

"Then I will provide you with strong escort to your patroness."

"How kind."

The djellabah-garbed easterners provided the only distraction, though she noted the disdain on some faces, both Roman and Italo, when they eyed them. She studied the foreigners.

"Your patroness is busy, milady. Do you wish me to find refreshment?"

"Ah, yes, do that ... please."

She exhaled when he left, her eyes going to the tall men once more. On the morrow, she'd try to capture their magic in stone. They exuded a potency, a quivering aliveness that intrigued her. Was it anger, or just an innate energy that seemed to pulse about them? Dwelling on how she'd begin reversed her boredom. Not once in the convent had she been bored, nor had she been in the company of Thorhallsson. All was changed. The sadness and sameness would've driven her mad, if not for her art. Not wanting to seem ungrateful, she kept her feelings to herself.

"You suffer ennui, I fear, beloved."

Finola started at the endearment. She couldn't get used to being espoused to Corin. Though he was every kindness, the intimacies jarred her. Since their betrothal bond had been signed that afternoon, it was acceptable to address her so. Only the vows of marriage separated them. To the world, they were now one. How had it happened? So swiftly. She'd needed time to discuss such a move with her guardians. Why had they signed and sent on the papers without such discourse? She was confused. She turned to him, trying to smile. "I find it somewhat airless."

He took her arm. "I, too, find it most heavy. Shall we walk in the garden?"

Finola hesitated. Why not? She could do so with impunity since they were now considered, in the sight of the Church, as truly wed. "That would be—"

A clanging bell interrupted her.

As the music stopped, the dancers moved to the side of the floor.

The Duc de Lyons, well past his prime with his ankles wrapped in batten, couldn't move fast. Suffering from the swelling disease strained his smile as he looked about him. The Duc de Seigne aided him to the podium.

"His leg should be elevated," Finola whispered.

"Not all adjurations keep him from a social life." Corin bent toward her, his mouth close to her ear.

Respected for their contacts, wealth and the power that went with it, the two men returned the bows of those they passed. Once on the platform they waited until the voices abated.

As though planned, the two turned and bowed to Finola.

Surprised looks from the guests mirrored her own. The announcement! So fast. She dreaded their words.

The Duc de Lyons cleared his throat and began to speak. "My friends, I have the honor this evening of announcing a betrothal. My friend, the Contessa di Marchi, has given me the singular privilege of announcing that Milady Finola Mac-Donnell of Iona, ward of Lord and Lady Sinclair, has exchanged vows with Lord Corin of Antioch, member in good standing of the Damascus Consortium. Their vows of betrothal are duly recorded. Thus they are bound and will exchange nuptial promises."

There were gasps, sighs, and a rush of persons toward Contessa di Marchi, who wore a silk domino and mask woven in the di Marchi colors of scarlet and black. The Contessa had remained at the side with her friend, Cardinal d'Ontini, and her confessor, Padre Antonio.

Others strained to see if they could find Finola in the sea of masks and costumes.

On the far side of the room, one of the caravaners ripped away his djellabah.

"Put it back on, friend," Tariq murmured, moving to conceal him. "There are some who would know you."

"Damn their eyes," Einar muttered, replacing the soft material around the lower part of his face, tossing the flowing ends back on his shoulders.

"You know the betrothers?"

"I do."

"They are the enemies you sought?"

"I didn't know it. Until now."

"By what connection do you claim them, Viking?" Tariq's question was a mere hiss of words, aware of the avid ears of the throng. Gossip was nectar to some.

"I sought to marry her." His chest hurt from the expansion of anger and betrayal. She'd been all to him. Now she'd tear him to pieces. It wouldn't happen. He'd stop her.

Tariq drew in a heavy breath. "And the man?"

"My close friend." Now an enemy. Corin'd taken his wife to be. The traitorous dog.

Tariq cursed.

"We go."

Tariq detained him, one hand on his arm. "'Twould not be

wise for us to charge through the throng. The revelers would question why we leave at such a time."

"Their lives are forfeit." One by one he'd take them down and tell them why. Curse their souls.

Tariq eyed him. "As you say. Not here. Not tonight."

Finola felt smothered by the well-wishers, webbed by their words and touch. When an arm went around her waist and she was all but lifted away from the throng, she could only be relieved.

"Are you all right, beloved?"

Corin's endearment seemed to weigh on her as much as the crowd. "I think I should retire."

"I'll take you to bed."

Alarmed, Finola turned to him. He had the right! In the betrothal bond was full permission to anticipate nuptial rites. She glanced around her, searching for an out, a way to put him off. She couldn't lie with him. She wasn't ready . . . "Wait. I had thought to sketch the easterners. Do you know them, Corin?"

Corin followed her gaze, his own disinterested. "No." He hesitated. "I could find a connection who would introduce you, perhaps the Contessa. If they knew you sketched—"

"Yes, yes, what a good idea." And appalling manners. To waylay a guest and tell them you wish them to be a subject of your next artwork. Finola was desperate. She didn't want to retire with Corin. Any excuse was better than that. How could she face marriage with a man she couldn't contemplate engaging in the same sexual delights that'd colored her relationship with Einar Thorhallsson? Yet, she was well aware that most marriages were not love matches. Rather, they were political moves designed to enhance a family, or a consortium.

When Corin would've left her, she put a hand on his sleeve. "What is it, Finola?"

Corin didn't repel her. She just couldn't contemplate intimacies with him yet. Einar Thorhallsson! Why did he have to die? She couldn't think of him now. She mustn't. Death had taken him. Her life was scarred. She stared up at the ceiling, the elegant rotunda no solace for her lacerated emotions. The night had been too depressing. To be intimate with Corin would be too much to bear. She couldn't. She cleared her throat. "I don't think we need ask the Contessa. Since she allowed the Duc de Lyons to make our announcement, it behooves us to address our guests."

Corin hesitated, then nodded.

Tariq's nudge alerted him.

Einar watched her approach, aware it was too late to slip away, not sure he wouldn't strangle the two of them.

"Forgive me, sir, my betrothed is an artist and she was very taken—"

Tariq bowed, touching Corin's arm, shaking his head. "My friend does not speak your lingo, signore. His common language is in the Mountain of the Clouds."

"That surprises me." Corin stared at the tall stranger. "I didn't think there were such tall men in that area."

"Many men taller than my friend. Beyond Tibet to Mongolla, good sir."

Corin shrugged as though he didn't agree, but wouldn't pursue it.

"What is it that you wish?" Tariq didn't loosen his djellabah.

Finola stared at the two men. Their eyes were much the same. "You both come from the same tribe?"

Tariq hesitated. "True, milady, but my friend is only rich, not learned as I am." He bit back a grin when he felt Einar stiffen at his side.

Finola's smile was unsure. She didn't know if the companion had insulted his friend or not.

31

When anger spreads through the breast, guard thy tongue from barking idly.

Sappho

Einar ground his teeth together.

"I . . . I would not ask you to sit. 'Twould be presumptuous, but I would enjoy perhaps conversing. You see, I can glean much information for painting or sculpting when I talk with someone." She tried to smile at each in turn.

Einar could've felled them both. Jade! She eyed him askance, as though she feared him. She should.

"Finola?"

"What? Oh. Pardon me. For a moment I thought of a . . . a friend when I looked in your companion's eyes . . . 'Twas foolishness. My nerves." She looked at Corin. "We might postpone the nuptials until—"

"Nonsense." Corin smiled at her.

"I should write to my guardians—"

"You wanted to sketch the gentlemen."

"Oh. Yes."

Tariq studied them. "It would be permissible to sketch us. I will contact you when all is ready."

Finola stared at him, her brow wrinkled in thought.

Corin touched her arm. "Finola? You've been given permission."

She pulled back, freeing herself from his touch.

Einar saw the sudden start, his eyes sharpening on her. Was she afraid of Corin? Foolishness on his part. His glance moved to his former friend.

Corin of Antioch, who'd been so adept at describing the positions that slave women would be twisted into for his delectation. Would Finola enjoy such variations? Anger erupted in him like a mountain in Sicilia blowing up its innards, the lava spilling and burning as his blood was doing.

In an abrupt move, he spun on his heel and strode away.

Finola gasped.

Corin's gaze narrowed on the departing figure.

Tariq spread his hands. "My friend is leaving. Forgive us."

When he disappeared in the throng, Finola shook her head. "How strange."

Corin shrugged. "The opinions of women differ in the east. Some do not countenance conversing with the soulless ones."

"They call women that?" Anger bubbled through her.

"They do."

"I like it not."

Corin laughed, leaning over her. As he opened his mouth to speak, a man approached him. He excused himself to Finola and began a whispered exchange with the man.

Finola moved toward the large receiving room. Her chance to return to the palazzo, alone. There were retainers aplenty who would escort her back to Palazzo di Marchi. Corin was as absorbed in business as the Contessa. If the man was a business associate it would keep her betrothed well occupied.

"Excuse me, milady. We've not been formally introduced, but your patroness had promised me an introduction to you. She is busy, so I cross the lines of propriety and introduce myself."

Finola turned and curtsied. "I do not—"

"I'm Count Sigla, signorina." He took her hand and kissed the tips of her fingers. "I've been told that you were friends

with one of my deceased ami. Einar Thorhallsson." He
winced. "You've blanched. Forgive me, signorina. I did not
mean to distress you."

"I . . . I know. I should be over it. His death was a great
shock." They used the stilted, formalized Latin much favored
by visitors to Rome, as a common language was needed to
override the glut of tongues and lingoes in the Eternal City.
Tears stung her eyes.

"I fear I've hurt you."

"No, no." Finola shook her head, taking deep breaths. "I
grieve for him. I'm getting better. I would like you to tell me
about him." She sighed. "Talking here is so difficult. The
heaviness . . . it's hard to get breath. I should like to leave."

"I will take you." Count Sigla beckoned. When an attendant
returned with her cloak, the count took it, murmuring to him.
He nodded and bowed. The count placed her covering around
her shoulders. "Allow me to escort you to your abode."
He nodded toward the vanishing attendant. "He'll tell the
Contessa where we are. When we reach her place, we shall
take a turn around her celebrated gardens."

Finola smiled, relaxing for the first time that evening.

The ride in the elegant dray was slow going but didn't take
long. They talked of many things. Consortia. Growing piracy.
The beauty of the western isles of Scotia, particularly Iona.
They talked of Antioch and its famous market. Neither mentioned Einar Thorhallsson.

When they reached the palazzo, they moved in tacit
agreement beyond the gates to the privacy of the gardens.

Relieved to be in the company of the courtly gentleman,
she laid her hand on his arm and moved with him to the
atrium.

The silence stretched like the fine tapestries woven in the
east, until the myriad forms in her mind had begun to jell
into serenity.

"I, too, grieve for good Einar of Icelandia, signorina—"

"We were to be married . . ."

"I understand. Though Corin of Antioch is most respected

in the marketplaces, west and east, he does not command your emotions."

Finola tried to smile. " 'Tis all so rapid. I've not gotten myself in order." She stopped in a haven of greenery, her face shadowed.

Count Sigla sighed. "I, too, miss the Viking. Not just his great bartering skills bruited about the world, but his ability to command the respect of decent and honest traders. This particular time his star was indeed rising. It was becoming his annus mirabilis. His name bruited far and wide, his talents and skills woven on the lyre."

Grief choked Finola. She had to swallow many times before she could speak. "I cannot credit his death." The Count called the present months and days Einar's "year of wonders." Now he was gone.

The count moved closer. " 'Tis been said . . . it could've been felo-de-se . . ." The count spread his hands, shrugging.

Finola gasped, staring at him. Then she shook her head. "No, no. It couldn't be. He didn't do away with himself." She bit her lip. Anger, grief, disbelief warred in her, drying her throat and making her blood pound into her head. "Felon of himself," the literal translation of the Count's Latin-Italo, made a mockery of Einar Thorhallsson. "He would not. He had too much to live . . ." She faltered. Turning away, she studied the night-black greenery. "That must not be bruited about, signore."

"I agree. There are those who set in motion the laws of piracy against him, making him persona non grata . . . even in death. As such his goods would be forfeit to the state, and as such to the consortia who would bid for them."

"Outrageous! Einar Thorhallsson is . . . was a man of honor. I'll not stand by and let it happen."

Count Sigla exhaled. "I'm an old man, wishing to be beyond the touch and magic of intrigue, but it snaps at my heels." His smile was determined. "I will help you keep his goods intact, signorina."

"Thank you, good sir. How do we do this?"

"We wait and watch. Einar had enemies. They will surface

... slowly ... now that he's dead. Those who couldn't thwart him in life may attempt to blacken his name, thereby conquer him in death."

"They shall not. I will remain in Rome to see that they don't." In the flickering light of the lanterns from Cathay she noted his astonishment.

"Where were you going, milady? Your nuptials come at the end of the month."

Finola sighed. "True. I'd hoped to get to my cousin in Scotia and talk to her about my nuptials."

"You're betrothed," Count Sigla whispered.

She nodded. "The old ways say I'm as good as wed, but there are differences now." She took a deep breath. "Betrothals can be broken."

"Not without the papal seal. Most hard to procure."

Finola winced. "I know." She sighed. "I thought it wouldn't matter whom I wed ... now that—"

"Einar was your true love."

"Yes. He was gone. Nothing seemed to matter." Lifting her head she looked into the gloom-shrouded eyes of the count. "I've changed my mind. Life matters. I want to paint ... to live alone and practice my craft—"

" 'Tis not wise for a woman to choose such an existence. Even in your wilds of Scotia—"

"Iona."

"Or there. 'Tis all the same. Women, alone, are prey for the unscrupulous."

"I will have dogs."

The count shook. "Such dreams are fantasy in our world, signorina, more unreal than the light and shadow caused by the hanging lanterns of Cathay." He gestured over his head. "These 'figaro' lights create a colored panoply that fools the eye. I would not have you hurt."

"I've lost much, been sorely wounded. I cannot find succor in Rome." Finola felt as though a dam had burst inside her. Saying the truth released her from being bound in the cocoon of misery that'd been hers since the death of Thorhallsson.

"I take it you do not have emotions for the lord of Antioch."

The flatness in his voice astonished her. "I like him. I would say you do not."

The count shrugged. "All kinds enter business. Some sharp, or dull, underhanded—"

"Which is he?"

"I don't know."

"He has the respect of a great many."

"He does."

"He is close to Viking, easterner and Italo. If he were dishonest he would not be."

"Very true." The Count moved back and forth in front of her, his strides jerky, as though what drove him was most unpalatable.

"Then why your antipathy?"

"Not antipathy . . . but, perhaps it could be called an unsureness." He inhaled. "I saw him beat a donkey to its knees. I bought the animal from him."

"Surely you know that in some eastern areas that's not unusual."

"I've seen it done, yes."

"Maybe it'd been recalcitrant."

Count Sigla nodded. "It was. And it is also true that my people have had trouble with the beast from the beginning . . ." He shrugged. "I come from a culture that doesn't value beasts as the Tartars do, that can be cruel to them. I find it vile to be so." He paused. "I've often judged men wrongly, or put weight on the wrong measure."

"But something upset you."

"Annoyed might be a better word."

Silence.

"To be truthful, milady, perhaps I am a bit jealous of your intended's power in business."

"But you're powerful."

"I don't own souls."

"And Corin does?"

"So I'm told."

"Could it be that there are those jealous of him?"

His smile gleamed in the gloom. "Indubitably. Most men

of his stature would have a host of traders watching them, many upset at the success."

Finola's teeth flashed in the semidarkness. "Then I must conclude you're not alone in your distaste of him." His chuckle balmed her spirit.

"I admit that the young who rise in the consortia are a constant thorn in the side of the elders. Their rashness seems excessive when we balance the long slow days of negotiations, the months of talks, quandaries that rise, friction of personalities that do more to cause financial schism than any Damascene blade could."

"You warn me against Corin," she prodded, feeling her way.

"It would seem that way."

The caution in his voice alarmed her. "Speak plainly, I beg."

Count Sigla cleared his throat. "I've been in business since I left my father's house to be trained. I've done little else that could absorb me so much. My beloved died very young and I was not inclined to repeat nuptial vows, so everything in my life began to revolve around bartering."

"I can understand that." Not that she comprehended where the Count was heading. Since she was in no hurry to take to her bed, she was patient.

"Corin of Antioch is a member of that group that storms over all barriers. He doesn't countenance any interference—"

"Nor do most in the consortia."

"You're correct," he exhaled. "Perhaps I'm too old, and it's his youth I envy." He shook his head. "I fear his inexorable methods, the goals that will not be tempered with thought, time, and the ability to refocus."

Finola moved closer. She needed to see his face. His features were contorted. "I find your revelations most wondrous, Count. Why they've been made to me ... about a man to whom I'm betrothed, I cannot fathom."

"Have I been stupid with you, signorina?" He took her hand, bowing over it, his leaf-dry lips grazing the surface.

"I would not say that. Though I must mention, with me, Corin of Antioch has been all goodness, all gentleness."

"I am glad."

In the flash of a swinging lantern, she thought she detected a look of relief. The darkness soon cloaked his features, so she couldn't be sure. "Is it because you fear for me, or the consortia that you seek me out to tell me this, Count Sigla?"

"I hear the anger and question in your voice, signorina, and I understand."

"You haven't told me why."

He faced her, his shoulders drooping. "Because I was a close business friend of ... Einar Thorhallsson." Her garb seemed to rattle over her bones, as though the tremor that took her had come from the heart and radiated from feet to head and back. "You cared for him."

"I ... did."

"You left his house."

"My patroness said it could cause gossip had I remained in the Viking household."

"True." He hesitated. "You left the Cup of Antioch with the Vikings."

Her head snapped up. "How is it you know this?"

He waved his hand as though it was an accepted thing. "Did you not trust the Contessa?"

"No. I thought the relic would be safer with such intrepid men. No cut purse would dare accost them."

"Yet, that was how their leader lost his life ... so 'tis said."

Finola exhaled. "'Tis true."

Count Sigla nodded. "His Vikings came to me when he was not to be found. They told me how he'd cared for you. As his men they felt incumbent on them to carry on this cherishing—"

"I've not seen one of the Icelandians, nor—"

"I know, I know. But they've tried to see you. They could not. The Contessa forbade it."

Finola turned away. "I know you speak true." She sighed. "I've tried to make her understand that I'm in no danger from them, but she has an innate fear of the Vikings, as do many of the Romans."

"Perhaps I will come to call one day, and take you for a ride in my new carriage. You could see the Vikings at my villa."

Finola touched his arm. "I thank you and I'd like that . . . but not for a few weeks."

The Count laughed. "You have work to do."

"You know?"

"Yes. I've heard about this wondrous art display that will be for all to see. High churchmen, perhaps the pope, will judge the entries."

"Yes." She leaned closer. "Please don't worry about Corin. He is all that is most pleasing." She'd all but made up her mind not to marry him. She couldn't mention that to the Count until she'd contacted her guardians.

He lifted her hand and put it on his arm. "I have done my duty for my deceased friend, Einar Thorhallsson. I know he cared for you, and he honored Corin as his friend." He sighed. "All is well now. The marriage will go forth."

"It would seem." Finola smiled at the man, but her heart was heavy. She hoped to change that. So much rested on the good offices of Iona and Magnus. Corin of Antioch would be a good husband for another. She'd go home. Her work would center her life now. None but Einar Thorhallsson could give the love she craved. Since she could not have that, she would turn her joy and sorrow into her work.

32

Love yields to business. If you seek a way out of love, be busy; you'll be safe then.

Ovid (Publlus Ovidius Naso)

"Milady, I like it much that we've been given permission to ride about the countryside." Dalia looked all around her. "I like the bustle of the market. One thing mystifies me. Why do we need such a large escort?"

"I was told that since the disappearance of a large contingent of workers from the household, the majordomo insists that we be surrounded by guards." Finola shook her head, feeling sad. "Reric and Gar . . ."

Dalia frowned. "I don't understand what happened. Think you they're enslaved?"

Finola bit her lip. "I can't think that. They wanted to be free. I wouldn't have known they were gone if you hadn't gone down to fetch them."

Dalia shook her head. "No one knows what happened. So many of them."

Finola's hands fisted in frustration. "I would give the Cup of Antioch to have those two back."

Dalia nodded, her mouth a tight line. "The relic is cursed. They've been doomed by it. We could disappear as well."

''That's silly, Dalia. It had nothing to do with the relic.''

''We shouldn't have taken it from Albai's.''

''He stole it from the Church.''

''Then the Church should've gotten it back. It went against good fortune for us to touch it. That's why so many are gone. Demons whisked them away.''

''Not so. They will be found. Every day the runners go to the market . . .''

''And return with no information.''

''They'll be found. Someone must've seen them.''

''One day they were there. The next they were gone . . . all of them. If the demons haven't taken them, why doesn't the majordomo tell us what it means that they should vanish so?''

''The majordomo was not eager to discuss it.''

''The slave, Horace, said that many workers have been abducted from households and put to the galleys.'' Dalia grimaced. ''He laughed. And they say the easterners are cruel.''

''You didn't have it easy in the kitchen.'' Finola squeezed her friend's arm.

''Very bad.'' Dalia glanced at her. ''Though I thank you for getting me upstairs as your maid. Not so many make slurs about my conception as they once did.''

''And you aren't slow to disabuse them of such.'' Finola grinned.

''Never!''

Their low laughs drifted back, past the guardians, the polyglot throng, to others who charted their course and kept pace.

Finola kept Dalia with her. Though Dalia depended on her, she also leaned on the handmaiden as her only confidante. Only one name was never mentioned between them. Einar Thorhallsson.

The crisscross clutch of tents and vendors was a distraction, though their slow-moving dray was not much faster than the market-day strollers.

''Milady, there is talk that you . . . we will be going to Corin of Antioch's home . . . soon.''

Finola swallowed. ''It's within his right to request that I

join him at his home." Why hadn't she heard from her guardians? Time was speeding by. She'd sent several messages.

Dalia squinted at the driver that drove the horses. "I would say more. 'Tisn't wise," she said from the side of her mouth. "The Contessa has many who report to her."

" 'Tis often better to say nothing." Finola didn't feel like pursuing the conversation either. Each day she was closer to the wedding. It was an effort to stem the panic. Why hadn't her cousin contacted her? She couldn't move to Corin's home as he'd requested. He'd begun to press her ... gently. She was running out of excuses.

At the center of the market they left the dray and walked. The Roman market along the Tiber was glutted with people, drays and tents that went up as fast as they went down.

"I do not see why I cannot come with you to this showing, milady. I've seen you fashion all manner of creature and person beneath your brush and chisel." Dalia frowned. "You've worked as though demons were in chase."

"So they are," Finola murmured.

"What say you? 'Tis not wise to call the black spirits into our day." Dalia shivered.

"They're already here."

Dalia stopped. "Milady, your doldrums do not presage happiness after nuptials. You have but two sunrises until your vows, milady. You must smile and be happy ... or run away."

"Where do I run? My guardians have signed the betrothal scroll. They've not answered my queries. 'Tis done."

Dalia stopped her. "Have you not love for Corin of Antioch? Does he frighten you?"

"No. Not at all. He's all goodness and gentleness. I could not ask for a better spouse."

Dalia shrugged. "Then wed him. You cannot go against the scroll. You've told me so."

"I have."

"Then I shall accompany you to the showing on that day, and watch as they applaud you."

Finola shook her head. "You can't."

"Why?"

"They allow no handmaidens in this. There will be a crush of churchmen, aristos, and other artists and their patrons."

" 'Tis foolishness. I'm allowed to attend your nuptials."

Finola's smile was tight. "I insisted. Then Corin added his support."

Dalia sighed. "I would've hoped for a happier visage, milady."

"And I wished that I might go to Iona before wedding Corin, but ... it won't happen."

Einar heard it all, freezing in place. He leaned past bolts of finely woven linsey-woolsey that, in the east, would be used to fashion the desert garb called the djellabah. In the west it was used for tunics and the rough garb of workers. Aware that Tariq still stalked the two women, he hesitated, pondering her words. So, she'd marry Corin. They'd betrayed him. She'd have his children!

Pain, anger, a rooted thirst for vengeance mushroomed in him like a noxious flood. He'd kill them.

Coming to an awareness of his surroundings, he realized he was well back from them. Moving in a serpentine pace toward them, he glanced over at Tariq.

The Bulgar eyed him, puzzled, inquiring. Einar gave a small shake of his head, keeping close to the females.

He counted the guardians again. Five of them, and two more remaining at the entrance to the market, guarding the dray.

Reason pierced the cloud of fury. 'Twas not a propitious time to make a move. A cool head would have a solid plan.

A need for secrecy had him moving away; the slight jerk of his head had Tariq melting toward him.

"Whence, Viking?"

"Back to our place. Now is not the time. Soon." He looked after the two women, fury and frustration limning his features.

"We're to kill them?"

"Probably."

"A waste of a beautiful woman. I like it not."

"Then stay out of the way." Einar ground his teeth, whirling away, plowing through the market like a bull on the loose.

Cursing, Tariq followed at a run. "Slowly, my friend. Think."

Einar cursed in Icelandic and Greek, but he stopped. He took deep breaths, fisting his hands to keep them from shaking.

"Where now?"

"I want a look at the scroll that says they are betrothed."

Tariq stopped in his tracks. "No!" He raced after Einar. "Darg has said it's been posted in the archives of the Vatican Palace. Who could get access?"

"I can."

Tariq groaned. "I've been in the west too long. Their madness is bound to bring about my death."

Einar spun around. "You're muttering."

"I'm preparing for death."

For the first time, Einar unbent. His smile was frosted. "Don't involve yourself, Bulgar. It could cost you. My enemies are legion."

Tariq shrugged. "As are mine. What difference which I skewer?"

"Eastern philosophy?"

"Mayhap it is. My father was a great warrior, so I was told. My mother was descended from a great tribe as well."

"You should stay out of the way."

Tariq smiled. "I accompany you, Viking."

Einar nodded.

"We forgot the blades at the armorer's."

"I'll send someone back for them."

When Einar and Tariq returned, they used a different way than the one used to go to the market. One *vicolo* wound into another, one crooked *strada* led through a maze of carts. Through the back grounds of a vacant palazzo adjacent to theirs situated on a little traveled via, they wended the path to the back of theirs. The new palazzo, which they'd purchased rather than leased, had been run-down and getting dilapidated. The Vikings had done extensive renovating on their purchase, explaining to the curious that a more commodious dwelling was needed for the groups of Vikings and friends that made extended visits in Rome. In reality its great draw was its isolation, away from the popular areas sought by aristos.

Darg met them in the back garden when thcy crossed from the vacant property to theirs. "Milord, you have moisture on your face. You're overtired—"

"No! I won't be babied." Einar strode around him and into the house.

Darg eyed Tariq. "What ails?"

"He saw the red-haired one that had been on his ship."

Darg's mouth tightened. "It burns in him."

"Her destiny is not tied to the Viking?"

" 'Twould seem not."

"We're to kill her, I believe."

"I don't know. I've talked to Count Sigla this day." His gaze slid back to Tariq, his eyes troubled.

"You still think not to confide in me because I'm Bulgar."

"A part of me does." Darg nodded. "Another section looks on you as Viking."

"I've been insulted."

Darg's rare smile was but a slash in his face. "Not so." He sobered. "I would have you listen to the words of the venerable count. He has told me that he talked with the lovely artist and told her not to marry Corin of Antioch. He would like to help her get back to her homeland." He frowned. "He said she wants that."

Tariq frowned. "Is this possible? Could such a deed be done when the vows are upon the woman?"

Darg nodded. "It has been done." He frowned. "There are some who'd turn their faces away at such a scandal. Others would not."

"How do you feel?"

"For me . . . I care not what others do or say. Lord Einar is above such plebeian responses."

Tariq shook his head. "It seems passing strange to put such value on a woman. I would want a bushel or more for such a ransom." He grinncd.

Darg eyed him, the small smile returning. The Bulgar sold himself as a rogue. The Vikings had come to view him another way. Their leader was freed. For that Tariq would get their loyalty. Despite Darg's wariness, he'd come to like the rogue. "It should not be done with the bond signed unless the participants would live in banishment . . . or one of the participants was dead."

Tariq nodded, his face a mask.

33

To go beyond is as wrong as to fall short.
Confucius

Einar sat in his room, his feet on the ornate fender of the fireplace, his toes almost touching the flame. Garbed in light cotton tunic, nothing more, he allowed himself to become mired in thoughts of Corin and Finola.

They'd fooled him! Not many could say that. They'd conspired against him.

Raging disappointment choked him. If he could, he would've vomited the hard core of angry disaffection that coated his being with an acid he'd never known.

Slamming to his feet, he pounded his hand against the stonework above the flames. He saw, heard, nothing as blood thudded through him. His raw heat demanded vengeance.

" 'Twould advance your cause to annihilate them?"

Einar spun around, snarling. Even his mighty Vikings would've backed away from his rage, waiting until a more propitious time to approach. "Leave!"

Tariq studied him. "We are of equal size, cubit and girth. I would give you leave to wrestle with me, if in doing you assuage your grief."

"Not grief, Bulgar. Anger."

"As you say."

Einar glared at him. "You question my veracity?"

"That you're spoiling for battle, I see. That you are truthful with yourself is not apparent."

The easy insults enraged him. When he curled his fingers into fists and would've charged Tariq, the other held up his hand. "An unfair contest. I would thrash you."

"What? I see you backing away. No stomach for it now?"

Tariq smiled. "I would relish our battle, Viking. In your fiery mood, I would turn you to pulp—"

Einar's roar brought armed Vikings into the room on the run.

"Milord?"

Taking deep breaths, he waved away his men. He noticed that Bela stayed. "Join them."

Bela shook his head. "I have a hankering to see you pummel each other."

His grin did more to soothe Einar than oil on troubled waters. A rough laugh choked out of him. Taking deep breaths, he stared at the two easterners who faced him. "You're fools for taking my ill temper lightly. I'm more of a fool for giving way."

Tariq nodded. "I wondered when you'd notice."

Einar exhaled, acid in his smile. "You don't honey your words, Bulgar."

Bela chuckled.

Einar's gaze switched to him. "I think I'll sell you to a galley master."

Bela shrugged. "I'll escape."

Einar laughed, his features lightening. Then he thought of Corin and he frowned.

"You go back to your deep thoughts."

Einar nodded, trying to shake free of the manacles of dwelling on Finola and Corin.

"Undermine them."

Tariq's whisper turned the other two sober, questioning.

"What?"

"Why flog yourself, Viking? Strip their hides instead."

Bela chuckled. "We could do it . . . on the day of the nuptials."

Tariq flashed a grin. "Too sweet to contemplate. Subtle, eastern. 'Tis too complicated for your western mind?"

Einar barely heard him. His mind flashed with the unthinkable. He'd never considered anything that would hurt Finola. Why not? She'd sliced him with the thousand cuts of Cathay. He'd seen the reality. The destruction of men in such a fashion was pain indeed. The slow chunking away of skin and bone, the endless screams, until finally the pathetic creature, no longer man nor beast, died of the towering pain and loss of life's blood. They'd done that to him. Could they be hurt if he disrupted their lives . . . for a time? "What upset there'd be if the bride . . . or groom failed to show up at the church."

"Indeed. The bride, I think, would be easier to steal," Tariq said, his teeth flashing.

"I will discover the hour and day, the driver of the dray." Bela rubbed his hands together. "What greater joy is there than games?"

"None other, 'twould seem," Einar said, his tones dry, watching his friends grin in gleeful acceptance of the moment. "Planning is important."

"Speed, more so."

"Silence is even better."

Einar stared at Bela. "You say my Vikings would betray us?"

"Nay. I say the workers in this place have ears."

"Good point, my friend."

"I have a thought," Tariq whispered.

"Speak."

Tariq, again, held their attention. " 'Tis my feeling she'll have the eastern girl with her." At their nods, he continued. "Best to take both of them." He held up two fingers. "Two. They will search for her . . . and the slave, thinking it an abduction for redemption, as is done in Rome. Better that the slave can't identify us." He shrugged. "Not that they would believe her. They would kill her."

"She's not a slave," Einar said, his voice harsh. "Finola

wanted her free." His Vikings had told him that Dalia had fared poorly, at first, in the house of di Marchi. Not as bad as Gar and Reric, but not well. Had Finola betrayed them all? She'd bound Einar to her. Had she called down his attackers? Ire rose like a flood.

"Calm yourself, Viking. We will prevail."

34

To lead them, but not to master them—this is called profound and secret virtue

Lao Tzu

The nuptial day dawned bright. The rawness was burned from the air by the early-morning sun. Not yet would it be warm enough for the garbage in the streets to turn fetid. The aristos had still remained in Rome, though many would decamp for Capri, where the water was warm and many new villas had sprung up on the ruins of Roman villas, more than a millennium old.

Finola sat in the window in a cotton shift that'd been fashioned for her in Antioch, as had much of her clothing used for warmer weather. She eschewed the use of linsey-woolsey underthings, since she'd discovered the Arabic fabrics that seemed lighter than air.

The heavy door behind her banged open, and she stiffened.

"So. You're not dressed. Where is that foolish girl you insist on keeping?"

Finola took a deep breath, turned and rose, sweeping up a colorful wrap from the chair back. "Dalia? She's in the bedroom, putting hot bricks on the nuptial garment, Contessa."

Contessa di Marchi's eyes narrowed. "I have not been successful in getting the Cup of Antioch returned to you."

Finola blinked. " 'Tisn't necessary. The Vikings will see that it's returned to the Church."

"I was sure you would want it here ... perhaps to carry with you to the Basilica so that you might present it yourself."

Finola shook her head. " 'Twould not be prudent. It could be stolen."

"Then you could've left here at the palazzo. I have many who would've protected it."

"I don't need it. It's safe with the Vikings."

The Contessa's mouth tightened. "You seem restrained for one who's venturing forth on the great moment of her life."

Finola tried to smile. She was well aware that the palazzo had been turned upside down for this day. Costumers, florists, decorators of all types had pranced through the halls, changing the palazzo into a gigantic garden of delights for the eye, the palate, and the ear, as the musicians tuning up downstairs attested. After the ceremony at the basilica, the entire congregation would walk through the city following the colorful dray carrying the bride and groom, in slow winding procession, back to the palazzo. Then the three-day festivities would begin. On the fourth day, she and Corin would leave and, with a cavalcade, they would wend their way to Capri and the Contessa's summer palazzo.

"Perhaps I miss my cousin too much. I was sure they'd come." Or at least send a message. It'd been over a month since her missive had gone to the Vikings, asking them to convey it to Sinclair land.

"And is such gloominess the reason you put off sharing your betrothed's domicile?"

"Perhaps." Finola had won that argument. Did it matter? Soon she'd wed a man she didn't love, one she scarcely knew. A good man. But Einar Thorhallsson still lived in her heart. "There will be none of my family to represent me at the nuptials."

The Contessa nodded. " 'Tis most upsetting that she would be ill at this time. But 'tis most understandable that Lord Sinclair wouldn't travel so far without her when they are expecting another child."

"I know. It's amazing. My cousin had not thought to have more than the three."

"She's been blessed."

"True." Finola sighed. "I've said all this to myself, Contessa." But it hurt. There'd be no one of her blood at the nuptials. None to stand with her. The fear that'd been growing inside her as the day drew near threatened to spill from her eyes.

"Would it help if I showed you the missive I received from your cousin and her spouse?" Her patroness removed a cylinder from the pocket of her gown, handing it to Finola.

Hands shaking, she took the scroll and unrolled it, scanning the words of good wishes and the mention of the approaching babe. It related nothing about Finola's letters to her. The two signatures of Lady and Lord Sinclair were scrawled across the bottom. Finola took a deep breath and handed back the scroll. "Thank you."

"Be of good cheer, child. Your family approves the match."

Finola nodded.

"I see you've done much drawing." The Contessa gazed around the sitting room that doubled as a studio for Finola, the large windows facing north bringing in the proper light for painting and sculpting. Scattered about the room were sculptures, finished or partly so, and many paintings, in oils and tempera. "Not that I admire the subjects. Why those?"

Finola shook her head. "I'm worried about my friends. It's been a turn of the moon, and there's been no word. It's as though they'd dropped from the earth." She swallowed. "Gar and Reric were dear to me. We shared many perils."

The Contessa shrugged, her lips tightening for a moment. "You think I haven't been inconvenienced by the loss of so many slaves. But that's what they do. They run off—"

"Gar and Reric weren't slaves. They were my friends. They would've told me had they chosen to leave. We suffered together." She swallowed, grief and frustration a heaviness in her.

"So you did. But now you must put that all behind you. I have. Today is the day you become a very important person.

Marriage to Corin of Antioch will bring you much prestige. And when you live in the east—"

"But we go to Scotia . . . to Sinclair land." Alarm shivered through her. Her heart pulled her west. She didn't want to return to Antioch.

"Of course, of course. But I'm sure you'll enjoy your return to Antioch. 'Tis where you did so much of your work—"

"No! I would hate it." Finola shuddered. "I don't like to think of it. The burning of the convent, the loss of my friends lives in my heart. Methinks I would like to travel to Scotland. Remain there."

The Contessa spread her hands. "That will be up to your husband. You will be subservient to him now." Once more she glanced around the room. " 'Tis getting cluttered in here. Just as well you have your own place, and a larger work area. For now, you must dress. Hurry." She turned, her wedding garb belling out around her.

Finola sank back in her chair rather than going to the bedroom. Worry choked her. What if Corin decided against visiting the Sinclairs after their nuptials? She wanted to see her cousin, to discover if she needed her. Finola was sure some of the blackness at losing Thorhallsson would be ameliorated by Iona's warmth and love. She shook her head. Not to be foolish. Corin was the most understanding of men. If he could he would consent to the visit.

Rising to her feet, feeling tired, unsure of the long day ahead . . . and the night, she had an almost overpowering need to flee. Hesitant, she made her way through to the bedroom, eyeing the paneling on one side of the bed where Gar had come to her that one day. Now her friends were gone.

"Milady? Your raiment." Dalia held the dress of gilt-crusted cloth of Cathay in her arms, a puzzled smile on her face. "What're you thinking?"

"Nothing." Finola tried to smile.

"If you wish, we can run," Dalia blurted, then grimaced. "Our chances might not be the best." She shrugged. "But we did it once."

Finola looked at Dalia, who'd become her closest friend.

"Thank you. I must go through with it, or disgrace my family."
She smiled. "But you are to come with me to the ceremonies.
I'm glad of that."

Dalia beamed. "As I am."

"You will enjoy the festivities."

Dressing became more lighthearted. Finola's doldrums
lifted a bit. When she donned the wedding garment and it fit
so well, she had to be pleased. It cascaded over her in the
softest folds.

Dalia looked her over, as she fitted the crown of gold
entwined with myrtle and thyme to her head. "You are most
beautiful. This day you will wed and your many works will
be taken to the Circus Maximus to be presented two turns of
the moon hence. Surely you can be happy, milady."

Finola took a deep breath. "I will try."

In too short of a time, both were ready to leave. A decorated
dray awaited them in the courtyard. It would be a quiet trip
to the basilica. The ride back to the palazzo would be far
more festive. Many Italos would line the main via to gather
the coins thrown by the bride and groom, and many of the
guests. A true Roman feast.

Dalia and Finola went down the wide staircase to the main
foyer, the vaulted area festooned with rich ribbons, tapestries,
and glorious flowers in every hue.

The Contessa studied her. "Are you sure you wouldn't like
me to accompany you?"

"No, you've told me tradition dictates the bride must ride
alone, except for a handmaiden."

"Or an attendant. Often it's the mother. I could be the
surrogate."

"No, I thank you for the courtesy. Dalia is fine. You ride
ahead as is customary, Contessa. We'll be right behind you."

The Contessa di Marchi's frown was a minute drawing
together of skin over her nose. "As you choose. I suppose
it's safe enough, though the rabble will be along the way,
screeching for their coppers."

Finola smiled. "I'm sure you've arranged for their recompense."

Her patroness shrugged. "I've also arranged drivers for the day. They will carry you and Corin back here. The rest of us will walk in *cavalcata*, as is the custom."

Finola bit back a smile. The Contessa thought the practice silly. She'd said so. The cardinal had insisted on the trappings. For the first time she was glad. She and Dalia could talk. She had a smothering sense of doom, as though it would be the last time she could converse with anyone. Bride's nerves!

Finola and Dalia waited until the contessa was helped into her conveyance and it left the courtyard, before entering theirs.

When she was inside the covered dray, the curtains were dropped. She grimaced at Dalia, whom she could barely make out in the dimness. "I would've preferred the fresh air."

"This must be another custom of the crazy *faranghi*." Dalia pushed at the heavy tapestry at the openings. "They keep out the air."

"They do." Finola lifted hers, seeking a place to hook it back. There was nothing. She held it for a few moments. The dray made a sharp turn and the motion had her trying to right herself. She dropped the curtain. Semidark covered them again.

"Not a good driver," Dalia managed, pulling at her clothes. "We'll be mussed ere we get to the nuptial place."

"The basilica is a very old church."

"Your god lives there, I know."

"He lives everywhere." Finola saw the flash of Dalia's teeth in the gloom.

"Then he must be many gods. I believe in the goddesses. I don't think they are as warlike as the gods, yours and any others."

Finola pondered the blasphemy. "I don't suppose it's any worse for you to call upon the goddesses. Vikings call upon Wotan, and they believe in God." She hesitated. "You might be right. The men, who call themselves God's servants, can be very bellicose. I don't think God is."

"Why would he like such if he wishes them to preach peace?"

"That I don't know."

"Men are fools, whether they believe in one God or many. To them all gods are male. Such stupidity. No women can be elevated to a level of man? Nonsense. I believe in goddesses."

Finola laughed. "Dalia, you and I could be burned alive for such heresy."

"Boiled, you mean? Like Albai would've done?"

Finola paused. What was the difference between the righteous and the heretic, or pagan? Not much. Degrees of burning?

The cart swayed again. They rattled over some rough quarry-stoned way.

Curious, Finola poked at the curtain, trying to discover where they were. "We should be close to the church by now. Though I've only been there once, I thought I would know the area. I don't know this."

Dalia was able to lift her curtain a bit. "We seem to be approaching a church, milady. 'Tis not so imposing to me."

Finola leaned toward her to look out that side. A sudden lurch almost took her and Dalia to the floor. They stopped with a rattle of wheels, the swaying dray almost toppling the women.

They were still tugging at their raiment and headgear when the wooden gate that served as a door for the sideless dray swung open. The sudden light blinded them.

Annoyed, Finola glared at the black outline of a man. "You should be more careful—"

"Never mind talking. Get out of there."

Stunned when the drayman caught her arm, Finola slapped at his grip. "How dare you—"

"Quiet!"

Finola was almost dragged from the conveyance.

"Stop!" Dalia shouted, reaching over to claw at the man's grip. "You'll soil her dress, scoundrel."

Another hand entered the dray and all but lifted Dalia over Finola. When she would've screamed, it was clamped over her mouth.

"Cease! Do you hear me? I am Finola MacDonnell—"

"You'll either walk, or I'll sling you over my shoulder. Which?"

Finola's mouth dropped. She stared from the hooligan with his face swathed in a linsey-woolsey cape to his partner, who held Dalia. "I'll walk. But this is not—"

"Quiet!"

Stunned, she walked between two of them; Dalia followed behind with two more.

The church they entered was dark, small. They passed through the gloom of the narthex to the nave. It was far too short to be the basilica, she thought.

Down the aisle, lit only by an occasional torchère, they moved in ragged procession. Balanced on a column the chancel, more clearly lit with clusters of candles, had a moonbeam gloom to it. Persons there seemed to sway and quiver as the candlelight sputtered in the breeze.

Finola swallowed, glancing around her. There was no one in the small church. Shouldn't there be guests by now? They'd been taken to the wrong church? She'd have to make the attendants understand.

When a priest came out of a chancel door, flanked by altar boys, she stared. One carried a thurible, its incense rising at every sway. The other toted a sconce, the array of light illuminating the altar. Finola exhaled. There'd been a mistake. She'd been taken for someone else. Easily rectified. No need to be concerned.

Other figures came from the opposite side of the chancel, hooded in a black cloak.

The leader threw back his hood and stared at Finola.

She stared back, shaking her head. Her hand went to her throat. "No!" It came out a croak. Her mouth parted, eyes dilating. She swayed, then sank toward the floor in a faint.

Einar was there before she hit the tiles, cushioning the fall as he looked down upon her.

"You've killed her." Dalia struck out at the man next to her.

He yowled and grabbed her, pinioning her arms. "What do we do, lord?"

"Bring her to." He lifted Finola, ignoring those who reached to take her. Glancing at the priest, Einar gestured him forward. "When she comes out of her swoon, we'll be back. Then we get on with it."

"Milord, the lady didn't seem overjoyed to see—"

"She is. Wait here. I'll return with her." At a slight motion of his head, the men lifted a struggling Dalia.

"If you've killed milady . . ." She sobbed.

"Hush! She's not dead." The Viking glared at her.

Dalia eyed the burden Einar carried, high and close to his chest. "Milady," she whispered.

35

I loved you once long ago—
Sappho

In the anteroom, Einar watched as salts were held under her nose. She sneezed, coughed. Her eyes opened on him. "So you see me, milady? Your treachery didn't work."

"Einar! You're ... alive!"

"Aye. To put a spanner in your works."

"What? Did you say treachery? I dinna ken your meaning." In her consternation, confusion, shock and joy, she'd switched to Gaelic.

"Drink the libation, milady, you have a meeting with a priest."

Finola blinked. "You're angered ... Yes ... the priest ... I know ... how did you ... ?"

"Now is not the time for your questions." He bent over her, lifting her to her feet. "Can you walk?"

"Yes. What happened to you?"

"There's no time for that."

"Einar, is that all you have to say to me? Have you been ill? Where were you? I thought you dead—"

"I'm sure of that." He turned to the men, gesturing that they precede him. Others left by a side door.

"Where do they—?"

"They'll be on watch against treachery."

"That's twice you've used—"

"Come, milady, your nuptials are nigh."

"Corin isn't here."

"You don't wed him. I'll be your spouse."

She gasped. "You can't. The law will be broken. The bonds have been signed."

"I am Thegn of Icelandia. You may choose not to wed me. If that's your choice, it will be bruited about Rome that you consented to lie with me without benefit of vows." Einar ground his teeth when she whitened. What was that to him? He cursed his hesitation. Had she not conspired to have him killed because she would wed another? No more treachery. He was going to expose all who'd turned Judas. "Don't blanch, milady. Surely you feel no qualms about this, after betraying me—"

"Betray? Me?"

"Milord Einar, the priest awaits."

So intent were Finola and Einar on their own exchange, he'd not thought of time.

"We're coming."

"Einar. This priest. Why is he here?" She felt a dizzying joy . . . and great ire that made her weak. Her hearing buzzed so that she couldn't believe what was said to her.

"To marry us, as I told you."

"Yet you call me traitor."

"I do."

"Then I shall not wed you."

"If you do not, there will be war. Against Iona, against Antioch. Choose."

"You're the traitor. You're betraying your friend Corin."

Einar shook his head.

Fury coursed through her like a flood. She struggled back from him, pushing at the Viking who would've aided her. "War, is it? Then, I tell you, you haven't seen war, Viking. If we wed, 'twill be a battlefield you'll not forget."

"Nor will you."

She staggered, the vehemence in his voice like a slap in the face. She'd grieved for him!

When Einar would've taken her arm, she jerked free. Chin up, lips pressed together, she preceded him from the anteroom to the chancel.

The priests and the altar boys were nervous.

"I am Father Paulus of the Abbey of St. Benedict." He coughed. "Milady MacDonnell, if you do not wish this nuptial to be exchanged, 'twill not be." The priest looked shaken when the black-cloaked Vikings closed around him. White faced, he stared at Einar.

Finola knew with a certainty that Einar would wage war. Would he kill a priest? Nothing seemed beyond the scope of his ire and vengeance. She'd not bow to him. Nor would she be the reason for a war to begin. How could she've ever thought she loved him? He was the barbarian most assumed Vikings to be. "I raise no objection." She exhaled, glancing away from the priest's obvious relief.

Panic rose like a summer storm, making her sway. What was her future with a man who hated her? The scandal that would commence because of their joining would be bad enough. The whirlwind of agony that could surface when she was wed to a man who hated her would be a pummeling to the spirit that would bring unrelenting anguish. Why? Corin was his friend. Surely he could see what a protector his friend was being when he proposed marriage to her. What demon possessed Thorhallsson, turning him ferocious, enemy to his loyal ami?

"Let us begin," the priest said, coughing over his nervousness. His hand shook when he gestured that the acolyte bring the candles and incense closer. He raised his hands and began the long Latin intonations, the blessings and nuptial phrasing that would precede the Mass.

Finola didn't know how many times she stood, then kneeled, repeating it over and over again. Grogginess assailed her. The combination of chanting, candle smoke, and the olibanum swung back and forth, almost in front of her face, made her queasy. The cloying dampness of the old church stuck like an old blanket. When she felt Einar's hand under her elbow, she jerked free, struggling to stay erect.

All at once she became aware of the cessation of chanting. She looked up and found all eyes on her. "I . . . I . . ."

"Your response," Einar said, his tone curt.

"Yes . . . ah . . . I will."

The priest's features cleared like sun popping through a cloud. He raised his hands, muttering a prayer.

Finola was sure he was thanking his Deity that the ordeal was almost over.

Then he raised both hands, murmuring the blessing. In perfect Icelandian, he pronounced them man and wife.

Finola stared at the priest. He was a Viking!

He nodded in encouragement. "I think your husband wishes to seal the vows, signora."

"What?" Confused, Finola turned to say something to Einar. His head was descending. She reared back, but he caught her close, his mouth settling over hers, his tongue touching hers. A familiar melting overcame her. Then she recalled what he'd said, intimated. How dare he! Touching her so intimately after all but proscribing her. She stiffened, intending to close her teeth over his tongue.

As though he read the thought in her mind, he pulled back, the acid in his smile attesting to his awareness of her intent. "Lady Thorhallsson, greet your people." Turning her to accept the bows of his men, he leaned down and whispered, "Now you're mine."

Her smile trembled. She acknowledged the men, then whirled to her new husband. "And you're well and truly caught as well, Thorhallsson." She knew the priest heard when he flushed, his mouth dropping open.

The unsettled man of God made another one-handed sign of the cross over them, muttering another blessing. "I must go. Go with God and be happy." He bowed first to Finola, then more deeply to Thorhallsson. "I will see you in deep summer, Lord Einar."

"So you will."

In the silence that followed, only the shuffling of boots and the deep exhalations of some penetrated the damp quiet.

"Time to go . . . wife."

Startled, Finola looked up at Einar. He hated her! She couldn't quite stem the shock of that. So be it! Scots knew how to hate back, very well indeed.

When he took her arm, she fought back the urge to draw her dirk from its hidden pocket and slice at him. He would pay for insulting her!

"Milady?"

"Come, Dalia."

Finola's friend exhaled. "Good. There wouldn't be a chance of killing them all."

Vikings who understood Greek glared at her.

"If there was a chance, I'd fight you," she whispered for his ears only.

"Bitterness, milady?"

Finola stopped, fury flooding her. "What did you expect? Obeisance?"

"You fear loss of reputation?"

"You needn't smile. To some a good name, a covenant are important."

"I agree. You made a covenant with me, as I recall."

"You were dead."

"Obviously not."

36

"It belongs to the Church!"

"My Vikings have cared for it." Einar shrugged at her ire, watching the blood rise in her face. Would her hair begin to crackle? It was the color of flame.

"The Cup of Antioch must be taken to the Church."

"You have it in your possession, Milady Thorhallsson."

They faced each other like combatants in an arena, unaware of the others who hovered in the great hall.

"I don't intend to steal it!" She glared at him.

"Can I be sure of that?"

"You can," she said through her teeth.

Einar inclined his head, staring at his very new bride. "You bristle like a fighting cock, as though to strike me ... after insulting me. If you were a man, I'd have knocked you across the room. You impugn my honor? You would've married my former friend, who is equally culpable. One day soon, I'll meet Corin and challenge him, settling his perfidy once and for all. The relic stays here."

Finola's head went back, her teeth clenched as hard as her hands. "Infamous!"

"So you say."

"I do. You're a brigand for keeping it . . . and for insulting me."

Einar shrugged. "Some would say I've reclaimed my family's property."

Finola swelled. "You didn't want it." When a muscle jumped at the corner of his mouth, she would've recalled the words. He'd confided in her. Trusted her. She bit her lip, saying nothing.

"It stays until I decide what is to be done."

She fumed. "I would go to my room. I have sketching to do."

"On your wedding day? Unusual."

His biting tones elicited titters from some of the staff. His one look silenced all.

Finola heard, blood climbing her neck to flood her face. "May I have your leave to withdraw?"

Einar inclined his head. "You're not a prisoner. You're my wife. Do as you please."

The word jolted her to silence. His wife! Dazed, she stared at him. She'd prayed for his return. She'd longed for him. He'd changed. The loving, sensuous man was gone. He hated her, called her his enemy. She was his wife, yet he despised her. What evil fate had taken the beauty from her life? First she'd lost him in death. Now, in life. She was cursed. Dalia had said the relic had been a curse on them since they'd left Albai's holding. Could it be true? No! She wouldn't blame the blessed Cup. It was Thorhallsson. He'd made her an outcast. Anger was a purgative. She wouldn't be downhearted! Thorhallsson was the brigand. Not she. She'd fight him every step of the way. Faugh! She'd thought she loved him. Nonsense! He was a treacherous Viking. He'd find out just what retaliation meant. He tangled with a Scot. He'd rue the day. "Come, Dalia." She'd gone but two steps up the stone stairway when she heard the husky whisper.

"Milady."

Finola spun on the stairs, almost oversetting herself. From the corner of her eye she saw Einar running. He steadied her.

She pushed at him, trying to see around him, steadying herself on the balustrade, trembling. "Reric? Is it you? How do you come here?" She started down toward him, arms outstretched, delighted, surprised. Dalia was at her side, voluble, welcoming. She barely noticed Einar taking her arm. "How . . . ?" She stopped dead, staring at the wan countenance, how her friend was held in Viking arms. She swayed. Dismay, shock, wonderment shook her. "You've been ill. What has happened? How is it we didn't know where you were? Why didn't you come to me?" She put her hands out to him, trying to smile when he grasped hers. He was so weak. "What ailed you?"

Gar pushed around the Viking carrying his brother, his eyes dilated, his mouth tight.

"Gar! How are you? I worried so. None knew where you were—"

Gar grabbed her hand, shaking it, gaining her full attention. He pointed to Reric's back.

Reluctant to see what she suspected, she moved his tunic, noticing his wince.

The Viking carefully shifted his burden to give her access. She edged the tunic away from his neck, gasping. "Oh! Who hurt you so? How dare they? You're free." Her accusing stare fixed on Einar.

"They're here recovering from the beatings and abuse they suffered at Palazzo di Marchi, milady," Darg said, speaking out even when Einar gestured him back.

"What?" Finola shook her head when Einar nodded, anger in every line of his body.

"It can't be true. I saw many of the Contessa's retainers, day after day. I never saw this. Many were cosseted, well fed." Her glance moved to a stony-featured Dalia, who stared back at her. "You suffered, I know."

"Others, too, milady," Dalia whispered.

" 'Tis true there was ill will among some—"

"The slaves in the stables were beaten. The majordomo turned a blind eye. Reric told us this, milady," Darg continued.

Finola opened her mouth, then closed it again when her

young friends nodded. "I'm so sorry. I didn't know. I . . . we . . . looked for you, Dalia and I."

Reric touched her arm. "I know you wouldn't harm us, milady. We had no time to . . ." His eyes fluttered as though the talking fatigued him.

The Viking lifted him higher in his arms.

"Are you so weak, my friend?"

Darg stepped forward. "He's much better, milady."

"I'm happy for that. And you, Darg? All goes well?"

The Viking nodded, his smile restrained.

"Wait," Reric demanded of the Viking who was going to cart him to the back of the hall. "Milady, I don't blame the Contessa, nor the majordomo. The palazzo was huge. Some of it well managed. Some not. The stables and sculleries were run by scoundrels who stole from her and abused her help. 'Twas slaves who did this to me," Reric finished, seeming fatigued.

"Have you medicaments enough? And the roots you need—"

"We're Vikings. We know of curatives. Reric is almost well," Einar said, his tone brusque. "He had good care from one who wouldn't betray us." Einar thought of the healer, how he had to remain hidden from the world of the aristos. Rome had an extensive underworld because much of its life was denied to too many citizens.

Finola spun around, teeth bared. "You knew of his infirmity, aware I would be searching for him, yet you let me wonder. You're a cruel man, Viking."

Einar shrugged.

"Nay, lady." Reric stilled the frowning Viking who carried him. "He saved us. The slaves abused us . . . as those did at Albai's holding—"

"Where are those slaves? The Contessa will have them lashed." Anger gushed in her. She noted how Dalia had moved to Reric's side, just behind Gar.

Reric shook his head. "I know not the fate of the slaves."

Gar started, biting his lip, his gaze sliding from Finola to Einar.

"Do you know of them?" Finola charged Einar, fury in every line.

He caught her hands. "Restrain yourself, milady."

"How can I? My friend has been abused. I would know who did this," she lashed out.

"We killed them. Bela and I. They're in the pit of caustic at the back of the stables," Einar said, his tone soft.

Finola factored what was behind the quiet voice. Gar's tension. "You killed them and dumped them there?"

"So I've said."

"This Bela . . ." Her eyes went from one man to another, discounting the Vikings.

"We did." Bela grinned when Finola fired a challenging look his way. "I'm Bela. I come from the Caucasus, milady, by way of the slave hells of the Mediterranean."

Finola glanced at Einar, who shrugged.

"He's one of us now, for good or ill," Einar said.

His grin exacerbated the ire that'd been simmering since the wedding. "If you were so innocent in all this, if there was no culpability on your part, why didn't you come forward and tell the Contessa what'd occurred on her premises. Surely you knew the majordomo would be searching for his staff, that he would've rid the household of those monsters at once."

"Slaves count for little."

Finola knew he was right. She was also sure he was goading her. "The Contessa runs a good domicile." The silence that followed was unsettling. The quiet gave lie to her words. Damnation! She wasn't wrong. "Contessa di Marchi has a well-defined sense of justice."

"That's for you to decide." Einar looked past her. "Reric needs his rest."

Whirling around, Finola flinched with the truth of that. "Forgive me for prattling on, Reric. Please rest. I'll talk to you later."

"Stay here, milady. You'll be happy. Gar and I are."

Finola tried to smile. She nodded. "Thank you. I will be staying. I'm . . . I'm—"

"She's my wife, Reric."

Finola scowled at Einar's bluntness.

"Glad tidings, milady," Reric said, smiling. "We will be happy, all of us."

She opened her mouth, then closed it, her smile weak. What would her friend say if he knew the details. "We will talk again."

He nodded, his head lolling on the Viking's shoulder.

Gar hurried after his brother.

Finola spun to face Einar. "Why haven't you told the Contessa?"

"A need for secrecy. I have enemies. So do they." He jerked his head up the stairs.

She swallowed, her lips tight. "You should've told me."

He gestured that she precede him from the receiving area into the great hall, indicating a chair next to the fire. Despite the spring day, the warmth outside, the stone walls held a chill. Most of the seasons a fire was needed, except in late summer when natural heat finally permeated the stone. By then, most were glad of the coolness that rarely left the stone domiciles.

Einar didn't sit opposite her. Instead he leaned on the back of his chair, staring at her. "Are you surprised I live?"

Taken aback at the question, she nodded. The acid in his sudden smile puzzled and annoyed her. "Why would I not be? You were pronounced dead."

"Apparently I'm not."

"Why didn't you contact me?" He was much thinner. How had it happened?

"To be set upon again? One *imbuscata* at a time, milady."

"*Imbuscata?*" Finola's fury rose like a flash flood. "You think I arranged an ambuscade for you? Is this your implication?"

He nodded.

Finola jumped to her feet. "Charlatan! Liar! Scoundrel! You accuse me of what you'd do yourself. Corin doesn't know what sort of friend you are."

Einar shrugged. "He should by now."

"What are you saying?"

"Most will have tired of the long stay in the basilica—"

"Oh. Dear Lord—"

"And the word will filter through Rome we're married. He'll discover it, just as most other Romans will."

"Lowlife," she said through her teeth.

"You're married, milady. You've lain with your husband before the vows. 'Tis meet that I make you an honest woman. I have."

She sank back in her chair, staring up at him. He'd torn her apart with his words. Anger, frustration, grief warred in her. If she'd had a weapon at that moment, she would've attacked. What would life be now? What could it ever be with a man who hated her? She'd loved him more than life. Now he doomed her to everlasting bitterness. He wouldn't forgive her. How could she forgive him? All was lost. Nothing left but her work.

37

We are quick to flare up, we races of men on the earth.
Homer

Einar regretted his words while they still hung on the air. Her face had crumpled as though he'd struck her. That was not his plan. He swallowed. She'd plotted with Corin against him. She'd have married him that day, scarce turns of the moon since she'd declared strong feelings for him. "We'll talk of other things." He couldn't temper the harshness in his voice.

"Will we? How can you speak to a fallen woman?"

"You're not," he roared. "You're my wife."

Vikings leaped into the room, swords drawn.

"Go!"

"Your bellow will bring the constabulary," Finola told him, chin lifted.

"It won't," he said, in a quieter tone. "There are high walls and space about the place."

"A veritable prison."

"No." His voice rose again. Swallowing his ire, he took deep breaths. "It's been bruited about Rome you'll be in an artist's showing in the Circus Maximus."

"What?" She stared up at him as though she didn't comprehend. The swift change of subject was unsettling. Her anger with Einar was underlined with great pain, the anguish of wanting him so much and having him reject her as traitor to him.

Was she still thinking of his words? He'd call them back if he could. She angered him. Theirs hadn't been a casual coupling. No. They'd joined and spoken private vows between them. They'd spoken of everlasting love. Now words of marriage bound them for all time. Many words of love were exchanged. He'd remind her. Had he been a fool about her? Did she think Corin the better man? Damn his eyes!

"I should go back to Iona."

"What? If you do, you'll be on my ship with me at your side. I won't let you out of my sight again."

She started to rise.

He put out his hand to stay her. "Tell me about your showing."

She shook her head. "I don't understand you . . . you hate me . . ."

"I've not said so, nor do I. Tell me of this display of artists."

She exhaled. "A host of artists will attend. I'm only one of many. If the day is sunny, it will commence."

"You'll attend?"

Her expression changed from glazed hurt, to shock, to hard-bitten incredulity. "How can I go? The reputation of the participants has to be as pure as "Caesar's wife," according to the specification. Talented, pious, without a hint of scandal surrounding the person." She glared up at him. "I don't fit that. I've broken my solemn betrothal." She took a deep breath. "Even you say that I'm—"

"Do not miscall yourself, Milady Thorhallsson. You belong to the highest order of Icelandians and Ionans. I'll not have you gainsay your station."

She lifted her chin. "You say your word is your solemn bond."

He nodded, his eyes wary.

"What does breaking my solemn betrothal make me?"

"My wife."

"I've broken my bond."

"So you have." He frowned. "Solemn betrothal? You had signed concessions from your guardians? From Sinclair and our princess?"

Finola nodded. "Of course. Why else would I've gone forth with it?"

Puzzlement gave way to blinding relief, then rage. He fought it, aware no good came from acting in ire. "This was done before you reached the Contessa's palazzo?"

Finola frowned. "I think not—"

"Must've been. How else could they've been procured for you? The ships that sail the seas are not as swift as the birds. They couldn't get there and back so quickly."

Finola bit her lip. "I hadn't thought of that. It must be so. Contessa di Marchi could've inquired of my marriageable state before I arrived."

"Why would she?"

"I don't know. I went over every exigency, trying to find a way out. I couldn't."

The hard core of resentment that'd smothered him with angst since he'd discovered her impending marriage crumbled a bit.

"Actually it could've been done anytime before I was posted to Antioch. Such inquiries about marriageability aren't uncommon, from patron to guardian. For all I know, Sinclair came and signed the contract in person."

"The princess had to sign as well."

"Yes. That could be."

"You don't know that?"

"I've seen the contract. I saw signatures. My cousin's and her spouse's."

"And you would recognize their writing?"

Finola hesitated. "I've gotten missives from my cousin. A few were done by scribes, others by her."

"Would you know their writing?"

"I should know Iona's." She bit her lip. "It must've been done as we said. They would've sent their blessing if my patroness assured them the banns would be posted with a man of honor. Such a person, presented by her, would set this in motion.''

"You're saying the Contessa is a friend of Corin's . . . of long standing?"

Finola was still. "Yes, I suppose that's what I'm saying."

"Yet, I never knew of this connection."

"Does Corin know of all your confidants?"

"No."

"There you are."

"I'm not so easily convinced."

"You're not because you don't want to be, Einar Thorhallsson." She lifted her chin. "Many marriages are contracted in such fashion, especially if the guardians are a great distance from their charge."

" 'Twas done in unseemly haste, methinks . . . and in too hidden a manner."

Finola bristled. "The Contessa is . . . was my patron. 'Twas her wish to see me settled. She might've had permission from my guardians from the time of my acceptance of her patronage."

"Then why weren't you told?"

She glared. "Why? I know not. I was told when your death . . . was such put forth." She felt a wrenching stabbing at the recollection of her pain when she'd been told of his death. "You were dead," she said in dull tones.

"Exaggerated, as we know."

She lifted her chin. "Yes."

"That's when you were free to accept Corin?"

"Do not hiss at me like a serpent, Einar Thorhallsson."

"Your answer."

" 'Twould seem so."

"You did not think it too hasty?"

"I . . . I beg pardon."

"No mention was made of wedding me. Yet in a short time . . . mayhap, hours after my "death," you're betrothed, your nuptials to occur almost at once."

"Not hours," Finola said. "Why do you have such fire in your eyes? What is your meaning?"

Einar raised his eyebrows. "You don't know?"

"I trust my patron."

" 'Twas done? Your betrothal recorded?"

"Yes. I broke the bonds. That's why I can't compete in the artists' show. At the moment I married you, I disgraced myself."

"Nay. You're the spouse of the Thegn of Icelandia. You'll be honored as such, no matter what the tongue rattlers say."

Finola looked away from him. "Many cruelties can occur when one falls from grace. My parents told me I must never forget my place. Shame is like a cloak. Once donned it becomes like skin, not to be shed in any season." She looked up at him. "Worse for a woman. Beyond the pale can cause banishment, shunning, even incarceration or isolation. The transgressions of a man can be overlooked. Never, in a woman. My cousin told me of one who was banished from Sinclair lands, who's probably dead now." She eyed him when he cursed. "What's wrong now?"

"Nothing to do with you, milady." Einar frowned, lost in thought.

"What say you, Einar Thorhallsson?"

He shrugged. "I ponder a vision of that time. Mayhap I was in Sinclair holding when it occurred."

Frowning, she shook her head. "I don't ken why."

He waved away her puzzlement. "You'll enter the Circus Maximus."

Finola was stunned. "Have you not been listening to me?"

"The criers will announce your name, milady."

Finola shook her head. "I cannot enter."

"You will."

"My wares were sent to the arena. They may've been discarded this very day."

"They will be in the competition."

Finola stood, trembling. "This day I've been shamed. The day of the competition I will be sliced in public, bleeding from a thousand cuts."

" 'Twill not happen."

"May I go to my room?"

Einar nodded. "Dalia will accompany you. We will have a light meal, then you may retire at will."

"I'll not share your bed."

He watched the blood rise in her face. "You have."

"Cur."

Einar nodded. "Mayhap, I am. Even a cur dog understands betrayal."

"I'm not the traitor."

"Are you not? Then you won't mind staying to your quarters for a time . . . until we go into society." He hated seeing fear on her face, the negative reaction to him. He wouldn't explain all that could threaten her. She would have to learn to trust again . . . or mayhap he would need to learn as well. Could he?

"Do you mean to humiliate me, then?"

Einar hardened his heart. Otherwise he would've scooped her into his arms. "In four days' time you'll make your entrance into society as Lady Thorhallsson. Until then, I leave you to your own devices." Incredulity scored her features. "Did you think I meant to ravish you, milady?"

"Mayhap I did."

"Mayhap I have no taste for traitors." He steeled himself when she swayed.

"Don't gaze into your shined copper when you trim your beard, Einar Thorhallsson, else you'll see the greatest betrayer of them all."

"Be still."

"I won't."

"You will," he told her in harsh tones.

"You, sir, are an unrelenting fiend." She whirled away from him.

He bowed.

When he raised up, she was gone. He began cursing, using every blasphemous word and phrase he could muster.

38

Cease to ask what the morrow will bring forth, and set down as gain each day that Fortuna grants.
Horace

The priest walked into the ornate room, a rolled parchment in his hand. He didn't disturb the woman who wrote so busily on the olivewood desk with corners and feet carved like gorgons.

She pushed one hand at the fall of dark hair that all but masked her forehead, much of its heaviness caught in a bejeweled snood. Well aware of his presence, she ignored it and continued posting in her ledger.

From experience, he was patient.

Making him wait gave her satisfaction. He wouldn't leave, nor did he mind. It gave him a chance to gaze around her room, tot up the price of each artifact. She noted he looked at the statue of Aphrodite, cast in gold. That was new. The tapestry wrought in silk threads from the caravaners from Cathay. Another acquisition. He pursed his lips. She knew he calculated the cost. She smothered a smile.

Glancing up again, her mouth curved in awareness at his intense scrutiny. He missed nothing. Checking what was new. Let him. So much for the asceticism of the clergy. Many of them were as acquisitive as the laity.

He'd be surprised if she told him she knew much about him. An unmarried woman, alone, had to have protection. Her network of spies provided that. He'd be bowled over if he knew that three of his most trusted people were in her pay.

Her gaze followed his for a moment, her smile widening. He'd be assessing the new painting by Aloisio, one of the young painters under her patronage. She inhaled, following his gaze around the cavernous room that was especially hers. Favored articles dotted walls and floors.

She looked down at her worksheet again. Once he left she could get back to it. "You want to discuss the scandal that hangs over the city like a low black cloud."

He started. "I know you detest being in the middle of it, but you've ridden out bigger storms. None could think you had a part in the unthinkable. You were in the basilica . . . waiting . . . waiting."

"Curse it! What happened? Four days since the fiasco, and no news. Have the girl and the handmaiden dropped off the earth? What a quagmire. She was in my care."

" 'Twas thieves."

She studied the priest again. Since the death of her spouse, the frail and aging Conte, he'd been coming around more often to the spacious palazzo she'd inherited. He thought wrong if he dreamed to have influence over her in any sphere. She controlled her life and di Marchi holdings.

He looked away from her. "This room is larger than some of the reception areas of the Roman palazzos."

"Yes, yes. You didn't come here to talk of decor."

He faced her, his mouth twisted. "Could the drivers of the dray have been compromised?"

She nodded. "I've just recently lost slaves." He pretended to be an ascetic. What would he say if she mentioned she knew of his warehouses? He'd begun small, buying goods from brigand caravaners, the commodities cheap and valuable. To his credit, she didn't think he knew that when he started. It hadn't taken long for his greedy soul to comprehend the savings on wares purchased from brigands.

She knew of the caravaners because of the spies in his

household, and because she used them herself. It didn't set well for a member of an illustrious consortium to do so, but she knew she was in a large group that did. Being discreet was the key.

Brigand caravaners preyed on the booty of others, carrying off both goods and monies. They often attacked some of the ones belonging to smaller consortia. She paid an exorbitant price to ensure the safety of her own. She accepted piracy, as most did, since many of the brigands were financed by the best families and some of the wealthiest churchmen.

The thin-lipped priest might mouth platitudes against it, but he didn't openly oppose them, nor could he when he was such an avid customer.

"Milady, you should protect yourself against marauders. You have treasures in this room many would covet."

"If you've heard something about the abduction, tell me."

"Piracy doesn't thrive in areas protected by the Church. Beyond those strong arms, the market in ill-gotten goods flourishes."

"Make your point, priest."

"To steal from heathens is not considered a crime. Perhaps the brigands were after her handmaiden."

"Faugh! The girl was worthless." She made another entry in her ledger, then looked up at the man in front of her. Spare of flesh, gaunt of cheek, he was the image of the clerical ascetic. Did his soul match his looks? If he was like those clerics who dabbled heavily in the lay world, it wouldn't. Her spies told her he did well in the world of business. Could his soul belong to other than the Deity? "And do you like the chalice you heft? It came from Tripoli, so I'm told."

His hand replaced the relic, then flew to his side, sliding into the sleeve of his cassock. "I know little of such things."

"Of course." Churchmen were much the same. They mouthed piety and abstemiousness, their avarice barely hidden. She wouldn't pursue the point. The connection to the priest was useful.

The priest tapped his nose, bringing his cowl closer about his neck, frowning around the room.

She followed his glance. "My husband liked this room." She shrugged. "At times, the preponderance of umber, ebony and glaring white plaster of the room can seem beyond cold, almost what the Greeks referred to as *obscena*, would you say?"

"I am not close to Greek things."

"Disarm yourself. I do not talk of heresy when I speak of Greek theater and how they described the distasteful, that which would be done off stage, like murder and mayhem, as *obscena*."

"I do not attend the theater. There is a vulgarity to it, a sensuality that offends. In the theater and the arts, they have forgotten subtlety, the gateway to mastery, mystery . . . innuendo, implication . . ." As though he'd said too much, he bit his lip and looked down.

"It saddens me that the di Marchi palazzo could offend."

His head snapped up, his eyes narrowing on her. "I did not say so."

"Then you do not look upon my paintings and sculptings with contempt?"

" 'Twould never be my intention." His eyes roved the intricate plasterings, the paintings done by masters, many going from floor to ceiling. The tinted and sculpted nudes were so lifelike, one could almost reach out and touch them.

"So! It pleases me that while you wait until I finish my posting, you feed your wondrous good taste by eyeing my collection."

The cleric's smile was starchy, giving the barest bow to the woman who now leaned back in her teakwood chair. "I confess to an appreciation of the arts, Contessa."

"Confess? You? What sin could you have?" She schooled her features into placid chiding when he pokered up.

"I'm on a mission from the cardinal."

"Go on." She picked up her quill and threw it down again, pushing back the emerald-studded ink pot, crafted in Venetian glass, styled after the craftsmen of the Nile. Her waving arm sent a jewel-encrusted sleeve sliding back, baring the healthy skin of her arm. She caught the cleric's eye upon it and her lips twisted in satisfaction. "Come, come. Tell me your message. I'm sure we both have work to do." She gestured toward her scatterings of foolscap across the surface of the desk.

"I would think you know, Contessa. Days have passed since the nuptial day—"

"We spoke of it," she said, her voice frosty.

"Foul play, think you?"

"Of course. I've had runners search. No trace." She sat forward, pushing a scroll toward him.

He picked it up, studying it. "You're most unusual, milady. Most of your fair sex can neither read nor write, nor would they do their own scribing." He pursed his lips.

"I can see you might not approve of my father's caprice." She cared not. They were used to each other, not loyal. They had a history, not an affection. Some of their goals were the same. The main one, now and tomorrow, would always be power.

"I see women on their pedestal, admired and respected for their chastity, restraint and motherhood, and they are happy women," the cleric mouthed as he often did.

The Contessa smiled. Prig! Empty vessel! He saw women as things, creatures to do his bidding, to lie, legs spread, flat on their backs when he wished to empty his seed. Let him pontificate! "Would not God wish me to use my knowledge?"

He hesitated. "I'm sure He would approve of your acumen."

She rose to her feet, kicking back the train of her heavy gown as though it were an encumbrance, not a work of art that had taken ten women many long hours of terrible eyestrain to fashion. She marched around the desk, head up, the fabric whispering with its weighty gems, its rich bronzy red a frame for her dark hair and eyes. "Get on with it."

"My mother was a saintly woman, who brought me to the friars when I was just a lad."

And no doubt his father had been one of them. "How good of her," she said. One day she would not need him. His power was growing. She'd have to watch that. Perhaps even now he was plotting against her.

He looked away from her. "I have not seen such colorful lancets. Have they come from Venice?"

"They have." She turned and prodded the fire behind her, welcoming the heat. "Have you ill news? Is that why you digress?"

"The heat is most welcome, Contessa. Rome has become dampish after the unusually cold winter, and the spring solstice carries ice in the wind."

"And have you come to tell me of the weather, padre?"

He shook his head. "The cardinal deems it necessary that we find the Ionan."

"I've tried." Damn! She'd scoured the city.

"The cardinal is displeased."

"It grieves me."

"What think you happened to your prodigy, Contessa?"

"I sense infamy. I don't know in what quarter."

He nodded.

"I should get back to business. Perhaps you could tell me why you've come, padre?"

Instead of answering her in the formal Latin they always used, he nodded, looked over his shoulder, then back at her, speaking in a spate of the lingua franca used in the streets.

The Contessa frowned, and rose. "You know I detest that speech, that I try not to have its roughness on my tongue."

"'Tis necessary."

"Why? I prefer Greek or Latin."

"There's a need for secrecy."

The Contessa shrugged. "None here speak the lingua franca that you mouth. 'Tis true. Proceed, then, if you must." She wrinkled her nose. "I prefer even some of the newer dialects to this."

The padre took a deep breath. "It grieves me to tell you this. The cardinal insists that the hunt be widened." When the silence lengthened, he moved closer, putting the parchment he'd carried down on the desk. "His writ says that you must equal the number of searchers he will put into the city and its environs."

Silence.

She glanced at the parchment, touching its crispness with one long slender finger. "I don't understand. I've done everything. We must wait—"

"I have faith that you search for her. The cardinal wants assurances."

"Why?" She frowned, tapping a nail darkened with henna against her front teeth. "Tell him that I have runners everywhere."

"She must be found at once."

The contessa shrugged. "I'm trying." She eyed the cleric. "I cannot believe this frets you."

The cleric stiffened. "I was to be on the altar on her nuptial day."

"I recall," she said. Sanctimonious!

"I've not told you all of it," the priest said, clearing his throat when she swung about, staring at him, her skirts settling about her person like bats' wings. "The cardinal wants the Cup of Antioch. It was left with her Viking friends."

She ground her teeth, rounding on him. "Does he think I didn't try to get the Cup? I did. Many times. She insisted on leaving it with the Vikings."

"He wants it back in the Church as soon as possible."

"What? He cannot have it." She slapped at another scroll. "I've requested the Vikings bring it here." She glared at him. "It belongs here."

The priest shook his head. "The Church thinks it's theirs."

"I don't care what a gaggle of red hats thinks. That Cup was in the di Marchi family—"

"And before that it was in an eastern family, who donated it to the Convent of Saint Mary."

"It was purchased by the di Marchi family—"

"It'd been stolen from Antioch by pirates many years ago when they absconded with one of the women—"

"Yes, and our family purchased the Cup while it was still in eastern possession. It should not've been returned to the convent. It should've come to us. It's ours." She stormed down the room, her overskirt belling out around her undergown of russet. "I've heard the talk among the prelátes, that the Cup surfaced to be returned to them." She shook her head. "I'll not stand for the seizure of Finola MacDonnell nor the artifact . . . I'll have them back!"

"The Patriarch of Antioch—"

"Think you it would be safer in a city plagued with ground shaking, padre?" She waved a hand. "Antioch is such a place. Would you deny it?"

"I cannot think anything of value would last in such upheavals as they have in the east. God has often been angry with the Antiochans, methinks."

"God, is it? Blame Him not for the stupidity of building a city where such evils occur. And that is not the only weakness to the bastion of Antioch. Do not the renegades storm down from the hills and assault its wealth time after time, Seljuks, Tartars and the godless Bulgars." She waited for his reluctant nod before storming up and down again. "The Cup belongs in Rome . . . in this house where it will be safe."

"Mayhap 'tis foolish for you to seek the Cup, Contessa. There are other great—"

"It belongs here . . . as does my ward."

"Will this obduracy not bring the scrutiny of the papacy? The di Marchi family has had good relations with the Church. The College of Cardinals—"

" 'Twould be more prudent to let it go. So you say—"

"Being out of favor with the Vatican could be costly."

"I'd like it not." Reason rose over temper. Though it would choke her to return the Cup, the priest was right. Years of goodwill toward her and her consortium could bring her a fortune.

"I cannot see how it can be gotten back . . . nor your ward."

"No? Well, it shall be done." She went to her writing desk, making her letters most carefully and clearly.

The padre coughed. "May I help you with the scribing?" She looked up, her smile pointed, then shook her head.

"Do not bother yourself, padre. I assure you I'm proficient enough."

"What will you do? Concerning the Cup . . ." He shifted uneasily. "About the maid from Iona?"

She smiled, dipping the quill once more. "I'll set out more runners, as the cardinal wishes." Her smile was acid. "I only obey."

The padre bowed his head.

39

Painting is silent poetry, and poetry painting that speaks.
Simonides

The four days passed at a gallop. Finola had thought she'd hate the incarceration. It wasn't such. She was told by a host of Vikings it was for her own protection that they dogged her footsteps. She'd come to welcome the care. Now and then, she had nightmares about Albai, and the constriction and confinement in the di Marchi palazzo. At Einar's holding she was free to do as she chose. Surely she lived in a dream. How many times he'd lived in her mind and soul. Now he was alive. Not dead! Her spouse! Her fantasy! She sighed. But unlike in her dreams, there was pain as well. She'd been rejected by her husband. Work was her great panacea.

She and Dalia roamed the grounds and gardens. Most of the time her mate, Einar Thorhallsson, was not to be seen. Angry, yet serene. It took effort to put the amalgam of emotion in perspective. She and Dalia talked of every subject under the sun. As though her tongue'd untied, her limbs'd unfettered, she chattered.

New utensils appeared. Chisel, granite, palette, brushes. Next to her bedroom was a wondrous place of northern light. Her creative juices cascaded. When she wasn't with Dalia, she worked ... and worked. Sculpting. Painting. Sketching. She couldn't stop when the light was good. Pieces evolved in rapid succession. A well of joy flooded her. She'd never felt more in tune with her art. Worries faded. She could've drowned in temperas, buried herself in stone.

She saw Gar and Reric whenever she wished, which was often. Reric seemed to grow stronger each day. Long conversations, laughter, shared memories of deeds that seemed impossible in the retelling were mulled and discussed, again and again. In tacit agreement Einar Thorhallsson was not mentioned.

"Today is the fete, milady. You return to society, they say." Dalia grinned as she grimaced.

They climbed the stairs after visiting the brothers. "Yes. I'm not sure how it'll go."

"Be at peace, milady. We're safe."

"So we are."

They entered Finola's chamber, a far larger apartment than she'd had at the di Marchi holding.

"Look, milady, something new, as always." Dalia unrolled the fabric. "'Twill make a beauteous gown. Before that the lustrous carpets and tapestries."

"Yes." Finola looked at the small jewel casket on the bed. The culmination of gifts. The obligatory treasure of gifts for the highborn bride. Did Thorhallsson mean to honor her, or mock her? She didn't approach, even when Dalia exclaimed, letting lengths of gold and ropes of gems ripple through her fingers.

"You must look, milady."

"First, I'll bathe." She couldn't clear the rawness from her voice. Why did the traditional gift make her feel like a commodity? She didn't want to touch the jewels. She must. Custom called for such adornment when she entered society as spouse.

"Milady, the thegn holds you in great esteem. This gift has spoken."

"I will choose something for this evening."

"Good."

Finola tried to smile. Her insides were churning.

"Don't be unhappy, milady. I have better feelings about this place."

"Good." Finola put aside her feelings. "Remember, Dalia, you're free, not a slave. Neither I nor the Vikings consider you anything else. I value your company, but you may choose to leave. You're free to dictate your life."

A well-worn smile crossed Dalia's face. "Milady, I'm not free because you pronounce it." Dalia looked thoughtful. "Not even here in the west am I so."

Finola stared at her handmaiden, pondering. Her laugh was caustic. "You're perceptive, Dalia." Sour mirth pushed her mouth wider. "So? We should enjoy what we can and not concern ourselves with aught else. Is that it?" At Dalia's nod, some of the bitterness segued to pragmaticism. "I won't sulk. I can work. If we can't change the world, perhaps we can fashion it more to our liking, Dalia." It might've made her feel better to rail at Thorhallsson face-to-face. She had enough ire for many battles. Since he didn't confront her, she'd build her own life, in his house, without him. He'd not enter her chambers to claim his nuptial rights. Fine. Let it remain such.

"I'm not sure of your words, milady. If you mean women should take what they can and run . . ." Her mouth twisted. "I say we must. We're trade goods, milady, not the most valuable, at that."

"We're not!" Finola's riposte cut across the room.

Dalia shrugged. "Think what you will."

Finola turned to the bathing chamber, mulling Dalia's words. She flung her overdress at a settle, ignoring it when it fell. "Commodities, are we? I'll see about that." She spun around, her dress whirling about her. "The Viking has provided a generous wardrobe, Dalia. I would wear the best for this come-out." She slammed back the curtain to the washing room, steaming water already in the metal tub. She immersed herself, looking up at Dalia, who washed her hair. "Did you know there are places where women don't believe themselves less than men, Dalia?" She sputtered when water splashed on her face. "I didn't live in such an area . . . but I'm one of them. Mayhap I've always been. My cousin can fight like a man." She jerked her head up and down. "So will I. My weapons will be different."

She swiped at the laving cloth being wrapped around her. "Dalia, my parents tried to tell me that a woman's place was behind a man—"

"So it is."

"No! I've never believed that . . . though I've just found my power to realize it." Teeth bared, she marched back to the bedchamber. "I was considered outré because I dared to enter a field populated by men. My dear grandfather overrode my parents' objections or I could never have proceeded with my learning. They had no right to chart my destiny, wishing me to marry at the tender age of fifteen summers—"

"'Tis done."

"They were wrong. I was not when I balked and went to my grandfather."

"You could've done nothing without a strong man to intercede."

"Aye. 'Twould seem so. That changes now. I will chart my life."

"Milady, you're espoused."

"Not enslaved."

"Same thing."

"No!" She slipped into the dressing gown Dalia held. "I won't accept that anymore. I'll do my work and kick aside any who try to put me behind a man."

"Does it matter how you think or feel? 'Tis a man's world, milady. Ever thus." She shrugged. "Don't be in a swivet about the way of things."

"I'm as good as a man. I'm not a chattel."

Dalia fixed her with a hard stare. "Did you imbibe too freely of the flowered wine, milady?"

"Faugh! I'm imbibing life, in pleasure, in my art, henceforth."

"Ah, I see. You'll be a courtesan, like the favorite in a seraglio."

"Never!"

The explosive negative had Dalia jumping back. "Milady!"

"I've turned over a new leaf." She went to the commodious clothes press. "I need a suitable garb this eve—"

"You could wear your elegant nuptial raiment." Dalia's eyes darted from her mistress to the clothes press. "This mood of yours is unsettling, milady."

"Good." She eyed the elegant draping of the nuptial garb. A great deal of material. "We'll make changes . . . starting with this. You're an accomplished needlewoman, Dalia. So am I. Together we will fashion a stylish, daring garb."

Dalia shook her head. "Choose from the others my lord has picked."

"No!"

"Is this the same swelling of the head that overtook you at Albai's?"

Finola glowered. "Don't be foolish. I was perfectly clear at the time."

Dalia groaned. "Not true. I like it not."

"Be strong, Dalia."

"I'm most uncomfortable with your fire, milady. I feel the burning already. I think it's my person."

40

So in the Libyan fable it is told
* That once an eagle, stricken with a dart, Said, when he saw the fashion of the shaft, "With our own feathers, not by others' hands, Are we now smitten."*
Aeschylus

Einar didn't have too long to wonder what kept Finola above stairs. He was kept busy by a stream of early arrivals. His invitations had been sent far and wide. Another palazzo had been leased for those who'd come a distance. Runners had been sent in all directions. Ships had been sent to Icelandia and Scotland, carrying goods and notices. Though it would be long past time when those invitations would be received, courtesy demanded that such an occasion be highlighted with announcements. Embossed with his seal and executed by the friars whose intricate work would make the missives keep-sakes, the word had gone out to the known world. The Thegn of Icelandia had been wed to Finola MacDonnell, daughter of the House of MacDonnell and Skene.

Many had been welcomed into the receiving area without the presence of the bride. This was permissible under the circumstances, though it frayed Einar's temper. Was she being intractable? Not impossible. The Ionan had more spirit than an Arabian steed, though she'd fly at him for making the comparison. Her smoky green eyes, much like the jade the caravaners brought from Cathay, would flash. They could smite a man with their fire. The coral cream of her skin could drive him mad . . . Damn her hide! Where was she?

"You're grinding your teeth."

Einar glanced at Tariq, who grinned. "She's late."

Tariq shrugged. "She'll be here. Ah, a friend approaches."

Einar turned, his smile welcoming. "Count Sigla. Welcome."

Sigla, eyes alight, looked around him, then back at Einar. "So, you Viking rogue, you come back from the dead and commandeer the beauty from Iona." He gripped Einar's forearms. "You will make her happy." His voice went to a whisper. "All are not as convivial as I over the news."

"This I know." Einar returned the salute. "What hear you?"

Sigla moved one shoulder. "Contessa di Marchi knows. So does Corin of Antioch. Gossip flies like birds in Rome."

Einar grinned. "So it does."

Count Sigla's gaze sharpened. "You invited them, no doubt."

Einar sketched the merest bow. "No doubt."

"Good. Disarm when you can."

"I subscribe to such a dictum."

Sigla looked around him. "You have many powerful guests, good friend. The consortia are well represented."

" 'Twas my wish."

"Arm yourself before the battle. Well met, my friend. Good strategy."

Einar cocked his head. "I count you as one of my weapons."

The Count grinned, his glancing sliding toward Tariq. "Of course."

"You've met Darg. This is also my friend, Tariq . . . from the east."

Sigla made the customary bow, a strange lingo rattling from his lips.

Tariq answered in kind.

The Count drifted away when an acquaintance hailed him.

"This Count is not stupid. He sought to catch me out. That's a little-known dialect he spoke." Tariq's mouth twisted when Einar laughed.

"He surprised you, Tariq."

"He did."

The receiving hall was packed. Though there was little to complain of, since attendants were everywhere with refreshments, there was tension. Guests smiled, greeted others, moving about the huge space. Etiquette demanded they not enter the great hall until the bride had joined them.

Einar was laughing with Tariq. The sudden hush had him swinging around, not needing the upraised faces to tell him his bride had appeared.

"Holy Wotan," Darg muttered at his back.

"Blessed be the Fates," Tariq whispered, scanning the crowd, noting some of the agape women and openly admiring men. "War," he muttered.

Curses rolled from Einar's lips, his hands balling into fists, his face contorted. Anger, frustration . . . and hot wanting that raged from toe to forehead were his torment.

"She's more a goddess than your wife, Viking," Tariq murmured, smiling when Darg hushed him.

The gown was simple. There was no adornment on that gold cloth of Cathay. In one drape it fell from her shoulders, touching her breasts and hips, clinging, swaying, belling out at the least air movement. In her hair she'd twined ropes of gold and topaz, her hands ungloved, sporting the heavy jewel-encrusted nuptial band.

Did his eyes deceive him? Could her wondrous form be seen 'neath the folds? No. She was covered. The illusion was erotic enough. Who fashioned it for her? Wotan curse the needlewoman.

Finola paused at the curve of the stairway, speaking to those near, smiling, at ease.

"She's changed . . ." Tariq muttered.

"True." She'd turned from woman to goddess. From that

to Circe. Damn her eyes. A sour amusement gripped him. She had the throng in her hand. She'd come to conquer. The glowing fabric, the fire in her hair were an amalgam of moon, sun and starlight. She'd claimed the firmament. It aureoled her from slippers to gem-entwined tresses. He stemmed the smile hovering over his lips. So! She'd proclaimed her independence of him by the mere expedient of a gown. The fiery Ionan always had the power. Mayhap she'd discovered the incendiary potency he'd found on meeting her. Not charcoal, sulfur and potassium nitrate, the compound called black powder, brought from Cathay, could equal her combustive presence. Would she level his abode? She was exotic enough to command all of Rome and the world.

He had a flash of irritation that the only bridal jewels she wore were in her hair and her left hand. But reason told him had she pasted them from eyebrow to foot, she couldn't have been more regal . . . more beauteous.

Many crowded near, moving toward her up the stairs. She raised both arms.

Einar's mouth curled into an appreciative smile at the sudden hush.

"I give you greetings, good guests, and as spouse to the Thegn of Icelandia, I give you welcome and a blessing that comes from this heart to yours." The formal Gaelic address was more in keeping with a royal greeting to subjects than from a bride supposedly married against her will.

It struck a chord. Male and female responded with full-throated ayes.

"She's managed to disarm and cajole, Viking. A capable woman, your spouse."

"Yes." He couldn't take his eyes from her.

"She had not been so undermined by the people, I would say, friend Einar."

"I agree with you, friend Tariq."

"There is much irony in such a moment. As an easterner, I applaud."

" 'Tis the intrigue that pulls you."

Tariq grinned. "She's a fearless one. A wonder to see, east or west."

"A worthy adversary. I could regret the nuptials," Einar murmured.

"The falsehood is in your face. You're glad to keep her from Corin of Antioch. Nothing touches the importance, though you don't say it."

"Think what you will."

"Frown not. I heard you tell Sigla Corin has been invited this eve?"

"He has."

Tariq chuckled. "I look forward to the entertainment." He nodded his head. "You've staved off the shunning that might've come, had you not invited so many powers in the consortia."

"Thank Count Sigla."

"He has corked any attempt to shut you out. I salute you, friend Einar."

"I'm humbled by your praise," Einar said, his cynicism not lost on Tariq, who chuckled. He'd not taken his eyes from his wife. So many crowded her, there was scarce room to move. She was making a serpentine approach to him, pausing long enough to be introduced or greet those she knew. In Icelandic, Greek, Latin and Italo she was at ease, moving from lingo to dialect with grace.

Admiration glinted in many eyes. Respect had replaced cool appraisal.

A facade? Or was she really as confident as she appeared? Braver than the white-striped cat of Tibet, yet shy as a newborn tern. Finola was so many persons, so multifaceted. Proud of her beauty, angry at those who stared, he wished they were back on the island . . . alone . . . together . . . as one.

When he moved, Tariq, Bela and Darg moved with him. The crowd parted. Einar faced her.

"Wife? Will you join me?" Behind her smile was a wariness. Did she fear him?

"As you say, husband."

He put her hand on his arm. "You didn't receive with me. You can lead our guests in to dine, at my side."

"I will."

Even her small hand heated him. He wanted her. The days since their marriage had been torture for him. He was sure she needed the time. Soon he wouldn't be able to stay away from her.

Their meetings had been few since saying their vows. Even to hold her hand made him harden with desire.

Finola stopped at the top of the two shallow steps leading down into the great room. Trenchers had been set up in three long rows with another table on a dais, perpendicular to the trio. Flowers were everywhere. In Rome the blooms came early and stayed late. Ablaze with candles and color, goldware glinting, catching the candle flame, the room radiated. "Beautiful. I would love to paint it."

"Do as you choose."

He would've said more, but a shuffling, raised voices at the entrance, drew his attention.

The majordomo stepped back.

Finola leaned to see around her husband, and almost fainted.

"Well met, Einar Thorhallsson. I've come to felicitate you." Corin of Antioch moved to the middle of a contingent, his dry tones whispering over the guests.

41

Finola gasped.

Einar took her arm, pulling her to his side.

She tried to free herself. The grip tightened. "You're creating a fuss," she hissed.

"Be still. I want you with me. Come, we'll greet the late arrivals, Corin of Antioch, Padre Antonio, and your patron, Contessa di Marchi."

"You have no shame."

"Why is that?"

"To invite them is to hurt them."

"To ignore them is to ignite war. Among barterers, that's the greatest sin. It impedes movement from one trading center to another."

She stared up at him. "True?"

Einar nodded.

"And that's the reason you invited them?"

"One of them."

His smile heated her temper. Tightening her nails on his arm, she moved with him. Even through her ire, she noted the strong muscles rippling under her hand. Despite a battle to push it from her mind, she couldn't blot out the memory of that strong body close to hers, the sinewy arms holding her. "I . . . I can walk by myself." He was all but carting her! She was flustered enough. Did she need to meet her patron and former betrothed out of breath and scarlet? She knew much of her botheration was acceptance of the relief she'd been feeling since not marrying Corin. "Wait. I can—"

"I know." Einar didn't look at her. He watched the new arrivals as he strode toward them.

"Slower," she said from the side of her mouth.

He smiled when he looked down at her.

The silence in the room vibrated with ripples of whispers, like wavelets on a shore, hitting, then slapping out again. Quiet. Few moved.

Einar stopped a few feet in front of them. He stared at each one in turn. "My wife and I welcome you to our home. We're happy you could join us." He turned to Finola, leaning down to kiss her cheek. "Aren't we, beloved?"

The endearment reverberated around the room. In polite society, a man rarely addressed his wife by her first name, let alone a love name. Such a gaffe seemed to have a positive effect. As though a new custom burst upon the scene, it beat a tattoo into the low sounds becoming part of them.

Startled, Finola nodded.

"You're quite flushed, my dear. Have you been working too hard?"

Finola inclined her head. "No, Contessa. It's more because I fear I've caused you stress. For that I beg your pardon."

The Contessa inclined her head, her mouth a thin line. "I'm sure you didn't mean to lapse. I knew you to be conformable." Her gaze strayed to Thorhallsson, who smiled. "Well met, Thegn of Icelandia."

"And to you," he said, his tone formal rather than friendly.

Finola cleared her throat. "I'm sure my . . . spouse would wish that you suffer no disturbance because of . . . of . . ."

"Your untimely vows?" Corin spoke for the first time.

"I would say ... timely," Einar interjected, his smile stretched.

Finola'd dreaded meeting Corin. "Sirrah, I ... I ..."

"My wife and I welcome you, Corin of Antioch." Einar's easy tone would've relaxed most.

Corin stared at him, implacable, unsmiling. He patted the sword at his side.

Vikings stiffened, touching their weapons.

Einar bowed.

Finola swallowed. "Perhaps ..."

Tariq jostled her when he moved closer to Einar.

Bela flanked him.

Darg moved up behind Tariq. "There's death in those eyes."

"So there is," Tariq said, smiling. "I feel I've met the man. Yet, know I've not. Passing strange."

"Watch him."

"I do."

Finola felt the quiver in Einar's body. She didn't have to look up to know there'd be menace there. It throbbed from his blood to hers. He hated Corin. Did he feel the same about her? Why did he marry her? To save her? He had. Anger and sadness rivered through her. How dare he bed her, make her love him, then call her betrayer! Who was he? Letting her believe him dead, so that she'd accept Corin. What humiliation. Pompous, unforgiving ... troll. None of his pain was her doing.

Her husband caught her hand when she would've moved back from him. When he would've tightened his grip, she pinched him.

He looked down at her, not by a flicker of eyelash showing what he felt.

He looked back at the guests. "My wife reminds me that I keep you standing. Join us at table."

Einar made a gesture. The harpist and lyre players began to strum. They were on a balcony above the great room.

As though on cue, persons moved to greet the newly arrived

guests, then curved in slow procession to the great room and the designated seating for dinner.

Einar looked down at his wife's white face, placing her next to him on the low dais at one end of the room. He settled close to her on the bench. "Why do you stare at the Contessa?"

She shrugged. "It's strange. I've thought of her as older. Tonight, in this bright room she looks different . . . younger." She lifted her shoulders as though she would cast away foolishness "She seems fetching in her raiment . . . looking almost familiar."

Einar nodded. "I've not had cause to seek her company over much since my affairs lie in a different direction, but I do not think she's advanced in age. Mayhap my age, perhaps younger."

Finola gasped. "Truly? Her husband was said to've been quite old."

Einar nodded. "Much has been said of the way he taught her about business. At his death she came into money and power." He looked thoughtful as his gaze stayed on the Contessa. "She's a force in the consortium. Most think of her as older. She courts that opinion, it would seem." His eyes narrowed. "Strange . . ."

"What?"

"At times I've had the feeling she thinks she knows me. I'm sure I would recall if I had had close discourse with such as she."

Finola studied her patron, feeling a dart of ire. "Perhaps one day I'll sculpt her."

"Indeed, it would be a challenge." Einar's attention was taken by another.

Finola ate little of the excellent meal and was glad when it was done. When the guests rose and ambled about the receiving room and terrace while the great room was cleared of its tables, she lost sight of her husband for a moment.

She knew the moment he was near. She could feel him though she didn't turn her head.

"You are little, wife. I would not like you to sicken."

"I won't," she said tartly.

"You fear nothing and have a strength that astounds, wife. Mayhap 'twould not be in my best interests to make you stronger."

She spun to face her spouse. "Enough. We should see to our guests."

"We have."

"We must move about the room."

"Your wondrous hair is as fiery as you."

"I'm more fiery than my hair, Einar Thorhallsson. 'Twould be well to remember that." His laughter squeezed her heart. How often they'd laughed and loved when they'd been on the island.

"Then you've become Icelandic."

"More than that, I'm Gael. We have more spirit than anyone." The chuckle at her back had her whirling. "Count Sigla! Good sir, I give you greeting and hope you supped well."

"I did." His smile widened. "I'm happy the Viking will soon learn his place, Lady Thorhallsson."

Finola laughed. "That would take a small miracle."

The count laughed. "Don't hide your smile, Einar. You must have great pride in such a spirited spouse."

"I do . . . and I'm careful."

"Faugh!"

Einar grinned. Count Sigla guffawed at her expletive.

Einar leaned down and kissed her cheek.

Finola flushed. "My husband can be unseemly."

Einar chuckled. "You must've learned that word from your cousin." He touched her cheek with one finger. "I'll explain . . . later."

Her flush deepened.

"Milady Thorhallsson, you must do me the privilege of dining at my home. I would give a fete to honor your vows. Would you wait until your family comes from Scotland?"

Finola smiled. "My gratitude. I fear 'tis not possible. My cousin won't be traveling for a time. She's enceinte, awaiting the birth of another as we speak."

The count looked puzzled. "I didn't know this. I've had pouches from Scotia. Nothing was mentioned of Lady Sinclair's confinement." He smiled. "I must chide my friend Sinclair. He's forgetful."

"Nor has he informed me," Einar said, his brow knitting. "I will send a ship to Sinclair land."

Finola nodded. "I would thank you."

"And you will include my good wishes . . . though Sinclair will have my ill will for not giving me his good news in the dispatches."

Finola laughed. "An absurdity, good sir. I know you think well of Sinclair, as he admires you."

"Thank you. He is an upstanding leader." He smiled back at her. When a passerby saluted him, he excused himself and moved away.

Einar was about to lead her to another group when an acquaintance tapped him, asking to be introduced to his wife. "Of course. Finola MacDonnell Thorhallsson, Angren Loose-mun of Oslo."

Finola was intrigued with the Viking and asked many questions. His craggy face would be wonderful to paint.

"What say you about the new bartering schedule, Einar Thorhallsson."

Finola enjoyed listening to her husband's discourse. He was knowledgeable, not pompous. Would she ever forget their time on the isle? She inched away from him, having the certainty it was the only way she could free herself from his aura. Making another move away from him, her hand fell to her side, noticing the slight bulge. Her fingers closed about the ring she'd removed on her wedding day. Corin's betrothal ring! She looked around for him. She had to give it to him. She had thought he may be one of the guests . . . but she hadn't asked. If truth were told, she'd almost wished he hadn't come. Then, she could've sent the ring to him by messenger. But, he was here.

Without thinking, she pulled it from her pocket, looking at it.

"Quite lovely. Didn't Corin of Antioch give it to you? I recall seeing it on your finger."

Finola stepped back, letting other guests mill between her

and her husband. "Yes, Count Sigla, he did. I want to return it to him."

"The ring is very eastern. I've seen another like it. A Tartar friend had one of similar brilliance. He long ago departed this life. Slain by brigands, so the story goes. His wife and child died with him. Very sad. I still miss him. A shrewd trader."

"You seem upset."

The Count nodded. "When I think of my friend, I get angry. The word was he was betrayed to the enemy."

Finola nodded. "I understand your ire. Treachery is the scoundrel's weapon."

"A false friend, I've been told."

Finola nodded, looking down at the ring. "I must give this to Corin."

"Let your husband do it."

"I'll not be cowardly." Her glance slid off Einar, who was deep in conversation with another Viking, back to Count Sigla. "I must do this. If you should see him—"

"I do. He's back against the wall. He has watched you for a long time."

"He feels betrayed, I'm sure." She shook her head. "I regret giving him pain. He was kind to me."

"He's a barterer, milady. He understands the maxim of reaching for something beyond his grasp. Not all we seek comes to us."

Her smile trembled. She touched the Count's arm. "You're kind. Will you excuse me, good sir?"

"Would you like my escort?"

"I have no need of it in my own house. But I thank you."

"Milady Thorhallsson. Well met."

"Corin, I'm uncomfortable with this, so I'll speak and be gone. I'm sorry for any hurt done to you. It can't be undone. Here." Stretching her arm its full length, she handed him the ring. "Count Sigla says it's a most unusual piece."

Corin took the ring, turning it in his hand. "I would make you a present of it, but it's been in my family—"

"No, no, you mustn't do that. I would be grieved if you tried to do so."

He took the ring, sliding it on his little finger. He smiled at her. "Could you walk with me on the terrace?"

Finola knew it would not be proper, but Corin had suffered pain and humiliation . . . because of her. She looked up at him and nodded. When he beamed, she felt less heavy hearted. Not just because she left him at the altar had she felt guilty, but because she was so relieved at not being his wife. He deserved more. "For just a moment."

"Don't do this because you feel guilty, milady. I don't blame you. 'Tis Thorhallsson—"

"We should set no blame, if you please."

Corin's lips twisted. "You I can, perhaps, forgive, milady. Thorhallsson will take time." He led her across a short space to tall doors, standing open to catch the breeze. The terrace was well lit with "figaro" lights.

She turned to smile at him, not far from the door. "Thank you for understanding."

"I don't. I just won't fight with you."

She nodded.

Corin took her hand, lifting it to his lips. "I've given you no remembrance for your nuptials. I will—"

"Nothing, please."

"I would like to—"

"What do you want to do?" The voice came out of the darkness.

Finola started.

Corin turned in one easy motion. "Thorhallsson. Don't you trust your wife with me?"

"I trust my wife." Einar moved to Finola's side, taking her hand and putting it on his arm. "Shall we join our guests, my love?" He'd not taken his eyes from Corin.

"Of course," Finola said, her husband's tension rippling under her fingers. It struck her how similar they were. Not in coloring. Corin's swarthiness contrasted with the lighter-visaged Viking. Their frames were similar. No wonder they'd been able to free themselves from the galleys. "Einar . . ."

"Yes." He didn't look away from his former friend.

"Corin holds no malice. I—"

"I do."

Agape, she stared up at her husband. "But there's no need—"

"Thorhallsson doesn't choose to listen, milady." Corin's voice was rough silk.

Finola felt Einar's rage vibrate under her hand. "Don't—"

"Be at peace, beloved." Einar's tone was as smooth and raw as Corin's.

Finola shivered. She stared from one to the other. They were gripped with fury. If they'd been a storm they would've flattened every olive tree in the garden. She felt burned by their rage. "You said something about our guests, Einar."

"I did. Well met, Antiochan." He turned, leading Finola from the terrace.

They paused just inside the great hall. Lyres, harps, flutes, drums picked out a lilting melody. Dancers swayed, dipped, swung apart, back together.

Finola took deep breaths, pretending to listen to the dance master's instructions. Einar, Corin. Friends once. Implacable enemies now.

"Shall we join them, Finola?"

She blinked. "Dancing?"

"Yes." Without waiting for another response, he led her into the set.

Others made room for them, smiling.

Finola couldn't blot the moments on the terrace from her mind, though she mastered the steps without too much concentration.

As they touched hands, she looked up into her husband's eyes. Like a spear in the heart, she wondered if she'd ever known him.

Einar leaned over her. "I would ask that you not see Corin."

They parted, moving in opposite directions.

When they came together, her hands were shaking, her face flushed. "You're ever quick to assume power over another."

"You're my wife."

"Yes." Why did he look so angry? "I've done nothing."

"I know." He caught her about the waist, swinging her in the air. Not traditional . . . in fact, improper.

"Einar!" She gasped, hearing the titters and outright mirth of those around them.

"Fear not, milady. Most would assume it an outlet for the pent-up passion of a bridegroom."

Fire rose in her, a suspicious quivering in her lower body. "You put me out of countenance, sir."

"Not so, wife. 'Tis only to show you my banked passion."

As he swung her again, she kept her eyes on him. As he was about to set her down, she let fly with one foot, catching him on the knee. It hurt her toe. Ample reward when he flinched.

Einar didn't pause. At the end of the set, he placed her on her feet, applauding with the other guests. When he bowed to her, the clapping increased.

"I might slay you, Viking," she said through her teeth, acknowledging her guests with a smile.

"You have a good kick, milady."

"Thank you." Her tone was honey sweet.

For the rest of the evening Einar never left her side.

42

A little thing indeed is a sweetly smelling sacrifice.
Judith

When she retired that night her head was whirling. Not even the back rub Dalia gave her took away her confusion.

"You'll sleep now, milady."

"Thank you, Dalia. Lie in on the morrow. Waiting up for me took your sleep time."

Dalia smiled, leaving the room.

Her candle was doused, she lay dozing, not stirring when she heard the door open. Dalia had forgotten something. In lazy fashion she looked to the door. Nothing. Surely she'd heard a sound.

"I'm over here, wife."

Spinning on the bed, she almost did a somersault. Mouth slack, she stared at the connecting door to Einar's quarters. "You! Why are you here?" Not once in almost five days since their nuptials had he come to her. Now he could with impunity! Faugh! "Go back."

"I'm your husband."

She pulled the covers up to her chin. "You can't come in my room. You haven't since we've married."

"You've had your time to settle, wife, to be alone, milady. 'Tis past time you slept with your husband."

"'Tis not done. Spouses don't sleep together. Women have their own rooms."

"You may come to mine."

"No."

"I'll stay here."

Finola spent the frantic seconds it took for him to cross the room to fabricate an excuse. Head injury. Fell when dancing. Sick to stomach. Ague. Palsy. Black humors. Possessed of demons.

"None of it will work, milady."

She glared at him. He moved into the shaft of moonlight coming from the lancet. She almost fell out of the bed. "You're unclothed!"

"I never wore anything when we loved on the isle."

"Cretin! Cyclops!"

"Two eyes, my love." He slipped beneath the bedcover, catching her under the arms, bringing her close. "And it pleases me to look upon you."

"Don't. You're only doing this to spite Corin," she blurted, risking his wrath. "I'll not be a pawn in bellicose games." She faltered but didn't look away.

"Not for all the vengeance in the world would I subject you to such, madam. There's no war in my heart when I want you. When I love you it will be because you want it as I do. We will mate in mutual desire. Beyond the bed we may scrap and battle. Not here."

She saw him take deep breaths, as though he forced his moves. He was gritting his teeth as he rose from the bed. He moved away from her. She couldn't smother the sob that broke from her.

He turned, gathering her up again. "Don't. I won't hurt you."

"You have." Her sobs deepened.

"No more, beloved. Your pain slices me." He kissed her tresses, each rivulet from her eyes. Desire to comfort overtook his towering passion. "Shh, little one. Sleep."

Her arms moved around his middle, not letting him leave.

"Release me, Finola," he said, his voice hoarse. "You

mustn't. I want to devour you now, kiss every part of you. I shake with the heat of you." He clamped his jaw and held her.

She kissed his chest, her mouth moving over his male nipples.

"Finola!"

"I didn't want to hurt you . . . or Corin."

"Thank you." Breath was forced from him.

She leaned back. "Einar." She let her fingers dance over his chest hair. "I thought you didn't want me. I tried not to want you."

"Did you?" He let his mouth rove over her hair, her eyes, her face, her neck. "Too long."

"Yes." She touched him again. He groaned. His hardness rubbed her belly. She curled into him, tightening her grip on his middle, pressing fingertips into his flesh. She looked up, letting her mouth reach for his. She kissed him for all the aching yesterdays, those lost moments when she thought him dead, for the tender mercy that'd reclaimed him, for not being able to bear letting anyone touch her but Einar Thorhallsson.

Tears coursed from her eyes. She was coming alive again, out of her cocoon. The release of grief, of anger, of rejection, angst and locked-up love, flowed from her eyes.

"Don't, beloved." His husky voice touched her as his lips were doing.

She ran her hands up his chest, over his shoulders, around his neck, as soft, satisfied sounds floated from her throat.

"Finola . . . I can't . . . I'm burning . . . I can't leave you." He enfolded her, slanting his mouth over hers in slow, melting hunger, his body beginning to throb as only she could make it.

"You drive me mad, Einar Thorhallsson." Helpless with yearning, he demolished her defenses. Her body, mind and spirit couldn't forget him, nor would they let her deny her need. His aroused body excited her, inflamed with her memory.

When he lifted his head, she was dazed, shaking, wanting. "Finola, do you really want this?"

Focusing on his words, she touched his cheek. "I didn't know you were alive."

Motionless, he stared at her. "I can't leave you."

"Don't." She leaned her head on his chest, as though it'd been moments ago they'd been on the isle, not harsh, abrasive weeks. "I would've helped you, Einar, had I known where you were." Fresh tears coursed her cheeks. "We looked and looked. No one knew what'd happened." A shaken sob escaped her. "Then a runner told Corin your body had been thrown into the Tiber."

"Did Corin question that?"

He'd hidden his menace, but she could hear it in the gentle tone. "He questioned everyone. He went himself to check. He didn't believe it. We were the only ones."

"Then he became betrothed to you."

"Yes. It was a protective action. I was alone. I couldn't stay with the Vikings. It went against culture and custom to do so."

"Yet you left your beloved Cup with my men."

She looked up at him, nodding. "Of course. I trusted them."

"Why marry?"

She sighed, her hands feathering up his chest to his neck, tightening. She shook her head, her long tresses cascading over his skin. "I told you. It was arranged by my guardians—"

"And yet this was not told to me when they commissioned me to look in on you?"

She was still. "I don't know. The Contessa said these contracts can be commissioned in secrecy. The principals not knowing until their signatures are required."

"And you think Sinclair and Princess Iona would handle it this way?"

Shaken, she bit her lip. "It's not like them, but—"

"Don't fret yourself. There's much we don't know. I'll find out everything."

"Yes," she breathed, blowing on his chest hairs.

"I want to love you."

"You're my husband."

His laugh was harsh. "I want more response than duty."

"So do I."

He chuckled against her neck. "You're beautiful, Finola MacDonnell Thorhallsson."

Much was unresolved between them. It didn't matter. She wanted his passion.

"I'm happy to be holding you, wife. Mayhap you won't sleep much this night." He chuckled. "I can be with you day and night now, milady."

"So you can." She couldn't catch her breath. His hands rubbed over her skin, making it blister with want. She was boiling with desire.

Rolling her on her back, he looked down at her. "Wife."

"Husband." They'd had so many missteps. She should fear him. She didn't. For a time they could be back on the island. A moment in time, theirs alone. Taken aback by his sensuousness, his open sexuality, his bold, unerring expertise in the art of love, she hesitated. Then he pulled her into the aura of love, and she forgot all else.

His mouth tormented, enticed, wooed hers, his tongue sliding over her lips, probing, touching, flicking at the dimple near the corner. His hands moved over her in constant building desire, tender, strong, urgent. Tantalizing, slow, his fingers tested, rubbed, inching toward the damp triangle of curls, then smoothing upward just under her breasts.

Titillated, out of breath, she moaned. The amalgam of delight and inhibition teetering on the brink of beauty. She wanted it. She'd be lost to Einar for all time. There'd be no turning back. She accepted. She fought it, her very resistance bringing them to an incredibly passionate precipice.

He blew in her ear. Barriers crashed. She reached for him, hunger in every gesture, her hands tugging at his chest hairs.

Breathing hard, his kiss became more demanding, his hands cupping her aching breasts but not touching the quivering nipples. He squeezed the flesh of her arms and shoulders.

Dying from desire, she clutched him. It'd been so long! When his tongue drove into her mouth, his hands moving over the nipples, she strained against him. Kneading, stroking, he brought her to an arching peak of emotion.

Restraint gone, they strove to pleasure each other.

Her hands flew over him, caressing, touching, opening to him.

He tore his mouth from hers. She groaned a protest. Then his mouth touched her breasts, sliding over the satin cream of skin, sucking on the nipples.

"Einar!"

Her keening cry brought a growl of pleasure from him.

Wild with sensation, she clung to him as his mouth moved between her breasts. Reaching her middle, he let his tongue invade her navel, imitating the rhythm they'd have in joining.

Moving lower, his tongue trailed over a hipbone.

Finola knew. How could she forget? Tense, her body beginning to writhe, she felt the building of the honey heat like none other. It captured her body, her spirit, her mind. "Einar," she breathed.

"Beloved."

Had he called her that again?

Lost in the sweet black wanting, his hand trailing over her legs as his mouth moved lower, she felt like flame. Then he was there, his tongue finding the hot message of her desire. Blinded by the flood of throbbing passion, she writhed closer wanting more ... more.

All strain left them. They were ready, wanting, eager.

His tongue entered, again and again, beginning the age-old cadence that had her calling his name.

He moved up and over her, his limbs tremoring. His hope of prolonging this first lovemaking in such a long time was shattered by her poignant giving.

Veins in his arms and neck stood out as he fought to restrain the ardor that'd overtaken him, that shook him to his toes. Nothing mattered but being part of her.

Easing into her warmth took all his forbearance. To bury himself in her and stay in that incredible sheath burned through him.

She arched her hips. "Einar."

At the whisper, he opened his eyes, looked down at her and was lost. This was no fevered manifestation. Finola was here. She was his wife. Her fiery hair was bronze in the moonlight that streamed from the open lancet, reflecting in the flame shadows from the fireplace.

"Please." Finola ran her hands over him. Blood thundered from one to the other. Want exploded.

He moved into her.

As aroused as he, she shifted her weight to take more of him. Holding him, pulling him to her, she writhed.

"Finola!"

"I'm here."

He caught her closer, lifting her hips to join more with him, thrusting into her, even as she drove back at him.

In the most explosive moment of his life, he knew he loved this woman some said betrayed him. It should've frozen him. Instead, it fired him. He took her, as she took him. So satisfying was the joining, the spill of seed, they laughed and gasped at their culmination and the wonder of it all. Cleansing the hurt, leaving peace and joy, they embraced.

Einar collapsed on her, bracing himself so as not to crush her. "I'm still on fire for you," he told her, his chest heaving. He moved to one side, catching her close, still connected. "You are all of passion, wife."

"As you are."

Sleep overtook them. They smiled when closing their eyes.

Was it minutes or a full turn of the hourglass? Finola didn't know. She'd woken. She moved clear of Einar so as not to waken him. Restless yet serene, she moved down the path of moonlight to the lancet, pushing against the casement, looking out and sighing. Her response had been total. She loved him. He was her husband. He thought her treacherous, but she didn't regret the joining. She'd reveled in it.

Wide awake, she looked back at the bed. She could only make out his outline on the sleeping platform.

He moved. The moonlight caught him as the coverlet slipped below his waist. A beautiful man. He'd been gentle, his lovemaking more wonderful than before. She'd not dreamed of such delights. Life could be bittersweet if he never came to trust her.

Shaking her head, her mind in turmoil, she was too churned to sleep. Rushing across the room, she pushed her feet into soft boots, draping a wrap about her shoulders. She moved to the door. Locked!

Irked, she glanced about her, noting the door to his chamber. Was that barred, too?

Unlocked! She opened it, the oiled hinges masking any sound. His anteroom. She closed the door behind her. That hall door was locked. Grimacing, she passed through Einar's room. She forgot the door when she noted the flickering sconces on the huge cedarwood plank used for a desk. She approached, not really curious, just at loose ends.

Bonds of debenture issued by consortia strewed the surface. They allowed members to purchase commodities on their good name, pay back the consortium with little or no interest. Among the papyri and scrolls were other missives. Finola sighed.

She noted the rolled leather. She knew what it was at once. Einar's scroll from his mother. She fingered it. The wax was broken. Had he read his mother's last testament to him? Taking a deep breath, she hefted it, took the leather-bound chair behind the desk, and arranged the sconce for better light. Settling back, she removed the scroll from the covering. Finola stretched it between two bronze weights, leaning over to read the diary of a woman—not knowing that the words would change her life and all of those around her.

43

From the memory of Griselda, daughter of Gjoll, I put this down for you, My dear son, Einar. My legacy is a tale of truth

—somewhere in the wilderness land of the Bulgars, bounding the great Volga, Vistula and Danubis rivers . . . 1034 Anno Domini

I remember it all. How could I forget. I left a life behind, my son. I shall try to explain.

At first it was a blur of misery. I was gone from you and your father. Then it changed. But I get ahead of myself. I shall begin at my clearest memory.

The diaphanous drapes swayed like the beautiful birds my captor kept in the walled gardens. Sometimes I felt mesmerized by the movement, lost in a nirvana that had no name.

"Milady, you've not eaten. The master will be angered."

At first their goodwill made me angry.

"Take it away. I, Griselda of Icelandia, will not eat." I didn't even watch the maid leave. They could melt from a room without a sound.

I had my own garden. Often I sat there, alone. The moon and sun said it was spring. It came early in the east. That day a cool breeze had sprung up from the north, sweeping down upon the river, that strange, twisting cascade of

cataracts my captor called Danubis. We didn't call it that
in Icelandia, nor do many peoples from the west and
north. It is of the Ister I speak, as the Greeks have called
the waterway for centuries. Now, in these modern times,
some of our boatmen, even, refer to it as the Danube, a
Celtic twisting of the Latin.

I have come to hate waterways, my son. I, a daughter
of seafarers. River, stream, ocean have become my nemeses, my foes. How can a daughter-in-law of the great Viking
Chief Thorfinn of Icelandia, daughter to Gjoll, who'd commanded an eastern fleet for the patriarchy of Antioch, hate
the sea? You would ask yourself that, my son, because
you love it so. How can I, daughter to the woman of
Antioch called Glynis, spawn of the family who'd had care
of the Cup of Antioch, and used the sea to make their
fortune, have such a great antipathy for the sea? It kept
me from you, beloved Einar. How often I'd dream of you,
recalling how I'd relate to you the tales of the great storyteller Snourri. Did you think me dead all that time, my
son? I, who had been wife to Gar, chief warrior and adopted
son to Thorfinn? Was I not mother to Einar, who would
someday inherit and earn great wealth in the world of
trade and be a warrior for Icelandia? I would think of you
so often as you approached two full turns of the sun in
age. My arms ached to hold my child. My heart called out
to you.

For many years I pondered writing this letter, copying
the scraps of journal I'd put down in the east to transcribe
for you. My coward's heart told me not to bare my soul.
My Viking soul told me I must. My life is shortening. I
know this. I want you to know everything. Birgit will give
you this when the time is right.

I'm not proud that I tried more than once to end my
life when I was in the east. I was guarded too well. Mayhap
'twas not the Christian way to do so. But how can a Viking
live captive? Ergo to choose to go from a heinous life
could not be a sin. Over and over I told myself this. I stole
a blade to cut my wrists. It was found. A scimitar left

behind would've been useful. To jump from the lancets was thwarted.

Many times I was chided by Atoli himself, leader of the pagans, that I must have a care for my life because he valued me. His concern made me uneasy. Shouldn't I kill myself before he tired of me and threw me to his men to be ravished? How could I trust him though he treated me with sweetness and care? Vikings can not be duped by such ploys.

Six wanings and waxings of the moon I was at his holding. I knew they must think me dead in Reykjanes. I was a lost woman anyway because each night Atoli took me to his bed.

The servants hovered over me.

"Milady, would you like a libation, cool water of roses?"

"Nothing, thank you."

Often when I looked out upon the sparkling serpentine called Danubis, I cursed it. The misbegotten water had brought me to captivity.

There were regrets. If only I hadn't accepted my mother's importunings to visit Antioch, to look upon the artifact that'd belonged to my family for centuries. The Cup of Antioch. Many in my mother's family thought it had restorative powers. Groups made annual pilgrimages to pay homage to the relic that the Savior might've used . . .

Viking ships had brought me from Reykjanes to the east down from the wild Sea of Norway to the North Sea, thence to the great inland sea, Mediterranis, then to the Euxine Sea, called by some the Marmora. During that journey that was sometimes rough, often smooth, I never thought of myself as captive of the seas. Being a captive so long has increased my hatred of my foe, water. My life could be forfeit at any time. Why had I been kept alive so long?

I was a fool to think that my mother and I would be safe in a convent among women who'd taken the sacred veil. The good nuns prayed to God, day and night, behind their safe walls in the glorious city of Antioch.

My mother's mission and mine had been a family pilgrimage, to pray with the sisters, to see and revere the Cup of Antioch that one of our antecedents had taken to the great city as testimony to the Faith. It'd been our ancestor's wish that a member, or members, of the family pay homage to the holy Cup each year. That the Cup had belonged to Saint Peter and had been used by Christ, I'm not sure I believe. I've accepted it has mystical powers, though it doesn't help me.

Another interruption.

"Will you not speak with me, milady? Our lord demands to know how you feel."

"I'm fine."

I soon sank into my reverie that centered about my capture.

Not once had mother and I been fearful, because we were in a holy place, praying and doing good works.

Even when we heard the muted clashes of weapons, most continued to pray. Who would disturb us? When the doors burst open we were shocked. Brigands, armed to the teeth, who laid about them as though they slaughtered cattle, not holy women, were amongst us in an instant. Some, like me, were captured. Your grandmother was killed at her prayers. I have asked about other captives and was told they'd been sold.

After a time I began to accept my fate. It seemed like forever I'd been at Atoli's holding. I knew I would remain until death, which I expected each day. Would I've been able to chart a course to where I was kept if I could've sent a message? I doubt it. By now no one would be looking for me, I was sure.

My son, I became with child, and knew that I could no longer attempt to escape or do harm to myself. Such a shock. Your own dear father, Gar, had not been able to plant his seed until seven years after our vow-taking. The heathen Atoli, who paid lip service to Allah and gave allegiance to nothing but his strong arm and mind, had held me but three wanings and waxings of the sun before I knew I was with child. How strange.

Do not be shocked, my son. I hold nothing back.

When Atoli approached me, his blunt words astounded me. I knew the women would've told him that I'd called not for bindings in my menses.

"Wildflower, look at me."

He had husky, gravelly sound to him, but he was always gentle, and he had been from the first day. I'd expected disdain in those black eyes. Instead there was respect. I'd expected ravishment, beatings, and there weren't any. He'd confused me with his serenity. He'd treated me with reverence when we were together and alone. He never sickened or repelled me. Instead he'd shown me a wonder between man and woman that I hadn't guessed. I stopped being ashamed of my body and its response. He was a heathen, yet he'd been nothing but good to me. I put my past behind me.

"Look at me, my blossom."

I looked up at him and saw love. I was as short of breath as he. His eyes were always soft for me. A barbarian? Mayhap he was. Not with me. Neither did he raise his hand nor voice to me. I'd fought him at first. Still he didn't retaliate. I couldn't hate him. There'd been no punishment or ill treatment. I gave up longing for Icelandia, my precious Gar, and you, my beloved son Einar. He would be walking . . . talking. I wouldn't see it. My heart squeezed with longing.

"Don't, my wildflower! Think not of past days. Your life is here with me. The women tell me you've missed your monthlies. That you've not called for the wrappings that would keep you clean."

My son, I was not used to his blunt way of speaking, though I speak so to you in this letter. No Viking, Briton or Scot would've spoken so . . . to any woman.

"Don't fear to tell me, Wildflower."

Atoli couldn't say my name, hence he called me Wildflower. "I'm with child, Atoli."

He fell to his knees when I said the words, pressing his face to my middle, his shoulders shaking, his hands grasping me in tender embrace. He told me our love was blessed. He called me beloved. I couldn't push him away.

I embraced him, touching his uncovered head, bare of the djellabah that usually adorned it. How much shorter their hair was than ours. I accepted that the rest of my life would be among the Bulgars because I would bear the heir to the powerful Atoli.

When he looked at me, I was both sad and peaceful. Sorrow filled me at the thought of not seeing you or my Gar again. Yet, I couldn't help the rush of happiness knowing I would have another child.

Atoli treated me with reverence. "I will teach you to love me, beloved." His embraces were both cherishing and exciting. "And I will make you my wife with much riches, beloved."

I felt honored . . . but hopeless. My world had crumbled as another was beginning. It shocked me that I didn't find his touch distasteful. Rather, his embraces made me feel . . . womanly. I had begun to love my captor. Unshed tears burned my eyes.

A full turn of the sun and seasons brought me another lusty son who ate at my breasts greedily, thumping my skin as he sucked. My new child was all beauty, a dark-haired boy with my deep-blue eyes, just as yours are. He had all my love, because to me there would be no other. You were deep in my heart, dear son, though I spent many contented hours with my new husband and child. Atoli was most attentive, not spending much time away from us. He showered us with gifts. He had married me according to his Muslim beliefs and put aside all his kadim and other wives. I was astounded and touched.

One day he told me he had to go among the hill people to trade and barter.

"They are coming to me, Wildflower." He laughed out loud and kissed me. "I will take our son to show them their future leader." He laughed when I was alarmed, reassuring me that there were many guardians for him and his son. "I and my son will be with you this evening, beloved."

That evening it grew late, I tried not to fret. Even when I heard a commotion I was not overset. Atoli and his men always arrived with great noise and fanfare.

When I heard the whistle of arrows, the clash of lance and scimitar, I armed myself. A Viking death! I no longer sought it. Were my husband and child safe?

Taking a knife and short sword, I prepared myself. I knew how to fight, taught as a Viking child would be. I prayed for myself, for my child and Atoli. Facing the ornately scrolled teak doors that'd been brought by caravan from the Indies, I took deep breaths.

The door burst open. A young archer fired. Not even the quick action of his comrade stayed his arm. It struck me in the head. I became insensate.

I heard the Viking voices from a long distance, incapable of answering them.

"Fool! She is our lady. If you've killed her, your life is forfeit."

"She lives. See."

They called on Wotan to help me. I wanted them to release me so that I could find my babe, my beloved second son. Then the blackness took me.

Many turns of the glass I slept. When I woke they spoke to me in Icelandic. I couldn't answer. On the ship was a slave who'd cared for me and my child. "Atoli . . . our son?"

"All dead, milady," Nasra, as she was called, answered me. "As soon we'll be."

I fell into the blackness again, not coming round for days. By then we were in cooler climes. I was told Nasra had died. I was alone, grief stricken among my Vikings. They thought I ailed because of mistreatment. How could I enlighten them? How could I tell them that I'd lost a husband and son, both of whom I loved?

I said nothing. I let the knowledge of my life with the

Bulgars die with Nasra. What would it accomplish to speak of my husband and son when both were dead?

Many moons later a larger Viking ship met our fleet of four. Gar was there to take me in his arms, to weep with me, to love me. I couldn't tell him that some of my tears were for my dead babe and the man who'd loved me. Lost forever. Atoli who'd loved me well. Tariq our beloved black-haired son with my blue eyes.

So, my son, Einar, you know the tale of truth, of when I resided in the east. I'm gone to join Gar, Atoli and my son, Tariq. I loved you. I loved them. Find love, my son. 'Tis my heartfelt wish for you. And forgive your mother, if you can.

Griselda

44

It was ordained at the beginning of the world that certain signs should prefigure certain events.

Cicero

This was the day of the grandest art exhibit in the world! So said Romans. Artists and their wares would come from everywhere. East, west, north and south would be represented by their best painters, sculptors, artisans. From hot, dark Afrique, the snowy tundras, mountains that touched the clouds, caravans came, people on foot, some traveling as long as five months. Talent stretched across the world descended on Rome for three days of judging.

Arbiters would stand beside the work they represented. The show had been an annual happening since the Circus Maximus had ended its fighting days. No longer wrestlers and gladiators battled. Now artist and artisan vied for the laurel wreaths that would be given to those most worthy. The commissions that could follow the judging could make one wealthy.

Guidons, designating country or habitat, flapped in the breeze. The sun was copper bright.

Finola was nervous. "You've brought all my works from Palazzo di Marchi. When did you do this? How did you manage?"

Einar shrugged. "A simple chore, wife. Be at peace."

"I am." She shook her head, unthreading her fingers. "It just amazes me that you were able to convince the Contessa ... Why are you smiling?"

"Vikings can be persuasive."

She should've pursued it, asked him what he meant. At the moment she was too anxious to care.

Vikings, including her husband, saw to the placement of the art.

"You've done well, wife. Your works are varied, distinguished and beautiful," Einar told her, standing at her side.

"I did little else when I thought you ... gone."

He leaned down and kissed her cheek, smiling when she reddened. "It's not like you to be so quiet."

She spread her hands. "I ... It's all so grand. I hadn't envisioned this. So many entrants, and spectators." She shook her head, wiping her damp hands on a square of linen.

He looked around him. " 'Twill be filled soon. Then the judges come and a coterie of spectators who've paid to follow them—"

"Is this true?"

"Yes. There are some who're so anxious to hear the comments of the judges, they pay drachmas to trail them."

"It sounds silly."

"You smile. Good." He kissed her fingertips.

All at once the cacophony of voices faded to a murmur. The judges entered in soft flowing robes, reminiscent of ancient Roman garb.

The judging was slow ... interminable ... painstaking. The sun rose high. Drops of perspiration appeared on many faces.

Einar arranged a shelter, wide enough to enclose her works, deep enough to hold the Vikings if they chose. It was open on the sides and supported by eight poles. "Drink this." When she balked, he grinned. "Not wine, milady. Just the fresh pressed juice of grape to refresh you." He all but forced her to nibble on biscuits at midday.

"You'll be too thin to hug, milady," Bela said.

Vikings stared at him, slack jawed. None should dare such intimacy with the Thegn's bride.

Einar's brows rose. When Finola laughed, he whirled to face her, grinning. He angled a look at his friend, who grinned back.

Tariq sipped his chilled wine. "Milady, you're surrounded by barbarians and heathens."

Finola shook her head. "I'm with friends."

Her simple statement seemed to rattle Bela and Tariq. The Vikings nodded, looking fierce, their glances at her warm and protective.

Einar leaned over her. "Again you ensnare my men. Kindly don't wage war against me. I don't relish standing alone against mine."

Finola's laughter pealed. Several looked her way admiringly. "You chase my angst from me, husband. I'm glad of it."

"You have no reason for concern. I've already arranged to buy many of your wares, milady wife. Mayhap I'm not a connoisseur, as the Duc de Lyons. I do know worth and salability . . . and what I admire."

Finola was aghast. "Einar! You mustn't. I would give them—"

"No!" Darg responded before his lord. "We are barterers, milady. You must be. Only the highest bidder gets your wares. I'll see to it."

"But . . ."

"Darg's right," Einar said, eyeing Bela and Tariq when they chuckled.

The afternoon waxed hotter. Without the canopy, they would've been uncomfortable.

"You must be bored, Einar. You needn't stay."

"I have no desire to leave."

"It's too hot for Vikings."

"Don't be worried. You've done well."

As the coterie of judges moved closer, she tried to smile, not looking at them. But again and again her eyes were drawn to the white-robed men.

Then the judges were there, as the sun waned. They looked, muttered and were gone.

Perspiration beaded her upper lip. "Seems fruitless. We should go."

"We stay." Einar gestured to a man wielding fans. At once the man moved behind the enclosure and began the movement.

"That's good," Finola said, smiling her thanks.

The blast of the trumpet cut through the sultry air. Silence. Then a speaker went to the podium. Though his voice would carry in the well-designed amphitheater, there were callers to echo his words.

When Finola heard her name, she rose, hand at her throat, speechless. She sank back, overwhelmed.

Einar lifted her up, kissing her. "The very small one I liked so much ... that I've purchased. The cutting of Antioch. You've won in your class. And your paintings have honorable mention. You've triumphed, wife."

"Yes, yes." She laughed and cried when the stolid Vikings hugged her, when Tariq and Bèla sounded their war cries.

When they left the Circus Maximus, Finola had two laurel wreaths and some ribbons. The household of Thorhallsson would celebrate.

When they rode together in the dray, Einar held her hand. "Did it help to wash away the pain when you did the cutting of Antioch?"

She nodded. "I needed to mark it in my life and put it aside." She blinked.

"What?"

"I've just recalled. I did another like it that day, when I'd just entered the market. Just a sketch. It was lost in the melee. She shook her head. "I've not thought of it until this moment."

"Perhaps your recollection will let you repeat the work."

"I don't know. I could try."

That evening she was feted by what she termed her family. Einar, his Vikings, Gar, Reric, Dalia, Bela and Tariq. Einar never left her side. She was happy.

That night they made passionate love, as always.

Had more of their barriers fallen?

* * *

They talked more. Every night they made torrid love. If now and then there was constraint, they fought it.

"You will have commissions. Will you accept them?"

"I . . . I hadn't thought. In our world women don't work, yet you ask if I would."

"It's your choice. You're an artist, deserving of praise. You're trained in your craft."

"I am. I think I would like to do some." That he would support such stunned her. Einar Thorhallsson had too many facets. She loved all of them.

"Good. Charge accordingly."

"Viking canniness?" She laughed.

He nodded, smiling.

A treasured moment. She looked forward to their discourses, more and more. Her husband was intelligent. He had knowledge of the world and differing mores and tongues.

She was thinking of her versatile spouse when she sat down before her palette. The sunny day gave good light from the north. Most other members of the household were on various errands. It was quiet. She let her hand lead her head, as it was wont to do. Antioch! It'd risen in her mind.

The studio fashioned for her by her husband off their suite of rooms seemed to echo with the sights and sounds of that fateful day. Her hand flew. Time and time again she took up a fresh charcoal. The noise, the bustle, the colorful tents and enclosures of the Antioch market rattled through her head to her hand. In a haze of memory and the need to transfer it to the stretched material in front of her, she lost track of time.

The cramp in her hand, arm and back had her pausing, taking a deep breath. As though she'd just descended from a mountain, her heart was beating a wild tattoo.

She focused on the stretched hemp. "Unbelievable," she murmured to herself. She'd sketched the market the same way she'd done that day. She'd not lost the image. Mayhap because of the trauma in the earth shaking and her abduction.

The child was there in the foreground as before. And the

man ... Corin! Surely that wasn't right. No! She'd superimposed his image over ...

Memories crowded in, stirring through her. Confusion had her frowning. Long moments she studied the rough sketch. She closed her eyes. The image jumped behind them. The child. Corin.

Jumping off her painting stool, she strode up and down the room. She'd talk to Einar. No, he'd see something in it that wasn't there. Corin? No. Too bold. Contessa di Marchi. Of course. She'd discuss it with her. Disgruntled as she might be about Finola's marriage, she was still a most pragmatic person. Who better able to help her solve the riddle of seeing Corin that day in the market? Could it've been an omen? Surely not. Mayhap nothing? More than likely.

She changed into a blue undergown, with a saffron overdress, loomed so fine it glinted like cloth of Cathay. She was determined to discuss her quandary, her unsettling reactions to the painting with the Contessa. Adjusting her kirtle woven with silver and gold, unembellished with gems, as was customary in daytime garb, she exhaled, feeling better now that she had a plan. The cloche headdress was loose and fringed about her face in azure lace.

She rang for Dalia. When she didn't arrive, Finola went to find her.

The house, which usually bustled, was quiet. Hesitating, she went to Einar's study, knocked, then entered. "Tariq?"

He smiled. "You're disappointed. I beg your pardon, milady."

He'd been seated at Einar's desk, rising at her entrance. "Please call me Finola. I call you by your given name." She felt like an intruder.

"You seek Einar?" He came around the desk, letting the scroll he'd been perusing roll up.

She had the sudden sensation she'd walked in on something. Had that been the scroll from Einar's mother he'd been reading? It looked the same. If it was, how had he felt? Had he drawn the same conclusion she had? She still hadn't broached the subject to Einar. Their personal life was progressing. She didn't want to throw oil upon the fire of his temper. If he considered her probing into his privacy, there could be strong words between them. She treasured the peace and joy of their union. Even though one day she must face him with what she'd found that night, it would have to be the right moment. She'd do nothing to spoil their growing closeness.

"Could I help you, Finola?"

She blinked, his sharp query pulling her from her reverie. "I was looking for Dalia."

"Ah, I can help you. She's gone to market with the major-domo. She was delighted to have her own drachmas to purchase some fabric."

"Oh. I should've gone with her."

"No, Finola. I think she liked the freedom of choice, of doing her own shopping."

Finola nodded. "I understand."

Tariq smiled, looking down once at the scroll, tapping it, then looking up again. "Einar went down to meet some ships arriving on the tide."

Finola smiled. "There'll be news from Scotia."

"You want to hear from the lovely princess."

"Yes." Her smile widened. "You have no idea how beautiful she is, Tariq. Beyond imagination."

"Then she must resemble you." He smiled. "I don't mean to embarrass you, Finola. Surely you know you have wondrous good looks." Her sudden confusion had him shaking his head. "Thorhallsson must be slower than I thought."

"Tariq! I must not tarry. If you will excuse me." His words embarrassed her. She'd never considered beauty a word connected with her, though her husband had called her beautiful many times.

"You wish to go out?"

She nodded.

"I'll accompany you, Finola. Einar would want you chaperoned."

"Thank you."

In a matter of minutes Tariq was able to get a public conveyance. The open-sided drays weren't comfortable, but they made as much progress as a horseman through the everlasting glut of carts, pedestrians, runners and milling people on every *strada* in Rome.

"Sometimes it would be more efficient to walk," Finola said, glad the curtains were hooked to the top and they had some air.

"Coaches are fashioned better in the east, Finola. The Italos have a poor idea of machinery."

"You're becoming western in your contempt of others' ways."

Tariq's lips twisted. "True." He glanced at her. "Einar has married a wise woman."

"I doubt you'd settle for less."

"I would. Fat, saucy, one who nods her head to all I say. That would be my choice."

Finola shook her head. "It doesn't fit."

"I'm a Bulgar from the east. At least I was raised by the Bulgars."

Finola took a deep breath. "What of your mother?"

His glance skewed toward her. "I know little of her. Why do you ask?"

She'd felt his stare like a knife. "Your blue eyes. Is your name a common one in the east?"

"Not uncommon. A family name . . . so I was told. Your interest in me intrigues me, Finola."

"We're here. Palazzo di Marchi."

"So we are."

Before the carriage man could blow his horn for entry, the gateman saw Finola and waved. He left his cubicle, turning the wheel that opened the tall metal barriers bearing the di Marchi emblem.

"Guardo, my best to your family."

"I thank thee, milady."

Then the wagon carried them up the drive to the portico.

Tariq was helping Finola from the carriage when the wide double doors opened and the majordomo appeared.

Finola greeted him, surprised when he bowed low. He'd

barely acknowledged her when she lived there. Had the Thorhallsson name and gold such profound effect?

"Well met, Milady Thorhallsson and Lord Tariq."

"Now I'm a lord. Wonders," Tariq whispered to her.

She smothered a laugh.

45

Once harm has been done, even a fool understands it.

Homer

The black-caped woman stood at the end of the garden, looking around her before she let the well-oiled door fall shut. No one else had a key. The peephole in it allowed her to check that others were not spying. None must know. Rome, at dusk, was intriguing and dangerous. She welcomed the cover of the foliage, the swaying shadows.

She'd left her comfortable home for this meeting with the usual excuse. Roman baths were salubrious, their mineral waters massaged her back. To all who cared to look, she'd walked to the end of the drive where she would hail a dray. She never took her own conveyance. At the curve of the drive, hidden from both the palazzo and the gate, she took a narrow path to the back of the holding, through trees and brush and out the rear gate. None but her used the way or the key.

Today, she'd not use the baths, though she needed them. Years back an inflammation of the chest had given her intermittent pain. Living in warmer Rome had been a boon. Her doctor had ordered the baths. One or two days a month she had the meeting instead.

In the grayish predarkness, she stepped carefully, not wanting to use a torch. At the far end of the garden was the gate. She opened it, looked left and right. The *vicolo* was all but deserted. She crossed to the other side, opening a wooden gate there. It was her property though few knew it. She closed it behind her and proceeded down a familiar path.

"You're still very cautious ... and, of course, able," a voice said in her ear.

She turned to the left. "And you still move quieter than a serpent of the pharaoh. Do we dally here?"

"Come inside. Even the stones have ears in Rome."

She let her hand move down his tunic until it touched the bulge beneath. She smiled.

"Yes, I'm ready, lovely one, as you are, I'm sure."

Passing down another tunnel of stone, they came to an iron door. He put a key in one lock; hers went into the one above it. The door swung open.

The opulence might've given them pause if they hadn't been used to it.

He leaned down, taking her mouth. "I like mixing business and pleasure."

"I admire your business acumen." Her smile widened when he nipped her ear.

"We didn't start as lovers. I'm glad our business led us to it, milady."

"As I am." She turned to him. "What name will you use when we meet the others?"

"Today, I am Aran of the Caucasus." He kissed her again, his hand going to her breast.

"Business first."

"Of course."

"Have you figured how we'll get the artifact?"

"I have plans ... not just for retrieval of it, but also for vengeance." He ground his teeth. "The one responsible for the years of anguish will die. I will have avenged my mother and father's death. I've sworn an oath."

"My vow is no less hot."

He nodded. "It will be done."

Her hand reached for him, squeezing. "I can salve your fury."

"Do." His mouth twisted, even as he caught her in his arms.

Sweet revenge could wait.

46

Every man's work shall be made manifest for the day shall declare it, because it shall be revealed by fire.
Paul 3:13

Finola rose to her foot. "We've waited too long. Her meeting holds her. I'll come another day." Annoyance creased her features. "Why didn't Francisco tell us she'd be overlong in her meeting?"

Tariq rose, shrugging. "He just said he was to keep you here because she wanted to see you."

Finola shook her head. "We've tarried over time—"

"Thorhallsson will think I've taken you captive. That—"

"So he will." The Contessa swept into the room, bowing as she moved. "I cannot tell you how grieved I was to hear you'd been waiting. That fool of mine never told me you were here. He's been dismissed."

Lips parted, Finola stared. "Dismissed? Francisco? He's been with you so—"

"He's been with the di Marchi family since boyhood." The Contessa's mouth tightened. "I'll not stand for inefficiency. He's gone." She spread her hands. "I understand if you wish to leave. First join me in a libation of forgiveness."

Tariq frowned, looking around him. "Mayhap we should come another time—"

"No, no, please, I'm devastated. Indulge me."

Tariq eyed Finola. His mouth was a tight slash. He went to the Contessa, holding out a chair for her. "Very well. One drink. I will get the refreshments . . . since no one will hear your summons."

Their hostess looked stricken, then pointed to a small table holding a tray, intricately carved gold goblets and a matching carafe. "We'll have wine. Then I'll talk to the chef about food—"

"No, we didn't come to dine, milady. I wanted to ask you about . . . Corin."

Startled, the Contessa inclined her head. "Corin of Antioch? I think he's left Rome, Finola. He saw no reason not to proceed to the bartering on the Volga. I think he intended to travel with Sigla."

Finola bit her lip. "I didn't know."

Tariq hefted the tray and brought it to the women. "Sigla's departure surprises me. Thorhallsson had dealings with him."

The Contessa shrugged. "He's a very busy man with interests far and wide. I imagine he tarries not in one place too long."

Tariq was still, then nodded. He poured thimbleful amounts of the heavy fruit wine, so popular with Romans in the afternoon.

The three toasted.

Tariq sipped his.

"I can see our Roman brew is not to your taste," the Contessa remarked.

Tariq shrugged, finished his. "Perhaps too thick a brew."

Finola sipped hers, agreeing with him. She was glad there was little in the goblet.

"So, Finola, in some way may I aid you in Corin's absence?"

"Thank you, Contessa. I wondered how long you've known him." She coughed. The brew slipped down easily enough, but the flavor was not to her liking. "I painted the marketplace in Antioch . . . the day I met . . . my spouse. The painting was lost when I was taken by Albai." She licked her dry lips. Her throat felt tight. "I began to re-create that picture. One of the persons . . . in it . . . was . . . Corin—"

"Who?" Tariq stared at Finola, then down at the goblet. He glanced at the Contessa, then tried to rise. "What's this?" He glared at her. "What've you done?"

"Not much." She gazed at the sagging Finola. "Tell me about Corin . . . and the Cup of Antioch."

"What?" Finola took deep breaths. "The Cup of Antioch . . . is . . . with the Vikings. You . . . know that. We should leave. I'm . . . unwell."

Tariq staggered to his feet. "Poison! You've put something in the wine."

"No." The Contessa shook her head, not moving. " 'Twas always there." She placed her untouched goblet on the table next to her, eyeing the two slumped over. She clapped her hands.

Two burly men appeared.

"You know where to take them. Quickly. Quietly."

It took both to lift Tariq. A third carried Finola.

The Contessa waited until they'd left, then strode to her study. "Einar Thorhallsson, my written words will bring you. Then the circle will be complete."

47

He has not acquired a fortune; the fortune has acquired him.
Bion

Cymbal and lyre set up the rhythm for the undulating dancers, draped in the diaphanous cloths of the east. The young and supple dancers would've done credit to the finest seraglio. If some of their rhythmic motions seemed too studied, perhaps the dilated pupils, their glazed orbs would be the reason. None complained or cried hysterically after being given the poppy nectar, and they were rarely discarded until the need for the poppy sent them into throes and hysteria.

Those they entertained were not from the highest order of man.

Bela was a lackey, a servant dressed in the drab garb of an Italo slave. He found it enlightening to hear all and see all. He didn't have to search the room to know that others loyal to Thorhallsson were there. He passed food and drink, listening.

"That one is a rare find." Albai pointed, tossing his gold goblet on the table. "Fill it!"

Bela smothered his anger at seeing the Tartar, murderer of many of his people, captor of the good lady belonging to Thorhallsson.

"I'm glad you find the entertainment pleasing," his host said, signaling for more wine.

Bela rushed to obey the one he recalled from Duc de Seigne's soiree. The Great One hadn't noticed him since he'd been a servant that night as well. He hovered behind the speakers.

"One of the older ones . . . and the youngest. I'll take those." Albai pointed to the dancers, licking his lips, belching, and making references to what he had planned for the girls.

Bela, used to such as Albai, still had to stem a shudder. Better the females be garroted now than be subject to the Tartar. He listened.

"What taste you have, my friend."

Albai nodded, not seeming to notice the irony. "We have business. You were to reclaim property of mine."

"It's been done."

Bela saw how the Great One's face contorted. His plan went beyond the property spoken of, it delved to the home of Beelzebub. Grief and anger tore him apart.

"The Cup is here?"

Bela stiffened. They referred to the artifact held by the Vikings that'd been shown to him.

"Not yet. It will be brought to you."

"Then give me the dancers until the Cup is brought." Albai stumbled to his feet, belching. "I would have sport."

"Last time your sport killed one of the dancers," the host said, his words sharp.

Albai shrugged. "Some have to die that the better of us live. I need sport. I will have it. You can get others if necessary." His eyes fixed on his host. "Do not put me off."

"I've not done that."

Bela backed behind the curtains. The fury between the two was palpable. 'Twould not serve Thorhallsson if it erupted before all was in readiness. He took deep breaths, eyeing his surroundings, the bustling attendants paying him little mind as they scurried to their chores. Soon. Bela leaned toward the opening in the curtains.

Albai tossed his cup, striking an attendant. "And I say you've put me off. That Cup has cost me much. The red-haired beauty and the slaves escaped, taking the relic with them." He banged himself on the chest, bringing cautious scrutiny from the other guests. "Gregor, my best eunuch, had to be disemboweled. Worse, I lost some of my precious steeds. My babies have not been returned to me. I will have recompense."

"Vengeance is on my mind also, my friend. Be patient. We'll both gain what we wish."

Bela could see behind the smile. The Great One would rid himself of the raging Tartar when he had the opportunity. His skin prickled with danger. It thudded through the room like a drum. He didn't fear for Thorhallsson. He had his Vikings. Where was the Bulgar and Milady Thorhallsson?

"How is it that the red-haired beauty is important to you? She must be given to me. I'll not change my mind."

"We will discuss it."

"No! You may be trade associate of Alp Arsian, the great caravaner thief, and a member of consortium. I, too, hold power, Bulgar."

"I know this."

How the Great One grinds his teeth. That he doesn't smite the Tartar is a small miracle. Bela had seen much in his life. He put little credence on evil. The Tartar made him shudder with disgust. For him, the greatest sport would be dismembering a man and listening to his screams, or tearing a woman apart with his man's root, getting his black joy as she screeched. Bela could fight, and had since boyhood, wreaking violence on the enemy. He didn't stomach attacking the defenseless. Honorable Bulgars were men who didn't need such sport. His eyes slipped to the Great One. Not melting silver was as hot as the hatred in his eyes. He would boil the Tartar in time.

"Then get on with it."

When someone came to his side and whispered, the Bulgar laughed. "The time has arrived. I will have my vengeance and you'll get your . . . recompense, Albai the Tartar."

Bela stiffened. Never had he felt so much revulsion. It coated his skin like the sludge in Romany. Nothing could grow upon it but fire. It would take great flames to burn away such ire. The room quivered with it. So it begins. He knew his part and would do it with relish. Where were Tariq and Lady Thorhallsson?

"Good."

A crash of cymbals slashed across his words. He turned, not quite taking his eyes from Albai. "Look your fill."

Dancers rushed off the floor to some applause, shouts, and ribald remarks.

Attendants came and ushered the other guests from the room. There were protests. Soon the room was emptied except for Albai, his host, and some guards.

Bela readied himself, eyeing the panoply through the curtains. The two sharifs were even to an untrained eye, which Bela's wasn't, combatants. They eyed each other, seeking a greater leverage, a power, over the other. Their acid antipathy touched Bela like a hard, wet hand. Those two must kill each other, existing in the same world had become anathema to them. He eyed the area at his back and sides. Few glanced at him. The only hope for a slave was in being unobtrusive, doing the assigned job, staying out of the way.

"Speak," Albai growled, reaching for a dish of honeyed figs.

The Great One pushed the dish out of reach. "We talk, not eat."

"I say you don't tell me what I must do or mustn't." Albai shook with temper, his multiple chins quivering with ire.

Bela edged his sword out from his voluminous robes where it'd been hidden. The Tartar was all but screeching.

The rusty muddled words, the slight hand gesture telegraphed the trader's fury. His host made a similar gesture.

In the blink of an eye armed men were facing each other. Bela swallowed, waiting the signal.

"I know you like to roll the ivories, my friend. Your choice and roll." The Great One smiled like Death.

Albai ground his teeth, then slumped back on his cushions. "Get on with it. I tire of your games."

"There'll be no more . . . unless you push me."

"We talk. Hurry it along. My men will stay."

"As will mine."

"So be it," the Tartar muttered.

"Albai, the prize you seek far and wide is within my grasp. She will be delivered to you."

"At how much cost to me, Bulgar?"

"None. Except—"

"What?"

"I wish to, first, use her as a bartering tool—"

"Her value is mine."

"Not for gold, but to set a trap for one who has needed a lesson in pain for many years."

"Who is this?"

"You needn't know. Is it a bargain?"

Albai nodded. "And when do I reclaim what's mine?"

"This very eve. My quarry enters the net as we speak."

Albai rose, rubbing his greasy hands down the front of his costly tunic, the cloth of gold barely covering his bulging middle. "I will wait." His narrowed eyes, almost swallowed in rolls of fat, fixed on his host. "She will be undamaged?"

"Yes."

"I'll not be cheated."

"Nor will I."

"It begins," the host spoke in sibilant tones.

"What?" Albai squinted at the man with the light behind him. "Who are you?"

The host ignored him. Rising, he bowed. "Well met, Einar Thorhallsson of Icelandia."

"Well met, Corin of Antioch."

Albai lurched to his feet. "This is your quarry? The Viking who took the flame-haired one to be his wife?"

"Yes," Corin said, clapping his hands. Another curtain opened. Finola was there, eyes dilated, clad in seraglio garb, supported by a slave. Tariq was nearby, his eyes no less dilated, naked, chained with two armed slaves on either side. He was torn and bloody. "Behold the booty."

Not by a flicker of an eyelash did the storm within Einar manifest itself. He couldn't let the rage move beyond his thin dam of control. Killing the one who hurt Finola could blind him, make him rash. He must not dwell on Finola, though even her name could make him tremble. "My wife. I'll take her so you might continue the orgy. I'd heard you were connected with . . . unusual business. Managing a brothel. Arranging contests between men and bulls." He inclined his head. "It would seem you've found work that suits your soul."

Corin's face twisted. "Have a care, Viking."

Einar shrugged and moved to Finola. In a flash armed men faced him. One eyebrow raised, he turned to Corin. "Not wise to come between a man and his wife." Did he smell brimstone, or was his flesh beginning to burn away from the hot anger in his innards?

"Did you bring the Cup? Both the girl and relic belong to me," Albai said, his stance menacing.

"Ah, the Cup. Yes, it's in my possession." His gaze went to his wife, then to Corin. "How foolish of my wife to ask your forgiveness. She didn't want to hurt you. Look how you repay her."

Stung, Corin's hand went to his blade. "I forgave her, not you. I used her to get you here."

"Here I am." He looked at Finola again. "This is how you'd have treated her had you wed her."

"I had thought to . . . then I became fond of her." He shrugged. "She's but a pawn. The bait needed to bring you to me."

"You've forfeited your life," Einar said, his tone easy.

Corin shook his head, his eyes burning. "You shall be the payer in this, Viking."

"She's mine," Albai blustered.

Neither man heeded him.

"I would say your vitriol goes deep, Corin of Antioch." No deeper than the acid that burned in him. Had there been other wounds to his wife besides the poppy nectar?

"It does, Viking." A muscle jumped at the side of Corin's mouth. "Your death will excise it."

"Then use your bitterness on me, since I am your target. Release my wife and Tariq." He did battle with his fury once more.

"No."

Einar took deep breaths. "Are we stalemated, then?"

"No. You are my prisoner." Corin's arm swept toward his guards.

Another door opened. "Einar Thorhallsson."

"Contessa di Marchi." He stared at her, his eyes narrowing.

"I thought you'd recognize me ere this, Viking." Her smile widened. "At first I worried. Then I realized you might not have noticed me among the throngs at Sinclair Castle."

"I had begun to find you suspect, milady." He smiled.

"Did you?" Her eyes narrowed, moving round the room as though she searched for a foe.

Einar frowned, his features contorting when another moved next to the Contessa. "I know you now, Padre Antonio. You're thinner, older. Once you were Abbot Thomas who betrayed the princess." His gaze moved to the Contessa. "And it didn't take lengths of time to figure you, milady, though I admit it took more time than it should. You see, I thought you dead, Elizabeth of Asquith."

"Banished," she said through her teeth. "I could've died. I didn't. Now it's my turn. You and the Ionan will die. I would've preferred Sinclair and his lady, but ..." She shrugged.

"You've become a witch instead of a woman." Einar baited her. His eyes shifted to the Padre Antonio. "He is your familiar?"

"Blasphemy," Padre Antonio said through his teeth.

"What would you know of that, spawn of Satan?" Einar threw the words like spears.

"Enough of this," Corin shouted. "He taunts you, fools." He inhaled. "I've waited too long for this. I'll not be put off."

"What is your complaint, Antiochan?"

Einar's query had the blood rising in Corin's face. "Quiet, Viking, at your peril."

The Contessa was furious. "Wait. Listen to me. I should—"

"Quiet!" Corin demanded, his voice harsh.

"You were a prisoner with me. I loosed your chains. Is that it?" Einar jabbed again.

"Your wit is wasted on me, Viking." He spat on the floor. "My covenant precedes anything you did. Once you commented on my good health, despite enslavement." His smile twisted. "I thought you knew, then."

"Not then, nor when you enlisted my Icelandic help in building your trade. Not until Finola did I begin to suspect."

"I aided you in our barterings, Viking. 'Twas not all one-sided."

"With friends, it couldn't be." Einar spat at Corin's feet. "I never had you staked out for the bulls."

Corin smacked the flat of his hand against a support. "How you and the Bulgar freed yourself I know not."

"Nor will you."

"Your vinegar goes past me, Viking." His smile was hard. "I stalked you. I meant to have your hide."

"So I've discovered."

Corin's eyes narrowed. "No. Never."

His gaze slid to the Contessa. "For a time I thought you held my wife in affection . . . until I discovered your liaison with this leman."

The Contessa would've flung herself at Einar, her clawlike nails reaching for his face, had not the priest grasped her arm.

Corin eyed her.

Her chin lifted. "Glower not at me, Antiochan. I ne'er broke the silence."

"There was no need," Einar said, smiling. "You've been watched for many moons, as have all your households." His glance touched the four who faced him.

"How dare . . ." The cleric's fury subsided when he caught the Contessa's glare.

"You were the unsuspecting," Einar drawled. "Persons, far and wide, in my pay dogged your ships, your people, yourselves. Though none of my sins could match yours, milady, I've not been banished. I understand it can madden one. The isolation foments brooding. Perhaps the Church and consortia will forgive your lapses because of it. I do not."

"You dare to castigate me when you're my prisoner," the Contessa snarled. She swung her arm at Finola. "See how cocky you are when you're strung up side by side and flogged 'til you die—"

"She's mine," Albai growled, spittle at the corners of his mouth.

"None will take her. Vikings own this place now."

Corin looked around him, his eyes narrowing at how few of his men remained. "You couldn't have brought your men. You wouldn't have been allowed to enter. This is as well guarded as a fortress." Corin cursed when Einar laughed. "Karoli! Come here."

Albai fumbled with his sword, gesturing to his men, who didn't move. "You'll be sliced . . . boiled—"

"Pig! Your life is forfeit." Einar's face glinted with menace.

Albai's eyes seemed to start from the sockets. Rage, like smoke, poured from his every orifice. He bellowed name after name. The few men near him stayed still. His other men had disappeared. "Come! At once! Your master speaks!" Albai's roars were enough to waken the spirits from the catacombs.

"No doubt they float in the Tiber as we speak," Einar whispered.

Albai pulled his scimitar, bellowing.

48

A semi-roused Finola screamed, her eyes focusing on the tableau. Einar was here! Where were the Vikings?

Bela burst from behind a curtain. ''No, no, sludge. Mustn't touch our thegn. Try me.''

Albai charged, his bellow shaking the rafters, his scimitar cutting through the air, his face red, contorted. Bela leaped to one side, smacking the leader along the face, drawing blood. Confused, out of balance, the Tartar turned, his arm wide. Bela moved inside slicing up, catching the Tartar in the neck, twisting through the jugular and dropping the monster like a stone with one lethal stroke. ''Die. You offend me.''

''Remove the dung,'' Einar said, some of his ire whispering through the room.

Bela and another Viking dragged Albai out by the heels, his bloodied face bumping on the tiles.

''Talk!'' He pointed at the Contessa and cleric. ''Don't move.'' He directed this at Corin.

Vikings seemed to come out of the woodwork. Many rushed to free Finola and Tariq, giving them cool drinks, covering them with fresh robes.

''Thank you,'' Finola whispered, sipping the libation, her eyes on Einar and the scene playing out in front of her.

''You can't keep me here,'' Contessa di Marchi blustered.

''As we speak, my people, Count Sigla and others, delve into your operations. Your palazzo is awash with people who will bring you down, and gladly. When it comes out what you've done to one who was in your care, the consortia will abandon you. Your power will blow away like ashes." His smile was sour. "I will see your holdings given to the poor." When she reeled, he turned his gaze on the cleric. "Think you the Church will back you when all is reported to them? The cardinals will deal with you . . . in varying ways." He pointed his finger at them. "Proscribed! As a representative of my country I set the seal on you. You can be killed with impunity by my friends and enemies. For those holding bonds and writs of trade on you, they will collect what's left of your holdings. The debenture holders may kill you."

The cleric folded his hands. "You can't. I'm protected by Cardinal d'Ontini."

"My runners are at his palace with the scrolls outlining the infamy of you and your cohorts." Einar shrugged. "I don't see anyone supporting any of you."

"You've killed a man in Holy Orders." The cleric's eyes almost started from his head. His hands shook within the sleeves of his chasuble. His face was parchment white.

"I do not associate the word holy with you. Enough of this." He gestured to his men, who went to either side of the Contessa and cleric.

Finola would've called out to Einar. Darg touched her arm, shaking his head.

"You don't hold all the cards," Corin said, backing away, drawing his sword. "Do you have the courage to fight me, man to man . . . brother?"

"Don't call me that." Einar's temper exploded. His hand dropped to his sword.

"Why? 'Tis true."

"Liar!" He fought to stem the hatred shuddering through him.

Finola couldn't believe what was happening. They'd been closer than brothers; now they were at each other's throats, determined that one should die. Not Einar. Her love. As they danced in front of each other, seeking a weakness, she felt caught in a macabre fantasy.

"To me you are my brother. For that, you die."

In a wisp of time they were caught in the swordplay of their lives, both of equal size and strength.

"You'll die, brother."

"I'll live," Einar riposted, darting away from Corin's blade.

Words faded as their skills, well honed and tested, brought the swords to clanging life.

Finola tried to struggle from Darg's hold. "No, milady."

Tariq moved to her side aided by two Vikings, their cloaks about him. "Stay, little sister. This must be done."

"Einar," she whispered.

"It has come too far, milady," Darg said, his face creased with concern. "None can stop it. In truth, they are well-matched adversaries."

"He's all of life to me, Darg. He must live. He's my spouse and my happiness. Tariq . . ."

"All will be as it should, Finola."

She shivered but made no further move.

"Milord will conquer," Darg said, edging her down on a low table, a gathering of Viking cloaks about her.

Einar felt the pain as Corin slashed down his side. He was strong and determined. Corin was in better shape. He would not lose to him.

"Kill him," Einar heard the Contessa whisper. Finola gasped.

"Shut up," Corin said through his teeth, dancing away from Einar's thrust.

Finola swallowed. "Darg, Einar is weakened from his long incarceration."

"Have faith, milady. He's not come this far to be undone." Darg never took his eyes from the gladiators.

Before Finola could say more, Corin feinted with his sword. When Einar moved to cover, the Antiochan sliced, catching him on the side.

Finola covered her mouth.

Vikings stiffened.

Einar waved them back. Reeling, backpedaling, he vied for position.

Again and again Corin tried to get inside for the coup de grâce.

Einar went wide, inviting him. When Corin moved to strike, he brought up his weapon in a short thrust to the middle.

None breathed or moved for long seconds.

Corin staggered. "You've killed me . . . brother," he said, expelling a long breath.

Einar caught him as he fell. "You would've given her to Albai."

Corin frowned. He shook his head. "No, I could not. I hated the Tartar. She'd become dear to me." He wheezed. "I feel nothing." He wheezed. "My mother made me swear on her dying that I would revenge her." He gasped. "I hated it . . . that I loved you . . . brother . . ." Corin grimaced.

"Hate ruled you when you took your covenant to Alp Arsian. He hates Vikings, too." Einar held the man filled with a bitter grief. Corin had been like none other to him. They'd shared much.

"I came to love you. I cursed myself for that." Corin coughed, blood coming from his nose and mouth. "I ask not your pardon. 'Twas my destiny." His head lolled to one side.

Einar shook his head, hugging him for a moment, then closing the eyes with two fingers. "Though I would not have you handled poorly, I ask you to mark not his grave. I would have his belongings given to the poor."

The Contessa screamed, cursing, screeching at the dead body held between two Vikings. "Fool! You failed me."

Vikings took Corin past her and the cleric. Then others took them away as well.

Einar stood and went to Finola. "Beloved, you have much to tell me." He lifted her into his arms. "Are you all right?"

"I am. And I do have much to speak of with you."

Bela returned. He opened his mouth to speak, when he noted the brightness of the Viking's glance when it rested on the Bulgar. He closed his mouth and watched.

Tariq stumbled to his feet, shaking off the hands holding him. "I read your scroll from—"

"Our mother."

Bela was astounded.

Tariq nodded, swallowing. "She loved . . . us."

Einar nodded. "Griselda was all of love. She could do naught else."

"You don't think my father a monster?" Tariq's stilted question had all assembled becoming still.

Bela watched, fingering his blade.

Einar pressed his side with one hand. The other he brought to Tariq's shoulder. "I'd noticed our eyes were the same. Though before I read the scroll I didn't think it remarkable." He hesitated, taking deep breaths, blinking. "I loved my mother. She was all goodness." He swallowed, a moistness to his eyes. "I never understood her sadness until I read the scroll. I hope she is consoled."

"I wish that I remembered her."

Einar's smile twisted. "She never forgot you."

Tariq nodded, swaying.

Einar gripped his shoulder. "Come, you must be attended, brother."

Tariq smiled. "So must you, brother." Then he fainted.

Finola wept. Bela swallowed a lump in his throat before going to heft the Bulgar.

49

So it is that the gods do not give all men gifts of grace—
Homer

"And are you up to it, brother?" Einar inhaled, swallowing hard. He'd had an affinity with the Bulgar from the beginning. To discover he was his kin had been a true revelation. After he'd read the scroll the night he'd found Finola with it, it hadn't seemed to register until he'd seen his brother and his wife in the hands of the enemy. It would've sliced him to the heart to lose Finola, and wounded him almost in the same way to lose Tariq. "We feared for you."

"Fool's game!" Tariq answered, his voice gruff, gritting his teeth against the trembling of his mouth. "I'm stupidly weak, but not soft . . ." His voice trailed. He shook his head. "How did it happen? I cannot credit how we found one another." He inhaled. "In a dungeon, preparing to fight bulls. Passing remarkable."

Einar looked away from Tariq, full shattered himself, and not just from the sword wounds of the hell-bent Corin. He took a deep breath, steadying himself. "My rib would tell you that our mother saved us . . . and she used the Cup of Antioch as her tool." Einar looked down at the relic in his hands. "All these years I've hated it because I thought it caused the sadness in my mother's eyes." He looked up, his smile twisted. "All that time she was torn, loving me and my father, loving you and your father."

Tariq winced when he changed position, holding up his hand to ward off help. "I tell you true, brother, I'm stronger, and getting more every turn of the glass." He hesitated. "From the first I sensed ... a truth between us. I thought it was because of our time in the arena fighting for our lives."

"I thought the same."

"Now I am here in your palazzo, among Vikings who are kinsmen. I'd swoon, but the barrage of aid would smother me."

Einar nodded. "Finola and the others have cosseted you to death." He laughed when Tariq rolled his eyes. "They love you, brother."

Tariq tried to smile. "I should smite you for trying to unman me ... though I would tell you I'm not untouched by it all."

"I, too, feel this tug." His voice trailed, eyeing the relic. "Mayhap our mother sought to protect us."

Tariq nodded. "You said another of your Vikings has told you such."

Einar's smile twisted. "Birgit. You'll meet her in Reykjanes." His brow lifted. "What think you? Would you see your homeland?"

"How can I disobey the call of my mother?"

His hoarse tones, the sheen to eyes so much like his own struck a shuddering chord in Einar. "Our mother is proud this day." His husky tones matched his brother's.

"Tell me of this Birgit."

"A wise ancient who once told me my mother understood the spirits, and now that she was one of them, she would reach out to me from time to time." He stared at the Cup of Antioch.

"So. This relic has joined us. In my world that would not be hard to understand. Our kinship is strong with the spirits."

"I, too, cannot gainsay it. It gives me pleasure to think of our mother's hand in this."

"And she was beautiful?"

Einar nodded. "Birgit would speak of her often, and I have fond recollections of her. In Icelandia we have cuttings in stone and wood of her. She had deep-gold hair with both Byzantine and Viking background. My father met her in Antioch when he'd gone trading. The Icelandians loved her on sight. They called her Beautiful Griselda. She became a trusted confidante of our good Queen Margaret, mother of Princess Iona." He glanced down at the Cup. "It was Birgit who referred to Finola as Swan East. She said I would sail to find her, and I did."

Tariq smiled. "You are truly caught by the wise ones." He paused, studying his brother. "And Corin?"

Einar ground his teeth, shaking his head. "The ultimate traitor. His bitterness ate him alive. All that vitriol ate away the goodness I saw. I was blind."

Tariq shook his head. "I think not." He looked away for a moment. "I think he grew to love you. That enraged him because he felt caught in a sorceror's web. He couldn't see the goodness. Blackness blinded him."

Einar took minutes to control the fury and grief that assailed him. "He would've killed Finola. Just being near Albai tortured her."

"To his credit I believe he couldn't have done that, even had he killed you."

"Mayhap. He had to die or the rot of that cruel triumvirate would've spread."

"True, brother."

"Our life begins from here." Einar nodded, then lifted his head. "They're coming."

Tariq grimaced. "Tell them I'm fine."

Einar laughed. "I'll try."

"You're sure you're up to it, Tariq?"

"I am up to anything." He grimaced at Finola when Dalia, Gar and Reric hovered over him. "Except more cosseting. I've been medicated, bathed, wrapped and powdered until I'm near death. No! No!" He hastened to assure them when he saw the alarm of those facing him, and how Einar chuckled.

"My injuries were slight, sister." He glared when a Viking put another covering on him.

Finola grinned at him. He was lying on a couch with trays of drinks and medicaments about him. Many of the Vikings had crowded into the chamber.

"I'll not let you tire yourself." Einar leaned down and kissed her forehead.

"I'm not tired. I'm glad to be home." She bit her lip. "Would you rather speak to Tariq about this . . . alone?"

Some of the Vikings rumbled a protest.

Einar shook his head. "They have a right to know of the scroll. Tell them."

Finola settled herself beside her husband. "My artist's brush saw Corin in Antioch the day of the earth shaking, when I first met Einar." She glanced up at him, smiling. "He watched me. I sketched him. The work was destroyed when Albai's men took the convent. The memory lived in me, so I did it again." She licked her lips. A Viking handed her some juice. "Tariq came with me to the Contessa's house because I thought she might know if Corin was in Antioch that day. It seemed a strange coincidence to me. What a fool I was to trust her. She drugged us, and we were taken to where you found us." She shuddered, then looked up at Einar. "You saved us."

"You were to be the instrument of her vengeance against the Sinclairs, who'd banished her for her crimes against their clan. With you thrown to the wolves, Sinclair would've come to Rome, she thought." Einar shook his head. "When she told this to me, I wondered at her audacity in trying to trick Sinclair. He would've seen through it."

Finola nodded. "I think so. He's as wise as you." Finola looked up at her husband, not noticing the smiles of the others.

"Corin saw to it that Alp Arsian abducted me, that I was put to the oars," Einar mused. "He'd banded with the outlaw Armenian shortly after his mother died. He'd told me that he'd tried to free himself from Arsian, and thus had been put to the oars as a traitor."

"Then you saved him, lord," Darg said, glowering. "I never trusted him."

Einar chuckled. "I'll listen to you more."

"So you should," Darg blustered.

Tariq shook his head. "I was brother to him, not you, Einar. The hatred fostered by his mother turned it to you because your mother . . . our mother enthralled Atoli, my father." He scowled. "Corin was not only evil. He was a fool."

"Had I thought I had a brother—"

"We would've scoured the world for you," Darg finished.

"I concur," Einar said. He touched the Cup. "We will return this to Antioch one day . . . together, brother."

The Vikings roared approval.

Finola's eyes filled with tears. "Your mother saved us all, Einar Thorhallsson . . . with her Cup. She would be happy that we've come together."

Tariq sighed. "I wish I'd known her."

"I knew her well," Darg interjected. "I will tell you all I know."

Tariq nodded. "Corin's mother must've loved my father."

"Or the way he lived," Darg said.

"His whole life was wasted because of his mother's bitterness." Finola shook her head.

Einar was grim. "He didn't have to fill himself with such poison. It was his choice. He died the only way he could. 'Twas his foolishness that gave his life over to his mother's acid."

Finola yawned. Her husband caught her up in his arms and strode from the room. "Einar! What will they think?"

"That I need to be with my wife."

She closed her arms around his neck.

50

But when a god-given brightness comes, a radiant light rests on men, and a gentle life.

Pindar

"In two days we sail for Reykjanes, beloved. Are you ready?"

Finola smiled, nodding.

Einar leaned down to kiss her. "Of course, first we go to Sinclair land."

"Einar!" She flung herself into his arms. "Oh. Thank you. How can I repay you?"

"Easily." When she inclined her head, he caught her chin in his hand. "You can love me."

"I've always loved you. I can do no other." Her voice was low, distinct.

"Then you have my life and all I possess, milady."

She reached for him when his mouth descended.

"Oh. Wrong time." Tariq's remark had them parting but not releasing one another. Neither felt confusion in the company of one so close to them.

"Come in, brother," Einar said, cuddling his wife. He'd come to full acceptance of Tariq as a sibling. More, he'd come to depend on him.

"I've pondered what you've said of Reykjanes. Though I'll no doubt die of inflammation from the cold, I hanker to see the place where my mother lived and died."

Finola freed herself from her husband, going to Tariq and grasping his arm. "You'll love it, as I will. You will meet my cousin and her husband."

The two smiled over Finola's head.

"Then, to please you, I'll come, little sister, and to see your babe at birth and become its guardian."

Finola and Tariq laughed.

Einar didn't. "Don't talk of this. Unseemly. Besides, Finola's but a child."

Tariq laughed. "I'll leave you."

Einar caught her in his arms again. "I should lock the door of our sitting room. None should disturb us, then."

"You love having him in your home."

"I do. 'Twas not right of him to talk so. We've been married too short a time."

Finola bit her lip. "I fear it's too late to talk of waiting."

"What's this?"

"Don't be alarmed. Tariq doesn't know. No one does. I just discovered it when I missed my monthlies." She took hold of his arms. "We are to have a child. Isn't it wonderful?"

"You're too tiny for bearing." Einar's voice was rough.

She laughed, shaking her head.

He buried his face in her hair. "You're all of life to me. You must be safe."

"I will be."

Reykjanes, Icelandia

"Birgit says she is like you." Finola brushed the damp tendrils from Einar's forehead.

"She's perfect, like you. Iona says it, so does Sinclair and Tariq. They are her godparents. They would know."

Finola laughed. "Do you like her name?"

"Griselda, after my mother. It's beautiful."

"You stayed with me all through my pangs. Iona said you were a bother."

"I couldn't leave you. Are you all right, beloved?"

"Wonderful. Light. Eager to walk with you in the mists, as we've done." She looked to the lancets. "I love it here."

"I love having you here, beloved. My people see you as their new princess." He leaned over and kissed her.

"I thank them all. They've been good to me." She inclined her head. "You mustn't be concerned. Birgit says our child is well. I would wish more—"

"No! . . . not for some years." Shaking his head, he dropped to his knees beside her cot. "I'll never laugh at Sinclair again. He's the only one who understood—"

"Iona says he bellowed just as you did." She grinned when he looked sheepish. She touched his cheek. "And are you happy with our girl child?"

"Happy seems a pallid word to say how I feel about our miracle, Lady Thorhallsson."

"There's a glisten of moisture in your eyes, Thegn of Iceland." She lifted her arms, glad when he caught her to him. "I'm in a fever for you, my husband. And I've just had a child. Shameless I am."

Einar groaned. "Don't speak of it, beloved. My teeth are locked together with the strain of thinking of you, awake or sleeping."

She embraced him, then pulled back. "What do Reric and Gar think? Dalia was ecstatic."

"They think their sister is most beautiful." Einar looked thoughtful. "They are pleased with the order of adoption . . . and their freedom. Birgit feels that Gar will talk one day soon."

"I believe her. All three have come to be confident and sure. Most wondrous."

Einar smiled, rubbing her back. "I like the role of father. Of course, Tariq says they are his, too."

She smiled. "He's become a favorite of our people, that brother of yours."

His smile faltered. He pressed his face to her breasts.

"What is it, husband?"

"You said 'our people.' You think of Icelandia as home." He cupped her face with his hands. "You've brought greater warmth than all our hot springs. Your kindness, spirit and energy make you queen, beloved." He smiled at her. "The swan who traveled east is the most beautiful of all her kind. Her wings spread far and wide from Iona to Reykjanes, touching all with her beauty and love." He put his face in her lap. "I'm glad you told me the tale of the swan that comes from Hibernia. I'm sworn to keep my swan safe."

Finola let the tears fall, her eyes bright with the promise of all the tomorrows with her Viking, her love. "The swan has come west and full circle. She is content," she breathed, sinking into his embrace.

Dorothy Garlock
touches your heart and soul!

Award-winning, bestselling author Dorothy Garlock brings romance and passion alive as no other author can! If you enjoyed *Homeplace,* you'll love Dorothy Garlock's other breathtaking romantic adventures.

"A gifted storyteller." — *Chicago Sun-Times*

- [ ] **SINS OF SUMMER** 0-446-36414-2/$5.99 (In Canada: $6.99)
- [ ] **FOREVER, VICTORIA** 0-446-36183-6/$4.99 (In Canada: $5.99)
- [ ] **TENDERNESS** 0-446-36370-7/$5.99 (In Canada: $6.99)
- [ ] **A GENTLE GIVING** 0-446-35990-4/$4.99 (In Canada: $5.99)
- [ ] **MIDNIGHT BLUE** 0-446-35522-4/$5.99 (In Canada: $6.99)
- [ ] **NIGHTROSE** 0-446-35607-7/$5.50 (In Canada: $6.99)
- [ ] **ANNIE LASH** 0-445-20037-5/$5.99 (In Canada: $6.99)
- [ ] **DREAM RIVER** 0-445-20676-4/$5.99 (In Canada: $6.99)
- [ ] **LONESOME RIVER** 0-445-20362-5/$4.99 (In Canada: $5.99)
- [ ] **RESTLESS WIND** 0-445-20932-1/$5.99 (In Canada: $6.99)
- [ ] **RIVER OF TOMORROW** 0-445-20366-8/$5.99 (In Canada: $6.99)
- [ ] **WAYWARD WIND** 0-445-20214-9/$5.99 (In Canada: $6.99)
- [ ] **WILD SWEET WILDERNESS** 0-445-20678-0/$5.50 (In Canada: $6.99)
- [ ] **WIND OF PROMISE** 0-445-20368-4/$5.99 (In Canada: $6.99)
- [ ] **HOMEPLACE** 0-446-35988-2/$5.99 (In Canada: $6.99)
- [ ] **GLORIOUS DAWN** 0-446-36182-8/$4.99 (In Canada: $5.99)
- [ ] **RIBBON IN THE SKY** 0-446-35989-0/$4.99 (In Canada: $5.99)
- [ ] **ALMOST EDEN** 0-446-36372-3/$5.99 (In Canada: $6.99)

Available at a bookstore near you from Warner Books